I AM
LILITH

MELANIE DUFTY

Sign up for the monthly newsletter at melaniedufty.com

First published in Australia in November 2020 by:

Melanie Dufty

melaniedufty.com

PO Box 242, Wembley

Western Australia 6913

This is a work of fiction. Names, characters, places and incidents are either the product of the author's imagination or are used fictitiously. Any resemblance to actual persons, living or dead, establishments, events, or locales is entirely coincidental. Artistic licence has been taken with historical facts.

Any use of information in this book is at the reader's discretion and risk.

Publication data:

ISBN: 978-0-6489378-6-9 (paperback)

Edited by Alida Winternheimer (USA) and Libby Turner (Australia)

Cover by White Mouse Design

Book interior design by The Book Design House

For Lilith, in me and in you

CHARACTERS

Thirteen priestesses of the Temple of Inanna and their star signs

High Priestess Lilith	Ophiuchus *(Oh-few-kuss)*
Priestess Gemekala *(Jemmeh-karla)*	Virgo
Priestess Urnina *(Err-neena)*	Leo
Priestess Tiamat *(Teeyah-mat)*	Libra
Priestess Doshina	Pisces
Priestess Ku-Aya *(Koo-ai-ya)*	Scorpio
Priestess Anunit *(Ann-noo-neet)*	Cancer
Priestess Lahamu	Taurus
Priestess Kammani	Aries
Priestess Beihani	Aquarius
Priestess Sabit	Gemini
Priestess Nin	Sagittarius
Priestess Ahassanu *(Ah-hass-ah-noo)*	Capricorn

Key characters

Adam, gem trader and leader of Uruk's army
Sabium, Lilith's twin brother and adviser to Councillor Semiramis
Menna, retired high priestess
Demsar, husband to Menna
Tadez, Lilith's attendant
Olgana, Uruk's head matron

Children

Aea (*Eye-yah*), High Priestess Lilith's seven-year-old daughter

Humusi, Priestess Gemekala's seven-year-old daughter

Nanni, Priestess Urnina's three-year-old son

Bazi and Eluti, young brothers working in the copper mines

Councillors of the six districts of Uruk

Semiramis (*Semmy-rammiss*), copper district councillor

Zamug, gem district councillor

Maida, arts, textiles and pottery councillor

Amarazen, building and infrastructure councillor

Benni, tannery and leatherworks councillor

Irkalla, education councillor

*The city of Uruk in the land of Sumer,
part of Mesopotamia, some 6,000 years ago*

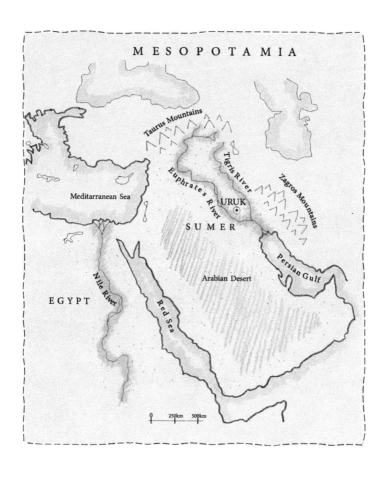

PROLOGUE

When you realise my place in history, you might wonder how you haven't known of me until now.

And if you *have* heard my name, you probably marked me as an evil seductress and baby killer, because if history wasn't ignoring me, it was demonising me. I was made an example of what happens to women who won't submit. It's true that, for a while, I lived up to my wicked reputation.

As I look down now upon the passing of thousands of years, I see that before the tables turned, I didn't really know what I was made of. For sure it wasn't Adam's rib.

But I grew strong in the dark, and the time has come when my voice can be heard once more, and I have something to say.

I am Lilith, and this story is mine.

PART I

CHAPTER 1

The girl, face hollow with hunger, came forward and dropped to her knees before me. She opened her mouth to speak, exposing the gap where her first milk tooth had fallen out. She must be about the same age as my own daughter, but that was where the similarity ended; where Aea was rosy and sturdy-limbed, this girl was skinny and bedraggled.

'High Priestess L-l-lith.' Sobs heaved the child's chest. 'Please let my brother stay.'

Her tears shone in the sunlight on the Temple of Inanna's reception terrace, where I was dealing with another group seeking refuge from the drought shrivelling eastern Sumer.

I rubbed my knuckles at the place between my bare breasts as I took a fortifying inhale, keeping the movement of my belly hidden from her people. The women and girls of her tribe rested beneath a pergola of magenta flowers, where my novices fed them honey cakes and tended their feet, bruised from days of walking through rocky desert. The men and boys had already been ushered into a separate cluster by my matrons, ready to be escorted from the city as soon as they were given barley bread and lentils.

A boy, clearly the girl's brother, came to kneel beside her and wrap a skinny arm about her shoulders. I averted my gaze to take in the vista of Uruk, the city stretching far below the mighty ziggurat that housed our temple complex. Beyond the elegant apartments and civic buildings that lined the plaza, laneways ran through the working districts where the men lived, giving way to fields of barley growing beside the Euphrates River. The lapis lazuli waters sparkled, but the river ran low. If the spring rains failed, our irrigation channels would not fill and the crops would dwindle.

I'd accepted some refugee men and boys over the last few months, but the numbers were not slowing and I had spread the word—Uruk would take no more.

A flash of irritation strengthened my resolve. Why did these people petition me when they knew I must refuse their men? I'd authorised an area downriver where these people could re-settle and, in the meantime, desert game and fish were plentiful. The women were free to join their men at any time, including this girl's mother, who had chosen the glamour of Uruk and the opportunities it offered her daughter over her son.

'Young daughter, I have said it—only women and girls can be taken in. The temple must prioritise for the good of all,' I said, more for the sake of her tribe than for her. The girl looked confused. In her innocence, she wanted to trust my words as if they came from the Great Mother Inanna's heavenly mouth, but how wrong they must feel in her heart.

I softened my voice. 'I am sorry. I cannot help your brother.'

I looked to the boy. As I held his gaze, my mind's eye began to swirl the way it did before a vision arose, and instead of willing it away, in my remorse I allowed it. The boy's face morphed into that of my twin brother, Sabium, wrenched from my arms when he lost his first milk tooth when we were seven. At that point, he was considered a fully incarnated male, unfit to live among the purity of the daughters of Inanna. That we were two halves of a whole until his exile made the contrast of our fates all the crueller.

Pain clutched my chest and I squeezed my eyes shut to clear his image, crossing a forearm over my bosom to touch the snake-shaped cuff on my arm and rub a finger anxiously over its gems. I barely noticed when my attendant, Tadez, appeared at my side and called in his courteous tones, 'High Priestess, an urgent matter calls you in the high temple now.'

I opened my eyes and nodded, grateful for his sensitivity in removing me from the situation. But when I tried to turn my back, I could not. Instead, I gathered my long linen skirt to crouch before the girl and boy, my throat as dry as if coated by the dust of their travelling shawls. Placing my hands on each child's outer shoulder, I held them together in a private affirmation of their unity and equal worth.

Then I remembered my duty to Uruk, and beyond that, to my secret vow to uphold the superiority of the feminine at all costs.

I hardened my heart, stood, and strode away.

Seated at my dressing chamber table, I rummaged through pots of face colours and perfume flasks until I found the pouch. I'd kept it since Sabium was sent to the copper mines but had not touched it for many turns of the seasons. Now, I opened the yellowing linen to look at my brother's hair and allowed rare sobs to rise and rack my body. Tadez had had to cut Sabium's hair on the day of eviction, when my brother had become subject to the grooming and dietary protocols which aimed to keep males as pure as their inherent coarseness allowed. Sabium had stared ahead with tears rolling down his cheeks as Tadez and I sobbed, watching the rich brown hair, as dark and glossy as the river otters my brother and I so loved, fall to the floor.

Holding the pouch to my cheek and closing my eyes, I was transported back through the years to the day I'd made a promise to Sabium.

It had been a good time to slip away, the hot afternoon keeping most of the city's women napping so no one significant would notice two children in the plaza gardens doing what they shouldn't. I recalled how I'd waved my finger in the air as I bounded down the temple steps, tracing out the new cuneiform characters I'd learned that morning, excited to teach them to Sabium. When I'd entered the gardens, I clapped my hands to scatter a couple of resident peacocks and ducked to crawl through a bank of pink frothy flowers and into the cavity of our secret meeting spot.

Sabium should have been waiting for me. I'd seen him slinking out through a servants' stairway. As I'd tried to slip away, our mother had called out and asked me to recite two of the many incantations I was learning, refusing me dismissal until I was word perfect. So where was he? Perhaps he'd stopped by the kitchens to trick the cooks into giving him some peaches or honeycomb.

I heard girls laughing and water splashing on the other side of the great flowering bush. Peering through the foliage, I saw five girls quite a few springs older than me clustered around the flush edge of the purification pool in the middle of the gardens. They held a small child's head under the water.

When they pulled the spluttering child up, I gasped. *Sabium*. The biggest girl, who wore a red skirt, laughed at him and asked, 'Do you still think you're smart, boy? Or must you follow the fate of the other braggarts drowned here?'

I scraped myself through the bushes. Time slowed and I recollected a healing lesson that claimed the back of the head held a sensitive spot. In mid-flight, I made a fist and slammed it into that place on the girl's head. She collapsed into the pool face-first, her back arching upwards and legs flinging high behind her. The others turned to me, stunned. Freed of their grasps, Sabium made a funny sound as he lay on his stomach and gulped breaths.

I helped him to his feet, his thin little boy chest heaving, and passed him the linen kilt lying crumpled on the ground where the girls had dropped it.

'What are your names? Who are your mothers?' I demanded, my back straight and shoulders wide, the bearing of a priestess even if I was still many springs away from my first blood moon. 'Do you know who you torment? This boy is the brother of I, Lilith, destined as your next high priestess.' I glared extra hard at the red-skirted girl, on her knees coughing, her hands clasped to her bare chest.

They all stared, taking in the fine white shawl wrapped around my waist that marked me as a temple daughter. None dared to speak.

I willed my mind's eye to send Sabium a message. *Don't worry about those horrid girls, I'll see to them.* He must have been the only boy in the world who knew how to use his mind's eye, because I had secretly taught him. Everyone believed males were incapable of learning the Mes, the hundred topics of the mother-wisdom. But Sabium was special, and every bit as smart as me. It was worth risking the wrath of our mother to teach him all I knew.

A few of the older girls dared to meet my eye, emboldened because their nipples showed the first signs of swelling to womanhood. They thought this made them better than me.

'Don't think you got away with this,' I said. 'I will remember who you are for the rest of my life.' I looked into their eyes one after another, each dropping their sneer under my frown. I sensed the one with the red skirt still had an air of contempt about her.

'Girl! What is your name?' I demanded. She had a strawberry-sized and -coloured mark across one cheek that would make it easy for me to recognise her in future, although I didn't have much to do with city girls.

'I am Semiramis,' she said boldly.

'Get out of here,' I snarled at her. The girls skulked away.

'Are you alright?' I turned to Sabium as soon as they were out of hearing, reaching my arms to embrace him.

'Get off me!' he snapped, stepping out of my reach.

'Why are you mad?'

'Because boys don't matter and that will never change,' he said, his voice wobbly. He swiped at the tears sliding down his face, mingling with the water dripping from his mop of dark hair onto his naked body.

I clasped his shoulders, my own teary gaze meeting his at exactly the same level. 'I'm going to be the ruler of this land one day, and I promise you—I will make things fair.'

I promise you ...

The padding of Gemekala's feet on my tiled floor brought me back to the present. She wrapped me in an embrace from behind, her juniper-scented hair falling past my cheeks like black curtains. Tadez must have told her of my upset with the refugee siblings.

'Lilu, there was nothing you could have done differently,' she said, squeezing my hand in her powerful grip. Without trying to engage my drooped gaze, she wiped my face and straightened my diadem, the lapis lazuli gem at its centre representing the energy of Ophiuchus, the thirteenth star sign, under which all high priestesses are born. My priestesses and I each represented one of the 13 constellations as defined by where the sun was at our birth, bringing the full spectrum of heavenly characteristics to our rulership.

Gemekala was my Virgo priestess, respected among the women of Uruk for her skill as a midwife and herbalist, roles she conducted with aloofness and fierce clarity. To me, she was far more precious. She was my cousin, my most trusted priestess, my proxy if I could not attend to my duties for any reason. And in the privacy of our temple enclave, she was the one who could make me roll about laughing with her riotous remarks, and the one who spoke the plain truth to me when others pandered.

'I'll run the rivers for you,' said Gemekala, lightly running a fingertip from each hand along several of the energy channels of my body, leaving a tingling trail as she cleared the blocked emotion in my systems. Immediately, I felt a little lighter, and met her eye to thank her.

'Come,' I said, standing and extending my hand. It was time to return to the reception terrace, where the people of Uruk came most days to see my novices for healing and advice. My 12 priestesses and I served there less often, but we did make ourselves available on the day of the full moon—today. We saw only to the more interesting cases or those brought by Uruk's most illustrious women, though in recent months I'd been called there more frequently to deal with refugee matters.

Back on the reception terrace, I took in with relief that the refugees had gone. I surveyed my novices and priestesses dotted along the length of the shaded terrace, busily proffering astrological guidance, diagnosing and prescribing remedies for health issues, and reciting incantations for all manner of situations for the city women. At the latter end of the terrace, a few of the younger novices consulted with boys and men.

Tadez rushed to my side to escort me to my consulting area, his gaze concerned as he placed a cup of hyssop tea in my hands and encouraged me to drink. He understood how deeply affected I was by separating the refugee siblings. As a humble temple servant, Tadez had always shown Sabium and I great kindness when we were young children. I'd made him my prime attendant the day I was ordained high priestess, the first man ever to be given such a venerated role.

I signalled a novice to bring me a worthy patroness, and soon one of the city's most esteemed artists was sitting in front of me.

'I don't want another child now, High Priestess,' she said, a hand on her belly. 'I'm working on new murals for the council chamber, so the Great Mother's creative power is flowing strongly through me—it seems to have started forming a baby.'

'And have you received a lover's shaft milk of late?' I asked.

'I accepted some only to flourish my art, not a baby.'

'Of course, his milk could not cause you to be with child, but it might have encouraged your creation.' My eyes broke away from hers as I spoke, straining to watch the tip of my finger scratch my nose. I did not enjoy lying, but perpetuating the belief that women create babies as a tree bears fruit was necessary to deprive men of purpose. It kept them malleable to temple rule and so held the prophesied future at bay.

The woman nodded.

'As such a creative woman, you should be very cautious about accepting men's milk,' I continued. 'It could tip your potency so far that you begin forming a baby. Your lovers should use a sully cloth unless you want to foster a baby's growth.'

The temple asserted that shaft milk was a poor and messy imitation of mother's breast milk, offering minor nourishment via a woman's gateway to a child she already grew. Generally, women had their male lovers use a sully cloth, but if a woman wanted a child, the temple's creed had always been that she should receive the milk of a few men to encourage her dormant babe to flourish. We also recommended an increased intake of pomegranate juice.

The artist nodded ruefully.

'Go to the dispensary and ask for a herbal tincture to make your womb inhospitable,' I said. 'Tell them to assign a novice to care for you the next few days with poultices to soothe your cramps.'

She gulped. 'And what of the soul of this baby?'

I obliged her need to hear the words. 'As the pomegranate tree rebirths her fallen fruits, so does a woman's womb. That soul will come again, through you or another, when the time is right.' I met her eyes warmly this time and grasped her hands to wish her well.

Tadez leaned in to whisper that one of Uruk's district councillors awaited consultation with me. From the corner of my eye, I saw our councillor of education, Irkalla, approaching. She held responsibility for ensuring the girls of Uruk studied the Mes, although to a lesser depth and exactitude than we temple women.

Standing to my full height, I looked down into Irkalla's face. I had seen her two days prior, when I had led the monthly council meeting. Encountering her again so soon was disheartening in my already low mood. The six councillors overseeing Uruk's districts—copper, gems, agriculture, building, arts and education—were wily and arrogant women, and I had little time for any of them. But they ensured our city was the most advanced in all the lands, and it did not serve me to offend them unnecessarily.

'What ails you, Councillor Irkalla?' I asked as pleasantly as I could.

She complained that a demon was sapping her vigour and despite her incantations to evict it, she'd felt it re-enter her ear that morning as she lay in bed. What gall she had, blaming her laziness on a demon.

I recited an impressive incantation and, to sate my ire, slapped her back three times, calling sternly, 'Be gone!' with each strike. I caught Gemekala's eye as she sat at her consulting area next to mine, examining a gouge on the thigh of a celebrated huntswoman. Our faces remained serene apart from the barest twitch of amusement at our mouths.

The throb of drums began echoing from across the ziggurat where our 50 or so novices resided and studied, providing me with a welcome reason to leave the reception terrace.

'I must attend some Mes lessons now,' I said to dismiss Irkalla. 'A full moon day is always special for our newest novices.'

Turning my back on Irkalla's grimace, I ascended to the next tier of the ziggurat, towards the novices' terrace, stopping behind a buttress to peer at the lesson in progress led by my Libran priestess, Tiamat.

Tiamat was directing seven junior novices in rolling their hips under a pergola of cascading jasmine, the perfume mingling with that of many other flowers in the ziggurat's sky-high gardens. My heart swelled to watch Tiamat, her dark amber hair hanging straight as a reed down her back and swishing from side to side as she moved.

Two novices at the drums stopped when they saw me and a peaceful hush descended. The only sound was the tinkling of water into a nearby pond, part of a complex of channels and pools that overflowed from one to another on all four tiers of the ziggurat.

'Look who is here—our High Priestess joins us,' Tiamat said, meeting my gaze with her shining hazel eyes. The novices stilled to behold me, postures adjusting to stand a little prouder in my presence. They raised their hands in the Great Mother's salute, thumb tips meeting and forefingers pointing down to make a triangle above their hearts, and I returned the acknowledgment.

'Greetings, Priestess Tiamat, novices,' I said with a smile. 'Please, continue.'

Tiamat bowed her head to me, the V-shaped point in her hairline centre clearly defined beneath the pink tourmaline in her diadem.

'Now you have opened the flow of your hips, place your hands upon your girdle of fire,' she said to the young women, positioning her hands over her lower belly in demonstration. She stilled a moment, closing her eyes in devotion to the complex pathways of energy that ran from a woman's lower spine and reached around to embrace and fill her belly with creativity, forming the girdle of fire. The novices followed suit, and they all began to roll their hips in sensuous circles.

'Let yourself move like the ever-changing ocean, to the ebb and flow of your instinct, for in doing so you please our Great Mother Inanna and stoke the fire of creation,' called Tiamat, a quaver of passion in her voice as she revolved her hips. Building the girdle of fire always drew forth a woman's truest ardour.

My own hips began to move in effortless sympathy as I admired the women, eyeing their lush bellies framed by low-slung shawls tied about their hips, their bare bosoms a glorious array of sizes, shapes and nipple formations. Life-force pulsated among us, each moving uniquely yet somehow with a pleasing sense of shared precision.

Tiamat continued. 'This practice helps you master the mesmerism.' She referred to the technique of expanding one's energy field to create a stronger presence, serving to enthral others. 'It strengthens the command in your voice, and the ability of your mind's eye to see beyond the superficiality of the manifest realms and into the mysteries from where you can direct creation. And of course it fuels your beauty, joy and ecstasy.'

Tiamat looked at me as she spoke, and I came to stand beside her as the drummers began a slow beat. We all moved as we would, the deeply felt emotion and fervour of our collective girdle of fire filling me with love for my women.

'You must not shrink in fear of the greatness you feel,' Tiamat called. 'You must practice your ability to hold the enormity of your fire, and only at the rightful moment may you release it. This requires discipline and strength to hold the power even as you surrender to it. Or you may hold the energy and direct it towards what you wish to create, or sometimes simply to magnify your bliss, a most worthy endeavour.'

She met my eyes in a smouldering gaze to welcome my comment.

'Such is the power of the girdle of fire,' I called over the sound of the drums. 'You need nothing more to create as you so will—from a babe to a great invention or work of art. As incarnations of the Great Mother Inanna, women carry the girdle, and only we can create anything of significance.'

'Let us chant,' called Tiamat in breathy excitement as we continued to move, and we all began a creation prayer, our jaws light as the words flowed melodically from our lips. The moment was so beautiful I almost forgot I'd just affirmed the priestess' great lie to my youngest novices, and although it was my duty to do so, heaviness began to creep into my heart.

They would probably never know the truth of procreation because none was likely to become a priestess—very rarely was one appointed, and only a novice who survived the rigours of initiation and had the correct star sign would do. If one of them did make it, she would vision with the Weird Sphere, an ancient crystal we kept secret in the high temple which offered many insights and showed the fated future. Only then would she learn the truth of a man's role in creating children, and why we must keep it secret.

CHAPTER 2

From the vantage of my outdoor bathing area as I stepped from the water, the rooftops of Uruk glowed with apricot light. Tadez's soft hands glossed patchouli oil over my skin as I tried to relax and let the beauty of the flowers growing beside my bath lift my heavy spirits, their lilacs, pinks and whites soft in the early evening light. He wriggled his fingers into the flesh at the base of my skull, tickling me the way he'd done since I was a little girl, and as my shoulders hunched I met his twinkling eyes with a small grin.

'Ah, that is better,' Tadez said, finishing the rub with a flourish down both my arms at once. 'After I dress you, shall I go to the Huluppu tree?' His foot tapped, betraying his eagerness to get back to styling the space for tonight's full moon ritual, a boisterous occasion to bring the Great Mother's blessings to the Earth.

'Go down to the tree now,' I said, indulgent of his enthusiasm. 'Send Gemekala to help me.'

'Thank you,' he said. 'I will do so as soon as I've given Yasmin her treat.' He surveyed the terrace, brightening when he spotted my python's green coils beneath the rambling vine she favoured as a resting spot. He took a bucket from behind a nearby buttress and went to kneel beside her, tutting words of affection as she began to feed from it. Every full moon, he had the servant boys catch a few frogs for this purpose, insisting they mercifully break the creatures' necks upon capture to save unnecessary distress.

Shortly afterwards, Gemekala joined me at my dressing table. I lifted my chin so she could paint a downward pointing triangle between my brow, feeling the sacred blue mark of the Great Mother Inanna come alive over my mind's eye. She slid snake cuffs up both my arms then placed one of my lapis lazuli diadems on my head. I reciprocated by straightening her own diadem, with its blazing yellow-green peridot.

The horizon was rippled in deeper orange tones when we emerged onto the residential terrace, the warm air sweet with jasmine and wisteria. My other priestesses and all the novices were admiring the full moon beginning to rise over the city as they awaited my presence.

'Mammi!' hollered Aea as she bounded towards me from where our terrace connected to the children's pavilion. The other giggling temple daughters followed her, some lugging babies and toddlers, eager to escort us to the Huluppu tree and longing for the day they became novices—and someday, maybe priestesses—and could join the ritual. Beside Aea pranced the dog she named Fancy, one of the Salukis we kept for their noble beauty and hunting skills, though I had retired this one from the hunt to be her dedicated companion. Aea flung her arms around my waist and buried her face in my belly with such enthusiasm it was impossible not to smile.

The cheers of Uruk's people, gathered to watch our procession, rose from the plaza as we descended the ziggurat steps, setting off exuberant honking from the peacocks that lived in the garden at the centre of the square. City children scrambled up the date palms that lined the concourse, ready to scatter blossoms on us in the hopes of a blessing. Aea swung my hand proudly as we led the temple group to the banks of the Euphrates, where the Huluppu tree stood, her ancient boughs outlined against the deepening violet sky.

Kissing my daughter goodbye, I entered the great dome formed by the tree's canopy and inhaled the rich living earth. Tadez had once again orchestrated a beautiful setting, with strings of blue lotus blooms hanging from the boughs and fluffy red sheepskins in the nooks of the rambling roots. I took my place in front of the tree's sacred gateway, where the trunk and broad roots had grown to form the shape of a woman's gateway that stood as tall as me. A novice knelt beside me, reaching into the gateway's hollow to draw out the polished gem wands we stored for these nights. I annointed each glossy rod—an array of black obsidian, rose quartz, red jasper, amethyst, amber—with a dab of blue lotus oil and murmured a blessing, then replaced it to be further blessed by the tree's emanations.

My lingering sadness over the refugees lifted as Gemekala joined me to sip from a beer jar, using reed straws to avoid the barley husks. I beckoned Urnina to sit with us, and we laughed as she shook her hips in a jaunty dance on her approach, her eyes glowing golden like the topaz on her diadem that marked her as my Leo priestess. Even on this full moon night when we all wore our hair loose, she'd managed to arrange her sandy mane in a voluminous style. Someone began to play a lyre and our chattering rose as we relished cumin-rubbed roasted quail, salads of sorrel, cucumber and radish, olives and barley bread, the servants stepping nimbly among us to replenish each platter as we emptied it.

No one else noticed Tadez waving at me from the edge of the tree's canopy. Another man stood behind him in the shadows, and as I lay eyes on his silhouette, a shudder of energy tingled above my scalp and ran down my spine. I sensed this interruption would bring trouble. Annoyed, I stood to see what was going on.

'Please accept my apologies, but I thought you would want to know,' whispered Tadez as I stepped outside the tree's hanging branches.

I held his gaze, waiting for an explanation. This was not a time to bring a strange man so close to the Huluppu.

'This man insists on seeing you immediately. It's something about the safety of Uruk,' Tadez continued. 'He said it couldn't wait.' Tadez's uncertainty irritated me. I did not see why the attendant of the high priestess would be swayed by a man's demands.

My crown continued to tingle, a new outpouring of energy running down my neck and arms so strongly that my shoulders shivered. This was not a common sensing of subtle energies. I moved forward to get a better look at the man eliciting such a strong sentience, my senses alert for information.

'What is so important it disturbs a celebration of Inanna, man?' I demanded of him.

The man faced me squarely, standing boldly without dipping his head in deference. He was a large hand's width taller than me, the tallest of all the temple women. His physical form was large though lean, but what startled me was his presence: it felt as pronounced as my own.

'High Priestess Lilith, forgive me. My name is Adam, son of Priestess Ayelet from the western Red Sea,' he said, his eyes on mine. I guessed he was about the same age as me, 29 springs in this life.

'What do you seek?' His mother's status in a faraway land gained him no pardons.

'I have news from a settlement east of here called Larsa,' Adam said, and gestured to a man several feet behind him with dried blood smeared on his chest and arms. With all my focus on Adam, I hadn't noticed him. 'This man's matriarch sent him here to warn you, High Priestess. He says six men from the north attacked them, stealing grain and gems. The invaders threw the matriarch to the ground and spat at her and...they cut her thigh open.'

A heavy hum swamped my head, causing the peals of laughter from the women behind me to sound distorted. I moved to block the view through the leafy curtains to the celebration, the frolicking women oblivious to our intense conversation.

Adam shook his head at such unbelievable acts. 'Of course, her men fought as best they could with their tanning knives, but one lies dead.'

'That is outrageous,' I said finally, my throat tight. Someone started to beat a drum and a lively song began.

'High Priestess, there's more. They said the Great Mother's rule is... over.' The words came out stiffly.

A fist grabbed my guts and my mind's eye shivered, giving a flash of the visions I'd seen in the Weird Sphere.

'Hah!' I made the sound to cover the sharp exhale of air trapped in my chest. 'What you speak of is nonsense. And why do you report this rather than letting the Larsa man speak?' I said, regaining control of myself.

'I know this man. Birru is his name. I live in Uruk but I often travel to trade. He sought me out for help as he is too overawed and exhausted to speak to you directly. He has run for days to reach you.'

Looking at the other man cowering before me, I sensed Adam's words were true.

I spoke to Tadez. 'See that Birru has somewhere to sleep. Have him come to the reception terrace in the morning for treatment, then I will question him. And ensure these two men do not speak of this matter to anybody else.' I casually waved my hand, dismissing them all.

'High Priestess, please. Your celebration. It may be risky to expose yourselves in such a way when those men could be nearby,' Adam said, reaching out to touch my arm, wisely stopping before he made contact.

I glanced over his shoulder at my head matron Olgana, her body twitching in readiness to spring into action. I shook my head at her. 'Any risk from men is laughable. Though my matrons may not find them so amusing,' I said. Olgana and her matrons, their hulking presence a stone's throw from the tree's perimeter, would happily push any man's head into the purification pool.

Adam remained still, eyes locked with determination on mine. They looked dark, but it was hard to say what their colour would be in the light of day. Without directly looking, I took in that he wore a common worker's sheepskin kilt.

'It is wise to have your matrons nearby, High Priestess, but I can gather some men I know to be strong fighters,' he said. His tone was earnest but I sensed a self-importance such as I'd never felt before in a man. 'In case there was any trouble and the matrons needed help.'

I laughed. Who was this man and why would he think himself qualified to comment on any of these matters? Audacious, yet intriguing. It was something about the way he stood in such full presence before me. Without premeditation, my attraction caused my eyes to widen into his for a moment. He held my stare easily.

'Leave now,' I said and deliberately turned so a waft of my patchouli-perfumed body went his way. I walked back through the canopy, aware of his eyes boring into me.

My heart beat strongly in alarm over the reported attack, and perhaps from the way Adam's presence affected me, but I pushed it from my mind—tonight my focus had to be on the ritual.

A novice poured rose water over my hands as the servants cleared the dishes and removed the cedar planks that had been our temporary tables. Urnina took a basket of blue lotus incense to place on the low fires around the inside perimeter of the tree's dome. Raucous laughter erupted as she squatted by one of the fires, her back to me. I peered past a few bare shoulders to see what the hilarity was about and spat out my beer as I joined in the uproar.

'What a lovely moon it is tonight, ladies,' Urnina screeched, now nude, her fingers between her legs and wriggling her gates as if they were speaking. Buoyed by our attention, she broke into a saucy song. A novice joined in by plucking the jolly melody on a lyre, and another added the beat of a drum. Soon we were heaving with laughter as Urnina tumbled over, her diadem falling from her head, but she kept her knees apart and her fingers at her gates as she lolled on a sheepskin rug and continued. She snorted sporadically in mirth as she sang of her vulva being like a fertile field seeking someone worthy to plough it.

The laughter washed away my tension and the remaining grief stirred by the refugee siblings, and when the milky disc of the moon showed through a gap in the boughs, I was ready to embrace my role with the passion it deserved.

Standing in front of Huluppu's gateway, I raised my arms until the women silenced. 'I am the thirteenth priestess, the chosen handmaiden of the Great Mother Inanna, Goddess of all creation!' I boomed.

The women contributed their own fervent calls, clutching their hands to their chests.

'Daughters of Inanna,' I called. 'Tonight, the moon blesses us with extra bounty as she rests in her own sign of Cancer, ruler of nurturance and fertility, and connects with Venus, Goddess of sensuality and pleasure. Our ecstasy is more powerful than ever. May it restore fertility across the land of the two rivers. May the Great Mother Inanna reach down from the Heavens to raise crops from the Earth's manly flesh.'

The women cheered, looking up to herald the moon resting on its lavish blanket of stars.

'As the gates to the full moon open, enter them in celebration of the life-force that runs through our bodies. Worship the Great Mother through your sensuality and praise the moon for showing us the rhythm of creative power.' I placed my hands over my lower belly, fingers splayed to cover the whole area. 'May your girdles of fire open the heavenly portals and fill our earthly coffers with abundance.'

The women positioned their hands the same way, bowing their heads in reverence. I nodded that they should come to take a wand from the tree's gateway, each choosing one instinctively.

The servants brought in amphoras of blue lotus wine, and we allowed the euphoric powers of the drink to take its silken grip. Elated gales of laughter swelled higher, and soon the women shifted around and adjusted their positions to be with those to whom she felt most drawn this night. Some of us lay across another's lap, played with someone's hair, or massaged a bared arm or thigh.

My priestesses Doshina and Anunit came to stand before me, marking their desire to lay with me tonight, and I welcomed them warmly. Two young novices who were part of Tiamat's class earlier that day edged closer as they looked at me shyly—neither had known my lap before. I smiled, our group set.

We lounged on cushions and leaned across one another to admire the moon as we sipped wine and breathed the heady incense.

Anunit told us how she had been looking forward to this after a few unfulfilling nights with her favoured lover of the moment. 'His udder teat leaks milk like a calving goat's,' she said, sighing dramatically and stroking her well-rounded thigh. 'Last night, I was so tired of his weepy teat I told him not to return until he can manage his flow. Such disrespect.'

We laughed.

I looked at Doshina, a popular lover at our full moon celebrations, both for her ethereal beauty and because she lay only with women and so was highly skilled in the arts of worshipping the female form. 'Then let us thank the Great Mother we have each other,' I said huskily, moving my hand further up her leg.

'Tonight the moon is full in our sign, Priestess Anunit,' said one of the novices, getting to her knees to inspect Anunit's diadem with its glowing moonstone, bringing her bare breasts right before her superior's eyes as she did so. 'One day, I may earn such a piece, far in the future, of course, when you retire,' she said, touching her simple copper headband that marked her as a novice.

Anunit cupped her own bosom. 'As a sister Cancerian, are your breasts also your most tender place?' she asked the novice, eyeing the young woman's dusky-tipped mounds. The novice leaned in to whisper a reply that caused them to collapse into one another in laughter, Anunit's delicious fleshiness enveloping the other's youthful limbs.

Around us, the giggling and murmuring continued, with occasional sighs of pleasure and the smacking of moistened lips on skin. The full moon's silver light and the glow of the fires shone upon our flesh and lulled us deeper into a sensual spiral that made me woozy with desire. But the moon was still climbing to her pinnacle and we could take our time.

I let one of my knees fall open, ready to invite further attentions, and the other novice leaned forward and made a show of adjusting my shawl over my breasts, deliberately letting the linen graze my nipples several times in pretence she was unsatisfied with how the folds fell. Doshina playfully swatted her hands away and pushed back the shawl to reveal my bosom.

'The moon is as full as your breasts,' Doshina murmured, nuzzling her head between them, making my blood thud at the prospect of her coming touch on my tips. When her mouth closed around one of my nipples, my chin dipped and I brushed my lips across the large aquamarine atop her Pisces diadem. I reached to stroke her ribs, then further outwards to find the novice's flesh, sensing she was feeling a little timid.

I became aware of someone's knee pressing against my left shoulder and turned to see Anunit arranging cushions to elevate the Cancerian novice's hips. Anunit kept a shawl draped over her lover's mound of Venus to enhance the excitement of its unveiling, a homage we used in these rituals to the moon, which hides then reveals her beauty as she wanes and waxes. I reached across to trail the amber wand in my right hand up the inside of the novice's thigh, my breasts falling together in a bounteous manner, Doshina's mouth never breaking contact with my flesh as she moved with me. The other novice ran the tip of a wand along my flank, my instincts telling me it was my favourite, black obsidian.

The man Adam came into my awareness. Was he nearby? Perhaps he hoped to hear the famously ecstatic moans of the temple women on full moon nights. A thrill ran through me at the idea. I let myself enjoy this titillating fantasy for a while before pushing him from my mind. Men were not permitted in the sacred space of a full moon ceremony, not even only in my mind.

The other novice's thigh now trembled against my shoulder, prompting me to resume stroking her inner thigh with the amber wand, and I let Anunit take it from my hand to pleasure her lover more deeply.

I hungered for all of them, to twine my tongue with theirs, immerse myself in their breasts, the lushness of their thighs, their soft bellies and the wetness of their woman's love. We moved instinctively into positions to best satisfy each other, drinking of and nourishing from the well of the Great Mother that lay between our thighs, mindless with desire as we were swept into a rapid tempest in our plunging, stroking and writhing.

We all rode the same swelling bliss as if we were one shared body, and I was dimly aware of my throat opening wide, sharing wild ululations of ecstasy with the others as we convulsed, our sacred water crashing forth into a sea of oneness.

The night was young and our urgency was mercifully relieved. We soon entered the next phase of our celebration, a timeless erotic trance taking us far beyond any sense of our individual identities and into the heart of the Great Mother. From here, we stilled the fire of our fervour to slowly relish the beauty of one another's womanly form, and at this kept well occupied until the moon began her descent.

Shawls and blankets were arranged over one another and through softened lids, we shared gazes, occasionally reaching a hand to stroke an expanse of skin plumped with life-force. The Great Mother Inanna was pleased with the depth of our eroticism and we revelled in her favour, content our celebration had been of sacred service and bolstered the fertility of all the lands.

Lying awake for a while, I thought of Adam and what he said about men defying the Great Mother's rule. I rested my hand over the area beneath my ribs to still the disquiet that lay there.

After returning to the temple the next morning, I went to the reception terrace to question the man from Larsa. I spotted him with a novice dabbing salve on his forearms, which looked to have been cut in the attack. I gestured her to direct him to me, then led him behind a hedge of white gardenias.

'How do you fare today...what is your name again?' I asked when he stood before me, his eyes downcast and cheeks blushed. I pitched my voice low so he would also speak quietly.

He flashed his gaze to meet mine for a moment before he looked at his feet again. 'I am Birru. Um, High Priestess.'

'Tell me more about the men who said they defy the Great Mother. What did they look like, what did they say?'

'They had beards and long hair, like wild shepherds. They spoke a different tongue, perhaps from a northern land.'

I nodded. Bearded men were held in contempt and disgust. Only shepherds who roamed the wilds defied the grooming protocols that required men to have short hair and shaved faces, and they rarely came near a city, at risk of being purified by matrons. 'Go on,' I encouraged.

'And they...they said they know...they know it's a lie.'

I felt the blood drain from my face. For aeons, my priestess foremothers had found it easy to maintain the lie, but it became more precarious since one hundred springs earlier, when shepherds shockingly claimed that males initiate pregnancy, based on what they saw with their animals. The temple mocked the notion as 'shepherds' foolery', condemning it as a sacrilegious and absurd self-aggrandisement from the crudest of men. When men had persisted in speaking the foolery, the temple had to take much harsher action.

I gave a small cough to hide a gulp. That the Larsa invaders wore beards suggested they were such shepherds, or at least sympathised with them. 'What else did you notice?'

He took a shaky breath. 'They had red marks—triangles—painted between their eyes.' As I tried to keep his gaze, a blurry red shape emerged in my higher vision, becoming a sharply focused red triangle, pointing upwards. It was a symbol I'd seen before, in the Weird Sphere. My heart raced and my head spun, the floodgates to my greatest fears raising another notch.

'Anything else?' With effort, I made my voice unflustered.

He hesitated. 'The man who cut our matriarch's thigh said her lap rights were...no more.' Birru spoke with his chin low, ashamed of repeating these sacrilegious words. Lap rights for all women were unquestioned, not only a right but a sacred duty to bring any man to her lap as and when she desired. It was crucial for bringing the Great Mother's blessings down from the Heavens, which in turn would stimulate the fertility of the Earth. To deny these rights was an affront to the Great Mother herself. It was heresy.

'Thank you, Birru. Be sure to rest at least a few days before you return to Larsa,' I said briskly. 'Go back to having your wounds dressed and request a balm you can take home for your matriarch's thigh.'

I called Tadez aside and instructed that Birru should be watched over by a matron to ensure he did not discuss the attack with anyone before he departed the city. The gossip of bearded men rebelling against the Great Mother's rule would spread like wildfire.

My insides felt like liquid as I went to fetch Urnina and Gemekala from where they chatted with some jewellery designers. I lifted my chin, indicating they should join me.

'What's happened?' Gemekala muttered as she came to my side, barely moving her lips, but I gave a tiny shake of my head. I led them up the steps to our private residential terrace on the next tier of the ziggurat. Once in my garden, its flowering plants and row of date palms sheltering us from the main priestess' terrace, I listened for anyone nearby. The only sounds were the cooing of white doves and water running into my blue lotus pond.

'I have more information about Larsa,' I said finally, satisfied of our privacy. I'd told my priestesses about the reported attack while we were still at the Huluppu tree, and they'd hoped it a one-off incident by some desert rogues. I paused, dreading what my next words could mean for us. 'The attackers appear to be bearded shepherds.'

Silence hung between us. Then Gemekala's face darkened. 'What? These men try to revive the shepherds' foolery?' Her black eyes flashed, but I saw her upper chest begin to move in irregular puffs, betraying her anxiety.

'I fear so.' I kept my voice low. 'They said they know about the lie.'

'Fools! It's a bluff by a few fools with heretical ideas. This isn't the first time men have tried to claim they are the creators of life.' Gemekala always spoke with such conviction and dismissive confidence, it was easy to think she believed her words.

'I'm sure this will come to nothing,' Urnina said mildly. 'No man would align with the shepherds' foolery after what happened last time.' I saw her shift uncomfortably at the thought that we may have to conduct a campaign of purification such as our temple foremothers had. They'd drowned dozens of shepherds, going on to kill thousands of other men as the foolishness continued to spread across Sumer. At some points, 50 men at a time were bound together and forced into the raging Euphrates during a particularly watery spring, as detailed on clay tablets in our library. The temple had carefully kept these stories alive among the population to discourage men speaking of such procreation theories again, under fear of ridicule and purification.

I shook my head. 'I doubt these men are intimidated by what happened last time. They sound beyond brazen. They said the Great Mother's rule is finished—the men of a hundred springs ago never said such a thing.' I took a shaky breath. 'The prophesied future could be rising.'

'A few men attacking a desert settlement doesn't signal that,' said Gemekala, ripping some leaves from a bush and crushing them, her fingers whitening with the force.

'We cannot underestimate any sign that the prophecy may be activating,' I said sternly. I knew she sought to reassure me, but her denial was unhelpful.

'We do not have to accept that future as fated just because our foremothers have,' said Gemekala. I inhaled slowly to find my patience with her—I knew what she would say next. 'I've long suspected that the Weird Sphere has been programmed in mischief, by an abnormal man who had some psychic power. It cannot be showing truth! I simply cannot see how women could ever bow before men.'

'Weird means fated! Everything the Weird Sphere has shown me rings as truth,' I said, extending my arm to show her the prickled flesh that rose, a confirmation of veracity. 'Our focus must be on *delaying* the arising of that future, even if I wish more than anything there was a way to change it entirely.' My endless prayers and visioning quests seeking a way to evade the dreaded future left me no wiser. I believed there was deeper meaning in why men were destined to tyrannise women and if only I understood, I might find a way to change our path.

For now, I must continue with the only strategy we knew—disempowering men further to ensure they did not rise. It left me queasy. I sighed heavily.

'If anyone can forge a better future it is you, Lilu,' said Gemekala passionately, an apologetic flash in her eyes. She saw my burden and sought to lighten it. 'But we can all agree on keeping men in their place. All this fuss, it's nothing the temple hasn't dealt with before.'

Urnina remained silent, squirming at the difficult conversation.

'All will be well,' said Gemekala, taking Urnina's hand and mine. 'Men do not have the wit to rise above women. They are dense as the Earth itself! All they offer that a bullock doesn't is sexual service, and only then if well-trained.'

'A bullock may be simple-minded, but it is far stronger than a woman. It will obey her only as long as it knows no better,' I said, unwilling to fuel her wry witticism. 'And if men find out the truth about procreation, they will become arrogant. We've always known that. We must take the Larsa attack seriously.'

'Of course,' said Urnina, re-entering the conversation with a gust of enthusiasm, indicating she had clarified her approach to the issue. 'But it was merely a few men. We mustn't give them too much influence to worry us. That awful future may not begin to unfold for hundreds of springs yet. For now, we rule the world, the favoured daughters of Inanna, and so long as we stand in her glory, we are unshakable.' Her posture augmented in dramatic leonine style, her cleverly made-up eyes inviting my agreement.

She embraced me in a cloud of jasmine perfume, and I let her think she had soothed me. I was loath to see my priestesses anxious, no matter how they tried to deny or hide it. As High Priestess of the greatest Temple of Inanna in all the lands, and guardian of the secretly held Weird Sphere, the burden of keeping feminine superiority rested on my shoulders.

I took my diadem from my head, feeling the slight indents it left on my temples. 'Let us hope this was just a few angry shepherds we can quickly quash. But what they said, and the red triangles between their eyes...' I paused, rubbing my forehead as a headache rose.

'Try not to overthink this when you're about to lead the city through the new year festival,' said Urnina in soothing tones. 'A successful Akitu will ensure our abundance, and that's most important right now, especially with the drought.'

'You're right,' I said. 'The Akitu events start in just a few days. As soon as celebrations end, I'll have scouts track those men and kill them. It must be kept quiet or the populace will wonder why I am taking a threat from a few men so seriously.'

'Indeed. Why would the Great Mother's chosen handmaiden be threatened by a few hairy brutes?' Gemekala's scowl was daunting, but the root of her fear sounded in the breathiness of her voice.

'Tombaya pecked me!' sobbed Aea, a red mark rising on the forearm she held out to me. The peacock eyed us rudely from where he stood. I kept him as my pet, enamoured by his great beauty, although he was often a nuisance.

'He doesn't like it when you try to pick him up. Shoo! Shoo, bad boy!' I flicked my hand towards Tombaya, who swished his train of feathers in a sassy arc as he turned to bob at a flowerbed.

I cradled Aea to my breast until she stopped crying, then whispered in her ear. 'How about I take you and Humusi to play at the river?'

Her cheeks, still shiny with tears, swelled with the force of her grin.

Later that afternoon, when the heat kept the city quiet, I watched Aea and Humusi—Gemekala's daughter—run into the shallows of the Euphrates where Huluppu's limbs stretched over the water, hearts glad as birds, with Fancy bounding at their heels.

I entered the tree's domain and leaned back against her gateway, taking off my diadem and closing my eyes to feel the swell of aliveness this place sparked in me. I listened to the cicadas chirping lazily and the girls splashing, taking my chance to rest in the awareness that I would soon lead the Akitu new year ritual. The city's building excitement soothed some of my anxiety over the Larsa attack. It was hard to take a threat from rebellious men too seriously when it was so evident how my people adored my priestesses and me, and the time-honoured traditions of our Temple of Inanna.

As I dozed, a presence welled in me and I opened my eyes to see an owl—a bird sacred to the Great Mother Inanna—gazing at me from one of the towering branches. She was a screech owl, my favourite for their wonderful array of calls. I had only ever seen such a bird at night and now marvelled at how her gold eyes glowed just as powerfully in the light. What was she doing awake and active in the bright of day? We exchanged a long look as she trilled, and I understood her message perfectly yet not at all. With a shudder of feathers, she bent her legs and took flight, swooping down past me and out through a gap in the boughs with stunning precision. Her wing beats reverberated in my chest, leaving me breathless even as I realised a man stood on the outside of the tree's canopy. He swept aside the branches and revealed himself, causing my heart to flutter further. Had Adam known I was here?

'Greetings, High Priestess,' he called, his smile as broad as the shoulders he held proudly. He wore the same sheepskin kilt I'd seen on the full moon night, and there were some scars on the smooth skin of his chest. His eyes didn't look as black as I'd thought, perhaps brown or murky green—it was hard to tell in the distance.

'Greetings,' I replied. 'What was your name?' I added, unsure of what to say as my belly grabbed with tension. It was ridiculous that a woman, especially one of my standing, should feel nervous around a man. I straightened my shawl and thought of replacing my diadem, deciding against it.

Our gazes locked. In the silence of my mind's eye, I asked his spirit, 'Who are you to me?' and in response, I was flooded with a powerful sense of knowing him. His eyes brightened as if he had heard my question in his conscious awareness and my brow furrowed in confusion—usually, only temple women were able to sense the thoughts of another, and only if we were not overly attached to the situation. Still, he did say he was priestess-born, so maybe he carried some of the far sight. It was very rare in a man, but possible, as Sabium had proved in our childhood games and secret communications.

'I am Adam,' he said politely. 'May I come closer?'

The only males permitted to enter this space were temple servants, yet I found myself waving him forward.

'What brings you here in the middle of the afternoon? Have you been released from your workplace for some reason?' I asked quickly, unnerved by my impulsiveness in admitting him. If Olgana and the other matrons were with me, would I have kept protocol?

'I do not bow to another regarding my working schedule.'

'What do you mean? Which woman do you work for that lets you decide your schedule?'

'I work for no woman, High Priestess, but for myself.'

The feeling of a man speaking so brashly made me think of Sabium. I scanned Adam's face, trying to understand from where this self-assurance arose.

He nodded at one of Huluppu's roots, an arm's reach from me. 'May I sit while I explain myself?'

After a suitable pause, I nodded to permit his request, my senses electrified by his presence. From the corner of my eye, I admired the long legs he stretched out, ending in large bare feet with sculpted arches.

'I am a travelling gem miner and merchant. I saw you and the girls crossing the plaza and followed you—since I am free to decide my own movements,' he said, eyes twinkling. I responded with a raised eyebrow, unsure of what to say. No male had ever teased me before, or at least not since Sabium and I were children.

The cicadas' song surged louder in the silence that followed, and I looked towards the girls playing on the other side of the tree's foliage. Aea's cheeks were rosy with mirth as she splashed in the water throwing stones, the dog leaping alongside her, while Humusi searched on her hands and knees for more rocks.

'Your daughter is lovely,' he said.

How did he know which of the girls was mine? Sensing our gaze, Aea turned our way. Her face lit as she ran towards us, calling, 'Adam, Adam,' Humusi chiming in behind her.

I hid my surprise while he flashed a charming grin.

'Well, hello. It's good to see you again,' he said to the girls, reaching to touch the dog's cream feathered ears and causing her to flinch politely. 'What's your dog's name?'

'Fancy,' said Aea, the gap where her tooth had fallen out making her lisp a little. 'I named her.'

'Seems a good name,' said Adam, looking at the dog's regal features and the elaborate beaded collar around her neck. 'She does look quite fancy.'

Aea smiled proudly.

'Young daughters, I see you are both fine throwers, but your techniques are limited—let me show you a new move,' said Adam, springing to his feet and taking the stone Aea held. He made a show of posing his body then skimmed the rock in several large hops over the water to the exclamations of the girls and the squawk and flutter of a pair of ducks.

I took advantage of this moment to study him. His hair was black, and a touch longer than male grooming protocols allowed, and his were eyes widely placed and angled slightly upwards at the edges, like a cat's. His face was elongated with a tall brow, long nose, and ears that stuck out too far and sat too low. The body was tall and rangy, and although his limbs appeared to move fluidly, there was a strong spring to his energy. His hands were huge. He was not conventionally handsome, but my eyes feasted on him.

'I'll try now,' said Humusi. 'I'm the better thrower.'

'Are you joking, cousin?' Aea pouted for a moment before she broke into a gappy grin, and the girls began one of their giggling fits.

Adam sat again, laughing. His forearms rested on his bent knees, the hands dangling casually in front of him. They were a little roughened, but not so much as those of a man who laboured as a gem miner, though I supposed he did say he was a merchant as well. The fleshy mounds between his thumb and wrist suggested he was a man of ardour.

Aea took a few figs from the basket beside me and handed me one, then leapt to take one to Humusi, who had climbed onto a low-slung branch. Pausing a moment, she held one of the ripe fruits out to Adam, who immediately took it, as if such intimacies were normal between them.

'Aea,' I said, my shocked tone making her quickly look at me. 'Is it proper behaviour for a temple daughter to offer food to a man?'

Aea watched me for a few moments. 'But Humusi and I know him.'

'Yes, Aunty Lilu, we know him,' said Humusi. 'Adam showed us a trick where he made pieces of red jasper disappear into his ear. Then he pulled them from our ears and said we could keep them.' She beamed at him.

I signalled the girls to go back to the water, calling after them to not go in too far. We watched as they re-entered the ankle-deep water, squatting in preparation for the figs' juices to run down their arms. Moments later, they squealed in delight, pointing upriver at the romp of sleek otters we often saw here.

I turned to Adam, my eyes narrowing. 'How have you befriended my daughter?'

'Both the girls came with one of your priestesses to the gem district, I think it was Priestess Urnina. She was interested in red jasper and mine is the finest available.'

'So you happen to meet my daughter, and you follow us this day. What do you want, man?' I stared intently into his eyes to find the truth of his motivation but I saw nothing. This man could hide his thoughts. My hackles rose alongside my fascination.

'Forgive my impertinence in following you, but there is something important I must report,' he said, and I wondered why he had not come to the temple to seek audience with me. It was clear he wanted to speak to me privately. 'I have more news about the men rebelling against the Great Mother.'

I held his gaze coolly, but my stomach constricted. I nodded for him to continue.

'Yesterday, I was downriver trading gems with the men you've denied refuge in Uruk. They said a group of bearded men visited and urged them to join a rebellion against the Great Mother's injustices, and 22 did so.'

Again, I felt the thickening in my gut and mind's eye as my world slipped another notch on its axis. I forced my features to remain composed.

He continued. 'I have heard these men are growing in numbers from other sources too, and that they have superior fighting skills and blades stronger than copper. I can help you with my knowledge of how men strategise to defeat one another, and I've seen every type of weapon there is.' His voice was charged with passion. Never had I heard a man speak in such a way.

'You have no ability to advise me. Do you think you tell me things I do not know?' I lied.

'Of course not, High Priestess. But Uruk needs to defend itself against these heretics in an organised manner, and I ask you to let me help—let me be of service to you and the Great Mother.'

His nerve staggered me—a man demanding to advise me on how to run my city! Men did not have the wisdom or insight to contribute in any significant way to rulership. Yet behind the surface of my irritation, my senses crawled with dread. I had never heard of men taking an organised approach to fighting.

'And what service could you possibly provide? How have you come to know such things?' I asked.

I felt his energy prickle with frustration. 'I've grown up travelling our land of the two rivers and beyond, as far north as the Taurus Mountains and east to the Zagros Mountains, and I have heard and seen many things.'

'What, the squabbles of quarrelsome men? And you believe such types could threaten the natural order of things?' His declarations quietly impressed me and I decided to change my approach. After all, I might need him. 'But I will consider what you are saying.'

I sensed the effort it was for him to remain silent. A few moments later, he held up his half-eaten fig with his thumb and forefinger as if toasting me with it, meeting my eyes with an insouciance I found both insulting and inviting, before he popped it in his broad mouth.

I looked back towards the girls, mindful he was observing me, and bit into my own fig. In a flash, he reached out an arm and dragged a couple of fingers across the dip in my chin where the red juice gathered, sending a shot of desire through my belly. I should be outraged at his presumptuousness in touching me, but I was thrilled at his boldness. My own emotions astonished me, and I could not allow this. I recoiled to glare at him.

'Get back to your quarters now, man. This is the second time you've interrupted me at this sacred place to drive your agenda on these so-called rebels. The notion! And now you touch me uninvited.'

He unhurriedly got to his feet and looked down at me. As I was prepared to order he be taken to the purification pool for his irreverent behaviour, he spoke.

'Please forgive me, High Priestess. I meant no disrespect. I only seek to offer you my service.' He backed away a few steps before turning to leave.

My heart was beating fast and my breath was high in my lungs as I watched him go, a gaping chasm of emptiness opening in my core. The feeling was familiar; it reminded me of the thwarted yearning I felt for my brother. I glanced up to see if the owl had returned, but she was gone and could not help me understand my feelings of intense attraction and repulsion. But I knew someone who could—Menna, my beloved predecessor, who had initiated me as high priestess when I was 18 springs in this life. I needed to discuss my odd feelings and this talk of rebel men with her. She would help me find clarity.

I called Aea and Humusi over to ask for details on their encounter with Adam in the gem district.

'Urnina took us to look at gems for a new collar and belt I'm making for Fancy,' Aea explained. 'Oh, and she needed some for the arm cuffs she's designing—we're not supposed to tell, but they're for you to wear at the Akitu feast. When she wasn't listening, Adam asked if we were from the Temple of Inanna and I told him you're my mother.' She smiled broadly, pleased to be able to tell me something important.

I smiled back, hiding my uneasiness. Was this man so determined to build a defence force that he had sought to enchant my daughter as a way to influence me?

Back at the temple, I also questioned Urnina.

'Oh!' Urnina's eyes widened. 'I'm sorry. I did not know it was the man you'd spoken of. He did approach me with his gems, fine specimens. His strong arms and odd face made me think of bringing him to my bed, yet he barely glanced at me. He just wanted to talk to the girls.' Her chin tucked inwards in offence.

The idea of Adam joining Urnina in bed caused me a twinge of antipathy that I quickly quashed. Urnina was not to be blamed for desiring to take lap rights with him. I linked arms with her and asked of her latest jewellery designs, unwilling to further contemplate the peculiar feelings this man evoked in me.

CHAPTER 3

Appearing as one squirming mass in the dark of night, some five thousand people filled the plaza below me and spilled along the concourse, awaiting the first stage of our Akitu new year ritual.

My priestesses stood in a semi-circle behind me in order of their astrological signs, starting with the fiery energy of my Aries priestess and moving around to the dreamy Doshina in all her Piscean beauty. My place was front and centre as representative of Ophiuchus, the constellation and sign of the winged serpent and first celestial daughter of the Great Mother Inanna.

The populace roared as I raised my serpent-entwined ebony staff, topped by a carved copper pine cone representing the conical-shaped pineal eye in the centre of the brain, the portal to the soul. My other hand lifted the not-insignificant weight of Yasmin's serpentine head as she slid slowly around my shoulders. In the light of the blazing braziers, the python's green iridescence shone beautifully against my black cow's hide mantle, opened wide to reveal my naked body. My every muscle tensed under the heft of the splendid Akitu headdress I wore, a gem-studded skullcap from which a pair of cow's horns extended.

A blast broke across the city as Uruk's most barrel-chested men sounded the horns, heralding that the white Akitu bull was about to begin his parade towards the temple. I could faintly see four men driving the beast forward, his great horns adorned with green ribbons in homage to the hue of Venus. Flanking the party was a group of city girls, shaking sistrums and ringing bells.

The men dragged and pushed the bull up the temple steps, lined with torches that gave me the sight of his figs swinging to and fro like a pair of stones. Sensing imminent death, the bull jerked his head, the men holding fast to the horns as their feet left the ground for a few tense moments. By the time he was brought before me on the public terrace, he stood calmly, as if resigned to his fate, occasionally emitting a gush of breath or clicking a hoof on the smooth mud bricks. His presence and milky white beauty moved me, and I took a breath to prepare myself to do what I must.

A hush fell over the people as they waited to hear my proclamations. 'Great Mother Inanna, Queen of Heaven and Earth! Mother of the Sky Snake!'

I put my staff aside and lifted Yasmin's undulant form towards Venus rising in the sky, the star's greenish glow seeming to grow more luminescent. Yasmin's ceremonial name was 'Sky Snake' in honour of Ophiuchus, and for the fact she lived high on our terrace, an unusual home for a creature that typically keeps her entire body in contact with the Earth.

The populace held their reverential silence.

'We thank you for the bounty of our Akitu new year, and for bringing us many daughters,' I continued. 'May your rains fall on the Taurus Mountains to fill our rivers. Open your heavenly womb upon our lands and fill us with your riches!'

Gemekala gathered her tiered white skirt and knelt before me, holding out a basket within my reach. I arranged Yasmin around her shoulders before grasping a handful of barley seeds and the bone handle of a curved copper dagger. Surprised that my hands trembled, I turned to fling the seeds on the ground before the bull and raised the blade to the violet-black sky.

In a customary gesture of respect to the bull, I sought his gaze as I approached, my breath grabbing at the depth of awareness shining from his black eyes. My compassion flooded towards him in my grief at taking his life, and I was staggered to feel it flow back to me ten-fold. Rather than any sense of self-preservation, this creature felt empathy for *me*. I had conducted this ritual every Akitu since my ordination, never experiencing such a connection. My heart ached with reciprocal gratitude as a vast feeling stirred in me, like a déjà vu.

Gathering focus to continue my role, I called strongly, 'Great Mother Inanna, we offer you this bull, a symbol of the sacrifice we each make when we enter the earthly realm of agonies and ecstasies. Your holy bull leads us back to the threshold of the gates of Heaven, wise and whole, that we may enter in your footsteps.' I paused, breathing deeply as I held the bull's fiercely loving stare, his body motionless without need for the men steadying his horns. My jaw quivering, I stepped closer, and with all my love I called out from deep within my throat, 'Praise Inanna!' and swept the blade across his neck, bringing a gush of blood that covered my feet and shins in warm wetness.

The bull's eyes kept mine in a timeless moment, and I sensed the sorrow I saw was not for the end of his life, but the pain I felt as the one to take it. I heard his silent acknowledgement— that to sacrifice what we love for a higher good can be agonising, whether done intentionally as I did now, or through the mysterious ways of soul destinies. Moments later, he collapsed, the men bending their knees to guide his fall as more blood pulsed out with his last heart beats. A sob caught in my throat to see such a force leave its body at my hand. Clasping the dagger, I lifted my hands above my head and tears streamed down my face as I dropped to my knees in gratitude to the bull, followed by the temple women and all Uruk's people.

The city people went in ceremonial silence to their beds, anticipating tomorrow's feast and fertility celebrations, but the night lay long before the priestesses and me. Back at my private terrace, I entered my outdoor bath filled with warm milk given by seven cows, the whiteness taking a pink hue from the bull's blood. I allowed my body to absorb the nurturance of the sacred cow's milk as the priestesses swished currents of warm liquid between my thighs in preparation for the ceremony. Tears flowed anew from my closed eyes, my heart raw with the compassion the holy bull had shown me.

Having emerged and been wiped with wet cloths, I was ready. The priestesses, now also naked apart from their arm cuffs and diadems, steadied me as I walked under the weight of the horned headdress to the next tier of the ziggurat, then up another set of steps to the high temple.

We paused at the entrance, flanked by braziers that threw light on the glazed mosaics of the façade, patterned in rows of zigzags, diamonds and triangles running around the building. Around the upper walls ran a wide band of rich blue tiles studded with yellow stones which marked the constellations. One by one, we touched the marble heads of the two pink lionesses guarding the entrance then stepped inside.

I lay on the alabaster plinth and took a last look around the temple before the ritual began, admiring the firelight bouncing off the copper wall reliefs depicting the Great Mother in her most glorified acts—birthing, making love, suckling, and destroying through storms, famine, and floods—surrounded by lionesses, snakes, cats, cows, doves and owls, her favoured animals.

The four men entered the high temple in silence and I shut my eyes, sensing them take their places around me. I knew they each wore a half mask depicting the bull's features. Warm oil perfumed with spikenard ran onto my body and they began to slide their hands up and down my limbs. I relaxed into the warmth radiating through the bedding, the plinth heated to ensure my senses were highly receptive, and listened to the fires crackling and the breathing of the men picking up force. My priestesses were silent, sitting in trance on cushions around the plinth and altar.

My attention was pulled to my breasts, plumped with blood. As I knew to expect, the man at my left shoulder began to tongue a nipple. After some time, his head retreated. A humming power was coming from my right side from where I awaited the next touch. I felt this man's lips enter my closest auric layer above my skin, taking my flesh to a heightened state of awareness and deepening the thrill of his touch when it came. I felt every nuance as his warm tongue dragged across my nipple, ending with a flourish. A shudder ran through my core.

It was now the turn of the man at my left to dip his face to my breast, but I was impatient for the other man's touch once more, bracing in exquisite tension when it was due. Finally, I felt his lips again, swooning as I fought the urge to loll my head. This eroticism would surely please Inanna. Next, I knew the men would take my nipples in their mouths at the same moment, and when they made contact, my throat dropped into a new level of openness, longing to roll out a low groan. Their tongues swirled and flicked, becoming more passionate as they endured their own struggle to discipline their touch, dizzy with feasting at the breasts of Inanna incarnate. All the while, my awareness of my right breast and the man who pleasured it was intense, the noise of his mouth moving on my skin like a crackling energy current.

I needed to know who this man was. I regularly lay with all four men participating in the ritual, chosen for their discipline and skill, but I did not recognise this man's touch. *Who is this?* I asked silently, opening my senses further to detect a response.

You know who I am, came the soundless response.

My eyes opened in perfect time as his head lifted from my breast. A thrilling bolt passed through me as I peered through the eyeholes in the bull's mask to the voracious black pupils behind it.

Adam.

A blast of rage ran through me, but I sought to smother it. Somehow, he had inveigled himself into this situation. I would deal with that later, but for now, I had to keep focused. His disturbance of the ritual risked the abundance of our lands, and brought danger to me. If I were to align with my lower sexual urges during such a sacred ritual, I risked binding my spirit to my body and bringing my hard-earned spiritual mastery back to a base state, recovery from which could take lifetimes. With a surge of will, I forced blankness on my mind.

The ritual continued, on and on, slowly building towards the break of dawn. The two men at the lower half of my body slid their hands up my thighs, around the oil-glossed curls on my mound of Venus, across my belly, repeating the motion as more warm oil was poured onto me. They circulated the energy, building fire and directing it upward to my heart, to assist me to expand my bliss. After a while, in synchronised motion, they slowed their hands and edged towards the fount of power between my legs, the pulse in my gateway in alignment with my heartbeat.

I became aware of more activity around me, the hushed whispers of my priestesses.

'It is time for the holy bull to enter. Sunrise grows nigh,' Tiamat announced.

The men stopped their caresses. I watched several novices struggle through the temple doors with a large object shrouded in linen. My lovers stood naked at my side, their masked faces hung in reverence and shafts swollen with respect, while the novices staggered to lift their load onto the plinth beneath my feet. The priestesses removed the linen, revealing the bull's white head with his magnificent curved horns spreading wide and his eyes black with impartial love, a love that radiated to all things without distinction.

The men manoeuvred me further down, lifting my ankles and resting them wide apart upon the curve of each horn, tying the green ribbons around them. I beheld the splendid vista of the bull poised at my gates, ready to escort me through the equinox moment and lend me his power in rebirthing my lands.

Longing to arch my back, instead I stayed still with my face impassive, closing my eyes again. Two fingers were placed at the top of my crevice and more oil drizzled between my thighs. I fortified my will. A few moments passed with the two fingers holding their slight pressure, then they slipped down and apart, making an elegant crescent movement on either side of my jewel before they met again at the bottom of my gateway. From here, after a pause, they retraced their movement, over and over. I let the sweetest sound emerge from my throat as if from Inanna's own. 'Ohm, ohm, ohm.'

As the fingers became more diligent in their ministrations, Adam's lips bent to my nipple again, the man at my left doing the same, and the sounds coming from my throat dropped an octave.

Tiring from the concentration it took to control my ecstasy, I opened my eyes a little in hopes of seeing the approaching sunrise. It wasn't long away. The incision in the ceiling above me was shaped as an eight-pointed star, showing a deep blue sky as richly hued as the lapis lazuli wand that lay on the altar.

'Prepare the wand,' said Tiamat. The men backed away as the priestesses stepped forward, focusing on their breath to build more energy, and sending it through their palms to the wand. The temple was fraught with excitement and the altered state brought about by the energy. So ready was I for the release, a waft of air could have set in motion the opening of my gates, but I steadied the energy that felt more powerful than all the world's bulls and seas combined.

We saw the first spot of sunlight at the edge of the altar, designed impeccably by the priestesses who had reigned hundreds of springs before us to receive the dawn equinox rays. The growing aura from the wand was palpable, and it flowed further as the sun's rays touched one end and gradually rolled up its length. Eventually the light touched the midpoint of the bull's head from where his horns sprung, and energetically rippled along each until it reached my ankles, entering my body as a vibration that ran up my legs and into the antechamber of my womb. I swelled in reverence as I bathed myself in the rays of the Great Mother Inanna and her champion, the holy bull.

The moment came to begin the opening of Inanna's heavenly gates. The wand was placed in my right hand, its power throbbing with the heartbeat of life. I rested it at my entrance then allowed it to be drawn inwards until it touched the final door to the divine abyss. Pregnant with an ecstatic power capable of rebirthing the city of Uruk and far beyond, I let the exquisite light radiate through me in flashes of brilliance. I felt the steadfast presence of the holy bull, sensing all he had graciously sacrificed to help me stand before the gates of Heaven, which I must enter with my own will and power.

The moment was exact. I splayed my heart and wilfully opened my being, and from the galaxy within it, a pinpoint of light appeared. In slow motion, it began to pulsate outwards as the explosion began, surging out in concentric circles at ever-increasing speed. A monumental flash of white light, so hot it was cold, took me far beyond my body, my being, and landed me in the black void of the Great Mother's womb, from which all begins and ends. Still further, higher, faster, deeper my essence was expanded through the peace of the black void, until I rushed beyond it and into Her pure light, endlessly brilliant. Infinite love and pure knowing were mine, unlike ever before.

My intent remained clear: to channel this energy to my people, the city of Uruk, our land of the two rivers and beyond to all. But in that moment, I knew it was unnecessary, for all is made of the same energy and has no need to receive what it already is, only to realise it.

The seawater that gushed from within me, the same water a babe floats on within the belly and can be drawn from a woman when Inanna is well pleased within her, was caught in the shallow dish placed between my legs. This would be mixed with the bull's blood and cows' milk from my bath as a libation for sprinkling over our crops and onto the backs of our female animals to ensure greatest fertility.

All was still.

We took our time walking back to our terrace in the early dawn light, and Gemekala helped me settle in my bedchamber to rest. The sounds of the priestesses making love with each other drifted blissfully into my ears as I floated into sleep, woken by Tiamat's lips on mine. I welcomed her into my bed.

As the sun reached the mid-morning sky on the fresh new year's day, we wrapped linen shawls around our waists and shoulders and began to emerge from our chambers to meet on our dining terrace.

Tadez served us breakfast himself, keeping the bustle of servants away on this special morning of rebirth. We devoured figs and yoghurt with honey, and warm barley bread, our senses pleasantly heightened following the ritual.

When I felt ready, I called Tadez. The priestesses hadn't realised there was an imposter, and I had not yet mentioned it, unwilling to disturb our peaceful mood.

'Why was that man, Adam, among the four lovers last night? What happened to Ureem?' I asked Tadez quietly as we crossed onto my private terrace.

'Oh!' he gasped, one hand flying to cover his mouth as he stopped in his tracks. 'My lady, forgive me. I had no idea. The four men were waiting in the vestibule in their masks when I went to collect them, and I assumed all was in order. I should have known. I'm so sorry.' His brow crinkled in distress.

'Adam is about the same size as Ureem, and the light was dim,' I said to soothe his conscience, ever sure of his loyalty. 'But as for those two men, there can be no excuse. Adam deceived his way into the ritual, though for what purpose I do not know, and Ureem must have cooperated.'

'Adam! That man cares nothing for protocol. This is the last time he fools me.' Tadez began strutting along my terrace with his shoulders hunched as if to contain his fury. My own anger rose as I caught him up.

'These men will be punished for putting the success of the ritual in peril,' I said, my brow wrinkling as I thought of Adam's pushiness at the Huluppu tree and the way he'd looked down at me before he walked away. I spoke quickly before I changed my mind. 'Have Olgana take them both to the men's burial fields. They will dig their own resting places in case they do not survive this afternoon.' I eyed Tadez to see if he baulked at the severity of my command, but he nodded sharply and turned. The fact Tadez, a man who would rescue the rat from a cat's jaws rather than see it suffer, was so goaded affirmed my approach.

'Wait,' I said. 'I will personally oversee the purifications. Not in the plaza gardens' pool. The brewery's well room will do.'

There was no reason to have the city talking about the disrespect these men had shown in the year's most important ritual honouring the Great Mother.

In the damp room deep in the ziggurat's belly, Adam and Ureem awaited me on their knees, hands fastened behind their backs and faces turned down. Olgana and several of her most menacing matrons watched them eagerly.

I took my time before speaking. 'Your graves await you. Whether you lie in them this day will be determined by how much purification you require.'

Even on his knees with his gaze down, Adam's proximity was causing my energy to throb, my enlivened body still connected to him after the ritual. I felt my face flushing and was glad for the dimness of the room.

'Ureem, you were trusted with the most revered role a man can hope to play, yet you failed me,' I said. 'What do you say?'

His tears made clean streaks down his dust-caked face as he raised his eyes and began to blubber that he had taken dizzy, remembering nothing beyond having some barley beer with Adam after the bull sacrifice.

'I am foul indeed, High Priestess,' Ureem said, his head now hanging low. 'I pray to the Great Mother I have not endangered the spring rains.' His anguish rang true to my ears. He was a controlled lover and a gentle man of whom I was fond, and I knew Adam had swindled him easily. I would not be surprised if Adam had slipped a sleeping tincture into Ureem's beer last night.

I turned to Adam.

'How do you explain your disrespect and deception, man?'

'High Priestess, I have no excuse. I wanted to be of service to you and ensure the fertility of our lands.' He spoke more loudly than necessary, the sound echoing around the room. 'Luckily, Ureem told me a little about his role before he became too drunk to perform it, but there was no time to discuss it without disturbing the ritual. I was foolish, and I take the water gladly.'

'I see,' I said, making my doubt of this story clear in my tone. I walked behind Adam, looking at his hands tied behind his back, filthy and reddened from the digging. I reached down to trail my fingertips back and forth through the well water, making a soft sound.

My volume rose. 'What is the truth of why you deceived me and disrupted our ritual?'

'I have told you the truth. I am sorry, High Priestess. Forgive me for being so lowly.' Adam's sycophantic words were misaligned with his air of insolence.

What an idiot he was, provoking me right before he was dunked at my pleasure. I now knew I must purify him myself, and hold him under to the crucial point. There was a sickening thud in my stomach, both dread and excitement. I came to stand before him, letting a few drops of water fall on his head from my hand.

I gestured to Olgana to move him into position. The rank tang of her sweat and the leather sash worn across her torso wafted as she brushed past me. I watched as she guided him onto his belly, his face above the flush edge of the well.

'High Priestess, shall I recite the rites?' said Olgana, looking at me with hollow eyes. Her exposed clay-red nipple was stiffened in excitement, or perhaps just the subterranean chill of the well room.

'No. I will,' I said. 'Stay close to ensure he does not struggle.'

I stood with my toes touching Adam's shoulder. 'In the name of the compassion of the Great Mother Inanna, you are to be purified of your delusions, weaknesses and filth. How do you respond?'

'I thank the Great Mother for mercy and I surrender my impurity,' he said into the water beneath his mouth, as if he was thanking me for passing the bread.

'You understand if your defilement causes you to resist the purification, you will require longer in the waters?'

He turned his dirt-streaked face to look up at me as he recited, 'I do, and I thank you, High Priestess.' In the dim room, his eyes were as black and hard as obsidian.

'We begin,' I said. Pulling my skirts high, I stepped one foot across him and squatted on his back, my thighs gripping his shoulders. I allowed my hand to caress his neck as I edged his face closer to the water, sensing when the tip of his long nose touched its surface. I felt his breath, pushing his head into the water when he had just breathed out. If he wanted to play games with me, I would beat him at it.

He was completely still. I knew the matrons would not be needed—this man would rather die than resist, an admission he could not cope. A thought broke into my awareness, of him at my breast, the feeling of him beholding me as I lay on the plinth. I knew this was what he thought of at this moment, and that he transmitted it to me. As I'd suspected, somehow this man knew how to use his mind's eye. I barricaded my mind against his invasion.

Pressing my lips together, I stared at the lamplights reflected on the black water, the barest ripples moving out from his head. I entered the private space inside myself where I had gone to ignore discomfort since I was a little girl. *A priestess must be in control of herself.*

For his own sake, I hoped he knew how to do the same. It appeared he did. Every sense in his body was palpable through my hand, and I felt the gasping call of his survival instinct, but still he did not move. Perhaps he would pass out, at which point he might gasp for air and fill his lungs with water. But his body was so slack—was it possible he had slipped away?

Panic engulfed me. A clammy sweat clung to my skin and in the chill of the room, I fought the urge to shiver. Focusing on my mind's eye, I sensed, *Do I let him up now?* The only sound in the room was the steady plop of water from the moss-covered ceiling. *No.* I must hold. If this man had a role in my destiny, he would survive. And if not, let the Great Mother take him.

He involuntarily twitched. It was subtle enough that no one else could detect it, but I felt a huge relief. I took my hand from his neck and he lifted his face, taking an urgent but measured inhale.

'Let that be a lesson to you,' I said, standing. 'I am not to be toyed with.'

After several more protracted breaths, he got to his feet clumsily, hands still bound, and looked at me with probing eyes. In a husky voice, he said, 'Thank you, High Priestess.'

He was as unbroken as when he'd gone in. I stared back unblinkingly for a few moments before I looked to Ureem, who was miserably awaiting his turn.

'Speak no more of this to anybody, either of you,' I said. 'You may both go now.' I looked pointedly at Olgana to ensure she registered they were to be released.

A tiny smirk played on my lips as I strode away, feeling Adam's eyes burning into my back.

The priestesses lifted their hands to form the Great Mother's triangular salute as I approached them in the kitchens, where we would prepare some of the sacrificial bull to eat at the feast. Dunking Adam had made me a little late, causing yet another disruption to the order of our ways.

Urnina seized the ruby red cheeks of the young bull, awaiting us neatly trimmed of sinew, and held them to her own rosy cheeks.

'Don't ruin me with your terrible cooking,' she spoke in a low mournful voice, moving the cheeks about in the rolling motion of a beast chewing its cud.

The women's rowdy laughter brought Cook and two of his juniors to peer at us from over a basket of lettuces, fearing the worst for our creation.

'I'll have none of your cheek,' Tiamat said, hands on hips. Amidst their hoots, I took the meat from Urnina and lay it in the pot heating over the cooking flame, unwilling to make jest of the bull after the connection I had shared with him.

As Doshina began to add a bowl of carrots chopped into eight-pointed stars in honour of Venus, Lahamu grabbed her arm.

'Wait! We brown all the meat first, then add onions, and lastly the carrots and pomegranate juice,' instructed Lahamu, who loved to cook, often coming to the kitchens on a slow afternoon to experiment with ingredients and techniques.

I felt more relaxed as we sipped barley beer to cool ourselves in the hot kitchen and sang buoyant songs, chatting about the Akitu feast and fertility celebrations to come that night. Our favourite temple cat, Dax, keen to be wherever we were, brushed against my calves. He leapt upon the benchtop and sat with his golden-spotted body held majestically.

'Look, Dax has ratter!' said Gemekala, and we all laughed as he wriggled into an even prouder posture, blinking his pleasure. Ratter was a description we used for cats basking in their own greatness after catching a rat, and we had come to use the term to describe any cat or person pleased with themselves.

The light mood felt the right time to tell the priestesses what had happened in the ritual. 'Sisters,' I began casually. 'I've just come from purifying Adam, the man who's speaking of a heretic threat.' I traced a fingertip over one of the spots on Dax's coat, not looking at any of them. I didn't want to make a fuss about Adam's subversive behaviour and cause alarm. They had been on edge since I'd told them the details of the Larsa invaders, especially Gemekala, though we maintained a façade of normality in alignment with our roles. Fear could spread quickly and we would not foster that state. I hadn't told them what Adam said about the heretics recruiting refugees either, preferring to wait until after the Akitu celebrations to address such weighty issues.

Of course, they expressed surprise.

'Whatever for?' Urnina asked.

I told them what had happened.

'Dunking doesn't seem punishment enough,' said Gemekala. 'They should be banded—tightly.' She turned to jab at the meat, her bare shoulder blades bobbing up and down. Any man who had been highly offensive, usually by losing control of his aggressive or rutting sexual nature or releasing his milk into a woman unbidden, was taken to Olgana and her matrons to have his figs and shaft banded with a copper ring. It was the level of discipline beyond the purification pool.

'No banding,' I said. 'However, I did have them dig their own graves in the common yard to torment them.'

Gemekala snorted, but I could tell she was pleased.

'Why would he so desperately want to be in the ritual?' said Anunit, wiping the back of a hand across her sweaty brow.

'To worship the body of the high priestess is not motivation enough?' asked Tiamat, leering at me. She was in bright spirits lately, her eyes lit by a new lover with whom she was besotted.

'Or perhaps he really thought he was doing a public service by stepping in. I've heard Ureem does favour a beer too many on occasion,' said Urnina, always keen to lessen the severity of any matter.

I shook my head. 'I'm sure Adam orchestrated it.'

Cook trundled past, peering at our progress, and we sniggered as Sabit mimicked his billowing cheeks and habit of rocking his big body from side to side as he fretted over his pots.

'The way you speak of this Adam, you're sweet for him, aren't you?' Tiamat asked, cocking an eyebrow at me. 'Will you be saving some of your meat for him?'

'I might,' I said with a smile. Most males would never taste the flesh of the holy cow in their lifetimes, but sometimes at the Akitu feast, we might save a titbit for a lover to boost his virility for the evening's celebrations.

After the cooking, I took a cool bath and Tadez brought me my beautifying mask carved from a piece of rose quartz to sit over my face, breathing holes at the nose. I dozed and allowed the emanations of the crystal to beautify my skin, leaving my face more radiant and my eyes with an extra sparkle. Later, Tadez slicked patchouli oil over my body and helped me into a long white skirt with seven tiers as can only be worn by a priestess, representing the initiation tests we must pass in relation to the seven energy centres of the body. I asked Tadez to send for Urnina to paint my eyes, then dismissed him to tend to his own grooming.

'Mammi,' said Aea, her voice combusting with excitement as she appeared at my door with Urnina behind her. 'Urnina has something for you.'

Aea carried Yasmin around her shoulders, red-faced with the effort to hold up the snake's weight. 'And Sky Snake is here too since she's the muse for the arm cuffs—oh! I've spoiled the surprise.' She looked up to Urnina, who smiled indulgently and bent to kiss the top of her head.

'I have a gift for you to celebrate Akitu,' said Urnina proudly, holding out her hands to present two glittering snake-shaped arm cuffs. They were lavishly covered with peridots, the same shade as Yasmin's pretty green scales, with a row of bright red jasper stones along the centreline and jet eyes. Gushing my thanks, I pushed them up my arms, twisting this way and that to see them from different angles.

'This shade makes your eyes greener than Venus,' said Urnina as she swiped green malachite paste across my lids. She was the most talented in the arts of beauty and design, and although not the finest-featured of my priestesses—that was Lahamu—she strongly radiated the loveliness of Venus. She touched up the blue lines of the downward triangle drawn between my brows with lapis paste. When she dabbed crushed mulberry on my lips, permanently blushed from the dye, she winked and told me, 'Remember to keep your lips wet for extra comeliness.'

'Can I choose your diadem?' Aea asked as she looked at my extensive range of headpieces hanging on the wall, and I smiled my agreement. Staggering a little under Yasmin's weight, Aea brought me her favourite. It boasted a dazzling lapis almost as large as my palm that sat above my forehead, the glowing copper headband studded with seven rows of stones in the colours of a rainbow. When she placed it on my head, I whispered in her ear, 'One day you will wear this. The day of your first blood, it is yours.' Aea's grin was so vigorous that her whole head moved with its force, and my eyes teared tenderly.

'No!' cried Urnina in stagey outrage as she dabbed at my make-up. 'Your perfect eyes!'

The sun was well into its afternoon arc when the temple women and children gathered for the feast. As I regarded my new cuffs, I looked at my breasts, satiny with oils, the nipples still swollen and darkened from the Akitu ritual, and my belly surged at the prospect of seeing Adam. Despite the vexation I'd felt at his intrusion, an excitement was rising within my core at the way he challenged me. It would make laying with him all the sweeter.

The populace cheered as we entered the public terrace. I took my place at the head table, laughing with Gemekala as servants dashed to and fro with huge fans, waving at the smoke wafting from the roasting fires below. From my cushions, I watched men carrying vats of barley beer and great wheels of bread into the plaza. Servant boys hurried out of the apartments lining the concourse, bearing platters of salads and pots of olives for the communal street tables.

I called Fancy to my side to admire the two new pieces Aea had instructed the jewellers make for her—the dog wore a pretty rose quartz and amethyst beaded collar and a matching belt around her narrow waist. Aea didn't hear me praise her creations, her focus on flicking olive pips at the other temple daughters sitting behind us and stifling laughs with

Humusi. The girls knew they had my indulgence today. Urnina sat at my other side with her little boy, Nanni, and the girls involved him in the game, although his fat little fingers were ineffectual and he giggled at his failures.

'Mammi, did the bull bring you before Inanna's heavenly gates last night?' asked Aea, now lying back across my lap.

'Yes, my precious white bird, he did,' I said, chuffing her cheek. 'He was unlike any before in his ability to do so.' Appreciation for the bull warmed my heart.

Nanni looked at me with wide eyes. 'Did the bull really go up in the sky?'

'His spirit helped me reach the centre of all that is,' I answered.

'What's there?' they asked in unison, their little faces turned up to me adoringly.

'Perfection.'

The childish wisdom in their eyes showed they understood, so fresh from the heavenly realms they hadn't yet forgotten.

'I know that place,' chirped Nanni, and I cupped the back of his head tenderly. Perhaps he felt I ran hot and cold with him. Sometimes it pained me to love him, knowing he had just a few more springs in the temple before he was sent to one of the working districts. Although Urnina and I would keep a close eye on his welfare, a widening distance would inevitably come between us. I put it from my mind and cuddled him close.

Tiamat was the first to ask for the lover she favoured to be brought to the table, the one who had lately so lit her with joy. He was a handsome man from the copper district named Anba, and I was surprised I hadn't spotted him before. He would've taken my eye with his air of confidence, lacking in most men. Other men hoping to be invited to our table waited in throngs at the bottom of the steps. I wondered if Adam was among them, but no. He was not the type of man that would do so.

Doshina had her long-term lover, matron Delondra, brought up next. The two women fell into each other's arms, Doshina's willowy slightness dwarfed by the powerful frame of the matron. When they weren't laughing and whispering, they fed each other pieces of meat, licking each other's fingers and kissing in between bites.

Most of us were in no hurry to bring a lover to our sides, preferring each other's company and our more sophisticated conversation through the late afternoon. When the six councillors ascended the steps, I pretended to be in deep conversation with Urnina, her lips twitching in amusement as she nodded vigorously in pretence. Tadez stepped forward to greet the councillors and seat them far from me, as he knew I would want.

My face lit as the retired High Priestess Menna, and her husband, Demsar, came to sit with me. I greeted them warmly and patted the cushion beside me, gesturing to Tadez to bring them beer straws. Menna had stepped down as high priestess 11 springs ago and moved out of the temple in order to marry Demsar—it was forbidden for a high priestess to marry, or for a man to live on our residential terrace.

'It's wonderful to see everyone enjoying such abundance,' said Menna, beaming as she surveyed the crowd. She was beautiful, her eyes crinkling a little at the sides with her frequent smile and the silver streaks in her dark hair sparkling. She wore flowing orange shawls, as she always did, and carnelian and malachite jewellery.

Leaning closer, I spoke low in her ear, rose oil filling my senses. 'I've been wanting to talk to you about a city concern.'

Her brow furrowed as I told her about the reports that men from the north were raising a heretical rebellion against the Great Mother's rule. I described the Larsa invasion, and how Adam wanted to help me form a defence force, and his report that the heretics had recruited refugees from the settlement downriver.

'There is a strange feeling around this,' she said, her warm brown eyes narrowed with seriousness. 'When I seek further information in my mind's eye, there is nothing there.'

'I cannot detect what will come of this either. But I've decided at the next council meeting to announce plans to take in some refugee men, and to provide more resources for their settlement. We need the goodwill of such men, although the council will push against it.'

'I do not envy you dealing with those women on such a matter.' She flicked her eyes towards the councillors, sprawled on cushions as a gaggle of boys fanned them. Menna's distaste for the councillors and politics was part of why she had chosen to step down. In her love of Demsar and her three sons, she could no longer pretend she considered males beneath her, and of course she could not publicly proclaim nor drive city agendas from such an eccentric belief.

'The council will think a threat from heretics is ludicrous,' continued Menna. She sighed. 'Sometimes, it would be easier if they knew about the prophecy.'

'Great Mother help us if they did,' I whispered, watching one of the councillors, who was heavily pregnant, slap a boy's hand as he offered her a peeled grape. 'They'd want every man killed except a few breeders.'

We shared a look of thin amusement.

People around the table were noticing our hushed voices, so I sat taller and sipped some beer, laughing at the children's antics. I watched Demsar stroke Menna's arm and brush her hair back over her shoulder, her face illumined with joy as she turned to meet his gaze. I had never known such feelings for a man and wondered what it would be like to love as they did. Menna had shared her lap only with Demsar through many springs, and I didn't know of any other woman who had kept only one lover for so long.

As the mood on our terrace became increasingly relaxed, a few more lovers were called up, and the crowds below caroused with greater enthusiasm.

Gemekala came to crouch beside me, gesturing at Tiamat and Anba with the large rib bone she gnawed. The couple was kissing deeply, limbs entwined. 'I think Tiamat will initiate the fertility rites,' she said, taking in every detail of the amorous pair. 'She kept him in her chamber until sunrise a few nights ago, thinking none of us would know.'

'So long as she is discreet, I can turn a blind eye,' I said. To maintain our energetic purity, no man was allowed to stay overnight, but we all understood that in the early flush of love, we might like to keep a lover until dawn. 'Maybe she'll be the first priestess in my reign that takes a husband.' A priestess was allowed to marry, although it was extremely rare any did.

Gemekala snorted. 'Like all fresh flowers, his appeal will soon droop. At his first snore, she'll no longer welcome him all night.' She put the cleaned bone down and met my eye with a spirited grin. It heartened me to see her feeling brighter, albeit with biting humour. She was gifted—or cursed—with particularly lifelike dreams and visions of the boded future, some of them tormenting her so deeply she preferred to deny the prophecy as false. Her fears made her reluctant to relate with men beyond their role at her lap, and even then she generally preferred women. But I had seen her stolen glances at Tiamat and Anba, and Menna and Demsar, as if she secretly wished for such a connection.

Emboldened by the beer and escalating mood, city women and their daughters ascended the steps to our public terrace to offer pink blooms or a single white dove's feather. Aea enjoyed every moment in her great pride in me, every now and then leaping to gather the white feathers piling up. She'd been collecting them as her most treasured possessions since she could walk.

Later, against the rose sky, we allowed uninvited men to approach the steps. Anunit gestured at a brawny man who placed a feather on the pile. He beamed with pride, delighted to be called to the lap of a priestess, especially one so fleshy and fragrant as her. As this man was not recognised as a regular lover used by any of us, Tadez pulled him aside to reiterate the rules for laying with a priestess—the hallowed experience must never be spoken of to others—and ensure he had suitable sully cloths.

I felt Adam's presence before I saw him ascending the stairs, a pleated leather kilt riding up his thighs with each step. His bare chest glowed in the late afternoon light, evidence he had oiled himself. I felt foolish for gaping at him and returned to chatting with Urnina, who knew exactly what I felt and smirked prettily. He knelt at the top step and called out to me.

'High Priestess,' he said with a slight dip of his head, holding out a white dove feather.

I brushed my hair back over a shoulder. Was I imagining it or was my right breast stirring in his presence, as though it recognised the source from which it had recently received such pleasure? I waved him forward and he knelt on the other side of the table in the space vacated by some of the children.

'Will you accept my offering of reverence?' he asked with a grin, reaching to place the feather on the pile. For a man who had dug his own grave and nearly drowned at my hands on this day, he was audacious. I couldn't stop my mouth from pulling up at one side.

'Despite your deceit and disrespect in intruding on a sacred ritual?' I said quietly, ensuring no one else could hear me.

'I hope I fulfilled the role as well as Ureem might have?' His eyebrows lifted earnestly.

For a moment I considered admonishing him, but instead a little gulp of laughter erupted from my lips. 'I suppose on that level, I can be merciful.'

We looked at each other a long moment.

'Have a drink with me,' I said, gesturing to the cushions next to me where Aea sat. She scrambled over my lap to make space for him. I smelled cedarwood oil on his skin as he sat and leaned forward to nod at Aea with a smile. Tadez appeared with a beer straw for Adam, his lips pressed together in disapproval.

'To Inanna and a bountiful spring ahead.' Adam glanced at my breasts as if including them in the toast, and I appreciated his reverence. We drank from the communal beer vat in front of us, the heat and drink soothing our jagged spark as we chatted about the feast and music. He casually took a jujube from a fruit platter although I had not invited him to partake of my table, and when he reached to take another, I grabbed his hand in irritation. My fingertips felt the moist puffiness of blisters, and I turned his palm up to examine it.

'Excuse the poor state of my hands, High Priestess. I had to do a lot of digging today.' How rebellious he was to speak so glibly of what must have been a traumatising experience.

He flipped my hand over and held it up. 'Your hands are elegant yet strong. Strong enough to push a man down—if he does not resist.' This time his voice carried an edge of darkness. I pulled away from his grip, deciding not to chastise him. He was the most scintillating company I could find and I still wanted him at my side.

He gestured to Menna and Demsar. They sat with the three boys Menna had borne over the springs she'd devoted her lap rights to her husband although, like all women, she had every right to lay with anyone she chose.

'Are those the retired High Priestess' sons?' he asked, nodding towards the teenagers. 'They look just like her lover, how can that be?'

The boys had the same distinctive dimpled chin, bright blue eyes and rangy frames as Demsar, making a compelling case that he'd had a role in creating them.

'Marvellous, isn't it?' I kept my gaze from his. 'Surely you know he is not only her lover, but also her husband. She loves him so much that she willed her womb to create her children to resemble him.'

I looked around in hopes of finding a distraction from the conversation, my eyes falling on Lahamu as she pulled away from her lover's caress to speak to the musicians. 'Listen, Priestess Lahamu will sing. She has a wondrous talent.'

We watched as the man playing a lyre with a carved cow's head protruding from the sound box stood to let Lahamu take his place, glancing up at her beautiful face in awe. Next to her was a musician with a bull lyre with a base pitch, another with a calf lyre that issued a high and sweet sound. They began to pluck the melody of one of our favourite hymns to Inanna. As her deft fingers strummed the lyre, Lahamu opened her throat and exploded in a passionate warble.

At the song's end, we applauded as the children shook their beaded rattles and clanged cymbals, and I laughed when Fancy wedged her muzzle beneath my arm to escape the clamour, sending up a waft of the geranium perfume Aea liked to dab on her fur. The girls began running around the tables, chasing one another in hilarious spirits, now an acceptable pastime as formalities were increasingly abandoned. I turned to Adam.

'Tell me about your life,' I asked, stroking Fancy's cream coat to soothe her nerves. 'How I did not know of you until recently?'

'I've been in Uruk only a few springs. I grew up travelling with a group of gem miners and traders, looking for red jasper mainly, but also carnelian, chalcedony, bloodstone—whatever we could find. I've seen many places and peoples.' He bent his head to his straw, taking a casual sip. 'My life has given me worldliness beyond the city of Uruk.'

He pulled a cushion behind his back and reclined further, reaching those big hands behind his head and revealing the lines of musculature in his arms, and the dark hair growing beneath them.

'I hardly think running round in the desert compares to the sophistication of the world's greatest city,' I said. Rather than argue his silly claim further, I changed the subject. 'You said you were priestess-born. Tell me again, who is your mother and where were you born?'

'My mother is a priestess of Inanna from Neotez, and I have barely seen her since she gave me up.' He looked down the wide concourse towards the river.

'Do you think of her often?' I asked, guilt grabbing my heart as I thought of Sabium.

'I don't think of her at all. She means nothing to me.' He kept his face turned away, making it clear he would not look at me while I spoke of her.

I would have preferred to be enjoying my time with him in the lead up to our lovemaking, but I was obliged to rebuke him. 'You disrespect your mother, who was merely following the priestess way. She gave you an honourable name—Adam means 'man of red clay', a celebration of the soil and the crops it grows.'

'I know what it means. But she had no regrets when I was evicted from her temple, as if I were a lesser being than a girl.' There was emotion in his voice.

I felt his grief within my own body, thinking of how my mother had also rejected Sabium coldly. *Forget your brother, Lilith. You must separate yourself from him*, she had said when I beseeched her to bring him back from the mines. I didn't know if her harshness was because her mind's eye showed that he would turn against me, as indeed he had, or perhaps she never allowed herself to care, knowing he must leave the temple as a child. Either way, I knew exiling Sabium hurt her, although she tried not to show it—her laughter never rang true after he left.

Adam sat taller, preparing to speak. 'High Priestess, forgive me for bringing this up at a celebration, but I must try again. I fear the heretics pose a great threat to Uruk. I implore you to listen to me.'

I exhaled strongly. Why must he keep spoiling our time together?

'I would have received word from other temples if this were a real threat,' I said quietly. 'And what place do you have, even with your pride in your so-called worldliness, to advise me on how to run this city?'

'The place from which I speak to you is not the concern. Your city's safety is. I beg you, let me take charge of building a defence,' he pressed in a low and urgent voice. 'Ignoring this is folly, and while you may cross the stars in your rituals, your naivety about this threat will hurt your city.'

I was stunned a moment by his outrageous criticism.

'Man, you are out of order,' I growled. 'Since your purification was ineffective, perhaps I should have you thrown into the pit.'

He thrust his beer straw into the jug like it was a spear and rose to his feet. 'I'm sorry, High Priestess. Again I have offended you when I meant to be of service.'

I waved my dismissal, although he was already turning away, forcing myself to smile a little for the sake of anyone watching.

It seemed the others nearby didn't notice the altercation, but I bristled with rare indecision about how to respond. Men had been dealt our harshest punishments for showing such disrespect to any temple woman, let alone a high priestess. Yet I could not bring myself to start proceedings, especially since I sensed there was truth in what Adam said. I put an end to the chasing game Aea and the girls played with a single sharp glare, my tolerance expended.

Menna gathered her shawls to shuffle close to me, resting a delicate hand on my forearm. 'So that's Adam. I felt his eyes upon me. Such a probing energy.'

'He questioned why your sons look like Demsar.'

We shared a worried look.

'I don't know why he challenges and attracts me so,' I said.

'There is a great light between you and he,' Menna replied, her eyes taking on a far away look as she connected with her mind's eye. 'And...a weird purpose. I sense it will impact far and wide.'

I leaned closer to her, rubbing the flesh prickling on my arms. 'What is this fated purpose? I do not trust him and he is infuriating, yet I am drawn to him so powerfully I feel out of control.'

'The fate of your mission is veiled.' Menna shook her head. 'We cannot always understand the weirdness of a situation, for it would change it in the knowing.'

My skin tingled further at her words.

'High Priestess.' A familiar voice, wheezing with effort, pulled my attention to a short and slight figure at the front of the queue of men. My eyes closed a moment, gathering myself to deal with the last thing I needed right now.

'Sabium.' I nodded a greeting as a wave of emotion rose to thicken my throat. Looking into my brother's hardened eyes, I knew he would refuse any effort I made at a warm connection.

'I'm here to pay my respects,' he said rudely, reaching into the pocket of his fine goatskin kilt, the garment of a quality no other man in Uruk could access—one of the perks he received in his role of councillor's adviser. He withdrew a bedraggled feather and tossed it on the pile.

'Although this occasion is not generally used for petitioning the temple, I pray you make an exception for me, your twin brother,' he said loudly, turning around to ensure the crowd of men on the steps below him were listening.

I hid my alarm, dreading whatever ploy he was going to use to undermine me.

'Did you know that in the last turn of the moon, four boys have been crushed to death in your copper mines?' he demanded. 'Two of them suffered for days, unreachable. Did you know?'

I flicked my gaze around to see who was witnessing his troublemaking, finding that every person within close hearing range watched with rapt attention.

'Councillor Semiramis has not told me as yet.' If the councillor of the copper district told me at all, it would be in context of how the collapse affected production. I glanced at Semiramis now, wondering how she would take to one of her advisers speaking so poorly of her portfolio's matters. With relief, I saw her attention was on the boy massaging her thighs, her eyes closed as she ran her fingertips over the strawberry-red mark on her cheek then down her throat in pleasure. Even in such repose, she radiated malice. She was the one who nearly drowned Sabium when we were all children. Now, he was one of her advisers, at my order—a few springs after I managed to bring him back from the mines, I insisted he be given the role to offer him a better life. Forcing her to take on Uruk's first male adviser had seemed just.

'I am sorry to hear of the suffering of the boys,' I added, my voice choked.

'Your apology means little to their broken bodies. What would help would be to use the cedarwood you grow for temple luxuries to scaffold the mines.'

Everyone on the temple steps and public terrace scrutinised me for my response. He knew he was immune to the usual repercussions any man would suffer for such insolence. Before him, my power was false, but at least I would maintain the theatre of it.

I waved dismissively, hoping no colour flamed my face. 'We all have the duty of celebrating this day to ensure the fertility of our women and lands, yet you depress it with a civic matter?' I said, hearing the shrillness in my voice.

We engaged in an unblinking stare, his green eyes similar yet worlds apart from my own. He had succeeded in upsetting the celebration and riled the men with his criticism of my temple. What's more, he was stupid, cornering me publicly so I could not agree to his petition without looking weak. My gut writhed.

'Let us hope the Great Mother won't punish us for your impertinence,' I continued. 'I will consider your suggestion at an appropriate time.'

At my nod, Olgana hastened towards him as her fingers hooked the copper band attached to her sash, and she made to put her hand up his kilt. I cleared my throat—she knew I forbade this tactic on my brother. Still, I allowed the matrons to lead him down the steep temple steps. The city would speak of his disruptive behaviour no matter what, so I had to show some repercussion. I sensed Semiramis' glare, now she had taken note of the fuss, and hoped the councillor would not punish him further. My throat choked with effort to hold back my tears, and I let Menna flow her love into my hand under the table until I regained composure.

Although the sky hadn't darkened beyond a pale violet and Venus was still a little low, I signalled Tadez to have the bulls' horns sounded. I would start the rites early so I could seek refuge in my chambers. I stood and expanded my aura using the mesmerism, drawing the invisible yet palpable shimmer of energy from my depths. I needed it to play my role with authority when my energy felt so low. The priestesses stood to assemble behind me and the city fell silent.

'People of Uruk, Inanna's most blessed ones,' I called, my serpentine staff high in the sky as I addressed the packed plaza below. 'Women, as incarnations of the heavenly Great Mother Inanna, rejoice in your sensuality to nurture life's bounty.'

The city cheered.

'Men, who are from and of the red clay of Earth, know this—the greater the ecstasy you evoke in the women you are chosen by, the more the Great Mother smiles down upon our soil and crops. Under Her star of Venus, let the Akitu celebrations continue!'

The horns blasted again as the people cheered and the tension of the day began to release as women drew their chosen ones towards them, a hush coming over the city. The scent of cypress branches placed on the city-wide fires wafted, the aphrodisiacal aromas permeating the air in support of the celebrations. I sat down, hoping to be unnoticed.

'Can I do something to comfort you?' whispered Urnina, her head reclining near me as two men kissed her feet.

It all seemed frippery. *Enough.* My head ached and there was a building pressure in my solar plexus. Reversing the mesmerism, I drew my aura in tightly around my body to make my presence inconspicuous and dull so I could slip away.

The draw I felt towards Adam had reopened the chasm of loneliness in my heart that had started when Sabium was taken from me. Why did I long for a deeper connection with a man? I had thought myself satisfied in the intimacy I shared with other women, Aea, nature, and my connection with the Great Mother.

But something was missing. I considered how Adam challenged me as much as Sabium, yet I dreaded to discipline either of them. As High Priestess, I must address their subversiveness or the structure of my society could be undermined, and at a time when a male insurgence seemed to be rising. Yet disciplining them because they dared to speak their thoughts and feelings grated against my own sense of rightness.

How could I punish a person in whom I saw a reflection of myself?

CHAPTER 4

Sated after the Akitu celebration, most of the city had gone to their beds as I entered the vestibule of the copper district's communal house. Sour sweat, clumsily tanned leather and stale beer instantly hit my nose.

Sleeplessness in my bedchamber had driven me here to find Sabium. I planned to give my brother a final chance to make peace with me, and it seemed best I come to see him rather than calling him to the temple.

So many springs had turned since I last tried to visit him here, and I barely remembered my way around. My eyes came to rest on a scrawny teenager sweeping the floor in a dark corner of the otherwise empty room.

'Take me to Adviser Sabium's chamber,' I called to him, relieved no one else was around to note my presence.

The teenager leaned the broom against the wall. He didn't realise who I was and didn't look at my face, yet obeyed me without thought. My sandalled feet peeled away from the sticky floor with each step as I followed him into another room, the boy stopping to take the single oil lamp that burned low near the door. The dark forms of perhaps a hundred men and boys slept on the barley grass-strewn floor, the smell of sweat rising off them like a haze. We picked our way around them and passed into an adjoining room, where more men and boys slept. The smell here went beyond staleness, heightened by the stench of human waste. A dozen babies and toddlers lay sleeping, one little boy sitting up to stare at our shadowy forms as we passed. Holding my shawl over my nose, I followed the teenager outside and along a colonnade, where I drank in the fresh air.

We continued on to a fragrant square courtyard, a hidden world open only to the black sky. The light of braziers showed gardens surrounding a central pond with marble benches at opposite ends, and doors marked a series of rooms around the square's perimeter, the accommodations of the copper district's matrons and advisers. The grand double doors with a pair of ibex horns as handles opened to the apartments of the district's head matron.

The teenager stopped in front of a door, a dim light showing beneath it. I knocked.

'Hello, brother,' I said quietly when Sabium opened the door, feeling renewed guilt for the way I had to look down to meet his gaze. He hadn't grown taller than an adolescent and his shoulders had never filled out, stunted from malnourishment and six years of rarely seeing the light of the sun.

'What do you want?' His face was sullen but I sensed his surprise.

'I want to improve conditions at the mines and I need your cooperation. Can we talk?'

He took in my appearance. I was dressed in plain white shawls, devoid of my diadem and snake cuffs that identified me as a priestess. I was here to meet him eye to eye, without my entourage and symbols of rulership.

Scowling, he stepped back to let me enter the simple chamber, undoubtedly of a humbler standard than those of the female advisers. His sleeping pallet was covered in linen and a wool blanket, the floor swept clean, his kilts and sandals neatly stored on a shelf. A bowl containing three peaches sat upon the table, still his favourite snack it appeared, and I was glad he had access to Uruk's finest fruits.

'Your coming down here like a common woman doesn't make me forget the way you abandoned me.' Sabium started in on me immediately, and my heart plummeted at the hopelessness of repeating this conversation over and over.

'I am here as your sister, who slept at your side from within the womb until the day you were taken from me. I did not have a say. I was a little girl.' Emotion welled in me despite my intention to be reserved. I knew he'd suffered greatly, but had it never occurred to him I had also?

He glared as his lower lip quivered, the pain between us as raw as the day we were separated. 'You did not have a say while you rested on your fluffy bed with your full belly? I was starved, beaten, forced into tunnels as high as your knee. I sent you endless messages with my mind's eye, but you did not help me,' he sneered. 'Even when I was half dead with the lung sickness, you did not find a way, although you think yourself all powerful.'

He coughed, his breathing laboured with the upset of his rant. The dust in the mines had left him with a cough that could sound like the dying agonies of a jackal, sometimes bringing burning fevers that drove him to the temple for herbs, although it stung his pride to need our help.

'I tried to get you back from the first day you were taken,' I said in pleading tones. 'As soon as I found a way, I did.'

When I welcomed my first blood moon at age 13, I'd used my right to request any gift the temple could bestow to bring him back from the mines, despite our mother's reluctance. On his return, she had him assigned to the copper district. Soon after, she was killed by lions during a hunting trip, without ever having seen him again. I tried repeatedly to connect with him, but he ignored or avoided me, filled with bitterness as he blamed me for his traumatic life.

Thinking of how he had suffered, I softened. I could not give up hope that his true essence was still within him somewhere. 'Sabium, please. Why can't we make peace?'

'Because you forgot your promise,' he snapped, anger crackling around him. 'You said you would not allow injustice when you had power, but you care only for your own privilege.'

I perched on the edge of his table, conscious of how much taller I stood than him. He began to walk back and forth in front of me as his familiar tirade rose in volume.

'You let boys die in the mines, you turn a blind eye to the abuse in the district houses, you cast out starving men and boys seeking refuge while you shelter the women. You have done nothing!'

My shoulders dropped and I stood to leave. He was like a child, seeing only the glamour of my position but none of the pressures. No matter what I did, he would hate me. I wavered as I touched the door, my feet like stones weighted to the ground. I laid a palm on the wall to steady myself, closing my eyes.

'You ask so much,' I said, turning from the door to face him once more. 'I want to make things better but I am confined by tradition and protocol. Do you see the responsibilities I face?'

The force of his glare told me he did not.

I tried again. 'I am going to order the mines be scaffolded. And I will make more changes gradually.' An image arose of the babies and young boys I had passed on my way here, along with remembrance of their stink. 'Starting with proper care for the boys of the district houses.'

He harrumphed. 'Your puny efforts are insult. Men are as worthy as you, with capabilities to further this society you won't consider. We should all stand up to you!'

'How dare you speak so seditiously! Don't you know I'd be compelled to have you purified if anybody heard you?' The thought chilled me. 'Oh Sabium, stop! Do not speak words that would make me hurt you. I came here to make peace.'

Sabium stared at me now with unforgiving eyes, unmoved as ever. 'Until I stand by your side, we will never know peace.'

'Another one?' I flung back my bedsheets to welcome Gemekala into my arms in the darkness before dawn.

She nodded, her face ghoulish in the shadows, hair in mad disarray and eyes wide with fear. She had been haunted by the same nightmare since we'd been children—a woman in a far-off time and place tied to a stake with kindling stacked around her. A man lit the fire to the jibes of a crowded public square, condemning her for being a midwife and herbalist, roles Gemekala was revered for.

I stroked her tumbled hair, swelling the energy of my heart to embrace her.

'It's just a dream, Gem, shh,' I whispered, but I knew the truth—she foresaw a future life. I had seen the vision once myself, when she had come to my bed for solace, my mind's eye pressed to her own as I sought to take her torments. I knew it was Gemekala's soul that finally left the charred woman's body, and I was her child, screaming and choking in horror as I watched my mother burn. Tears ran silently down my cheeks as I held Gemekala now, feeling the irregular pumps high in her chest as she struggled to breathe, hearing the faint wheeze in her lungs. Her breathing became like this whenever she was frightened, as if the smoke and constricting terror of that distant experience affected her in the moment.

'Lilu, I'm afraid.' She whimpered in my arms. 'This talk of a rebellion. We must be harder on men. We cannot let such things unfold.'

A ravaging hopelessness pulled at me and I fought its jaws, expanding my energy with a gust of strength. She was right—that horrifying future must not eventuate.

Yet it *was* wrong to treat men and boys so harshly, and betraying my conscience became more difficult every day. All I could do was try to negotiate between the two pathways, preventing men from uprising while treating them better, but not so well they could take advantage of the leniency. I knew it was a poor strategy, bringing no ease to the sickening thud in my belly, but what else could I do?

As Tadez and I approached the grand home on the western edge of the plaza, the roar of a birthing woman rang out. A novice had summoned Gemekala this morning to attend the labour of Zamug, councillor of the gem district. Now, as the sun hit the mid-sky and the birth was imminent, I had been called to bless the mother and child.

I was about to let myself into Zamug's front parlour when I noticed Tadez's pallor.

'You may wait outside,' I said, grinning wryly at his squeamishness. Men were not built to be amid the might of childbirth.

In the central courtyard, Zamug squatted over a pile of barley grass as she gripped a rope slung over a large pomegranate tree's limb, Gemekala kneeling before her. Two novices held Zamug's arms to ease the weight on her legs between contractions, their faces glowing with the rigour. They grinned greetings.

'Councillor Zamug, you must control your push on the next rush. Let us ease this babe through the gates of life,' urged Gemekala, who prided herself on keeping perinea intact. She flicked her hand at a novice for another hot compress to aid the stretch of Zamug's bulging gateway.

The next convulsion visibly pulsed Zamug's belly, and she fired a mighty wail, pulling hard on the rope.

'She comes!' cried Gemekala, unable to contain her excitement as the baby's shiny black curls appeared. I raised one arm to the Heavens and pointed the other towards the Earth as I spoke the birthing rites. Gemekala crouched lower to peer at the crowning head, reaching her fingers into the bowl of lard next to her and smearing some around the puckered little scalp. Zamug's face shone with the glow of an ecstatic birthing mother, her heavy-lidded eyes rolling back as orgasmic pressure danced with agony. She lolled her head as she allowed Gemekala to probe for the baby's neck.

'Let's see this baby!' rallied Gemekala, satisfied the neck was not roped. Zamug's grunt turned into an open-throated howl, and suddenly, the ears appeared, then a pink baby rushed into Gemekala's hands, followed by a gush of hind water.

A timeless moment of pervasive peace embraced us all. Gemekala held up the baby, its limbs jerking and eyes squinting at the rude emergence into the bright world of air.

'It's a boy.' Gemekala used even tones, but still Zamug's face dropped in disappointment. In spite of the baby's sex, Gemekala radiated joy as she beheld the spluttering boy, her eyes spilling tears. Her forehead was reddened where she had scratched at her mind's eye during the night, as was always the case the day after one of her nightmares.

We helped Zamug recline on the prepared bedding, the white linen dotted with red flowers fallen from above, and the novices swiftly laid warm sheets of wet linen perfumed in jasmine over her belly.

I caressed the baby's slippery arms and thighs as he took to Zamug's nipple, murmuring blessings upon him as if to compensate for the lack of welcome he received from his mother. Wetness swelled in my eyes and I closed them, pretending prayer as I gathered myself. An odd feeling arose, then a swirl of confusion as I registered the distant sound of yelling. Anxiety struck at my belly and a moment later, I heard the front door burst open. Tadez was shouting something, knocking over an amphora that clattered on the tiles of the parlour in his haste.

'My lady!' He gestured at me wildly from the edge of the courtyard. 'Uruk is under attack!'

I met Gemekala's stare in a flash of dread as I rose to my feet, the disturbance causing the baby to break his latch and squawk in outrage.

'Stay here,' I called over my shoulder as I raced outside to the plaza with Tadez at my heels, instinctively turning towards the concourse. A man was running towards us, waving his arms and shouting. Screaming and yelling rose from somewhere nearby.

'In the gem district!' the man yelled at us. 'Men with daggers!'

The breath sucked out of me.

'Do not go!' Tadez tried to reach out for me, but I was already running ahead.

The fracas became louder as I neared one of the lanes leading off the concourse and into the labyrinth of the gem district, pushing my way through people running from the scene.

I took in the chaos. Blood on the compacted dirt laneway, a wide streak of it left by a dragged body. In an instant, I found its source, one of our city men, dead, with two men crying and pawing at his body. Glancing up the laneway, I saw the fight had moved on, rapid movement and flailing limbs making it impossible to tell what was going on.

Several people knelt around a woman slumped on the ground further along the laneway. I shoved my way in to drop down beside her, seeing a gaping wound on her belly and a deep slash across the top of her bosom. Blood flowed from her at a horrifying rate.

Yanking off the shawl I wore over my upper body, I knelt and pushed it onto the belly wound, the more ghastly of the gashes, and began to whisper an incantation for the semi-conscious woman, an urgent plea for the assistance of the Great Mother. Her blood was warm under my shins and I increased the power of my incantation.

More shouting pulled me out of my trance. In shock, I saw flashes of Adam wrestling with an invader, my view impeded by the people hovering around. I screamed at them to stand back, the injured woman forgotten in my panic that Adam might be killed.

Staggering to my feet, I rushed towards the fight, the two men swinging punches and Adam blocking the invader's glistening dagger with his forearm, wrapped in a leather kilt.

I heard myself shouting, 'Help him!' but no man came to help Adam, whose eyes flashed to meet mine for a moment. After making a hard blow to the invader's head, Adam grabbed him in a headlock and brought him to his knees. Both men panted in the haze of dust kicked up in the fight, the invader in submission.

The other invaders had run away before I'd had a chance to see them properly, but at least we had one prisoner.

'Tadez,' I said, taking a shaky breath as I eyed him hovering anxiously by my side. 'Have someone bring the injured woman to the temple now.'

'Yes, but first I must attend to you.' His face was ashen as he looked me up and down. I took in my appearance, finding my hands covered to the wrists in blood. From the knees down, the front of my long skirt was soaked, the redness bright against the white linen. A bloody palm print lay over my heart, where I must have placed my hand.

'Adam,' I called. He still held the man tightly. 'Are you injured?'

He shook his head.

'Take the prisoner to the head matron's chamber now.' I kept my voice strong. 'Tell her I said to prepare the rods of truth.'

Back at my terrace, Tadez helped me wash. His hands shook as hard as mine, and it took a little fumbling to dress me in a fresh skirt. As he wrapped an official shawl around my shoulders, I gathered my focus to instruct him. 'Have the pit prepared and spread word to the city—everybody must be in the plaza at sunset to watch the prisoner die. And see if that Larsa man, Birru, is still in Uruk. I want to talk to him.'

The other priestesses were waiting in my garden when I emerged.

'Who is the injured woman? Is she alive?' I asked.

'Her name is Iltani. She is a fine artisan, and the mother of three daughters,' Urnina said, her eyes red with weeping. 'I know her. She helped make the snake cuffs I gave you. She's alive but her wounds are severe.' Her eyes filled with new tears.

'You should go to Iltani now, and ensure only the best of our novices are treating her.' I looked to the remaining priestess. 'Sisters, who will come with me for the rodding of the prisoner?'

None looked too willing to be part of the truth extraction. Finally Ku-Aya agreed, her skinny neck and jerky nod reminding me of a desert ostrich.

I turned to leave.

'Wait,' said Gemekala, stepping forward to squeeze my hand with an unusually loose grip, her muscles weakened with trepidation. 'I will come with you.'

I led them down the main temple steps, the people of Uruk staring at us as they milled in the plaza, buzzing with speculation. They grew quiet as we passed. The whole city had heard of the invasion by now and awaited more news. If they did not already know, they would soon realise we were going to the head matron's chambers, and what that meant.

I paused outside the door to steady myself. The cloying scent of honeysuckle incense hit my nose as soon as I opened the door. After the blinding midday sun, it took a moment to adjust to seeing the large room, lit with oil lamps at each corner, an extra one on the instrument table where Olgana stood with her back to us. She fussed over her seven rods of truth, placed in ascending size and levels of texture.

Each head matron of Uruk crafted her own set of rods from clay when she took over from her predecessor, expressing her creativity as to how she progressively increased their power to extract truth. Olgana's rods were glazed bright blue with her fine paintings on the handles—flowers, rabbits, deer and birds. In my reign, she'd had opportunity to use the rods just a couple of times—men were usually willing to tell us anything we needed to know at the purifying pool.

Two snarling matrons held the prisoner by his arms, one of them gripping his figs in the pacifying hold, with four others standing close by. The rodding bed was neatly prepared with fresh barley grass covered with white linen.

Adam stepped forward from a dim corner. 'High Priestess, the prisoner does not speak our language,' he said, his face bloody and one of his eyes swollen. 'He is from the far north, where the rebellion has its roots. I speak some of his tongue, from my years travelling the lands.'

My eyes bulged. I was to be reliant on Adam for the interrogation, forced to trust him to translate correctly? He seemed to be involved at every turn of the disturbing occurrences in my city of late—was fate bringing us together, or did he will himself to the forefront?

'There must be others in Uruk who speak this language,' I said to the matrons.

'We can look for a travelling merchant somewhere in the city, or one may show up in the coming days or weeks if you want to wait,' said Olgana.

I inhaled, closing my eyes a moment. There was no other option but to proceed with Adam's translation.

'For now, if I may be of service, it would be my honour,' said Adam in gracious tones, though I detected smugness that I must accept his offer.

I just had to hope he would not use the language barrier to push his agenda, and that he would bring me meaningful information. I nodded sharply. 'Progress, for now.'

I faced the prisoner. He was an older man with swarthy skin as rough as a desert tree's bark and spattered with blood. He had a grey-streaked beard longer than any I'd ever seen, making him look more animalistic. His worn leather kilt had pockets that looked to be designed for holding weapons, and tough leather cuffs extended from the back of his hands to his elbows. He kept his chin high as he stared back at me with contempt, but I could see fear in the way he held his muscles. My gaze was drawn to the red smear between his eyebrows. At first glance I thought it was blood, then dread sank through me—it was a red triangle, pointing upwards, the opposite direction to the blue triangle priestesses wore on our brows.

Drawing a breath into my lower belly, I spoke from its power. 'Tell the prisoner this—his attack on the earthly home of the Great Mother is heinous and he will die this afternoon after he answers our questions. Inform him this can be as unpleasant as he chooses.'

Adam relayed the message. The prisoner spat with noisy bravado on the mud brick floor, his dry mouth conjuring merely a speck of spittle.

Gemekala stepped forward in a flash and thumped his cheek. 'Watch your manners, man.' He winced from the strike, and the matron's tightening grip on his figs.

'What's this?' said Gemekala, grabbing his beard and yanking it to force his chin into a position of subservience. Desert dust gathered in the bushy beard puffed into the air. 'He wears animal hair like a shepherd.' Her words forced their way out aggressively, but I heard her struggle for breath. She released him, holding out the hand that had grasped his beard as if it were contaminated.

Nodding at the matron to relieve the pressure of her hold, my face remained impassive as I stared at the man. 'Adam, ask him this—who is he to attack my city?'

The question was translated and the man held my eye as he spoke a couple of sentences, his voice trembling with fear and malice.

'He is from the far north of our land, almost as far as the Taurus Mountains,' Adam translated, stepping forward to stand halfway between the prisoner and we priestesses, as if he sought to shield us from the man's psychic daggers. 'He says his name is Zambiya of Sippar...and that he does not yield to a woman.' Adam looked steadily into my eyes to register my response.

I hid my shiver of revulsion at this unprecedented insult. 'Tell him he will indeed yield to me when he is rodded.'

I nodded to Olgana, who held the first rod, the size of a well-stiffened shaft. She slid her hand up and down its smooth length, eager to start proceedings. Four of the matrons took hold of the prisoner to force him towards the table. As the man realised what was happening, he paled and broke into a furious rant at Adam, flashing yellow teeth. This sudden change in temperament was shocking—surely he had known the essence of what was to follow? Adam's face remained blank as he ignored the torrent of abuse.

'Adam,' I called over the hollering, 'What does he say to you?'

Adam shrugged. 'He says you are evil and I am pathetic for doing your bidding. I'll cut off his tongue if he insults you further.'

'Olgana, gag him for now,' I said loudly. He would not be ready to speak the truth for a while, and I could not bear the din.

He was forced belly down onto the rodding table, especially designed for the purpose, with a two-foot-high apex over which the prisoner's hips were dragged into position. One of the matrons held his head as Olgana stuffed his mouth with linen and bound it in place. Still, he flashed wild eyes and made jerky movements as best his restrained body could, furiously grunting.

'Get on with it,' I said. My gut constricted at the stink of the prisoner's fear and the perverted excitement of the matrons, as thick as the sickly incense. These women were prized as Uruk's best matrons, yet they were repulsive to me. My hypocrisy sickened me further, for they acted on my orders.

Olgana took her time removing the prisoner's kilt, folding it meticulously and placing it on the table next to her rods, her unhurried pleasure causing my teeth to grind as I contained the urge to shake her.

The other matrons adjusted the prisoner's raised hips again, pushing his knees wider. I refrained from looking at the presentation in any detail, reaching my senses out to connect with Gemekala and Ku-Aya, and the three of us rallied in a united front. I felt Ku-Aya's vengeance—she would take a peculiar pleasure in this. Gemekala's anxiety caused her aura to quiver, but I knew she would remain uncompromising in seeing the situation through.

'High Priestess, if I may suggest we help the prisoner loosen his tongue for the first two or three rods, before we remove the gag?' Olgana said in a reasonable tone, and my chin jerked a nod.

Olgana carefully smeared mutton lard on the man's orifice with her forefinger, her thick bow legs bending a little as she leaned in to peer at her work. She took the first rod and nestled its tapered end between his buttocks, their paleness sharply delineated against his otherwise dark skin.

'Man,' said Olgana pleasantly to Adam. 'Remind the prisoner that we can use the larger and more textured rods if he finds it hard to express truth.' A sheen lay over the fine hairs above her lip.

Adam spoke to the prisoner, setting him off on another enraged but muffled rant, which turned into a stifled howl as Olgana plunged the rod into him. She held it up to the hilt for a while until he managed to calm himself, probably in the hope she would retract it if he quieted.

Adam asked him if he was ready to speak truth to us, eliciting fierce grunting from the prisoner that was clearly a refusal of cooperation.

Great Mother, help this process go quickly. I brought blankness across my heart, ignoring the nausea causing the room to sway around me. I caught Adam's eye as he tipped his head to the chairs beside him.

I turned to my priestesses. 'This may be a long process, shall we sit?' We did so gratefully, breathing as shallowly as possible in the suffocating room as Olgana began twisting and pushing the rod into the prisoner with sensual attention. Still the prisoner refused to cooperate, and larger rods were employed. All the while I looked past the scene on the bed to study the fresco at the far end of the chamber, depicting two white storks in flight above the sparkling river.

When Olgana put down rod number three and picked up the next, the tips of its barbs painted green, I spoke. 'Remove the gag. Adam, ask him how many are in his community, where they camp, and what they plan, especially regarding Uruk.'

Olgana's face was glowing with fervour as she untied the gag then raised a hand to gesture she needed a moment. She pressed the man's trembling buttocks to still him and nestled the rod, as thick as my lower forearm, at the man's bleeding, gaping hole to warn him it could be called into use at any moment. She gave a self-satisfied nod to Adam.

The man was sobbing and rambling, and Adam spoke over him, translating my questions. The two men engaged in an exchange of words, then the prisoner burst into shouts of rage. Olgana waited eagerly for any sign she should proceed, but Adam shook his head and turned to address me.

'He says he is of a band of two hundred men, and they camp to the north east of Uruk, waiting for more heretics to join them. When they have amassed in sufficient numbers, they will attack Uruk.'

Bile rose further from my stomach, along with the beginnings of an uncontrollable spasming. I took controlled breaths into my lower belly to steady myself, clasping my shaking hands together on my lap.

'I see,' I said loudly, the extra force designed to keep my voice steady. 'Ask him why only ten men attacked us. Why would they make such a futile attack on the largest city in all the lands?'

Adam spoke with the prisoner, then reported the attack was not designed to take over the city, but to warn me that the days of the Temple of Inanna would soon be over, and to take a few gems while they were at it. I asked about the red triangle between his brows, and the prisoner confirmed my dread—it was the chosen mark of the heretic rebellion.

Gemekala's thigh trembled beside mine. The foretold male uprising was unfolding before our eyes.

'Was he part of the group that attacked Larsa?' I said, straining to keep my concentration on what I needed to ask. The prisoner said he was not.

'Ask if he and his cohorts are shepherds,' I said.

After a short interaction with the prisoner, Adam responded. 'They are not shepherds. They wear beards because they laugh at the grooming protocols, and say it is women that should be better kempt.'

At this, Olgana gave the man a jab of the rod, causing him to squeal. I continued with my questions, fighting to keep my head clear in the swirling density of the room. The stench of the prisoner's shit and the iron tang of his blood caught at the back of my throat and I gagged a little, turning it into a cough to disguise my strain. At times, the prisoner garbled on and on, apparently explaining something to Adam, but I couldn't be sure all the information was translated. Frustration throbbed through my veins as I watched helplessly.

'High Priestess, shall I employ rod number four?' Olgana asked, her normally hollow eyes filled with zeal.

I turned to lean my face into Gemekala's neck, greedily inhaling the biting freshness of her juniper perfume, and whispered, 'Can you think of anything else I must ask?'

She kept her chin steady as she shook her head, the inflamed skin on her forehead standing out against her blanched face.

'We're finished with the rods now,' I said, looking pointedly at Olgana. With a sigh of regret, she removed the tip of rod four from between the man's cheeks, to his sobs of relief. Rod number five was the furthest any man had lived through. 'Get a barber here to shave that hair from his face and head. Do not touch him unnecessarily. And give him some water.'

A knock sounded at the door and Tadez's muffled voice called to me. The door swung open to reveal Birru, Tadez hovering in the background with his head down, unwilling to catch so much as a glimpse of the rodding scene.

'Come in, Birru,' I said, waving Tadez away. He quickly shut the door.

Birru reluctantly came to stand where I pointed, giving him the best view of the panting prisoner lying with his face to the side, eyelids drooping. Hopefully the man was not so altered in his appearance that Birru could not recognise him.

'Is this man one of the group that attacked your settlement?' I asked him.

Birru shook his head. 'No, this man is older. But he does carry the same red mark between his brows.'

My belly sank further. If the prisoner was not one of the Larsa invaders, it suggested the rumours about the existence of multiple heretic groups were true.

I turned to Gemekala. 'Send the novices and matrons to find any travelling merchants in the city who may speak the northern tongue. The people are primed to see this man die as the sun touches the horizon, but in the meantime, we must try to verify the information.'

I sensed Adam's offence that I doubted his translations. 'High Priestess,' he said, keeping a neutral tone. 'May I come to see you this evening to discuss the interrogation and the prisoner's weapons further?'

I nodded, keen to escape Olgana's chamber as quickly as possible.

As the priestesses and I began the walk back to the temple, a woman, old enough that she kept her wise blood every new moon, stepped in my path. Looking into her kohl-rimmed brown eyes, I recognised her as the mother of Essa, a woman murdered last spring by one of her lovers. It was one of the most shocking events Uruk had seen, at least until now. When Essa birthed a deformed baby, the district matrons put one of her lovers, a clean-shaved shepherd, to the purifying pool because it was assumed it was his sour milk that hurt the child. Shepherds—whether clean-shaved city fringe dwellers or the wild bearded ones we rarely saw—were frequently blamed for any number of social problems. He survived the water but strangled Essa that night, and I had of course sent him to the viper pit.

'High Priestess, we have heard Iltani is badly hurt. Will she survive?' The woman's voice was dignified, but I sensed her anguish. The pain of losing a daughter was surely one no woman could recover from.

'Her wounds are severe.' I spoke gently.

'I implore you—what is becoming of our society? The second woman in one turn of the seasons subjected to violence at the hands of men.' Her fingers curled around my wrist, bringing coldness down my spine. 'We heard the invaders were bearded. Were they shepherds from the wilds?'

I rubbed her hand reassuringly as I removed it from my wrist. 'They don't appear to be, despite their facial hair. The one we captured dies this afternoon, and the council meets tomorrow to ensure we bring these issues to a swift end.' I did not mention the notion of a heretic rebellion, but as I walked away I wondered how much longer could I downplay the threat.

'Oh my darlings, do not worry yourselves. Your work will soon be done and we can go home,' the viper keeper crooned into the seething pit of greasy black snakes. Even I found those snakes repugnant, nothing like my sweet Yasmin, with her green elegance and peaceful black eyes. Like the rods of truth, I rarely called the vipers into service, only a few times in my reign so far, unlike my distant temple foremothers who were said to have been quick to engage the pit at the slightest offence.

We had not found anyone else in the city who spoke the northern tongue, so I would accept Adam's interpretations, with caution. If he'd lied about or misunderstood any of the prisoner's words, it would not change the course of my response in any major way—that the heretic camp must be destroyed in the near future.

For now, the prisoner must die.

The crowded plaza was in the long shadow of the towering ziggurat, the snake pit a stone's throw from where I stood on the temple's wide lower steps, the priestesses standing tall as reeds behind me. A pretty sunset was beginning to streak the sky and I aligned myself with the beauty, letting it support me through this experience.

A few steps back from the pit stood the councillors of Uruk, and behind them their advisers, including Sabium, all ready to enjoy their privileged viewing position. The crowd was parting at the far end of the plaza to make way for the procession of the prisoner, jostling to vilify him. Women and children sat atop men's shoulders, everyone leering to get a better look, crying out, 'Teach him a lesson' or 'Damn his soul'. Each proclamation drew a wave of cheering from the crowd, unified in outrage. Several matrons flanked the naked man, stumbling and doubled over in pain, and made no effort to shield him from the abuse, such that I almost felt sorry for him. But a vision of Iltani's guts and the gaping flesh at the top of her breasts brought me back to my senses. The poor woman was in agony as she clung feebly to life.

Now neatly shaved, the man was pushed to the ground a few steps in front of me, dark sunspots standing out on his ash-white face. Although gagged, he occasionally roused himself to shoot hateful looks at Adam, standing behind Olgana. Good. The prisoner still had enough life in him to scream when he went to the pit, carrying a warning to any men who might sympathise with the heretics.

Although it was late in the day and we were in shade, the heat was still high. Sweat prickled beneath my arms in a maddening itch, and a drop ran down my back beneath my formal cobalt mantle worn for council meetings and other serious city occasions.

I nodded to have the bulls' horns blown, the sound setting off honking from the bevy of peacocks in the central plaza gardens. Grasping my serpent-entwined staff, I turned my back to the crowd to herald the high temple atop the ziggurat, spreading my mantle to display the eight-pointed star of Venus appliquéd across its back. After allowing them to absorb the display, I turned back towards the crowd.

'People of Uruk,' I called from my lower belly, drawing on the power of my girdle of fire to project my voice. I resisted the urge to adjust my gold headpiece, feeling the peacock feathers sprouting from the back of the headband bobbing with the movement of my body. 'This day, a group of ten men attacked our city in a horrific offence of violence, theft of gems and flagrant flouting of grooming protocols. We captured one of them, and during questioning, he insulted the supremacy of the Great Mother.'

I paused, letting the crowd murmur.

'We will now witness him receive the Great Mother's compassion through the viper's poison, serving to alchemise his putrid soul into annihilation.'

The crowd cheered. Although few of the people could hear me, my message would spread around the city before the sun had set.

'I ask you this—if you know of any men questioning the natural rule of the Great Mother, you must inform the temple. This message will be reiterated through the district matrons.' The people muttered righteously. I wondered how they perceived the notion of a man questioning the superiority of the feminine. Knowing nothing of the prophecy or the lie about procreation, they surely saw heresy as ridiculous and entirely futile misconduct. Or at least the women would. I wondered how many men held resentments over injustice to males, as Sabium and Adam did.

'Bring the prisoner forward,' I called.

The blast of Sabium's hate forced its way through me like a foul wind, and I caught his eye as he stared blackly at me. My efforts to seek peace with him had done no good, and I'd sworn to myself I would have him punished the next time he defied me. Still, in my guilt at ordering the execution of a man, a fate that had never been put upon a woman, once again I found myself looking away.

I refocused on the task ahead. 'Olgana, prepare the man. Remove the gag first.'

She pulled the wad of linen from his mouth, and he yelled something as loud as his hoarse throat could conjure.

The crowd craned to see Olgana pull the man to his feet, faeces and blood coating his legs. Her eyebrows raised perkily as she tied his ankles with reed rope and flung it over the wooden frame. Two matrons held his elbows as Olgana's bulky shoulders hoisted the rope and he was pulled off his feet, his head hitting the mud brick ground with a thud. Soon, he dangled over the pit.

His body twisted as he sought to rant at Adam. As the prisoner's body swung towards him, Adam reached out and thumped the bobbing head with his fist. The barrage stopped, and blood flung from the prisoner's mouth as he spat out what looked to be a fragment of tooth. I flinched, straining to keep my anger at bay in this public forum—Adam had no right to touch the prisoner without my order. What's more, he had risked quieting the man's wretched screams. Yet I had no choice but to continue and hope the public assumed Adam had acted on my say so.

'Great Mother, take this man into your bosom through the poison of the black snake,' I called. Olgana looked eagerly for my signal, as a pup focuses on a stick about to be thrown. The viper keeper hovered next to her, muttering worries that her snakes could be injured if the prisoner entered the pit forcefully.

I held my staff above my head, pausing for effect. As I slowly lowered it, Olgana squatted on her hulking haunches dramatically, although the man's weight would barely affect her. She let the rope out in time with my arm's slow downwards movement, the prisoner hollering and twisting. A sound like a hundred dragonflies buzzing assaulted my ears and confused me a moment as I sought the source, before realising it was my own stress and fury.

I fought to keep my gaze cool as I watched the dark hole consume the prisoner, his body writhing like the snakes he would soon meet. Soon, his shrieks echoed in surges as the vipers began to strike. The wait was excruciating, his screams becoming high-pitched and throaty as paralysis set in on his jaw. Eventually, all was silent. I did not know how long it would take him to be transformed from his suffering into the embrace of the snake's medicine. A man who had chosen to contest me, the Great Mother's chosen handmaiden, was a fool, but still I hoped the alchemy was swift.

'How do you fare?'

I looked up at Gemekala, the night sky a massive expanse above her from where I lay in my bath. After leaving the pit, the priestesses and I spent the early evening discussing the attack, agreeing a loose plan to increase matron numbers and train them in using weaponry. I would firm the approach at tomorrow's council meeting. For now, I tried to soothe myself in the warm bath that Tadez had dosed with lavender oil, its violet energy helping to purify my aura of the day's atrocities.

'Fine,' I said, meeting her eyes with a glum grin—we both knew that was a ridiculous description. We laughed a little, and I sat up to make room for her to join me in the water. Her black hair fell past her waist to brush her hips, and she gathered it into one thick braid then coiled it about her head as her bosom jiggled with the effort.

'How do you really feel?' she asked, dropping her skirt to the ground then climbing into the bath.

'Sickened. I don't want to speak further about the prisoner.' I shuddered as visions, sounds and smells from the matron's chamber and the viper pit appeared before me. 'What I am thinking of right now is Adam's behaviour at the pit—he was outrageous, striking the prisoner! And all the while, I felt the weight of Sabium's scowls.'

'Adam is arrogant—I do not trust him at all.' She flung a foot out of the water and rested it on the bath's edge. 'And why must Sabium still hold such a grudge? After all you've done for him. He crawled his way out from those rat holes to become the most privileged man in Uruk thanks to you.' Her sardonic chat could not cover the trauma I knew she had suffered this day.

'It was cruel though, was it not, that Sabium was ejected from his home and forced to slave in the mines?' I asked, queasiness gnawing through my belly.

'I suppose so,' said Gemekala with a shrug. 'But boys become men, so the line must be drawn. Anyway, in recent times, some mothers have shown more care for their sons.'

'But what of all the women who abandon their sons to the district houses or the mines and forget their existence? There is no one to ensure they're not mistreated.' My heart clutched as I thought of the toddler that watched me stride past him in the copper district's communal house.

'There's a reason we must keep boys strictly managed. We need to be firmer than ever. We've just seen the second woman in the last turn of seasons attacked by a man!' She eyeballed me. 'Lilith, if we're soft, their brutish natures will take over. It's for their own good as well as ours.'

I said nothing, knowing she could not relate to my desire to be fairer to males. Sensing my disconnect, she leaned forward to peer at me. 'Don't these men know they're only good for working, serving or sexing, and even then, just barely.' When I met her gaze, she rolled her eyes with a small smirk, inviting me to join in the droll griping. Sometimes we did this.

'Yes, or for drinking their fill of barley beer and brawling,' I contributed, willing to lighten the density of the day.

'Their minds are thick with simple thoughts, useless as old sully cloths.'

'They'd better have a good skill or work hard, if they're of no use in our beds.' Our laughter grew louder.

'Those types have nowhere to put their udder teats except the goats or each other,' she snorted.

Urnina's laughter announced her arrival. She carried three cups and a jug of warmed goat's milk and honey, a pouch of herbs soaking in it. 'We're better off with real goats' teats than men's,' she said, kneeling down to pour us each a cup.

Dax sauntered over to sit at the bath's flush edge, braving my wet hand to rub his cheeks against it, purring ecstatically. Gemekala reached past me to pet him.

'We make an exception to no males living on our terrace for you, glorious boy,' she crooned softly, scratching his light gold breast and chin. Tombaya's sharp cry broke the moment, the bird approaching us with his plumage fanned out impressively. 'But I'm not sure we should allow the same for that vain bird. He shouldn't be here, no matter how pretty he is, the way he torments Yasmin and screeches incessantly.'

'I love him, and you needn't worry,' I said, smiling a little. 'Tombaya would never win out against that snake.'

Urnina patted my hand. 'It's good to see you feeling better. We can relax now we've decided the matrons will deal with these horrid heretics.' She smiled affectionately.

'I am not relaxed about it,' I said, my chest tightening as I forced my attention back to my responsibilities. 'It could take many months to build matron numbers and train them, and it seems there are growing numbers of these heretics.' I watched Urnina's face pale at my insistence on facing the threat. 'The more I think about it, I think we may need the physical strength of our men to assist. We certainly don't want to put the lives of matrons at risk. I feel this situation is truly dangerous, more than we've registered.'

Urnina shuddered. 'Now you say that, I'm thinking yesterday a woman came to the reception terrace to be purged of an evil dream. She dreamed of men killing women. It did quiver the snake in my spine to hear of it.'

'Why didn't you tell me?' I spoke sternly.

'I should have, but I didn't want to worry you,' said Urnina, eyes widening with culpability. 'And there's something else I should have mentioned. I passed two men yesterday in the plaza who had stubble on their faces.'

I sighed in exasperation at her avoidance of difficult topics.

'Why didn't you have them purified?' demanded Gemekala. 'They disobey the protocols. Not to mention the offence of them bringing such coarseness before a woman's lap. We must not let men get away with any infringement.'

'Perhaps the answer is in being kinder to our men,' I said. 'If we get stricter, it could make them sympathise with these heretics. It might be better to give a few allowances, like turning a blind eye to an unshaven face.'

Gemekala's mouth opened in shock and Urnina's eyebrows knitted in concern at my radical statement. I tried to convince them. 'Consider how making our men happier will strengthen the city at a time of threat. Being harder on them could accelerate the prophesied future rather than delay it.'

'It's true that being kind gets the best behaviour from children,' said Urnina, quickly taking to the idea of a more pleasant strategy. 'So perhaps you're right. As ever, the most important thing is that we stand in our glory as Inanna's supreme daughters.'

I refrained from rolling my eyes at Urnina's unhelpful advice and stepped out of the bath, ending the discussion.

The women retired to their chambers, needing their rest before taking the next shift at Iltani's bedside in the midnight depths. I feared the woman's wounds would kill her by sunrise.

I wrapped myself in linen shawls and sat on my garden bench, Dax on my lap, annoyed to find myself waiting for Adam. A screech owl broke into hypnotic trilling from a hidden location near my terrace.

'What do you tell me, wise owl?' I whispered into the darkness, and the bird answered with a piercing screech that ran through me. Was this the same owl that had come to me at Huluppu?

Tadez appeared and announced that Adam was waiting for me on the reception terrace.

'Bring him to me here,' I said, ignoring Tadez's pursed lips.

'Finally,' I said brusquely as Adam strode towards me, his swollen eye now showing the dark shadow of bruising. Dax sat up, his huge ears tilting slightly back as he glared at Adam. 'How dare you hit the prisoner today.'

'Forgive me, High Priestess, I wanted to shield you from that man's hatred, and I hit him to silence his abuse.' He frowned slightly, as if annoyed that I did not appreciate his actions.

I looked at him with narrowed eyes as Dax jumped from my lap and strolled away. 'Let's discuss the interrogation,' I said, irritated with his pompousness. 'Tell me something useful.'

'There's something I didn't want to translate in front of the matrons. I thought you'd want to hear this first.' I nodded impatiently for him to continue. 'It's worse than we thought. The prisoner said thousands of men are gathering, with their eye on Uruk as their first target.'

I rose to my feet, speechless for a few moments. 'What rot is this! You said there were two hundred men, and now there are thousands? Why would I give credence to that brute's word, or your word he said it, for that matter? If this threat were substantial, I would have heard warning from other temples.' I spoke strongly to hide the panic that washed through me and weakened my limbs.

'The other temples would not know because the heretics are focused on Uruk—take down the most crucial city, and the rest will soon follow. And that brute was not the only one speaking of the rebels gathering. If you talk to the refugees downriver, or to travelling gem miners and merchants, they will tell you the same. What I've heard those heretics did to a woman in a far north settlement to show how they despise the Great Mother, I cannot burden your ears with it.' His gaze cast downwards for a moment in a manner that scared me.

I held my face in what I hoped was an unreadable arrangement, and began pacing my garden terrace. He fell into step beside me.

'They believe there is a male god that is the ruler of all there is,' he continued, this time looking at me with what could be a little pity.

'The desert sun has burned their tiny minds beyond reckoning,' I snapped. 'Even if there are significant numbers, they are too stupid to defeat us with their aggression.'

'High Priestess, they appear to be strategising in sophisticated ways. These heretics are calling themselves an army and using a new word— war—to describe the large-scale fight they will bring to you.'

I kept walking, my chest heaving. I could not risk hoping the reported numbers of rebels were false. There was no way the matrons could fight thousands of men. I stilled and took a slow breath, about to authorise what Adam had petitioned me for since the day I met him. The feeling of inevitability was unpleasant.

'Very well,' I said. 'We will train a group of men to kill any further invaders.'

'High Priestess, may I lead those men?' His eyes leapt into life as he seized upon this opening. There was something deep in his drive— he sought a mission, a purpose. Like all men, he had never been able to pursue this part of his nature, untrusted with any serious decisions. 'I have knowledge of the land between the Euphrates and Tigris, and details of the settlements. I know about fighting and weapons and how a man thinks. If you build your own army, our greatness will be unthreatened in this new time of war.'

He spoke with a tremble of excitement, and I couldn't help but feel inspired by his clarity. I believed he could do what he said. This odd feeling of a man offering decisive action felt like a strength I could lean on. Perhaps he could help me make Uruk an even greater city and ensure its continuing supremacy.

'Why do you so badly want to lead my men?' I sought to penetrate his mind with my gaze to sense the truth of his response.

He met my eye with the boldness of a bull. 'I want to be of service. If that means we must go to war, then I want to assist.'

'What is war? Some word promoted to glorify men's squabbling.' I questioned him to gain myself a few more moments so he wouldn't know my decision had already been made.

'I have something that may convince you. Again, I wanted you to hear this before anyone else.' He struck a hand against an object belted at his waist, then drew out a knife. 'I took this from the prisoner. It is made of a metal far stronger than copper and it holds a sharp edge for longer. If this is what the heretics use against us, we stand little chance.'

My heart sank further as I took the dagger, feeling its weight. It was a more muted colour than our burnished copper knives. 'What is it made of?' I asked.

'It's called bronze. It comes from the north, where a new metal called tin is mixed with copper. We need to access our own tin and make bronze weapons if we're to stand against these heretics.'

I handed it back to him, keen to release the sinister metal from my grasp. 'Put that away. I've called a council meeting tomorrow at midday. Be waiting nearby with this blade in case I call you in, but watch your mouth. The council will not take kindly to a man explaining this.' I was glad I had reprieve until then to gather my thoughts, away from the intoxicating effect of his presence.

He dipped his head in agreement, eyes never leaving mine. There was a mutual recognition that went deeper than the short time we'd known each other. My practiced blank expression was harder to arrange than ever and I wished I could let myself surrender into him, if only for a few moments. It was a relief to have a man meet me with full presence, to have him support me.

Before I knew it, he reached out and cupped the back of my neck, drawing us towards each other.

'You are my High Priestess, and I will help you protect this city. Let me solve this problem for you,' he said, face dark with passion. My eyes magnetised to his lips as they moved towards mine and encompassed me in a kiss of such fire, my guard was forgotten. I cared nothing for my pride as I allowed myself to surrender, in equal parts ecstatic and terrified.

He kept one hand behind my neck and slid the other down to cover the flatness of my lower back, sparking my girdle of fire to fill my belly with sensual life-force. He pulled me into him, and I let my hands snake around his neck to touch the muscles I'd felt when dunking him.

The minor stubble on his face scratched my skin as his lips consumed my mouth, an unfamiliar sensation. Why was he coming before me without being clean-shaven? But the sensation was oddly stimulating in its newness, and I had no further qualms as he guided me backwards to the pillar beside my blue lotus pond. I allowed it to support me as I relaxed deeper into him, thoughts obliterated in the fiery moment.

My tongue reached out to taste more of him, and he met me with his, both his hands on my jaw and holding my head backward a little as his head tilted to one side, then to the other, plunging deeper into the kiss with each swoop. One of his hands dropped to clasp my throat and his thumb ran along my jaw line, eliciting a low growl from my throat, my entire being an abyss of desire to receive him. Overcome by passion, he broke the kiss a moment to murmur, 'Let me rise,' into my neck and ear, and I did not stop to ponder what he meant as he rained kisses across my cheek before feasting on my mouth again, my body molten against him. Certainly, his staff had already risen to the occasion, marking its desire against my thigh.

'Come to my lap,' I whispered with all the promise of Inanna, breaking away from his kiss to pull him in the direction of my bedchamber.

'No, here, before our great city,' he said, drawing me to the alabaster bench between two date palms that framed a magnificent view by day all the way to the river, but now showed blackness. He guided me to sit on the cushions, and I leaned back on the balustrade as he knelt before me, kissing the inside of my thighs with his eyes locked on mine in the dim light. His hands ran up and down my legs and over my hips to unravel my shawl from about my waist, yanking my shoulder shawl away and casting both aside.

He dragged his palms over my breasts, massaging them rigorously, his hands everywhere at once, then losing patience, he splayed my thighs and beheld my gates in the lamplight as I offered myself proudly. With a guttural grunt, he lunged at me, slurping at the tide of wetness that had risen so quickly in response to him, and I sought to quench him as I grasped at his cheeks. His hands slipped under my buttocks and held them firmly in his fists to push me into his face. I moaned as his hands pulled me apart, taking my hips wider, the tip of my toes pointed on the ground as his tongue thrust in and out of the abyss, up and down, none too careful nor precise as men were trained to be in this art, but all the better for it. I let him continue for as long as I could bear it before I yanked his head back and snarled, 'To my lap now.'

He lifted his glistening face and stood, pulling me to my feet and guiding me to sit on the wide top of the balustrade, the plaza an endless fall below me. Standing before my open thighs, he clamped his massive hands around my hips and began to enter me. For a moment we were still as our energies united, stunning me with the vastness we instantly found together.

Gradually, we moved, my eyes only pulling from his when they rolled back in my head as we moved like discordant waves slapping into one another in the sea, each pushing or pulling to our own combative agenda. Then, a new power surged in him, and he gripped me like a vice as his thrusts superseded my writhing and he moved as fast and hard as a coppersmith's hammer. His gaze was wild, and I felt like punching him, smashing my fists on his chest, as much as I wanted to love him until we disintegrated into oneness.

A shock arose in me. 'Adam, wait,' I choked, pushing him back. 'Your sully cloth?' I reached down and squeezed the base of his shaft. He knew the consequences but I didn't know if I could trust him to hold his milk. He winced, shaking his head, and pressed his palm hard against my heart to push me back until I released my pinch. He stared at me as he appeared to gather his focus, then re-entered me and struck at me relentlessly, on and on, until a ragged cry of ecstasy tore from my throat.

Only then did he pull back, his eyes meeting mine in a flash of knowing before he turned his hips and, with a wild grunt, released his milk into the blackened vista of Uruk.

CHAPTER 5

Although the priestesses and I had taken turns in small groups at the bedside of Iltani, she left her body with a small gasp as I held her cold hand. I'd sat beside her since the pre-dawn depths with Lahamu and Doshina. Shocked by such violence shown to a woman's tender flesh, we'd cringed as we dabbed sesame oil and honey around the gaping wound in her belly to try to stop the blood and purify the foulness the knife had released. All the while, we repeatedly uttered healing incantations, but it was useless. Her mottled face became peaceful as she traversed the realms between life and death, helped by the extra dose of poppy tincture I gave her to ease the pain and quicken her departure.

We cried and rocked by Iltani's body for some time before I realised the sun was mid-sky. The council would be waiting to discuss our response to the invasion. Before we could attend, I had to stop by my chambers to dress in official garb and gather the other priestesses.

'I can't believe we're dressing you in this for the second day in a row,' muttered Gemekala as she draped the cobalt mantle around my shoulders. Urnina was silent as she painted my eyes and re-pinned my hair before placing the gold diadem with peacock feathers atop my crown.

On our way to the meeting, I stopped at the looking pond, lined with obsidian. The water was highly reflective on both a physical and psychic level, enabled by the revealing powers of the black stone. My chin lifted as I consciously radiated Inanna's power throughout my aura with the intent to see myself as the councillors would—tall and strong, a full bosom held proudly, my neckline elegant, my face resting in noble beauty. The councillors must bow to my guidance, and I could not afford to show any quiver around such ambitious women. They had no idea of the prophecy and would scoff at the idea that men could be of any serious risk to our society.

The sun beat down on my back as I led the priestesses down the ziggurat's steps and towards the cylindrical council chambers, its copper dome tarnished blue-green. Throngs of women gathered in the plaza, tolerating the midday heat in their desire to seek news on Iltani and exchange whatever information they had. They stepped back to bow their respects, their eyes pouring over the details of our appearance and their minds nosily probing for information. I pulsed out a wall of energy. The news of Iltani's passing would reach their ears soon enough.

The councillors were already seated at the round table when we entered the chamber, each wearing a copper collar as wide as a spread hand bearing the gems symbolising her portfolio. Despite giving birth the previous day, Zamug was at the table, the swaddled baby suckling at her breast. Everyone stood as I approached my chair, the priestesses moving to their area of the mosaic-covered bench running the edge of the room, filled with the councillors' advisers and matrons.

'Greetings Councillors.' I nodded around the table, keeping my eyes from Sabium, whose presence hung resentfully on the adviser's bench, the only man in the room. I felt the colour in my face rise under his daunting glare. Thankfully, the clear quartz skylight at the centre of the dome removed the need for lamps that would have increased the stifling atmosphere.

'Councillors, I have grave news. The woman attacked yesterday, Iltani, daughter of Ikurtum and gifted jewellery artisan, is dead. Despite our best efforts, the Great Mother welcomed her back into the bosom of the otherworlds before the sun hit the mid-sky.'

I let the room take in the news, dropping my head in respect as I stroked the polished cow horns forming the armrests of my chair. 'I will officiate at her funeral before sunset in the gem district. We will all place our gifts in her coffin to ease her life in the otherworlds.' The councillors murmured their agreement.

'As you all know, there was also a man killed in the attack. I believe his name was Luninni,' I continued. 'I expect he will be buried this afternoon. Having just given birth, Councillor Zamug probably has not yet given the man's friends and brothers leave from their duties to attend the burial fields, but I'm sure she will have her advisers see to it?'

Zamug waved towards her three advisers, her other hand clutching the baby absentmindedly. 'Rest assured, High Priestess, I have managed that, and ordered a reed basket be provided for his body,' she said in lofty tones. I held her gaze a moment, letting her know I was cognisant she had not already thought of organising any of that herself.

I continued. 'As you know, both victims were stabbed during yesterday's attack, which is disturbing enough. More concerning is that we are receiving reports of a growing group of rebellious men who have their sights on Uruk. They want our city, our grain and beer stores, but most outrageous of all, they seek to undermine the Great Mother's natural supremacy.'

Pausing, I let them take in the statement, expecting irate reactions from just one or two councillors. Most were so sure of their superiority they would pay little heed to the ludicrous concept of men as a threat.

'These men are heretics!' cried Irkalla, always quick to take umbrage at any slight, thumping a palm on the table.

I had asked my priestesses to stimulate indignation, and their righteous murmurs now rose from the bench, encouraging some hissing from among the advisers and matrons.

'Blasphemers!' spat Zamug, sufficiently riled to join in.

'Indeed we are dealing with heretics, and they try to threaten us,' I said, pleased my ploy had worked. 'We must take the safety of our city seriously, especially based on the information extracted from the prisoner who met his end last night.' I neglected to tell them that thousands of men were reportedly gathering—I needed a certain level of outrage raised over the threat, enough to justify building a defence force, not to set the city into panic, but not so little as to cause complete denial.

Dudu, pompous in her greatness as the ruler of Uruk's prolific agriculture portfolio, which included overseeing our bakeries and breweries, stood. 'If I may speak, High Priestess? The very existence of heretics is a disgrace, and the murder of one of our women is heinous indeed. However, Uruk is the greatest city on Inanna's green Earth. There can't be a threat from a bunch of hairy desert scruffs, no better than shepherds, with sun-curdled brains and shaft milk.'

She looked at Benni, councillor of our tannery and leatherworks district, and the two only half-hid their sniggers.

'Do you naysay me?' I said, drawing my power up from my lower belly. I was not to be questioned. Quickly the edges of Dudu's lips turned down. I continued. 'There are already settlements in the far north where men are claiming to be superior to women. After the attack on our city, we are compelled to take action for the safety of our people, and most of all, to avenge the insult on our Great Mother Inanna.' I looked from one councillor to the next to engage her in the severity of this matter. They all quickly nodded except Semiramis, and I held her eye until she gave a small jerk of her chin.

Dudu licked her lips. 'High Priestess, forgive my impertinence, but have we verified these reports?' Her tone wheedled after my admonishment, but her arrogance remained palpable.

'I've been told by a source I consider reliable—the man who interrogated the prisoner in his own language, Adam. He shows grave concern for the safety of Uruk as the Great Mother's earthly home,' I said evenly, seeking to disguise my niggling doubts about this man. 'He has grown up travelling our lands and beyond, as far north as the Taurus Mountains, and he is from the western coast of the Red Sea where his mother is a priestess of Inanna. Additionally, yesterday I sent two novices to our sister city, Ur, to ask High Priestess Daggartum if she's heard anything of these heretics. Our best runners and canoeists are with the novices so word can be brought back quickly. I've also sent scouts to find a few men that attacked the small settlement of Larsa, who appear to be of the same heretical group. But the terrain is vast and it could take several moon cycles to complete the mission. What's more, it appears we now have a larger group of heretics to contend with.'

The councillors looked wary.

'That all sounds concerning indeed, High Priestess, and I'm relieved you've taken such wise action,' said Amarazen, councillor of building. I could tell she'd paid little notice to what I said about the heretic threat before praising me. Her self-interest shone in her eyes like braziers, hoping to gain my support for her longer-term petition to build a luxurious new residential complex for herself and her leading women.

I fixed her with a cold stare and said nothing, letting the pause in the room hang. These women were too petty and decadent to continue the farce of consulting with them. As the handmaiden of the Great Mother, the decision to build an army was ultimately mine, and I would not be subject to their little wills. Taking several breaths into my girdle of fire, I gathered my energy and expanded my aura with the mesmerism. Menna had often told me this technique should be used with discernment in service of the good of the people. *It's a fine line between using the mesmerism to convince a less evolved soul to follow what is for their highest good, and using it to bamboozle and manipulate others.* Right now, it was necessary to pacify the arrogant councillors and influence them to agree my agenda.

The councillors stilled, sensing the power that came upon them without realising its source or purpose. Always impervious to my sway, Sabium broke the stillness by coming to stand behind Semiramis. I bristled, sensing he had found the opportunity he'd been waiting for to undermine me in this forum.

Semiramis listened to his whispers, then sat back to look at me. 'High Priestess, if I may speak. Apparently the marauders carried some interesting weapons.'

My brow furrowed—how did Sabium know that?

'What does this Adam say?' she continued. 'Do we need better weapons ourselves?'

Semiramis was already thinking of the potential for expanding the copper district's portfolio. A shift occurred as the other councillors' minds ticked over, considering how the rebel threat could offer opportunities to grow their own power, and I allowed it to continue a while. It served my purposes.

'Adam is nearby and will answer your questions,' I said, gesturing to Tadez to fetch him.

Loud enough for all the councillors to hear, Sabium stage-whispered in Semiramis' ear, 'We know some advanced settlements across Mesopotamia have already started to use a new type of metal, but Uruk's leadership has been a little, um, delayed on these new possibilities.' He wheezed with excitement at criticising me in front of the council.

I surged the mesmerism again before I spoke. 'The knife taken from the prisoner is made of a different metal, made by melting copper with a new type of metal called tin. It's called bronze. It is stronger and stays sharper than copper alone.' I ignored Sabium's eyes burning into me as he realised his ambush had failed—he had not expected me to know.

The councillors sat a little higher. A new metal—this was exceptional.

'Where is tin mined?' said Semiramis.

'In the foothills of the Taurus Mountains,' Adam called out as he entered the chamber, striding towards the table. He wore a leather kilt studded with copper, a more impressive garment than I had seen him in before, and held the bronze dagger. He must have been waiting right outside the double doors, eavesdropping. The entire room stared at him, taken in by his grand presence and the shocking sight of a man holding a dagger.

He made everyone else fade into the background. My features remained pious but privately my mouth watered as I remembered the feeling of him the night before, the way I felt expansive and vulnerable in his arms, the way he made me forget everything but the rapturous moment, unlike any man ever had. My fingers flicked as I cleared my mind, cross at myself for thinking like a girl in a first flush of love, and during a crucial council meeting no less.

His behaviour was impudent, strutting in and speaking so boldly. Yet I could not show offence or the council would turn against him.

Instead, I said, 'Ah, Adam. Show the council the knife.' He met my eyes with a slight tilt of his head, as if we shared a plan, and walked towards me.

'Wait a moment,' broke in Semiramis, the strawberry mark on her cheek inflamed with excitement. 'If my advisers and I may see the item first, High Priestess?' she added as she realised the rudeness of her interruption.

I nodded, and Adam handed her the dagger. She turned it over, smelled it, knocked her knuckles against the blade to listen to its resonance, and pushed her fingernail into it to gauge hardness. Satisfied, she held its utilitarian bone handle so the blade pointed at Sabium, who jumped up from the advisers' bench to take it. It struck me as odd she offered it to him ahead of her two women advisers. Sabium and Semiramis had hated each other since childhood. He must have won her trust and respect—or maybe it was a shared loathing of me that bonded them.

Sabium took his time examining the knife before passing it to the other two pouting advisers.

'The dagger was taken from one of the heretics who attacked us yesterday, as you know,' said Adam, still standing near Semiramis and sounding relaxed, as if he spoke at council every day. 'I also have this one—' he took out a smaller dagger from a scabbard belted around his hips '—which I traded from a merchant. He said there are a number of places in the far north where tin is mined, and that these men are accessing it in large quantities. Bronze is a mix of nine parts copper and one part tin, making it far stronger than copper and able to stay sharp for longer. Our soft copper knives have no chance against this superior weaponry.'

I sensed the women stiffen—they prided themselves as leaders of an exceptionally advanced civilisation that must always be ahead of all others. As if Adam sensed their response, he added, 'We must have bronze for our defence force, and of course we will design the world's best weapons.'

'Man, what do you mean?' said Benni. She was not an easily impressed woman. 'It's the first I've heard about Uruk having a defence force!'

'Councillor Benni, forgive my forwardness. In my desire to protect our city, I got ahead of myself,' said Adam, bowing his head. 'These heretics are calling themselves an army and seek to bring a large fight upon us. War is the word they are using, and we need to defend ourselves against it.'

Under her glare, he sat on the adviser's bench with his gaze down, wisely deciding not to push her further. Behind their snarling faces, the women around the table seemed unsure, looking at me for direction.

'Councillors,' I said. 'After yesterday's events, I am heeding the threats. We must be prepared for more attacks and with greater numbers of men, and if they have these weapons, we are in trouble. We need to be ready to defend ourselves.'

The room bristled with a mix of excitement and denial.

'Council, may I speak?' said Adam. The councillors looked at me, and after a suitably long pause, I nodded. He stood and paced around the table, stopping by my side. 'Uruk is entirely undefended,' he said. 'Even if we had stronger weapons, our men have no idea about fighting, beyond the odd brawl. If we do not have an organised approach, no matter how big our city is, the enemy could overpower us. Councillor Amarazen, in your wisdom as head of building, you've probably already thought of erecting a wall around this city to make people enter and exit at one point we can control. It could also help manage the approaching refugees. Your portfolio's role is crucially important in the defence of Uruk.'

His lack of political savvy shocked me. Although the councillors were partial to sycophancy, the obviousness of his attempt to ingratiate himself as important in our defence strategy was disappointing.

An angry crease appeared on Amarazen's forehead, as though hearing flattery from a man was a waste of her time. 'Who are you to tell me the importance of my portfolio, man?'

Zamug cut in. 'Man, you are a gem miner and merchant in my district, are you not? So why do you speak of things you know nothing about? You belong in my portfolio, doing what you were born to do.' She leered at his long shapely thighs as she spoke, causing his lips to twitch in irritation.

'Apologies, Councillors,' Adam began, frowning so his bruised eye squeezed almost shut. 'If you look at the logic, you'd be interested—'

'Pah!' said Zamug, lowering her eyebrows. 'A man's logic sees as far as his udder teat extends. You register only the slivers of truth shown by the physical world, so don't speak of your silly logic to *us*.' Disturbed by his mother's vitriol, the baby began fussing. Zamug held him out towards her advisers, his head falling backwards in her carelessness, and one rushed to take the now howling infant outside.

'Adam, sit,' I said. Best he shut up before riling the councillors further. He obeyed, legs opened far wider than a man's should.

Amarazen, seeming to have come around to the idea after her initial offence, spoke. 'Although it is unprecedented, and rather shocking, I agree we may need a defence strategy. I've been thinking for some time of the need to build a wall around our perimeter.' She fingered a bright orange carnelian on her copper collar, and I could sense her imagining the extra resources and importance she could take from this opportunity. 'But this will take a great deal to organise if we need to release men from their daily work to build walls and train in a defence force—an army.'

'Exactly the problem, sisters,' said our councillor of the arts, Maida, sweeping a bejewelled hand around the table. 'Have you considered the impact of such a path on our artists? Who will fire the kilns and smelt the copper for our designers, harvest the oils for our perfumers? Ask yourselves—what is more important,' she said, her heavily made-up eyes filled with charismatic angst, 'having men run around tussling, or supporting the culture of our city?' She'd risen to her feet, frizzy white hair clouding from under a lavish headband of large flat gemstones chained together with gold.

The councillors were enchanted by her sumptuous performance, lulling them back into the comfort of believing in Uruk's impenetrability as the world's greatest city run by the world's most accomplished women.

'Indeed, Councillor Maida,' I said, hiding my delight as an idea rose. I had the answer to my prayer to better manage the refugee situation, legitimising the entrance of some men and boys to Uruk. I could even send for the girl's brother I'd had to turn away. 'The art we create is so valuable that it alone could attract covetous eyes. We must not let these heretics threaten our art or our city. Here is our solution—we can use refugees to do some basic tasks. There will be less impact on our usual activities when our own men are released for training.'

'Those refugee men caused the drought that drove them here in the first place and deserve no sympathy,' Maida said, scowling. 'They have offended the Great Mother to bring dryness upon their fields.' I held her within my cool stare, willing her obeisance. 'But I suppose they could be put to work, so long as they are monitored closely for signs of disagreeability.'

'The temple will look for appropriate refugees, and they will be closely monitored by the matrons,' I said, pleased I'd found a way to bring more of those men into the city without mentioning the heretics were trying to recruit them. 'Councillors, are we agreed on building an army?' I said, projecting a thought wave from my mind's eye that they should all agree.

'Yes,' said Semiramis, 'And we need to investigate this new metal immediately.' She was excited by this brand-new industry rising—war.

'We'll need to send a contingent upriver with our biggest barge straightaway, with 20 oxen to pull it,' I said, looking at Dudu to ensure she received my command to release the oxen. I turned to Zamug. 'We need gems to trade—be generous. Getting tin is the priority use for our gems right now.' I felt Maida flinch at the idea her artists would be deprived of materials.

I looked at Semiramis again. 'And of course, we'll need extra bitumen to fuel all the smelting. See to that.'

The room was soon filled with activity as the advisers were called to their councillor to begin forming plans.

Adam stayed seated and I allowed myself a shared glance with him. I had council agreement to build a defence force, and it felt good to have achieved our goal.

'Councillors, before you go,' I said, standing. 'Adam has good knowledge of weaponry and defence, perhaps more than any of us. Use him and his knowledge. He is at your disposal.'

'He may be of use to prepare our weaponry,' said Semiramis, looking him up and down appraisingly. 'Thank you, High Priestess. Sabium, bring Adam back to the district with us.'

Sabium ignored me when I sought his eyes, bending his head to Adam to speak quietly. Men on a shared mission.

CHAPTER 6

As awareness crept into my waking moments, I remembered with pleasure that today was the Akitu picnic. It was the culmination of the new year celebrations for the temple inhabitants, a break from all the formal rituals and the ever-probing eyes of the city. After the commotion caused by the invasion, it was just what we needed to restore a sense of normalcy. I stretched luxuriously, knowing I would be spending time with Adam in my favourite place, the sunken grotto half a morning's walk from Uruk.

The thought of him pulsed desire through my body, and I writhed slowly, lazily massaging my breasts and tweaking my nipples. Reaching down, I pressed my palm on my triangle, grinding my hips in a sensuous circle as I opened my thighs. Indulging my lusty impatience, I swept my fingers down my crevice, dipping into the wetness to allow a gliding caress upwards to my swelling jewel, down again, over and over, forcing myself to receive the intensity of the sensations without flinching. As the tension bloomed, my other hand twisted in my linen sheet as I braced and let the force explode, my belly clenching as I quivered in pulses, all the while conjuring visions of Adam pleasuring me as I knew he would later that day. I'd never been so desirous of a man and it thrilled me.

My cares aside for now, I happily went about my ablutions. I pushed the new cuffs Urnina had given me up each arm and selected a red shawl embroidered lavishly with gold thread and bordered with lurid blue peacock breast feathers, then tasselled with many tiny copper beads. I wrapped it about my waist as a skirt then threw one end over my shoulder. As I laced my red walking sandals, Urnina swept into my dressing chamber, beaming and embracing me, her signature scent of jasmine on the air.

'What would you like today?' she said. She began combing my hair and pulling pieces up to try a few arrangements.

'Something special,' I said, tingling waves of anticipation rippling through my belly at the thought of seeing Adam. I was roused enough to enhance my beauty for him.

She looked more closely at my face and smiled. 'Hmm. I see you have given yourself the best beauty treatment. No cosmetic can give such well-flushed cheeks and bright eyes.'

We laughed heartily as she continued playing with my hair. 'It would be comely to have layers of varying thicknesses cascading a little. Like mine, but with braids,' she said, twisting to show me the back of her head. Her voluminous tresses were piled above a new priestess' diadem with a large golden topaz, matched to glowing topaz-studded cuffs I hadn't seen before. They must have been commissions she'd designed to wear on this special day.

'Take all the time you need,' I said as her meticulous fingers began to work through my hair, perfumed and softened with jasmine oil. When she'd tied off each braid, she arranged them in a snake-like mass atop my head, securing it all with jewelled pins. After applying my make-up, she placed the diadem I'd selected over the arrangement and stood back to admire her work with a satisfied smile.

In front of the ziggurat steps, the plaza was a hive of activity. Our temple congregation was more than one hundred, including the priestesses, novices, some retired priestesses, all the temple women's daughters and young sons, as well as some of the older boys who had been fostered out, plus the favoured city men who received a coveted invitation. Delondra, her powerful body draped in soft blue shawls rather than a matron's leather sash and skirt, stood alone as the only matron invited, watching eagerly for Doshina to descend.

Dozens of servants milled about, the strongest men carrying jars of barley beer and heavy carpets, and younger ones hauling sacks filled with all manner of foods, cushions and tent equipment, softened animal hides, lyres and drums. Four young sheep and three pigs were tethered ready for the long walk ahead from which they would not return, along with two milking goats who would add their bounty to that of the grotto's resident goats. Some of the servants began to head out of the city so they could establish camp before the main temple procession arrived.

'Mammi, don't look,' said Aea, stepping in front of a sack as if her small form would block my view. Feeling indulgent, I turned away. She and the other temple children had planned a performance for us, directed by Tadez who I'd freed to spend several afternoons rehearsing with them. They'd all remained secretive about it, refusing to tell me anything, although Aea had asked if she could borrow some items from my dressing chamber as props.

'I'm not looking,' I said over my shoulder, spotting Tadez whispering in Nanni's ear and helping the little boy tuck something else into the sack. Tadez looked especially refined today, wearing a white kilt with a colourful beaded belt, a light gloss of oil evident over his chest. His physique was still attractive although he was old enough that grey strands ran through his lustrous and well-styled dark hair. I allowed him to keep his hair longer than grooming protocols dictated, though of course his face was always kept well-shaven. He was excited he would soon see his lover, Udul-Kalama, the grotto caretaker who ensured no itinerants stayed beyond refreshing their water bags and resting one night.

Urnina walked towards me, holding Nanni's hand as he looked up adoringly at his mother. A gaggle of temple daughters trailed them in hopes Urnina would focus her radiant smile upon them, maybe slip them one of the tiny gems she carried in a pouch at her waist for just such a purpose.

She ignored them all now, squinting a little in the morning brightness. 'Are you sure we should stay overnight?' she said in a low voice only for my ears. 'We could still make it a day trip. Those heretics might be running around out there.'

'Of course we're staying overnight,' I said breezily. 'We will not change our traditions because of those heretics. And we have what Adam is grandly calling "guardians" to accompany us. Look—some of them are rather strapping too, despite their silly hats.' We shared a smirk, looking at the hundred or so men wearing red rolled headcloths standing around the edges of our assembly. They'd been selected by Adam to form the beginnings of Uruk's defence force. The men looked pleased with themselves, sporting copper daggers at their belts and carrying slingshots, clubs and bows, proud as children flaunting new toys. A dozen hunting dogs circled around them in agitated movement, keen to run in the open desert. Our male guests looked sulkily at the guardians, envious of the novel air of confidence they emanated.

I spotted Adam talking among the guardians. He wore a smart new red leather kilt but no headcloth, to set himself apart from the others as the leader, I supposed. When he looked at me, I lifted my chin to gesture him over.

'Your guardians await you, High Priestess,' he said as he neared, eyeing my appearance appreciatively.

'I'm sure they'll be unnecessary. The Salukis, whatever are they for? We're not hunting.' He looked a little disappointed at my response, so I continued in kinder tones, 'But still, it's good to have you all with us.'

'The dogs might alert us if they pick up any scent or sight of heretics.'

'The dogs are trained to detect prey, not men,' I said, slowing my words to disguise my impatience at his silliness.

'Then I will personally guard you.' His eyes burrowed into mine and he offered me his arm. I smirked as I took it, ready to share a day of celebration with him as my chosen paramour who also happened to be the leader of my fledgling army. Aea spotted us and raced to greet him, Fancy trotting alongside with her long legs flowing their feathery fur and together, we led the temple assembly out of the plaza. Two boys with date palm branches woven into parasols hastened to my side although the sun was not yet fierce.

Before we reached the outskirts of Uruk, Lahamu instigated a song and when I joined, my voice rang with passion that sought to delight Adam's ears. Later, I offered him some dried fruits Tadez brought to me, and we chatted about the grotto. He said he'd visited it once or twice when he was travelling the land of the two rivers as a gem merchant.

'My legs are tired,' Aea said, tugging on my hand when we were a little way into the desert.

Tadez called out immediately from a few steps behind us. 'Lady, your sled is ready.'

He gestured over his shoulder to the wooden and copper sled, dragged over the desert sands by a white ox wearing white peacock feathers on her head, carrying a low, ornately carved throne. Tadez's fingertips delicately pushed Adam's shoulder, moving him aside as if he were a distasteful morsel of food in order to settle me on the throne and put Aea on my lap.

The grotto's submerged location meant it could not be seen until you almost stumbled into it, and before the sun was high in the sky, the lush greenery suddenly appeared before us. Cheers erupted as we thought of swimming in the pool twinkling below us, and drinking of its cool waters.

Adam called out to the guardians, instructing some to scout the surrounding areas for unusual activity, and others to take stations around the ground level ledge of the grotto with the dogs.

At my instruction, Adam would join the picnic assembly along with Tiamat's new paramour, Anba, who was also a guardian. The other guardians would remain at ground level, although from the smouldering looks the temple women gave them, their company would have been well appreciated at the party. There was a mysterious spark the newly appointed guardians carried. It must have something to do with them wearing the red headcloths that marked them as part of a group with a particular purpose. It seemed to enliven them.

Adam took my arm as I stood at the edge of the cliff looking down on the grotto, as if he were trying to protect me from stumbling. I considered flicking it off—why should I be any more at risk of falling than him?—but I let it be, the burning pleasure of his touch titillating me.

The grotto had once been a massive cave with an underground spring-fed pool. Something had caused the cave to collapse, forming a grotto surrounded by rocky walls, with half the pool now shaded by the remnants of the overhanging cavern. It was an oasis, with date palms, cedar and cypress pines interspersed with lush clumps of flowering bushes, wild iris, jasmine, honeysuckle and primulas, and masses of ferns on the perpetually wet rocks around the cavern.

The lavish picnic was still being set up on a shady clearing beside the pool. Brightly coloured goat skins and cushions were liberally scattered in a large open-sided tent on top of wool carpets and reed mats, and a second tent for the children to sleep in was being erected nearby.

The carcasses of the sheep were already roasting, the aroma whetting my appetite for our first feast of the day. The pigs, unaccustomed to long walks, snoozed in a pen fashioned from sticks, oblivious that they too would soon meet their end when they provided their flesh for our evening meal. Tadez had checked Cook's menus with me the previous day so I knew they would be cooked with wild garlic and tulip bulbs sourced from the grotto, served with cumin-speckled carrots and a host of other side dishes.

'Let's go down,' I said to Adam, and Tadez appeared at my side with Aea. I took her other arm, and the four of us began to pick our way down the most accessible entry point into the oasis, the cooler air greeting us.

Tadez could barely focus on the footwork required as he held the eyes of his beloved Udul-Kalama, waiting with his trained wolf, Teba, at the base of the cliff. Tadez and Udul-Kalama had grown up together in the communal servant house, one of the places unwanted boys lived along with those whose life work was the role of temple servant. When I made Tadez my prime attendant, his status earned him better accommodations in the lower levels of the ziggurat, but he continued to love Udul-Kalama. Several springs before, I'd agreed Tadez's request that his lover be excused from the communal house to become grotto caretaker after the previous one was killed by wolves. The circumstances at the communal house must have been dire for Tadez to want his lover sent here, as the distance meant they rarely saw each other. Tadez had said Udul-Kalama would value the isolation and healing powers of the grotto. I had wondered at the time what the matrons had done to scar him.

As we neared the base, I told Tadez to go ahead and greet his lover, and with pleasure I watched them exchange repeated embraces and animated words.

Once in the grotto, the children stripped off their tunics, no longer needing to protect their skin from the harsh desert conditions, and ran straight into the emerald pool. Some of the older ones called an impromptu race to the back ledge of the cavern.

I stopped to wipe the kohl from my eyes with the oiled linen Urnina handed me, preventing ghoulish streaks on my face when I entered the water, and as I opened my eyes again, Adam was in front of me.

'Ah, so that's what you look like without your cosmetics,' he said with a grin.

I snorted a little in good humour.

'Shall we cool ourselves?' I said, unravelling my red shawl and letting it fall to the sandy beach, my body naked except for my arm cuffs and diadem. His eyes burned, fixed on mine as he dropped his leather kilt, and I too resisted the urge to freely behold his nakedness. My heart and belly swelled with the joy of erotic life-force. I watched his lips curl in a smile, then he turned and strolled casually into the pool. I followed, walking proudly with my eyes feasting on his rippling buttocks, my hands itching to grip them.

The picnic assembly frolicked in the pool as the sun climbed higher and hotter in the sky. Adam indulged Aea's requests to be thrown in the air so she could splash into the water, prompting Humusi to want the same favour, then Ku-Aya's daughter, then more of the temple girls. We all barked with laughter as they clambered over him and he pretended to sink, the gaggle of girls dragging him up again.

'Come, young daughters, enough now, or I will have no strength for the rest of the day.' He laughed, turning towards where I stood in the water. In response, I bobbed my nipples above the water line for his eyeing.

The clanging copper discs of Tadez's sistrum called everybody's attention. 'Esteemed residents of the Temple of Inanna, and guests. Your feast awaits you,' he called from the little beach, gesturing to the low tables set up in the open-sided tent behind him.

The air erupted with bells and drums and the robust whine of reed pipes as the musicians commenced playing. Gemekala and I laughed as Fancy swam past in a long cream streak, Aea and Humusi paddling behind her, pretending to be dogs. After emerging, we dabbed our bodies dry with linen cloths while evading Fancy's wet shakes.

Urnina pulled me aside, holding her pouch of beauty aids, and we darted under the old willow at the edge of the beach, its sprawling limbs fanned by the fronds of surrounding date palms. She passed me my red shawl, its blue feathers and beads tickling my ribs as I tied it at the centre of my chest, a more relaxed outfit for the afternoon ahead. She deftly repainted my kohl, adjusted my hair and diadem, and opened a small bottle of patchouli oil mixed with finely powdered mica to gloss over my body and make it twinkle in the sun.

I gestured for Adam to join me on my cushions and when we were settled, the servants began placing a lavish array of platters before us, the choicest cuts of roast meat, salads of lettuce, cucumbers and radishes dressed with coriander, lemon juice and sea salt, green beans with butter, olives, barley bread to dip in oil. Adam offered me a morsel of roast lamb with his fingers which I accepted, my lips sliding over his thumb pad to receive the juicy well-salted meat. We both sucked thirstily on the straws in our shared barley beer jug as the music wailed wantonly and the chatting and laughter grew louder alongside. The morning's long walk followed by the boisterous swimming had aroused the thirsts and appetites of all, and the jugs and platters needed to be refilled several times.

I suggested a game of 20 squares with Tiamat and 'Guardian Anba', as she mockingly called him, the couple clearly enamoured with one another. Adam and Anba arranged cushions and jugs of beer around the clay board, and each couple engaged in a race across the squares based on the outcome of the way we threw knucklebones. As the afternoon deepened, we snacked on goats curd with honey and sliced oranges sprinkled with pistachios, and the games became livelier. Our ribbing fought with the music and the increasing variety of singers taking to the sandy stage in front of the tent, including some of the more extroverted men who sang earnest love songs.

'Adam and Anba, won't you sing for us? Something bouncier,' I said, playfully prodding Adam in the ribs. He leapt to his feet, pulling Anba with him, and they stood to the side of the stage while I gestured Tadez to have the current performer ushered off. Adam said something to the musicians, and a twangy tune began from the harps, the other musicians joining with gusto. Anba and Adam began to sing one of the bawdy ballads that always raised everybody's spirits to new heights.

I exalt our Lady
Her sweet thing
With my own
Let me be at her lap

Adam continued to sing as he gestured theatrically that he had forgotten something. He darted behind the tent wall to re-emerge a few moments later with a frizzy lettuce held to his crotch.

Her pubic hair is a sweet lettuce in a moist ditch
Her triangle is sublime
My lady, I bow before you

Tiamat and I were grasping each other in hysterics as Adam jiggled the lettuce around and Anba got on his knees to serenade it, each man singing wholeheartedly. The audience cheered when the song ended, the musicians still jangling its last notes as Adam returned to my side. I leaned closer to him, pleased with his rambunctiousness.

In the relative quiet, a sudden cacophony of barking rose from the hunting dogs stationed around the top of the grotto's walls, echoing ferociously. Fancy scrabbled to her feet and joined in, deep-chested body squatting with the force of her bark and her long front legs splayed outwards. Beyond the dogs' racket, there was a high-pitched buzzing noise. A shock of fear ran through me as I leapt up to follow Adam out of the tent to the beach, almost tripping over the others also rushing outside.

'Aea! Humusi!' I yelled, looking frantically around for the girls, but above the din of the dogs and the shouting of the others, I could barely hear my own voice.

Some of the guardians looked down from around the top of the grotto walls with confused faces, the dogs jerking wildly at their sides, and others scrambled down the steep entry wall.

Were we under attack? As I tried to place what was happening, the whirring noise stopped.

Across the pool, I saw the servants gathered at one end of the cavern's ledge with most of the children. My hands were still clasped over my chest, but relief coursed through me as I realised some of the children held clay buttons, popular toys that spun on strings to make a humming noise. The sound had been magnified by the echo of the rocky dome to the delight of the children, oblivious to the trouble they caused. Aea and Humusi looked bemused, wondering what all the fuss was about.

'What were you thinking making such noise!' I shouted across the water at all of them. 'Do you want everyone across these lands to know our presence here?' As soon as the words came from my lips, I regretted them, shocked by the transparency of my own fears. I had not realised I was so on edge about an attack.

Menna came to stand beside me to offer her support, and with quiet presence, I quickly regained composure. Demsar joined us, putting his arm about Menna's shoulders as we watched the children swim back to us. Menna's three sons emerged first from the water and stood in a row, their gaze on the sand. Adam paused to stare at them, and I could tell he once again noted how they looked like Demsar.

When all the children were gathered in front of me on the sandy shore, I calmly instructed them to never make such a racket again. Satisfied, I turned and linked arms with Menna to head back into the tent, laughing to show everyone the celebrations were not to be dampened by this silly misunderstanding. But still my heart thumped and my limbs felt weak.

When the sun had sunk and we'd partaken of our second feast, Tadez again rattled his sistrum.

'Ladies, Inanna's own, and men,' he cried, sashaying the length of sandy ground in front of our tent, marked out as a stage by a brazier burning bright at each end. He had changed into a smart orange kilt that swished behind him as he turned around and came back again, one wrist high in the air flicking the instrument rapidly.

I leaned in to whisper in Adam's ear, letting my lips brush his lobe. 'He's made that kilt out of one of my shawls.' We shared a smile. Tadez was always keen for any opportunity to change out of his usual garb, and had a stylish streak.

Tadez stubbornly waited for us all to settle into silence before continuing, his respect for the arts strong. Adam plumped the cushions around us and ensured our beer was within arm's reach as we leaned back together, taking mint leaves to chew from the platter passed around.

'The daughters of the temple have prepared a special performance for you,' announced Tadez. 'With a little of my help,' he added magnanimously, attempting humility but unable to hide his pride in driving the theatrics. I knew he was shining extra bright under the gaze of Udul-Kalama, who stood in the shadows to behold his lover on stage.

'Welcome to the spectacle of Inanna's descent to the underworld, told in a simplified tale,' Tadez called, his free hand sweeping in a gesture to the ground. 'It is the story of the dying of the false self and being reborn whole, of descending into the depths of hell in order to find true Heaven and the sacrifices this demands.' He now gestured to the sky, thick with stars and showing a quarter moon, a tinkle coming from the sistrum he still grasped.

'The star of the show is Aea, playing Inanna herself,' he boomed, and applause broke out as she stepped flamboyantly from behind the tent's side curtain to greet her audience, all of us ready to be easily pleased.

Aea wore two honeydew melon rinds strapped to her chest as breasts, a red linen skirt, and one of my diadems modified to hold a pine cone, symbolising the pineal eye as the doorway to the higher realms. She twirled to show us her costume and we clapped our appreciation. I glanced at Adam, wishing to share my pride with him. He murmured hotly in my ear, 'She has her mother's glorious bosom.'

'And Humusi stars as Inanna's shadow, Ereshkigal, queen of the underworld,' continued Tadez as the applause settled. Humusi appeared in a black cowhide mantle that dragged on the ground all around her—I suspected it was my ceremonial mantle—and stood behind Aea, popping her head over her cousin's shoulder with a ghoulish expression, eliciting playful booing from the audience. Gemekala and I exchanged proud grins.

'And we have the stern guardians of the seven gates to the underworld which Inanna must pass to claim her wholeness,' said Tadez, bowing with a flourish to welcome seven girls, all in the space between child and womanhood. They emerged in single file and clumsily lifted Aea and Humusi at the hips as we cheered. Aea's back slumped ungracefully and I tried to catch her eye, raising my chin in little jerks to tell her to straighten up, but she was convulsed in laughter and paid no heed.

'And now welcome the kind little clay creatures that soften Queen Ereshkigal with their compassion, convincing her to resurrect Inanna from the death she experiences in the underworld,' he said, as two girls, the daughters of Sabit and Lahamu, emerged from the tent side and bowed to the audience, their faces and bodies smeared in clay.

'And of course, all of our helpers,' said Tadez.

A group of boys stepped out forlornly, the young sons of the temple women and some older fostered boys, the latter looking awkward at being in the presence of their priestess or novice mothers. I knew at least some of them had been forced to attend. My heart felt jagged as I watched their downcast eyes and the way they held their bodies without confidence, as if they didn't feel the right to take up the ground they stood on.

The entire cast and helpers shuffled back behind the tent's curtain and we all quieted. Tadez stood still for a few moments to build the anticipation of the audience, then began his narration in a resonant voice.

'Once there was a Goddess named Inanna, who lived in Heaven and knew only light. But she did not know how wonderful life was, as she had nothing to compare it to. She felt half of herself was missing. Inanna remembered that she had a sister, Queen Ereshkigal, who suffered in the underworld in rage and grief because her husband, the holy bull, had died.'

Aea, as Inanna, merrily skipped onto the stage and knelt to place her ear to the ground, one arm holding her melons in place, to enact hearing the call of the other half of her soul.

Tadez continued, enjoying the captivation he held us under with his theatrical presentation. 'Inanna knew she must unite with her sister if she was to find wholeness. She says goodbye to her favoured paramour and begins her journey to the underworld.'

Aea acted out the goodbye, waving to a temple boy.

'She must pass through seven tests of initiation, each one veiling her more to the truth of who she is. Only then will she face the real test that will take her beyond endurance,' called Tadez. 'If she passes all these tests, and unites with her sister, she hopes to re-emerge to the light of day as a whole being, and from then on will know herself as beyond day and night, up and down, hot and cold. She will know the "otherness" that is the creative essence of life and use it to manifest her will. If she doesn't pass, she will remain in the hellishness of being forever thrown from one end of an opposite to the other in turmoil and tedium.'

He performed a sweeping bow and walked backwards to the side of the stage. Humusi emerged, the black cow hide mantle pulled over her head so she looked like a dark shadowy figure. Tadez gestured to her and continued his narration. 'Queen Ereshkigal is the opposite of Inanna, the part that is unloving, unloved, abandoned, sexually unsatisfied and full of rage, greed, self-spite and loneliness. She blames Inanna for separating her from Heaven and causing the death of the holy bull.'

Nanni and another young boy rushed forward, each grasping a pine branch, and held them to form an arch. Urnina beamed with pride, though Nanni's little arms could barely hold the branch and it drooped lower than the other boy's.

The judge of the first gate to the underworld, played by Ku-Aya's daughter, Tyne, entered the stage to stand by the arch.

'I am here to go to the underworld, may I pass?' said Aea.

'Yes, but first you must give up your connection to your spirit,' said Tyne, her face as sharply angled as her mother's.

'You ask too much,' said Aea.

Then the shadowy figure played by Humusi stage-whispered, 'See! You'll never make this journey. You're not ready to give up what it takes to become whole.'

Aea tilted her head and considered the situation before reaching up to the diadem and taking the pine cone from its resting place. She looked at it wistfully, showing her reluctance at giving up her soul connection and thus locking herself into perceiving only the physical world. Then she handed it to Tyne, who gestured for Aea to enter the first gate of the cedar branches.

We clapped at this brave choice. Adam and I leaned in simultaneously to sip from our straws in the jug before us, our noses almost touching, and we chuckled. I leaned further into him as we sat back again, breathing deeply to catch more of the faint scent of his skin.

Another boy walked onstage carrying a strip of linen. He was followed by the judge of the second gate, played by Anunit's daughter. She wore her mother's visioning headband, a copper band suspending a lapis lazuli stone over the mind's eye between and just above the eyebrows, designed to stimulate the pineal eye and assist the far sight of a priestess. Anunit tried to look vexed because her daughter had taken the sacred headpiece without permission but, like me, she could not hide her fond indulgence.

'I am here to go to the underworld, may I pass?' asked Aea.

'Yes, but first you must give up your sight,' the judge said.

'That's silly. You ask too much,' said Aea, and Humusi whispered theatrically, 'I knew you wouldn't do it! You're not ready to give up Heaven to know Earth. Best you go back to your old life and stay the same forever.'

Aea again tilted her head in a showy contemplation of the situation, and nodded to the boy to proceed. She let him tie the linen strip around her eyes, then stumbled blindly with her arms reaching in front of her to the tittering of the audience.

Next was the third gate, and a boy entered the stage floor with another strip of linen, which was tied around Aea's mouth to prevent her clear expression, and she made comical muffled sounds through her gag. At the fourth gate, she agreed to lose her heart with a dramatic nod. In response, a boy untied the shawl holding her melon breasts in place, and they fell to the ground and rolled in opposite directions to represent the loss of earthly love and its accompanying broken heart, making us guffaw at the ridiculous sight. The fifth gate saw Aea's hands bound with reeds to represent the loss of earthly personal power, then at the sixth gate she dropped to her knees to represent the loss of shallow self-worth and value. Finally, when she reached the seventh gate, the judge said she must be stripped naked, and her skirt was untied. She was nude, bound, gagged, blindfolded and on her knees.

'Hah!' cried Humusi as Queen Ereshkigal. 'You finally meet me face to face, stripped of your heavenly assets. And all for nothing, for I will torture and kill you. You were a fool to think you could master your shadow. You cast me to the dark by separating me from my holy bull, and I will now keep you from the light forever.'

Aea cowered theatrically, and I felt a little queasy seeing her this way. Even with my understanding of the path of initiation, it was hard to see my little girl face such a situation, if only on a stage. As a mother, I was not sure I wanted her to take such a difficult path.

Tadez came in with his narration again. 'Inanna had paid dearly for her descent into the Earth, but this was not enough. Now she is tested beyond all expectations as Queen Ereshkigal torments her.' Humusi pretended to beat Aea with a stick, eliciting squeals that turned into laughter as Fancy leapt onto the sandy stage to growl at Humusi. Aea broke out of character to stroke the dog's head and offer reassurance all was well.

The audience continued to laugh heartily at Fancy's antics, and my eye was drawn to Ureem, this year among the temple women's chosen paramours. His soft grey eyes showed joy rather than the fear he suffered when facing purification alongside Adam. His mirth now sent his cheeks to his eyes and caused them to crinkle, and I recognised Aea's face in his. I had taken on the milk of several men when I wanted a child, unwilling to know which was the crucial contributor, but it was clearly Ureem as I had secretly noted over the years. My heart constricted at how easy it was to recognise a man in a woman's child and how Adam seemed to know this, although Ureem, like most men, seemed oblivious. Or perhaps he did not dare make the connection with the dangers that spouting shepherds' foolery would bring.

'Ahem,' said Tadez, waiting for one of the helper boys to lead Fancy away, then continued, 'Queen Ereshkigal now turns Inanna into a rotting green piece of meat.'

Aea fell to the ground, playing dead, and Humusi stalked around the stage looking triumphant while the audience booed and hissed. Humusi pretended to ponder what she'd done, plonking herself next to the body of Inanna, and putting her chin on her hands in the glum realisation she'd lost half of herself. She cried noisily. 'Waahh.'

Tadez was gesturing furiously to the two kind little clay creatures who were due on stage to join Humusi in wails of lamentation, and the girls finally sprung out giggling from behind the tent side, wailing in sympathy. 'Waahh.'

'Kind little creatures, you have transformed me with your compassion, what wish can I grant you?' Humusi said. 'I offer you all the grain and fertility you want.'

'We ask for what you most want to give and what is most difficult for you to give,' one of the girls said.

'What is that?' asked Humusi, feigning perplexion.

'To resurrect Inanna, who has lain dead for three days. She passed the seven tests and is now veiled to the higher truth of who she is. Only the most difficult challenge remains—for you to forgive her. No longer blame her for forsaking you to the shadows, and you will be free and whole.'

Humusi agreed and instructed Aea, 'My light half, arise from the dead so we can be whole!' Aea leapt to her feet and embraced Humusi, Fancy again running onto the stage to be part of the fun.

The girls embraced. 'Thank you, sister Ereshkigal,' said Aea. 'The loss of your holy bull made you become my shadow, so I could discover who I truly am. Now you and I are whole, the purpose of his sacrifice has come full circle. The seven veils are lifted so we can see the truth once more, and we can re-enter the gates of Heaven as an evolved soul.'

As Queen Ereshkigal, Humusi nodded, then said, 'There is one more thing. You must make another sacrifice before returning to the Heavens. What do you give?'

Aea contemplated the question by pursing her lips and looking up thoughtfully. 'I give you my favoured paramour, who is unripened by the underworld, and so cannot love as the holy bull does. I sacrifice him so he may come to know what it is to wholly love.'

Satisfied, Humusi and Aea embraced again.

'The cycle of destruction is broken and rebirth is nigh,' said Tadez, stepping forward from behind the tent side. 'Through losing her assets then reclaiming them, Inanna rejoices in their gifts where before she could not appreciate them. She is ennobled by this experience, and knows life and death, shadow and light, purity and filth are necessary counterpoints to one another if we are to be masters of creation. She knows that without them, we are but half a being who realises not who they are, and until we accept them as part of us, we are imprisoned by them. She can live on Earth as it is in Heaven, and use the opposites with wisdom to create new life.'

Aea and Humusi remained beaming in their embrace through Tadez's narration. My eyes filled with tears, touched by their innocence as they expressed the essence of initiation I had been through myself with the humourless rigours of a priestess' training and tests. Adam's hand, which rested on my upper arm, increased its reassuring pressure, as if he sensed my shifted mood.

Tadez went on. 'Inanna has completed her journey. She knows she and her shadow are one and together can create in ways that complement rather than oppose. She realises if she didn't know the experience of living on Earth, she would remain stagnant, never changing, and have a yearning within her that would be forever unsatisfied. She is whole and fulfilled. And that is the end.'

He bowed with a flourish towards the cast, who mustered to take their bows, our rapt applause and cheering staying strong until our hands and throats hurt.

I stood to embrace Aea, congratulating her and the other children. When I thanked Tadez for his superb directorship, his eyes spilled with tears, running streaks of black kohl down his cheeks. Udul-Kalama emerged from the shadows to praise his lover, and I turned away to give them space. I would dismiss Tadez early tonight so they may reunite properly after so many moons apart.

After the excitement of the play, the younger children began to rub their eyes and yawn, and were taken to bed. More beer was brought out, pleasingly cool from the jugs being submerged in the coldest parts of the pool all afternoon, and the music started again. Blue lotus incense burned in dishes set out around the edges of the tent to enrich the decadent ambience.

Tiamat and I took sides against Adam and Anba playing the board game again, but no one was really engaged. Tiamat whispered in my ear a plan for cheating, and we snickered and sought to distract the two men by stroking and massaging one another's limbs, the men's eyes on us, as we sought to secretly move our pieces further across the board. I caught the eye of Gemekala and Urnina, who sat next to us with their two guests, well-built brothers from the agricultural district, and we smiled, all of us taunting our chosen men by stretching out our bodies and preening and stroking one another to whet their appetites.

The music was calling me, and with it a desire to dance for Adam. I stood and sauntered to the centre of the sandy stage, my arms swanning out as the party clapped and cheered their encouragement. My head tipped back and I closed my eyes as my twirls and twists began, the entire tent urging me on as my head lolled loosely in a graceful trance.

Tiamat joined me, sensuality sparking between us as I trailed my fingers along her arm in welcome. Instantly, we synchronised our movements and as my hips undulated in writhing circles, the red tasselled shawl tied at the centre of my chest parted and swirled with each slink of my torso to reveal the curls at the top of my thighs, where I'd patted a little patchouli oil to add gloss and perfume. Tiamat wore her shawl low over her broad hips, tied well below her navel, revealing her lush belly and the curves of her waist. She brushed her pointy breasts, tipped with large nipples as purple as fig skin, tantalisingly against my arm as we danced.

I relished Adam's rapt stare, which never wavered although I withheld my eyes from him often, making my gaze all the more alluring when I offered it the way a woman knows to do. As the dance deepened in rapture, I met his eyes more often as my hips quivered and shook with increasing speed and my arms snaked upwards. My bare feet slapped on the Earth, my erotic life-force sparking wildly as I almost crested simply from basking in the light of his beholding.

Gemekala and Urnina came to join us and in the ease of our connection, we undulated around one another freely. I signalled Adam to come to me and he held me in his sights as he slowly approached. All the while, I never stopped moving for him, bending my head forward as I shuddered my shoulders, flinging back the cascade of snake-like braids that had fallen from their pins. He took me into his arms and crushed his lips to mine, holding my face upwards to meet him in a luscious kiss while the women danced around us.

Life was magnificent.

I wandered to the edge of the pool, looking up at the quarter moon in the sign of Gemini, the twins. At its heart, Gemini is about mastering duality—shadow and light, love and fear, high and low, and I reflected on the perfection of performing a play on Inanna's descent at this time. Gemini also symbolised the two lovers or the twin flame couple, the two halves of one soul that separate for a time to know themselves, then rediscover each other to become whole again, deeper than before. This journey of wholeness is ultimately experienced within the self, but can play out through one's partnerships.

I'd always felt Sabium was my other half and been confused and saddened by our disharmony. But maybe Adam was my twin flame, although we also seemed to have plenty of friction in our connection. Still, nothing in the earthly world could be perfect. Could Adam be my true love?

I never thought I'd truly love a man, not the way Menna loved Demsar, and until now that hadn't concerned me. But it had become dull to always be above men and although Adam was difficult, I relished the way he met my eye.

As I gazed upon the stars perfectly reflected in the blackness of the water, the picture broke apart with a series of splashes. Turning, I saw Adam grinning and preparing to skim another stone across the pool.

'Shall we take a walk?' he said.

A good omen—he appears as I think of him. Smiling, I held out my hand to meet his palm, huge and warm against my own. We strolled beyond the fires circling our camp and continued towards the other side of the grotto.

'Let's hope no hungry wolves or lions have their sights on us,' I said. 'Or heretics, for that matter.'

He made a sudden growling sound, causing me to jump a little, my nerves still twitchy from the fracas with the dogs. Laughing, he put his arm around me and pulled me close as we walked.

'So is that what you went through to become initiated?' he asked, referring to the play. 'Is it safe to say you're a whole woman, master of your shadow?' His tone was irreverent but it made me feel less self-important, and happy he wanted to know me.

'I suppose there are similarities, in essence at least.'

'Is it all so shrouded in mystery a man cannot know what it entailed?' he said, trying to tease me.

I heard his request to know something of my true self and answered earnestly. 'Many aspects of initiation can never be spoken of to one who is not also initiated, but I can tell you something of it.' I waited to see if he showed an acceptable level of gratitude before I went on.

'Will you then need to kill me?' Again he teased me, too proud to admit he wanted to know.

I was tired of silly cat and rat games and decided to continue. If he was my true love, I wanted to share this with him. 'When I was 18 springs in this life, and Menna planned to retire, I asked her if I could attempt initiation to become the next high priestess, in line with my destiny. On the next full moon, I was taken to the initiation chamber and lay in the sepulchre with the stone lid closed over me, where I must spend three full days. I had to take myself into a trance without succumbing to the fear that I wouldn't make it through, and I was tested in each of the seven levels of life's mastery.'

He watched me carefully, surprised I was telling him so much.

'Each experience, starting with the most primal level, felt completely real in the moment. There was no awareness that it was occurring in something of a dream state. Only when the level was passed would the realisation arise that it had been like a dream. It felt like the time that passed during each test was years. It felt as real as this moment with you.'

I knew he wouldn't understand, as I wouldn't have either until I experienced it.

'Did you feel scared?' he asked.

I snorted. 'At times, I was stiff with terror that I was inescapably confined in hell. But my training was instilled deeply enough for it to rise to my awareness. I remembered the key lesson that we are not in truth a physical body and thus we cannot be imprisoned. I remembered our true essence is free and once I affirmed it with commitment, that test was over. But it was terrifying. It took a tremendous focus in the moment to claim the truth. If I had remembered the lesson but not claimed it with full confidence, I would not have passed.'

'Do novices ever die during the process?'

'It happens.' My head drooped in regret. Several springs ago, when a priestess was about to retire, a novice with the correct star sign asked to attempt initiation. Although I had sensed she was not prepared, after she asked three times, I had to agree. It was a terrible wait while she lay in the sepulchre as I prayed beside it. When we opened it, my dread was confirmed—she was dead. I continued, 'Such novices panic during a test, believing it real, and allow fear to have its way, and they cannot pull themselves back to truth. They suffocate, as the air is so limited that only a trance-like state is survivable and we cannot hear them through the stone lid to help even if it were appropriate to intervene. If they die, their consciousness aligns with the experience they became stuck on. Through many incarnations, they will have to work it out in the physical world to regain their consciousness to the level at which they fell. That is the risk of initiation.'

'Why would you risk that? Is there not another way?'

'It is a path of accelerated initiation. There is another way, but it takes many lifetimes to achieve. Temple women train to understand the tests and practice how to master them in an intensified experience.'

'You must have trained hard, to have made it,' he said.

'Since I was half Aea's age. My mother impressed upon me constantly the need to master my bodily needs and desire for comfort, and to control my emotions. To survive initiation, I had to be a master of the lower desire nature yet also know how to fully enjoy the bodily pleasures. My mother began to teach me the Mes from a younger age than the other girls so I learned something of the hundred topics of the Mother-wisdom—I'm sure you must have heard of them? Things like ritual, architecture, healing, mathematics, astronomy and astrology, the use of the mind's eye to sense the future or choose the best path to take, music and dance,' I explained, glancing at him to gauge his reaction.

'I know what the Mes is.' He sounded annoyed that I had assumed his ignorance. 'And do you train your own daughter so intensively? She is destined as the next high priestess, is she not?'

'She is, but not because she is my daughter.' He looked at me questioningly and I remembered that of course he knew little of the temple's conventions nor of astronomy and astrology. I had never spoken of such sophisticated topics with a man before, not since my childhood when I taught Sabium all I knew, and I reminded myself to be patient. 'It is because she is born under the Great Mother's sign of Ophiuchus, like me, as high priestesses must be. Aea has started novice lessons and training now she is seven springs old, but I have no desire to drive her as hard as my mother did me.'

I felt my lips purse as I thought of my mother. She had always said my destiny would require so much of me that every bit of my training would be crucial, though sometimes I felt she was merely harsh on me, as she was in the way she turned Sabium away without concern for his path. I did not sense it was necessary to push Aea in her training. Although I did not know her higher destiny, I felt what she most needed was all the love and happiness I could share with her.

'Were you ever allowed to play?' he asked.

'I played a lot, with my brother. Do you know Sabium is my twin?'

'Yes, he told me.'

'Oh, did he?' It felt strange to know Adam and Sabium had spoken of me, but it was only to be expected now they were working together on developing weaponry. Without awaiting his response, I continued, 'Sabium and I were inseparable until he had to leave the temple.'

His eyes darkened at the mention of a boy's eviction.

'Go on,' he said. At least he did not look away from me this time when I spoke of this practice.

'My mother would sometimes not allow me to eat for a whole day as part of my training, but as Sabium could not take the sacred path, it mattered not what he did. Sometimes our mother would make me sleep on the hard ground, or sit in the sun for long stretches with no water. But remember, the physical mastery is the easier part. It's the training in the higher mind and the spiritual tests that are the most difficult, and the most perilous if not mastered.'

Adam looked at me intently and I continued. 'I felt sorry for my mother when she would cry and say one day I would understand she was preparing me to handle my future, as if she saw great challenges upon me. But most of all, I felt sad for Sabium. He was so upset when I had to suffer, and our mother was so cold to him.' My voice cracked as wretched guilt and sorrow tore at my heart.

Adam gripped my shoulder more firmly in a demonstration of comfort. 'How did you cope when Sabium was taken away?' he asked. 'If he was the closest person to you, it must have hurt you terribly.'

'I was devastated,' I said, wiping a hand quickly over each of my eyes. Discreetly, I took a couple of breaths to steady my emotions. 'We had always been beside each other except when I was studying, and I taught him everything I learned. He knows a lot for a man.'

Adam snorted. 'A man is as intelligent as a woman. If men were taught the Mes, they could offer more to the city.'

His statements could be considered heretical, but the truth in his words made me respond in even tones. 'It's true that Sabium is as intelligent as I, but men may not have the higher sensibilities of women or the attunement to the mysteries of life. They do seem to be as smart when it comes to things like reading and writing.'

He was quiet a moment. 'What happened to Sabium?'

'He was sent to the copper mines in the Zagros Mountains.' My voice choked as I thought of his suffering. 'In veneration of my first blood moon, I requested he be brought back and given a comfortable position in the copper district. But though I helped him in every way I could, he hated me still.'

I avoided looking at Adam as we sat on a rocky ledge at the far edge of the grotto pool, my tears welling. Every day since Sabium had been taken away, I'd felt ripped in two, and although I'd come to live with it, the emptiness and pain were so near the surface in my every moment.

'By the time I entered formal novice training when I was 13 springs on this Earth, I was far ahead of the other girls in my skills,' I continued. 'The physical mastery lessons were easy for me, and I was able to focus on increasing my knowledge. I started training in the sexual arts and learned that a priestess' ecstatic abilities are the seat of her higher power. When I felt ready, I chose my first lover, and learned to train a man in how to elicit the ecstasy of the Great Mother through me.'

He huffed. 'Men don't need a temple woman to learn that—we are naturally wise in how to draw forth a woman's pleasure. And a woman doesn't have to be a priestess to know ecstasy.'

'Yes, but an average woman does not have to use her sexual power in service of the entire land.' I kept my patience, for he was like a child thinking the squelching of clay could be equated to a sculptor with a lifetime at their art. 'She need only enjoy the pleasures Inanna bestows upon her body—a sacred endeavour, of course, but for a priestess, the power is also used for higher purpose.'

He ignored my comment. 'Is it true the priestesses have some sort of magical crystal sphere that holds the secrets of creation?'

I laughed to cover my alarm. How did this man have any inkling of the Weird Sphere? 'That would be convenient. Wherever did you hear such a thing?'

'I don't know. Some men have spoken of it, saying you have a special sphere that gives you the knowledge of the world.'

'Really!' I scoffed, wondering how this rumour had begun. With the heretic threat rising, it was more crucial than ever that no one knew about it. If men realised the future it boded, it would fuel an uprising. 'Even if there were such a thing, a man would probably not have the insight to see anything within it.'

The familiar feeling of Adam's aura prickling in frustration washed over me, but he did not respond out loud. After a long silence, he spoke again. 'So how did it come to be that you are high priestess?'

I was relieved he had moved on from asking about the Weird Sphere, and answered gladly, 'Sabium and I were born in the month of Ophiuchus as well as under its moon sign. Ophiuchus is one of the 13 zodiac signs, you must know that much of astrology? Ophiuchus is ruler of the 13-month lunar year, sitting between Scorpio and Sagittarius on the zodiacal belt. She is the Sky Snake Mother, the winged serpent bearer, the unifier of Heaven and Earth. Because I was born in her bosom, I was marked as the next high priestess. That's why my mother pushed me so hard in my training.'

'Well, apart from a bit of deprivation from your mother, your life sounds pretty charmed,' he said with bravado.

His flippant words felt like a slap and I stood to walk away. I had shared myself with him more openly than I had with any man, feeling relief at telling him of my background, yet he would scorn me.

He came to my side and pulled me to a stop, grasping my hands to his chest.

'I don't mean to mock you. Those who don't walk the priestess path also suffer and master themselves, but we are not recognised for it with pomp.' He held tight to my hands. 'The men of Uruk work hard to make it the great city it is, and do so without privilege and without proper food. Lentil stew and bread, day in and day out! We are denied any of the city's significant roles or any chance to give an opinion.' He spoke with seriousness, his eyes boring into mine.

I could condemn him as a heretic for this, yet, again, I knew he spoke some truth. 'You're right, men do give a lot. But it is not the Great Mother's way for them to rule, and they must humbly accept their place. I'm not denying that men suffer and grow, but the priestess path operates at a whole different level. You cannot compare the two.'

He dropped my hands.

'You know not what you say,' he said. 'Without men, the city would crumble. You don't understand our importance.'

I flinched a little. 'Adam, watch your place.'

'No, you listen to me. I was cast out by my mother as if I were worthless dross. Going without water and food for a day? That is nothing. The matrons of my city starved, beat and molested me. They crushed my spirit as best they could, forcing me to worship at their disgusting laps. One of them tormented me to the point I would sooner die than continue living that way. She consumed the life-force of young boys, forcing us to perform acts upon her and twisting our ears to pulp, or squeezing our figs so hard it felt they would burst.'

His voice shook with vitriol. 'That matron tormented us by forcing our sexual responses so our minds would be shamed at the way our bodies betrayed us. Through the season turnings, she brutalised younger and younger boys. When I fought back, she had me strung up by my feet and beaten. My mother must have known—she laid cold eyes on me in the street occasionally, but she was too busy opening her thighs to an endless stream of men to care about me.'

I pressed my lips together, horrified to hear of the abuse, yet unsure I could let him get away with criticising his mother in such a sacrilegious manner.

Sensing his overstep, he took a long breath and spoke with more control. 'When I was 13, I ran away into the desert and would have died there, but it was not my fate. A group of travelling gem miners found and revived me. So yes, I know my place, and it is as the master of my own life and body, regardless of what you say I am.' He trembled with indignation.

A sickening anxiety rose in my heart and belly. I had always known males were treated badly, but from up high in the temple, it was my duty to rule society so the prophecy did not eventuate. I could not afford to give many allowances. Even so, my conscience throbbed.

What I knew the matrons did in the communal houses was bad enough. But an even uglier feeling rose as I considered the boys I saw brought to the chambers of Beihani, revered as a priestess who kept her wise blood. Those boys were barely old enough to sprout hair on their figs. Surely she would not treat them with cruelty? But I'd noticed they looked pale when they were sent away, their heads hung low. I suspected she had strange proclivities she played with on their young bodies. I'd considered her lap rights as unquestionable as any other woman's, and assumed all males enjoyed a woman's attentions. But I also knew sexual activity could be unpleasant. On the rare occasion I put a stop to sex that wasn't pleasing me, it surprised me how distasteful it could be. I dreaded to guess at how awful it was for boys forced to perform all manner of sexual services for women they hated. My stomach turned.

Adam continued in strident tones, eager to make full use of my sympathetic ear. 'We are forced to shave our faces as if our natural form is wrong, told we are so rank we must wear perfumed oils, believed to be without insight or wisdom. You rob us of our confidence and purpose in every way. Can you imagine what it's like? To have no choice in how we live our lives, to bow to women's demands and still reap mostly scorn?'

'Adam...' I didn't know what to say. I wanted to soothe his heart, to fill him so deeply with my love that all his pain was pushed out. I took his hand and held it to my lips, relieved he let me kiss it, then pressed my cheek into his palm. I needed to think about what he'd said, and all the messages and events arising of late—the heretic threat, the upsurge of my pain over Sabium, the impact Adam was having on me, all of it stirring my grief at the mistreatment of males. Since Adam entered my life, my conscience was shaken. I could no longer pretend the society I ruled was unchangeable. Surely treating males humanely did not necessarily mean they would rise to crush women?

A profound emotion was stirring from the depths of my soul. Who was this man to me to make me so conflicted? Again and again I'd asked this of myself. He was not just another lover. He felt like a lost part of me I longed to reunite with, to make peace with. I recognised with clarity—I am in love.

Sitting together back in the main tent, Adam and I listened to the sweetness of Lahamu's voice and the tinkling of the lyre as she sang a love ballad. After our conversation, a pleasant rawness connected us. I allowed my head to rest on his chest, his arm around my shoulders. I turned my face a little to inhale more of his skin, craving to know more of his essence. The thud of his heart moved right through me, synchronised with the pulse of yearning in my belly.

Around us, couples were kissing, hands were caressing, sighs of pleasure were being uttered. I tipped my head back to seek his lips and he came forward, our mouths meeting in a languorous kiss. If I opened my mouth wider and devoured him the way I desired, the fire in my depths might take over and squander this precious moment with the urge to relieve my base instinct. Best we savour this blessing, the gift of Inanna's sensuality bestowed upon all.

Although I wanted to explore his body, I kept my hand softly on his chest, feeling the curve of the muscle beneath my palm. There was a delicious game of seduction and he was a worthy playmate—he was in control of the male's rutting nature and I knew I would not need to deal with the tiresomeness of him getting beyond himself.

When I could resist it no more, I slid my tongue to meet his, tasting his liquid thirstily.

Desperate to draw him inside me, I swung my leg over his hips, my arms either side of his shoulders as I pulled myself up to hover over him.

'Take me to the deep,' I commanded huskily. Although we had coupled with raw passion the night of the invasion, I sensed this man had more to his lovemaking. He carried the power to join me in infinite space in which the stars and the Great Mother dwelled.

His throat yielded a low growl at my words, but a moment later, he pushed me back.

'Not with all these people around us.' He sat up, pushing me firmly back by the shoulders. It was natural and celebratory to be witnessed in the act of sexual worship, but that he desired me in private raised my excitement.

He stood to pull me to my feet, then grabbed a blanket and tucked it under one arm, picking up an oil lamp with his other hand. We stepped past the squirming bodies to get outside, where fireflies shot past, brilliant flashes in the night sky. When we reached the willow tree, he parted the leafy curtains that fell to the beach to let me enter the tree's cupola. He followed me in, setting down the lamp and tossing the bedding on the sand, still warm beneath my feet from the day's heat.

We stood facing one another, and my heart surged open as I saw into the blackness of his eyes. The enormity of his soul caused an inner tremble in my core. I reached to the knotted shawl at my chest, the red linen almost black in the dim light, and slowly untied it. As it dropped to the ground, I felt my breasts elevate, reaching out for him, keen to push against his chest, to feel his hot breath. My chest rose and fell visibly as I stood still, powerfully thrilled as his gaze left mine to take in my body.

Under his watch, I let my hands run over my breasts, cupping them in offering to him before I dropped them, their gentle bounce filling me with aching desire. I let my fingertips trail down the contours of my belly to brush over my pubic curls, displaying my body in invitation, twirling my fingers over my mound of Venus to almost imperceptibly open my crevice to his sight.

I waited for him to show himself to me, my breath in my throat as he unwrapped the shawl around his hips. His staff sprung upwards at a jaunty angle as the fabric dropped to the ground, and my mouth and gates filled with more wetness at the sight. He was distended with his desire and for a moment, I smiled in delight at this wondrous sight, and he joined me in a sudden laugh that erupted from the glorious tension of the moment.

'Come,' I whispered, holding out my hand.

He stepped forward, and knelt before me, placing his hands on my hips. He leaned forward to nuzzle my triangle, inhaling my smokey readiness. I lolled my head, feeling my wetness pooling in oceans of desire, allowing the deliciousness of the moment to continue although I ached to feel his face burrow into me. But I had already experienced his rough and wild lovemaking, and this time I wanted to know the nuances of his art.

Obligingly slowly, the tip of his tongue reached down and dragged lightly up to the top of my crevice without drawing it apart. We both groaned a little. I felt lightheaded, my legs weakened. He did it again. And again. Still he left me wanting, over and over.

'You torment me well,' I breathed, and he tipped his head back to gaze up at me.

'I will torment you to bring forth your best,' he murmured.

I closed my eyes as he returned to the slow stroking of his tongue up and down, adjusting my stance to open my legs a little more in the hopes he would dip inside me.

'I will lay down,' I said, starting to feel impatient, and he drew back his head to laugh a little as he helped me recline on the blanket.

I pulled him to my mouth and we kissed deeply. Lazily, he trailed the back of his hand from the hollow of my throat, over my heart and down to the top of my mound, and back again, refusing to increase the pace. Our mouths moved in rhythmic slowness, feeding our erotic trance, and I wanted to drink all of him into myself.

Finally, his hand rested at the centre of my chest and my breasts pulsated, their consciousness registering he was about to caress them. I revelled in his patience and control, knowing I could surrender into it, and sank back a little more into the blanket beneath my back to present my body.

As he kissed me, he stroked around my breasts, carefully avoiding my nipples as his hand glided, gradually picking up speed. My body was limp with desire, longing to yield but in acceptance of when he would give me more. He pulled back to meet my eyes with ardent presence, cupping one breast, pausing, then dragging a thumb across my nipple. I shuddered, touching his arm, imploring him to do it again. He did. Back and forth he thumbed my left nipple, the one that had missed his caress during the Akitu ritual, as if in recompense.

'And the other?' I whispered.

'Already?' he said, but he reached across to my hungry breast and pleasured it in the same manner. I absorbed the exquisite sensations, throbbing to be opened. I reached to stroke the springy hair at his crotch and cupped his firm figs, then swished my lightly gripped hand over his stiffness.

Swamped with fervour, he bent to kiss me again, probing my mouth, then broke away, biting and mouthing along my neck as it elongated in response. He shifted his body further down and pushed my breasts together so his tongue could swirl from one to the other with the shortest distance separating the sensations.

Panting with increasing desperation, I struggled under his weight to open my legs and offer my ripeness to him, whether his fingers or mouth or shaft—I wanted it all. I started crooning, the noises effortlessly emerging from my softened throat, and I felt my core lifting higher and higher as my gates prepared to open. I held myself at bay for now, for the sheer delight of intensifying my fulfilment.

'Come to my lap,' I said, my frustration getting the better of me as I pulled at his arms to move up and enter me.

'Not yet, lady.'

He kissed my belly, across from one hip to the other, pausing over my womb to lap at the skin with a warm, flat tongue. He reached to spread my legs wider, moving his body further down. I held myself proudly, swooning with arousal as he took in my sacred gateway.

He placed a palm on my mound of Venus, dragging it back to jut out my ruby to greet him, his face pulling back a little to behold this spectacle before he placed his lips around it. His other hand appeared at my gates and he pushed a finger a little inside me, gently beckoning on the place that throbbed with oceanic power. I felt a flash of jealousy for the women he had learned these skills with, quickly forgotten as his tongue danced over my jewel and I became mindless. The fire between us was combusting into a light explosion that could not be held back, and I reached down to yank him under his arms to come up. I pushed him to the side and onto his back, straddling him, dangling my swollen breasts with their distended nipples above his slick mouth.

'Adam!' I cried, all-out desperate for him to plunge into me. I positioned myself over the tip of his staff, nestling around him, and pulled on my discipline to pause. Our eyes mated, and at the right moment, I slid my hips smoothly down to take him into the divine abyss. A searing ecstasy of fullness consumed me and opened my throat in a gasp. I undulated my hips, letting my spine wave and writhe as I pleasured myself upon the length of him, his hands moving without pause all over me. He pulled my lips to his, and with great will, I stopped moving to give my entire focus to the kiss, letting the higher energies build and our souls expand together in an ecstasy far beyond that our physical bodies could offer. I resumed my writhing, allowing the flow to build until I felt like sobbing with passion, moving my hips in hard smacking thumps against him. Unable to hold himself much longer, he flipped me onto my side and pulled my leg over him, taking control of the strokes.

Undone with the frenzy, my palm pounded his back to urge him on, my other hand grasping at one of his buttocks as I ground him deeper into me, demanding he meet with me with every fibre of his being. His eyes held mine, as present as a lion's before its killing bite, and I opened my core to let him take it. I let him disintegrate me into nothingness, the power of all women throbbing through me as I soared in mighty waves into the All That Is, seeing his face transform into that of an otherworldly masculine presence.

Then a flash of knowing filled me—Adam had taken me to the gates of Heaven as did the holy bull. Such a feat could not be achieved by a mere man. Ardent gratitude filled me, for I sensed a potential in our union that was beyond my comprehension.

We collapsed, his arms tight around me as he smothered my neck with kisses and murmured into my ear, 'My love, my love' over and over, and I wondered if I heard tears in his voice, or perhaps it was passion that made him sound so raw. Together we coasted in the finest lightness of being, luxuriating in the succulence of skin on skin, inhaling each other's scent and the special perfume we made together.

'Let us rest. You'll need your strength for your first day of training,' I said, softening more deeply into Adam's arms as we lay sated in my chamber in the darkness before dawn. Since returning from the grotto two days earlier, Adam had been busily planning the commencement of army training, reporting to me on progress in the early evening, then spending most of the night in my bed.

He dotted kisses on my forehead, rubbing my back down to the top of my buttocks and massaging the flat space there, threatening to awaken my girdle of fire yet again.

'I will never tire of you, it seems,' I murmured, tipping my head back to kiss him.

He sat up a little, resting on one elbow so he could look into my eyes in the dim candlelight. 'Are you serious about that, Lilith?'

'You call me Lilith now, do you?' But I liked the sound of my name on his lips. I continued. 'Yes, I am serious. Since the day we met, I've been drawn to you with a power I do not understand. Do you feel it too?'

'I do,' he said, eyes shining. 'I swear on my love of the Great Mother, I've never known what it is to love a woman before you.'

'Then we are in love.' I relished the words.

'Yes, we are in love. I wish you would marry me and we can show the city that a man can offer value alongside you, and quell this rising talk of rebellion. You can be an example of a woman with a man by her side.'

He looked at me expectantly, and I laughed. 'You as my prime consort is enough. Already I listen to you on matters of state,' I said.

'My love, you only listen to me in privacy, not in front of the council or your temple women.' His tone was taut. 'We have the chance to show Uruk you are willing to listen to men. With the heretics touting their ideas, it's a matter of time before the men of Uruk also question why men are treated as inferiors. Since you and I want to be together, why not marry me so we can show the people our ruler is starting to see the value of men?'

I didn't want to further disrupt these intimate moments but I had to be clear with him. 'Never has a high priestess distracted her focus by taking a husband. It is forbidden.'

He held my eye in surly silence.

'Come to think of it, I don't want to be married anyway,' he said finally. 'It's grossly unfair a man must devote his body only to his wife in case she gets jealous, while her lap rights are unquestioned.' He readjusted himself to sit a little higher.

'Jealousy has nothing to do with it. Married or not, a woman's ability to create new life is ripened by her sacred lap rights. Men have no such need.' I used a brisk tone to cover my lack of conviction.

'A man's milk can help a woman grow her baby, so he has some role in the creation of new life, even if you say it's minor. Maybe shaft milk is more significant than you say.' There was a crack of hurt indignation in his voice. 'Why doesn't a man have a right to contribute to a child's life after it is born, if his milk has partly nourished it?'

'Any one man's contribution is negligible.'

My tone was dismissive but as a woman in love my heart heavied at denying the truth to his face. I decided to share something more profound with him, first breathing into my throat to open the tightness my lies had brought. 'But part of me senses you are right—there may well be a new era afoot where men will be treated with more fairness, and even play a greater role in the raising of children.' I paused, realising I felt so softened after our lovemaking that perhaps I'd spoken too frankly. 'But changing the traditions of my temple is not something I will entertain. Ruling Uruk is my focus. And you may call me Lilith only in private.'

He was silent, a certain tension anchoring around his jaw.

I didn't want to think more of this. It had to be enough that we had spoken of our love for one another.

The piercing cry of Tombaya rang out from my garden terrace. Dawn was close. I felt Adam's embrace stiffen in anticipation of my next words, and I smiled apologetically. 'My love,' I said softly. 'You must leave now before the sun rises. You know the rules.'

CHAPTER 7

The sound of clanging metal and hollering men had drifted up from the plaza since soon after sunrise. Mid-morning, I invited the priestesses to join me to inspect the inaugural training session of my army.

'I can hardly wait to see the chaos going on out there,' said Ku-Aya. 'This is a feat of organisation beyond those thick matrons. Even with the temple's orders, getting the district supervisors to release their men from work for a whole morning is quite an accomplishment.'

'Actually, Adam is organising this training. The matrons were instructed to allow his input and advice,' I said, sitting on the raised edge of the looking pond to lace my sandals. 'The councillors were also cooperative and gave their men leave from work without fuss.'

'I cannot imagine the matrons are pleased with all this—imagine how Olgana will react to Adam telling her how things should be done,' said Anunit, her mouth turning up on one side.

'I'm eager to see Anba in fine fighting form,' said Tiamat. 'He was so busy preparing for today he did not come to my bed last night.' Her brow contracted delicately.

Gemekala remained silent, a small scowl on her face.

I stood, brushing down my long skirts and peering at my reflection in the obsidian-lined pond. I tweaked my nipples to rosy them for the public appearance, then fiddled with my hair.

'I wonder who you preen like a peacock for?' teased Urnina, and I smiled without taking my eyes from my reflection.

I led the priestesses down to the plaza. I didn't have to look back to know we'd all assumed the serene expressions we wore in any public space, and wouldn't change them even as we took in the bizarre sight ahead of us.

Beneath my calm demeanour, I was stunned. I had never seen, nor imagined, a sight such as this. A thousand men filled the plaza and concourse, engaged in a flurry of combat situations, their bodies flying about in ways I'd never before seen men move. The expansive view from the top of our steps showed there was an organised structure to the exercise, with zones set for different purposes. At the far end of the concourse, men flung spears and slingshots into the river shallows, then there was a section for hand-to-hand combat followed by a zone with tables holding samples of prototype leather items and newly forged weapons. In front of the ziggurat, the plaza was being used for practicing combat with copper knives that glinted in the sun.

Adam's guardians, in their rolled red headcloths, were easy to spot among the crowd. They wore hardy sandals and protective leatherware on their forearms, and enthusiastically yelled commands, praise and criticism to their charges, who seemed to lap it up with veneration. I sought out our matrons, difficult to pick out through the fray. Whenever I did spot one, she was scowling and looking out of place among the jubilant men.

Dozens of city women sat on the lower temple steps, staring in amazement at the peculiar activity, and they jumped up to let us pass when they realised our approach. I surged out the mesmerism to ensure they'd see no falter in our procession, and didn't slow as I led my priestesses straight into the men jabbing and thrusting with knives. They fell back to open a path before us and I kept going, a speck of someone's sweat flying onto my arm.

The titillation among the men was palpable, and although they stepped aside and bowed as they noted our passing, I sensed their impatience to return to the lively shouts and grunts of their training. Was this...hostility? Towards us? As this thought crossed my mind, a sparring man glared at me, causing the hackles on my neck to rise. My alarm increased as I registered a pungency in the air that went beyond the stench of a crowd of working men. My heart tightened as I realised—this was the scent of aggression. I was allowing my men to become more brutish, even if the purpose was to defeat the far more threatening heretics.

Urnina mirrored my concerns, her mouth close to my ear, 'The men are loving this—feel the emanations. I fear the fighting is awakening their gross nature.'

'They're puffed up with self-importance,' muttered Gemekala from behind me. 'Our men have ratter!'

I did not comment, unsure how I felt about the confidence so evident in my budding army. We reached the end of the plaza and began along the concourse, getting a closer look at the samples of weapons and leatherwear set up on the tables. I'd released one hundred cubits of copper from our coffers and authorised the slaughter of 20 sheep and 20 goats, their hides to be dried without the full tanning process to create a stiff leather for protective gear—vests, arm cuffs and sandals with shin guards. Some of the extra meat would go into the army trainees' soup, which I'd agreed at Adam's request. He'd also wanted me to release 20 cows for their tougher hides, but I had admonished him. The notion of using the Great Mother's holy cows for such a purpose! More leatherwear and weapons were being made to cater for the rest of the army, but it would take many more days before all were equipped.

As we passed into the next zone, I recognised Adam's booming voice ahead in the crowd of sweaty men. Soon, I spotted him instructing two men wielding batons that clinked and cracked with each strike, circled by 12 or so eager spectators, including Sabium. My brother wore the red headcloth that marked him as a guardian, a token fighter only since his frail constitution meant he could barely defeat a kitten. But I knew that what he lacked in physicality, he made up for with cleverness that would make him a resourceful tactician. As a young child, when his size and constitution were on the tall and strong side, he'd driven plots to have Cook bake an extra batch of crescent moon-shaped honey cakes that were produced at every new moon. The day before, Sabium would mention to Cook how a dog had nearly tripped him or that he'd stubbed his toe on a wonky brick. Then he'd use these comments to back up stories that a batch of cakes had been knocked in the dirt by an errant dog or that I'd stumbled on a skewiff brick when we were delivering the cakes to the priestesses, and we'd scoff the extra cake in our secret space in the plaza gardens. Or Sabium would convince the bakers to give us a loaf of hot barley bread, and we would eat it with honey he'd scam from the agricultural district, giving a lie that our mother needed some urgently in the dispensary.

'Do you want to be felled in your first battle? Raise your fists, my friend!' Adam bayed at one of the combatants with fierce joy, slapping him on the back.

Sabium stared at Adam with unabashed admiration, causing me unease. Why were the two men most important to me, apart from Tadez, aligning with one another? That Sabium was one of the guardians was odd enough, but to see his adoration of Adam was disturbing. I supposed I couldn't be the only one to enjoy Adam's charisma.

I had to jab the shoulder of a man in the spectating circle to get them to notice my presence, so entranced were they by Adam's show, and when they stepped aside, I moved to the front. Adam was holding a wooden baton, slashing it in long motions through the air to show the trainees how it was done. I watched as the weight of the baton made the muscles on his chest bob and the sinews in his arms dance. He met my gaze with customary single-focus while he continued his flamboyant tirade at the men. The two men fighting were tiring, their arms dropping with fatigue, and Adam urged them on relentlessly, 'Raise yourselves, men. Let me hear your voices!'

He seemed reluctant to drag himself away, an unexpected affront to me as his high priestess and lover. Just as I was about to turn my back, he called out to the men, 'Continue under the command of Guardian Sabium.'

Sabium stepped forward proudly and Adam nodded encouragement before coming to stand before me.

'Well, High Priestess, how do you like our fledgling army?' he said, his ribcage heaving from his exertions. He was animated, his eyes filled with fire. Sweat dribbled down his temples and I caught the grit of his leathery odour, strangely unrepugnant.

'I'm amazed you've arranged such a set-up in a couple of days,' I said, uncertain if I was truly pleased with this feat. It was all happening so quickly. While it was a tremendous help to have him organise training so successfully, already I sensed the men were looking to him as their authority figure. Was this the price I must pay, less control to protect my people?

'I've achieved more than this. If you visit the tannery, you'll see the men and boys working hard to make the leatherwear. They are accomplishing so much, thanks to the temple's generosity, of course. With your bountiful contribution of copper, your brother has the district churning out new knives at a remarkable pace. Those will have to do until we can start making bronze.'

Sabium's jealous glare burned into me as he watched us talk. 'Come on, men!' he shouted with what strength his lungs could muster, watching Adam to check these galvanising cries were registered. 'Waken your strength!'

I rolled my eyes and returned my focus to Adam. 'Proceed with the training and report to me this evening at sunset.' I needed to know more about the army's progress, but what's more, my mouth moistened at the thought of him at my lap tonight. I turned to go.

'High Priestess, wait,' he said, coming closer. 'I need to talk to you about something else. Guardian Anba is not here today. He was eager to be at training when I saw him yesterday, and I can't imagine why he's not here. I asked a couple of men from the copper district but they don't know his whereabouts. Do you know if something has befallen him?'

'I don't know,' I snapped, immediately feeling my anxiety rise though I did not know why. Perhaps I was irritated at Adam's presumptuousness in thinking I kept tabs on a man just because he was one of the guardians. 'But Tiamat may wish to investigate. I'll ask her,' I added to soften my words, although he seemed unconcerned by my curtness.

'Another thing you should know,' he said, speaking more quietly. 'The men are angry that Luninni, the man killed in the heretic attack, was buried in a reed basket without any gifts to ease his journey in the otherworlds. The men are asking me why they should risk their lives to protect this city when it does not honour them? The woman was given a state rite with your blessing and buried in a clay coffin filled with gifts.'

I was about to scold him for challenging me, but my conscience prickled. 'I have heard your concerns. Now return to training.' While he did have a point, Adam was getting ahead of himself, again, thinking that because I favoured him he could speak out of turn. That I understood his grievances and was inexperienced in dealing with male sassiness continually saw me err to lenience. I must watch myself, lest he push even further beyond the station of authority I had granted him.

After the nasty look the trainee had flashed me earlier, and the general frenzy of aggression around me, I was tense. This was not acceptable. I had to set ground rules for the army's behaviour around women.

Tiamat approached me on the way back to the temple, her mouth barely moving as she spoke quietly in my ear, conscious of the need to keep our business private from the men around us. 'I sense something has happened to Anba. I asked Sabium where he is, and he said he did not know. But he was hiding something—his emanations were agitated.'

My gut tightened in the knowing this would not end well. 'Have Councillor Semiramis come to the temple right away with her head matron,' I muttered. 'Surely they will know what's happened.'

As we marched back towards the temple, my temper rising at the increasing surety something foul had happened, Olgana's booming voice called me. I turned to watch her striding through the crowd, shoving men aside.

'High Priestess, something terrible has happened.' Her tears alarmed me. 'A matron in the copper district, Puabi. She's been strangled.'

When Tadez came to announce the arrival of Semiramis and the copper district's head matron, Shagshag, I was sitting with the priestesses on my terrace, discussing what might have happened and how Anba might be involved. We all sensed calamity, and I tried to keep my head clear to deal with what was about to be revealed.

'I will send for you as soon as we know what happened,' I promised Tiamat, her face tense with worry. I would not let her come to the interview—Semiramis and Shagshag surely knew Anba was Tiamat's favourite paramour and would not reveal as much information in her presence.

I squeezed Tiamat's shoulder and led Ku-Aya and Doshina to the reception pavilion on the other side of the ziggurat. Semiramis and Shagshag waited in the shade of a bougainvillea, avoiding the afternoon sun, and my wrath increased as we watched them hurry over. The sight of Semiramis aggravated me. I felt the same acrimony between us as when Sabium and I were seven and I faced her at the purification pool.

'Semiramis.' I addressed her without preamble or the use of her title. 'I am shocked I had to call you here to explain how Puabi was killed—the murder of a matron! How did I hear of this only now when her body was found this morning?' I made myself large and intimidating with the mesmerism as I glared at her.

Her cloudy eyes flashed with panic.

'High Priestess, I'm sorry. We were trying to put together what happened,' she said quickly. 'I didn't want to come to you with half answers.' She dipped her chin in an imitation of respect.

'The murder of a matron is utterly unprecedented, yet you fail to tell me as your first priority? There has never been a more shocking event in our city! And what of the man missing from your district, Anba, what do you know of that?'

'High Priestess, please forgive me, I hoped we'd find the two men who went missing before I told you what happened to Anba.' Semiramis was sweating, her squat head pulled back a little from the blast of my rage.

'Two more of your men are missing?' My alarm was growing by the moment.

'Yes, I didn't have a chance to tell you. They killed Matron Puabi then it seems they ran away to join the heretics. They'd spoken of it to some other men.'

My in-breath was controlled as I glared at her, shock coursing through my veins. The situation was even worse than I'd expected with my own men now apparently joining the heretic uprising.

'Matron Shagshag was more involved in last night's events, she can best explain,' Semiramis said, nodding towards the towering woman standing a step behind her.

Shagshag spoke reluctantly. 'We thought it best to deal with it as quickly and quietly as possible so as not to disturb you nor raise a fuss among the population. We didn't plan to go so far, but this Anba! We've never heard anything like it, the way he insulted us, refusing to obey us. He resisted the purification process and it took all of us to hold him, even with his hands bound. When we let him up to see if he had humbled, he said he'd rather die than worship at our laps. We had to purify him completely, there was no other option.'

She paused, overwhelmed with the ferocity of my stare as I took in that Anba was dead. My heart grabbed painfully as I recalled meeting his merry gaze as we played 20 squares just a few days ago, him singing with Adam with such good humour, the way he and Tiamat had laughed together until they snorted.

'How did Puabi come to be strangled?' I snapped, eager to push on with this interrogation.

'The other two men didn't resist their dunkings and we showed them the Great Mother's mercy. Their hands were bound and they were passive, so we left them with Puabi while we went to fetch Councillor Semiramis because, well, we knew she would want to be involved.' Shagshag shot a look at Semiramis.

Of course the matrons had fetched Semiramis—they'd killed a priestess' prime paramour and hoped their district councillor would know how to minimise the consequences. I nodded in an angry jerk, urging Shagshag to continue.

'When we returned to the well, Puabi was dead and the men were gone,' she said. 'We're sure they've run away to join the heretics.'

'You know Anba was the prime paramour of Priestess Tiamat. Did he not report this to you and ask for her intervention?' I demanded.

'It was such a fracas with all the shouting and struggling, it was hard to hear anything clearly,' Shagshag said, her head low.

'Do not lie to me, woman!' I spat. 'Do you have no respect for my mind's eye?' I turned to nod at Doshina, who was awaiting my signal to fetch Tiamat. We stood in silence, the tension rising as I stared unblinkingly at Semiramis and Shagshag. I felt Tiamat's energy before I heard her feet slap on the mud bricks, her aura pulsing with rage.

'Priestess Tiamat,' I said, holding out my arm to welcome her to my side and placing a hand on her back to offer support. My throat tightened with dread at what I must tell her. 'It is my sorrow to tell you...Shagshag and her matrons killed Anba.'

Tiamat's intake of breath was audible. A moment later, she stepped forward and yanked Shagshag's leather sash, shrilling hysterically, 'You will be sorry!'

I knew Tiamat had already sensed Anba's soul had departed, but having such a thing confirmed was devastating. Shagshag cowered like a sorry dog as I spoke. 'It is clear Anba asked for your intervention, and Shagshag failed to respond.'

Tiamat's energy was swelled out in a most impressive field, giving the illusion she was as big as Shagshag.

'What consequence do you wish to see, Priestess Tiamat?' I asked, my brow menacingly low.

Tiamat let go of Shagshag's sash and shoved her backwards. 'I wish to see Shagshag banished to the desert, where she will die of heat and thirst if the jackals don't eat her first—though even they would find her repugnant,' she said flatly, and the bulging of Shagshag's eyes almost made me laugh. 'Perhaps she will make it back to the uncivilised land she hails from, and they are welcome to her.' Tiamat's lip snarled in contempt as she insulted Shagshag's rustic origins in the lands to our east, from where most our matrons hailed.

I nodded, and turned to Semiramis. The woman was quivering in dread. I would be happy to also see her banished, but feared if I issued such a harsh punishment to a councillor, it would be said that I was penalising powerful women due to events connected to the heretic uprising. It would cause additional upheaval in a situation already bound to erode the city's stability.

One corner of my upper lip snarled in disgust as I addressed her. 'You are devious and inept, attempting to hide serious events from the temple and failing to correctly manage your district's matrons and matters. You are stripped of your position on the council, and will leave your apartments by sunset. You will spend the next three turns of the moon alone in the exclusion hut.' If we had to severely punish a woman, she was sent to an old fisherman's reed hut by the river, with food delivered wordlessly to her doorstep by a servant. 'After your sentence is up, I don't want to see you lurking around. Find accommodations in the outer areas of Uruk with the shepherds for all I care. Stay away from the temple and keep your head down in the city. If you do not, you will rot in the desert. I warn you, do not tempt me.'

Semiramis stared at me wide-eyed with shock. Tiamat yanked her by the shoulder and spun her around to unclasp the councillor's collar, pulling the symbol of power from her and letting it clang to the floor.

I turned my wrath on the skulking matron. In a cold flat tone, I said, 'Shagshag, be gone by sunset. If you are seen again near this city, you will become the first woman to go to the pit.'

Beside me, Tiamat's aura wavered and I knew she could not contain her grief much longer, so I declared, 'Ku-Aya, tell Olgana to oversee their punishments in the sternest fashion. Both of you, take your feet from this hallowed temple now.'

Ku-Aya pointed at the vestibule and the two women began to walk towards it, stunned at the dismal turn in their fates. Ku-Aya followed, jabbing the back of one then the other with her finger.

Tiamat waited until they were out of earshot before she crumbled into sobs, stooped with her hands tearing at her heart.

'Anba, I'm so sorry I was not there for you,' she cried in pained passion. 'I'm glad you refused that revolting woman's lap. It is an outrage you were treated this way.'

I half-carried her to a pergola, pulling her down onto the cushions and into my arms as she sobbed and gushed words of love and regret to her lover's departed soul. Her body shook with the force of her grief and my heart bled for her—we had both fallen in love with men who stood by our sides as equals, and to lose such a precious connection was unthinkable. I was deeply saddened that a fine man like Anba had been demeaned and killed in this way, and under my rule. Men were frequently purified at the discretion of the district matrons, with no system or justice to the approach. If men were obsequious, as most were, the matrons generally let them up, but it was not unusual that a man was fatally purified if he too greatly offended the matrons or the city women—or the temple, for priestesses and novices ordered purifications too. My hands buzzed as I thought of holding Adam's face beneath the water, suffocating him at my will. Once I had ordered the purification of Sabium when his public slurs at me had been too outrageous to ignore, instructing Olgana to be lenient in fear his lungs could not cope.

Remorse wracked my soul. The temple should have a duty of care to men and boys, but this had always been neglected in our anxiety to keep the prophecy from activating. Helplessness at the predicament wrestled with desire to make changes to our justice system, and I tried to push it all aside. Right now, the political situation I faced was more pressing.

Whispering coos of comfort, I wiped Tiamat's face with my shawl as I held her. We stayed wrapped in the embrace until the sun moved into mid-afternoon and her sobs finally quietened. Leaning my forehead to hers, I willed her my strength. Impressions flooded my mind's eye as I sensed the loss of Anba would impact her immensely. She would spend many, many lifetimes seeking her true love again, even giving up on the quest for some time. I barely dared to feel the depth of this loss for fear of glimpsing my own—that half of our very souls were bound and kept from us.

After I escorted Tiamat into the arms of the other priestesses, I told Tadez to bequeath a clay coffin not just for Puabi, but also for Anba, and to provide generous gifts of milk, butter, grain and beer to be buried with both.

Then I sat alone in my garden. A deep unrest was upon me. Although I hadn't banished Semiramis, I had thrown her off the council. It was scandalous, and would cause more unsettlement in Uruk at this chaotic time. And how would I deal with the backlash from the murder of a matron, the symbol of feminine law and order in our land? Puabi was the third woman murdered by men in a short period of time, showing a dire pattern emerging that had been inconceivable two springs ago.

'If I may say, removing Semiramis from the council is not a wise decision,' Adam said as I paced around my chamber, the sun now nearing its late afternoon point. He had finished ranting his upset at the murder of Anba and was now thinking of how these events might affect the army. 'Without Semiramis, how can the district produce the weapons we need? She's run that district for 20 springs. Let Matron Shagshag be the example here, she is the wicked killer of Anba. Allow Semiramis to remain as councillor.'

I stopped to look out my door towards the river that sparkled in the distance. 'No, you may not say. I do not trust Semiramis. She is a liability to this city.'

Adam did not comment for some time.

'You cannot afford to get rid of Semiramis,' he said carefully. 'Things in the copper district will fall apart without her. Two of her three advisers are halfway up the Euphrates with the tin convoy. Who will drive the district?' His voice was controlled, but frustration pulsated from him.

'Sabium knows enough to keep things running at full capacity,' I said, turning back to face him. Sabium would no doubt try to use this unrest to propel himself into a position of greater power, but I had little choice. 'I have other concerns. I'm worried about the novices I sent to Ur. If I don't get news in the next few days, I will take the temple barge downriver to speak to High Priestess Daggartum myself. For all I know, Ur has been attacked by these heretic rebels.'

'Should you be travelling at this time?' Adam asked, alarmed. I wasn't sure whether I appreciated his concern for my safety or found it condescending. 'I don't think it's safe for you to risk going to Ur. And the safety of Uruk is surely our prime concern. If that journey is necessary, perhaps I could go for you?'

I snorted, not sure if my amusement was at the idea of sending a man to speak to a high priestess or his presumptuousness in advising me.

'Regardless of your opinion, it does seem best I stay in the city now to settle this issue with Anba and the missing men,' I said. 'If I've received no news by sunrise four days from now, I will go. You may accompany me. I would appreciate your company.'

He bristled. 'I have more to offer than my company.'

'Yes, but your company is...pleasing.' I sat beside him, tired of this argument.

'How will you manage the situation with the missing men?' he demanded. 'This situation will have the army speaking more of injustice. I've heard some men have been sympathising with the heretics' cause.'

'Then you must keep them in line, if you are fit for the leadership role I've given you. Anyway, it was just two men who were foolish enough to leave the greatest city in the world,' I said. 'Most men are happy to be part of our army. Did they not enjoy their first day of training, and meat with their lentils, and time away from their usual tasks?'

He shook his head. 'It is not enough. The men will be angered by the death of Anba and glad that matron was killed by men who then walked straight out of this city to join the rebellion. Those men carved a pathway others might follow.'

My chest thumped as I tried to downplay it. 'The so-called rebellion is just a mob of hairy shepherds and some bleating followers.'

'No, they are organised fighters who will kill for what they want, and now they're attracting Uruk's own men.'

While I gathered my thoughts, I stared at the fresco at the far end of my bedchamber depicting a deer in a garden. Adam was right. With the instability of the city, I needed to take immediate and radical action—

something to show I was breaking with tradition to honour men more. And a city-wide celebration was always the best way to win over the people and redirect their talk to something positive. Something like...a wedding.

'Maybe you're right, Adam,' I said slowly. 'We need to show the people of Uruk a new way of being.' I paused to inhale slowly before allowing my next words from my lips. 'Perhaps...I will marry you.'

'You would marry me for politics?' He looked away, hurt.

'Don't be hypocritical. You forget you suggested we marry for these reasons yourself.' I sighed, turning his chin so he would meet my eyes. 'We love one another, that's a given. Our marriage would mean much more than a shallow political arrangement. If I thwart the ancient tradition that says a high priestess must not marry, it would give the men hope. They will trust that I am creating a better future and it will soothe any heretical notions.'

'You want to use me to placate your men.' He sounded offended.

'No. My desire is born of love for you and to support the greater cause to bring fairness to men. Do you not wish to marry me?'

He sighed, looking at me a few moments as he decided his next step. He pulled me into his arms and kissed me, hard, the fire lighting easily in the familiar ferocity of our passion. The callous drowning of Anba and pain of Tiamat's loss drove me to love Adam from a new place, and I writhed with him so deeply I sought to taste his soul. My grief blended with aliveness, bringing tears that dripped down onto his face.

Later, the balmy air of early evening caressed our naked skin as we lay on my bed. I could feel he had something to say.

'What is it?' I murmured, touching his lips with my fingertips.

'I love you.'

I smiled and burrowed my face into his neck, inhaling his musky manliness. 'And I you.'

He propped himself up on one elbow and gazed down at me, kissing my forehead, my jawline, my lips.

'I do want to share my life with you as your husband. Together, we can ensure the ongoing primacy of Uruk and inspire the people with positive change.'

'Yes, we can.' My hands cupped his cheeks as I rolled on top of him.

CHAPTER 8

After darkness fell, I let myself into the antechamber of Menna's spacious apartments on the northern edge of the plaza. After stepping down as high priestess, she had moved into this complex so she could have Demsar live with her, refusing to live on the elitist western edge where the councillors would be her neighbours.

As I entered her front parlour, the sounds of lovemaking rang through the space, coming from Menna's bedchamber on the other side of the courtyard. I pushed apart filmy curtains and stepped outside to wait for her among the date palms and flowering plants, wrapping my shawl around my shoulders against the night air. The cries crescendoed and shortly after, their murmurs drifted to my ears. I smiled; still they acted like new lovers after so many springs together.

Demsar's fawn-grey cat, Star, greeted me with a long, warbling meow as she slunk over to rub against my ankles. I sat on a bench beside a mass of white moonflowers and welcomed her to my lap, dipping my forehead to receive her nudges. I sent Menna a message from my mind's eye, *Come outside.* Shortly after, she emerged into the courtyard from her bedchamber, one of her orange shawls flung around her small body, her hands flying up gracefully to form the downward pointing triangle over her heart in the Great Mother's salute.

'I need to talk to you,' I whispered after we embraced, aware I did not want Demsar to hear our discussion. I trusted him as I did Menna, but what I had to say was highly controversial. The tinkling water running through Menna's lotus ponds muffled our voices but still, I leaned close to briefly explain what had happened with Anba.

'I am considering radical action,' I said. 'I want to make Adam my husband to demonstrate I'm giving men more societal importance. Considering what's happened today with Puabi and Anba's deaths, and two of our men joining the heretics, it may be a prudent way to calm rising resentments.'

She raised her eyebrows. 'What do your instincts tell you?'

I was silent a few moments. 'I am torn. Perhaps my love for Adam and grief for Tiamat are influencing me to make decisions that could be disastrous.' I paused, feeling a small premonitory shiver. 'It could soothe an escalating situation. Or it could encourage men to pursue more power while women criticise me for facilitating it.' I looked at Menna, seeking guidance in her serene expression. 'I'm confused.'

She nodded slowly. 'Confusion doesn't mean you don't know what to do. It means you do, but don't want to see it.'

Her words sent a thrill of truth quivering down my spine.

'Yes, I do know,' I said quietly. 'I know the prophecy is activating, and I must take this action to moderate the situation as far as possible.'

She nodded. 'Then why are you hesitating to claim this path?'

I gathered the will to articulate my deepest fear, difficult to speak aloud even to Menna. 'What if I'm wrong? Marrying him could accelerate the prophecy unfolding at its worst.'

She tilted her head a little, staring at the orange glow of the brazier at one corner of the courtyard, almost burned out. Through the long silence that followed, I cupped Star's tapered muzzle to feel her warm breath on my palm. Menna turned to meet my gaze in the dim light, still waiting for me to explain myself further.

'And in the shorter term, I'm worried the city women will see me as weak and indulgent of men,' I continued in a rush of words. 'Without knowing about the prophecy, they won't understand what I'm trying to avoid. But I cannot reveal it without also fuelling the heretics.' A familiar feeling of helplessness tensed in my solar plexus.

'You could build on your reputation for being broadminded—everybody knows you took on the first male attendant and were behind Sabium becoming an adviser. The people of Uruk already know you as a progressive, and see this has benefited society.'

'Yes, I can promote how fulfilling it is to have a lover that is more of an equal as progressive and exciting, but it's flimsy. I doubt the populace will appreciate me flouting temple traditions. The city will want to know why I deem it my right to change the rules.'

'The people may be more ready to support you than you believe,' replied Menna. 'Many women have told me my marriage gave them hope for finding such romance themselves, and the men tell Demsar they are heartened he is so valued.'

'But you didn't break any rules. I fear I am arrogant to take such a decision.'

'Your motives are pure. As high priestess, you best serve Inanna not only through worship and ceremony, but also by being a great politician and following the truth of your heart, and you do this well. The city can accept new trends and will probably admire you for it. They need not realise the depth of the political situation you face with the heretics. And those reasons aside, aren't you in love with Adam?'

'I am.' A flush of love warmed my core as I thought of him. 'We argue, but it's refreshing to have a man I relate to as if my equal. And it's not only me that has felt equality. You and Demsar feel it, and Tiamat and Anba felt it too. It's rare, but appears to be increasing.'

'Poor Tiamat,' said Menna, shaking her head. 'I saw how she loved Anba.'

'Tiamat's grief makes me realise how I don't want to lose Adam, whether to a heretic's blade or because of arguments about injustice,' I admitted. 'It makes me think of my childhood promise to Sabium to make things fair, and...how I have failed.'

A long silence reigned before Menna spoke. 'There's something I never told you. I promised your mother I would wait until you were ready to understand.'

My mother? 'Go on.'

'When your mother birthed you and Sabium, she lost a lot of blood. I thought she died but she later told me she went to the Heavens for a brief moment and saw that you and Sabium shared a soul plan to push us all forward to a better era, one where someday, men and women will stand side by side in unity.'

My neck and shoulders rippled. 'What else did she say?'

Menna looked at me thoughtfully. 'She knew your destiny would see you torn apart, and the pain of that must run deep enough to drive you to make changes that impact far and wide. It pained her to be part of separating you.'

I stilled as I took this in. Star blinked up at me, reaching her paw to lightly tap my chest. My heart began to thump with revelation. 'I have always felt it so strongly, that Sabium is part of me, equal to me. It's the pain of losing him that has prepared me to make changes.'

'You have been primed to make our society fairer since you shared the womb with Sabium,' she said, grasping my hand in excitement.

Knowing filled me. 'Yes. But my first step must entail more than just marrying Adam.' I paused, a new idea emerging. 'I could change the marriage agreement to offer husbands equal lap rights. It's ideal as a beginning.' I rubbed the area between my eyebrows. 'I feel the foremothers frowning upon me though.'

'Pay the ancient dead no heed,' said Menna. 'We can't stop the tides turning towards a new era where men take a different role. We know it is weird, as did our foremothers. Anything you can do to make it a more harmonious transition is helpful. As for Adam being the one you take these steps with, I feel you belong together. But...I also feel such dread, without knowing why.'

The tremulous trill of a screech owl rang out through the courtyard, the sound chilling my blood. I spotted two glowing yellow eyes in a pomegranate tree, gripping Menna's hand as we waited for the trill to descend into silence. After a long moment, the owl emitted a soft, low hoot. I sighed heavily. 'I sense the owl says the situation is as we see it—both dangerous and necessary.'

Menna nodded, her gaze still on the owl.

'I will proceed,' I said. 'The wedding has to happen as fast as it can be organised. I need a big statement to deflect attention from the strife of today. Marrying the popular leader of our army under more equal terms will accomplish that.'

When I returned to the temple, the waxing moon was high in the sky and I told Tadez to have a novice light the braziers in the high temple. I went to

Tiamat's chamber where she lay limp on her pallet, worn out with grief, the other priestesses huddled around her. They made space for me to join them.

'We will all go to the high temple to sit in devotion,' I said, wiping Tiamat's face with a cloth moistened in lavender water. Not only would devotional practice help Tiamat feel better, the news I had to share with them all about the wedding would be better received when we were all more aligned with higher wisdom.

'Come, Tiamat,' I urged, my fingertip tracing the V-shape at the centre of her hairline lovingly as she remained motionless. 'We can pray for Anba and reflect on these calamities.'

We pulled Tiamat to her feet and escorted her upstairs to the high temple, where Anunit lit spikenard incense. We each took a devotional collar of rose and clear quartz to amplify our heart energy and a polished black obsidian egg, then gathered our skirts to sit on cushions around the altar. I held the egg to my mind's eye, asking it to reflect the wisdom of the Great Mother to me then, with two fingers, opened my gates and slipped it inside. The obsidian was cold, but not unpleasant against my inner flesh, quickly warming as I used the strength of my gateway to draw it deeper within. The egg throbbed its power, and I let it release the stress I carried in my shoulders and belly from the day's events. When I felt the bridge was made between my physical and energy bodies, I spoke an invocation and offered prayers for Tiamat and Anba.

We fell into silence, allowing the eggs to pulse life-force throughout our beings and stoke our girdles of fire. I soared into an expansive state of consciousness, and the two light serpents began writhing up my spine, seeking to unify at my crown. A strong sense of knowing lay just out of reach, as if a veil stood between me and the realisation...

As I pulsed in gentle waves of bliss, I felt peace in my decision to marry Adam. Although I recognised I did not yet see the entirety of the wider situation, I knew it was the right choice, one that opened a path of hope for balance, for the boded extremes of masculine domination to find a gentler path. Tears of gratitude moistened my eyes.

We emerged from our state of connection and grounded ourselves, most of us sharing radiant smiles as we removed the eggs.

'Priestesses,' I began, my voice soft in the peaceful atmosphere. 'We have all offered our prayers for the soul of Anba and to ease the suffering of our sister, Tiamat.'

The women murmured their agreement, Urnina reaching out to touch one of Tiamat's slumped shoulders.

'We are facing the greatest threat ever encountered by our temple, far worse than the era of shepherds' foolery,' I said. 'I have a strategy for distracting the city from today's shocking events, while also taking a longer-term approach to addressing the rising tide of men's dissatisfaction.' I paused, looking around at each woman briefly to prepare them for my next statement. 'I am marrying Adam at the next full moon.'

I felt the energy in the high temple drop as they took in what I'd said.

Urnina was the first to recover. 'Oh Lilith, how wonderful,' she said as she favoured me with her brilliant smile, her first thoughts of love, not politics. 'He is so special to you, I know.'

I smiled, grateful for her devotion to me and her unfailing positivity. Ku-Aya was the first to voice her displeasure, as I'd anticipated.

'I'm shocked beyond words,' she said harshly. Her beady eyes were sharp even after the bliss of our practice. 'With men getting cockier, why would you give them more positive attention right now?'

'This change is necessary to prevent the prophesied future being as extreme as we've seen in the Weird Sphere,' I said, confident my oracular powers were unquestionable. 'I feel that we can moderate that future if we take positive action now. And perhaps men are evolving out of their coarseness.'

'I don't think so!' Ku-Aya's chest swelled with ire. 'They're strutting around like feral ratters, full of their own importance. Councillor Dudu told me this morning some of her district's men were heard complaining about returning to the fields after one morning of army training. Even those refugee men you took in to do basic chores have been less than humble.'

Ignoring her, I continued. 'The wedding will be seven days from now, when we will be holding a city-wide celebration rather than our usual full moon ceremony. The marriage will not follow tradition, to demonstrate the temple's progressiveness to the people of Uruk.'

'What do you mean by progressiveness?' asked Gemekala, her chin lowered as she looked up at me apprehensively.

'Our wedding vows will be different. The marriage terms will not force him to serve only at my lap, allowing him the same rights as me. These terms will also be extended to all married couples,' I said, readying myself for their reactions. There was a subtle intake of breath around the circle.

'But Lilith!' cried Gemekala. 'Controlling men's sexuality is the crux of keeping them in their place!'

Ku-Aya held me in a piercing glare. 'Why would we encourage men in thinking their rutting should have free expression? There is no such thing as lap rights for men!' She pointed at me in a rage, her pointy breasts rising and falling quickly under her devotional collar. 'This the beginning of the end. You might as well hand over power to men now!'

'Sister, please,' said Urnina, brow furrowed in distress. 'We should not use such confrontational tones in the high temple.'

'Silence, Ku-Aya,' I said, my voice low but warbling with power.

There was a tense silence before Gemekala said, 'There must be another way you can create what is needed.'

'All of you, stop fussing like fretting ducks and listen carefully. I don't care if you believe me for I know it is so. I have answered your questions, now you must accept my wisdom.'

The women silenced, with no choice but to accept my command.

'Listen,' I said. 'Publicly, we will give little focus to the reasons Anba was purified. Instead, we must fuel outrage for the other two guardians as murdering betrayers of the Great Mother and our city. To minimise talk about Semiramis, we spread rumours she has been inept for some time.'

They all nodded, even Ku-Aya.

'And encourage plenty of sensational gossip about the passionate love between Adam and me. It will please the romantic streak in women and the proud new military vanities in the men.'

The women nodded again, and I allowed the space to settle. Tiamat lifted her pale face to fix her swollen eyes on me. She had been silent during the heated discussion, deep in her grief. My heart swelled in compassion for her loss, the love opening my willingness to see how frightened all the priestesses were. I softened my tone. 'Sisters, I hope you can come to see this marriage offers many benefits in service of our city and the future, and few drawbacks.'

Gemekala nodded, her steady black gaze communicating she chose to trust me. 'I respect you have reasons and knowing beyond what I can see. But it doesn't mean I like it.' She sighed, and her expression took on better humour. 'Hardly anyone wants a husband anyway. Giving equal lap rights in marriage will soothe the men with the idea we're treating them better while not meaning any real change.'

The alchemy of Gemekala's wit saw an improved energy settle in the high temple. It gave me hope the priestesses would come to support me, not only formally as they must, but also in sentiment.

Tadez did little to hide his displeasure when I told him of the marriage, but when I explained I was establishing equal lap rights in married couples as part of shaping a fairer future, he became more supportive. Despite his lingering misgivings, Tadez loved nothing more than creating an occasion, and he took to the task like an excitable peacock.

'Alert the gardeners,' he commanded the servants. 'I want a tower of purple irises and baskets of blue lotus blooms, a sea of jasmine. And armfuls of bird of paradise. Festoons of hyacinth. Boy, go to the shepherds and fishermen. Tell them we need a feast worthy of this occasion, no expense spared, as authorised by the High Priestess herself.'

I left him to his grand designs, confident all would be well.

'Mammi? I have something for you.' Aea stood shyly in the doorway of my sitting room where I studied my ephemeris, contemplating what the stars boded on the day of the wedding and into the coming months. I'd told her of the marriage as soon as the priestesses were informed, and she was happy. She adored Adam.

'Come in, my white bird.' I held out my arms and she raced into them, turning her face to receive my kisses. 'What do you have?' I rubbed her smooth back, bare above the white shawl temple daughters wore around their waists.

'Wait here,' she said, and darted out the door, reappearing moments later dragging a large sack.

'What's this?' I asked enthusiastically, getting to my feet.

'It's for your wedding day.' She looked up at me, swinging her little arms at her sides.

'Well, can I see?' I rubbed my hands together in glee, and she wrangled the sack closer.

My mouth dropped open when I saw a white feather protruding from the mouth of the sack. Since she'd taken her first steps, Aea had collected every white plume that fell onto our terrace, where doves came to peck at the crumbs we threw them in their esteemed status as one of the Great Mother's favoured birds. She also kept all the white feathers given to me as offerings, and still more when the cats caught a lax dove and left plumes in the wake of the scuffle.

My eyes filled with tenderness.

'Your beautiful dove feathers! You want me to have them?' My heart swooned at the sweetness of her gesture. She nodded proudly.

'Thank you.' My voice was husky as I welcomed her to my arms again, nuzzling her cheek as she lay her head on my shoulder. 'This is the most special gift anybody has ever given me.'

Her face lit with joy. 'You could make a cloak with feathers all over it to wear at the wedding,' she said.

'That is a glorious idea! There looks to be enough to put them on both sides.'

'Tadez can help, and Urnina too,' said Aea, beaming.

'Shall we call for them now?' An uprush of happiness inspired me to get started immediately. 'Let's talk about how this will be crafted and ready in time for the wedding. I will be the most spectacular woman who ever took a husband.'

The dawn air was cool in the high temple on my wedding day. I shut the double doors, pulling the bar across, and found my visioning diadem. When the dangling lapis lazuli touched the space between my brows, my mind's eye began to hum. Kneeling before the rose quartz altar, I felt for the groove in the carved base, pulling open a secret compartment to lay my hand on the Weird Sphere. I drew it out. The cool, smooth crystal was the size of a newborn's head and as clear as the space of nothingness. When visioning began in earnest, rainbows of colour emerged to shimmer into moving pictures. Or, the sphere could be held and its visions seen internally within a priestess' mind's eye. Each priestess saw only what the sphere chose to reveal, or perhaps what she was ready to see, but all of us had seen future scenarios where men tyrannised women in unfathomable ways.

The first time I'd used it had been shortly after I'd emerged from the sepulchre as an initiated priestess. At my next red moon, when a woman's veils between the realms are the thinnest, I visioned alone in the high temple for several days and nights, as tradition dictated. I'd been staggered when the sphere showed me the process of procreation. I saw tadpole-like creatures, which I intuitively knew lived in a man's shaft milk, with one pushing its way into a bubble held somewhere within the womb, causing a flash of light as they united. I'd seen it split into two, four, then eight parts and more, until the form of a baby started to emerge, always female. About half the babies would become male at a later stage of development.

Sitting cross-legged on the alabaster plinth, glowing white in the early light shining through the ceiling's star-shaped incision, I let the Weird Sphere radiate in my hands. Its light pulsed like a heartbeat throughout my being as I breathed into my lower belly and expanded my energy until I was no longer contained by the boundaries of my body. Silently, I asked for the message I'd felt called here to receive.

The purity of love I always felt in the Great Mother Inanna's presence intensified, and as my trance deepened, the sphere showed me two flames—one blue and one red—dancing together. I knew the blue flame was feminine, and was the larger and more active one. It wound around the red masculine flame, intertwining with it in endless movement. Then each flame began to untangle from the other, and the energy dropped. A fear rose within me. *What's this?* I called.

I watched as the masculine red flame grew bigger and took its turn intertwining with the blue flame. My vision expanded and the flames were at the centre of two larger red and blue flames. And these were within grander ones. On and on into eternity, flames danced and intertwined, in different ratios of each colour, becoming more unified and equal the more expanded my vision became. One day, I knew this balance would be experienced on Earth, and I realised my yearning for equal partnership was my knowing of this.

A different energy, with a whitish golden colour and feeling, swelled inside me. *Who are you?* I asked silently.

A soundless voice of purest love spoke to me. *We are one and the same.*

In direct knowing, I felt all was well with Adam and I, a dance of our wills afoot at the level of our human characters. But beyond, we were representations of the twin flames. We were helping to bring forth a new era in our world.

Afterwards, a sense of rightness remained deep inside me, but my mind was agitated. I couldn't shift my worries about the uncertainty of the future. Grand visions aside, how would this new era look?

On the afternoon of the wedding, Urnina soaked my hair in almond oil and rinsed it in rosemary water, leaving it more lustrous than ever. She coiled it around her fingers and forbade me from moving while it dried, then pinned it up in harmony with my wedding diadem, more extravagant than any ever created. Based on Urnina's design, Uruk's artisans had worked day and night to create the piece, consisting of three diadems, each smaller than the one below it, fastened to a wide gold band. The first diadem, which covered my forehead, was formed of large interlocking rings, while the second and third were made of hammered gold willow leaves. Above the diadems were three gold stars on stems, studded with lapis lazuli and red jasper. I wore a necklace with heavy rows of crystals— lapis lazuli, malachite, red jasper—centred on a pressed gold lotus held in a circle sitting above my heart. The freshly polished snake cuffs Urnina had given me at Akitu were on my upper arms, still my favourite pair.

Aea came to join Tadez and Urnina when it was time for me to don the white-winged mantle.

'Oh, Mammi,' Aea breathed, taking in the spectacle as I spread my arms and twirled to show how the feathers tiered on both sides of the floor-length mantle.

I enfolded her in my winged embrace and whispered in her ear 'Thank you, my precious white bird, for this wondrous gift.'

'Lilith.' Urnina's topaz eyes shimmered with tears when I turned to face her. She withdrew a perfume vial tucked in the waist of her skirt, her hands clasping mine as I took it. 'May this bring you as much joy as I felt in its creation. I hope it captures your truest essence as intended.'

My smile was wide as I pulled the stopper and inhaled, eyes closing as I felt my aura expand and tingle delightfully.

Urnina said it was called Lotus of Lilith, to represent my journey of spirituality, symbolised by the lotus growing through the dark waters to reach the light. Her description evoked the fineness of truth in my heart, but unease remained, and I suspected my initiation in the sepulchre was not all my soul asked of me to reach enlightenment.

I turned my focus back to enjoying the perfume. Notes of frankincense, sandalwood and blue lotus melded with other oils, so skilfully combined I could not determine them. It was rich yet light in its musky sweetness, and surely her finest scent creation. I thanked her and applied a dot of the perfume to the pulse points on my neck.

The priestesses wore diadems of blue lotus blooms with golden yellow centres, woven with froths of jasmine. Their long cloud-white skirts sat low on their hips, fastened with a gold-threaded knot above their pubic triangles that framed their bellies invitingly. Each wore newly commissioned necklaces, composed of rows of coloured gems, atop their breasts.

Through the week, they had mostly come to accept the wisdom in my decision to marry, and though we were all nervous about how the changes would unfold, we happily put our concerns aside to focus on the celebration and the sense of newness throbbing through the city. Even Ku-Aya made a show of swallowing her gripes as she came to kiss me, and I received her with grace.

From the vestibule, I peered at the sea of people waiting below, sensing the men and boys stood a little taller. The populace had taken well to news of the marriage—word on the streets was that my liberalism in changing tradition to wed Adam heralded an exciting new era.

Gemekala came to stand beside me, and I ran my hand lovingly down her waist length hair, shining blue-black beneath her floral diadem.

'Well, Lilu,' she said, her dark eyes glossed with light. 'You are leading this change in alignment with your truth. I am proud of you.'

She pressed something hard and cool into my hand. I gasped as I looked upon the small black obsidian arrowhead, an amulet I gave Gemekala when we were little girls mastering the art of archery.

'You blessed this to help me always find my target, and I have held it to my breast for courage and strength so often through the years,' she said in a voice wavering with emotion. 'Now it's time for you to take it back with the blessings amplified. Lilu, may you find your mark in creating a just society.'

I touched the shiny black sliver to my lips and closed my eyes, whispering thanks when I could find my voice. She pressed her lips to my cheek in a waft of her crisp juniper scent, then backed away.

A surge of joy rose in me and I kissed Yasmin's head, her serpentine body rolling around my shoulders. I was serving the Great Mother and Her cycles of change, and uniting my city against the heretic threat by allowing men a better place in life. And I was marrying the man I loved.

The crowd roared as I took my pose, holding my staff high in one hand and supporting Yasmin's head in the other. I stood proudly as the drums beat and Uruk stamped its feet in unison in the late afternoon sun. From across the plaza, the crowd opened and closed around Adam as he began his procession towards me. The cheering rose louder as he began to ascend the temple steps, lined with guardians resplendent in their military leatherware and red headcloths.

Sabium stood on the highest step, closest to me, looking out of place among the other men. Adam wanted Sabium to take this prime position because he was my brother and the acting head of the copper district, and I'd agreed. I sought my brother's eyes in hopes of sharing my joy with him, and as he met my gaze, a throb of bittersweet love burgeoned between us. I sensed he was almost proud of me, of the way I was taking action to improve fairness. Tears filled my eyes, but a moment later, I felt him snap the barrier between us back into place, and he turned away. I pushed him from my awareness to focus on Adam, the drums increasing their beat with his every approaching step as my heart thumped in synchronicity.

Passing my staff to Gemekala, I opened my arms to shoulder height to receive him, the mantle a pure white background for my naked and bejewelled body. The voluminous mantle was tethered at my wrists, giving me the feeling of being a winged goddess, heightened when Yasmin lifted her head high as if heralding the groom. Elation filled my body and soul.

When he reached me, the drums ceased and the city silenced. He was dazzling in a red leather kilt belted with a wide bronze girdle, which I heard he'd commissioned with the first meagre supplies of the metal obtained from travelling merchants. It had annoyed me he'd taken the rare bronze for such a vanity. Glowing cuffs circled his wrists, studded with red jasper, custom-made from gold I had released from the coffers as a wedding gift. On his feet were gilded sandals, laced up his calves and tied below the knee. His chest was sheened with cypress oil and his head and face expertly shaved, highlighting his unusual beauty and the endearing way his ears stuck out.

He knelt before me. 'I give myself to you in marriage under the blessing of the Great Mother Inanna,' he said, looking up at me. He stood and began his parade around me in three circles, with each pass our eyes smouldering.

On the final circle, he stopped in front of me, and when he took my hands, the life-force between us crackled as I stated, 'I receive you as my husband under the blessing of the Great Mother Inanna.'

'I pledge my love and body to you for so long as we are married,' he said, and I repeated the same. Adam held out his left hand, and I my right, and Urnina wrapped a length of reed around our wrists and tied the knot of Inanna. We turned to face the people and raised our joined hands to the roars of adulation. Adam turned to me with a smile, and as I returned it, he twisted his huge hand to completely enclose my own. I tried to pull my hand out, but it was held fast in his grip, on display to the people of Uruk. Across my mind's eye flashed a red flame, so large and bright it blinded me a moment, sending a jolt through my being.

As we left the terrace at the completion of the ceremony, I said quietly, 'Why did you grab my hand in that way?'

'When our hands were raised? My love, I was simply holding you in my embrace.' His eyebrows knitted, perplexed by my hostility. 'I'm sorry if you didn't like it.'

'I love the feeling of your embrace, but not when it seeks to dominate me.' Seeing his miffed expression, I let it go. 'Shall we?'

Since a high priestess had never before taken a husband, the ritual of our wedding day was mine to decide. I was drawn to use the high temple to offer our first married union to the Great Mother, in service of all. We ascended the steps and came to stand between the pink marble lionesses guarding the entrance, the space before us fragrant with blue lotus incense and glowing with a hundred candles that cast their light across the polished black floor. The noise of the city's continuing celebrations hummed softly in the background, faint from these lofty heights.

I led him to the plinth, covered in softened black cowhides and cushions, turning to lean against it as he stood before me. With his head shaved as was traditional for a groom, and his oil-glossed skin shining in the light, he was utterly beautiful—a male divinity, if such a thing were possible. He stared at me as his hands rested on either side of my diadem, lifting it from my head and placing it at the head of the plinth. He unclasped my dove feather mantle at the base of my throat and from each wrist, letting the tips of his fingers dance on my skin. The pull of attraction between us was immense, but I remained still as he slipped the mantle from my shoulders, the plumes brushing my nipples and causing a throb to rise from my core. He reached past me to lay it on top of the plinth, making a white-feathered altar for our union.

After removing my necklace, he delved his hands into my armpits and lifted me in one haul so I sat on the plinth, his eyes level with mine. One of his hands rested between my breasts atop my pulsing heart, and we kissed slowly as his other hand reached around to rest upon the base of my spine. I allowed my back to arch under his touch in the hopes he would intensify it. The energy was already tormenting me with the urgency that comes of an untempered sexual greed, and I breathed into my lower navel to store the power until its rightful release.

He pulled back from the kiss and looked at me, his eyes drugged with desire as he brought both hands to rest lightly over my breasts. A fierce heat emanated from my nipples as though piercing the centre of his palms, causing his eyes to widen. My head waved a little as he made a tiny circular movement over them, one by one. He paused, and did it simultaneously. I leaned back on my elbows, my breasts thrusting upwards, and he leaned over to kiss my heart, to lick it, and I watched as he moved to nibble at one nipple and then the other.

My surrender to pleasure was already becoming too great and I tipped my head back as he continued, relishing the feeling of opening my heart to him upon the altar of my Great Mother. In bliss, I gazed at the star-shaped incision in the temple's ceiling and out to the deep blue night sky.

In the fullness of time, I felt a delicate fingertip between my gates, erupting a low moan from my throat. As he pleasured me, I dropped back against the soft feathers and turned my head this way and that, nestling my cheeks against the soft perfumed mantle, writhing my arms and stroking the textured bed until I was ready for more. He leaned forward to put his mouth on mine and I felt the hotness of his shaft awaiting my invitation.

Sitting up, I kissed him eagerly, sucking on his mouth, sometimes breaking away to bury my face in his neck and bite and mash my mouth against it in mindless passion as he continued with his fingers inside me. I clasped at one of his hard buttocks, squeezing it viciously, as my other hand wrapped around his shaft and swirled up and down with vigour. In response, he twisted a hand in the loose hair at the base of my skull, using the grip to push my face further into our wild kiss...it was time.

I pulled back my mouth and we locked eyes.

The tip of his shaft immediately drew in towards my core, such was my openness to receive him, but I held him still to let the charge between us build. Timeless moments later, I nodded almost imperceptibly as I let the will of the Great Mother open the gateways, and in a smooth dive he entered me fully, eliciting a wild moan from my throat. I wrapped my thighs around his back, linking my ankles and pushing him into me, and together we found a slow rotation of our hips. His right hand spread broadly against my lower back, its energy fuelling my girdle of fire. It felt as if his shaft had become a wand of light, energetically piercing me up through my core to expand in my heart, as if an unstoppable channel of bliss had been opened.

Something different, hitherto unknown by me, was happening. My breasts were becoming alive as never before as I ground them into his chest, filled with love and life, opening up into the expanse where there was no boundary. The energy expanded more, reaching forward to penetrate him, seeking to pierce his heart. Confused but overcome by the unstoppable need to do so, I surrendered and let the light flood out of my bosom and into him, feeling the two of us as one being. He received it and circuited it back through his shaft and around to me again, the rays bursting up to our minds' eyes and crowns of light. It was as if the ritual of our marriage opened a new flow between us, allowing me to accept him more fully into my field than I had ever allowed a man before.

At that moment, as the gates of rebirth began their unstoppable opening, a massive energetic force rose from Adam that overwhelmed me, his power expanding and rising above me, moving beyond my crown and into the higher realms. It seemed he was trying to flip the poles of my very being, and I felt myself falling down, down, down, a terrible plummeting from a great height. In a gush of fear, I had no sense of where he or I began or ended, and all became red before my mind's eye. In alarm, I willed a wave of power to block this energy that felt as if it were inverting my very being. I pulled upon the strength from deep within my core and flung it outwards with all my force.

No!

Pushing his body away from me, I spluttered in shock. I was prepared to offer equality to him, not to let him rise above me. Must the redness engulf me?

'What happened?' I gasped.

'I felt only ecstasy.' He looked a little smug.

I stared at him, doubting his words. Surely he had felt the strange energy? 'Calm down, and ensure that does not arise again.'

Hesitating a few moments, I took a grounding breath before I felt ready to embrace him again. We made love once more, and as soon as I felt sure the swamping would not occur again, I allowed myself to surrender into bliss, my mind's eye blasting open with such light it was as if I stared at the sun.

'Are you alright?' he asked as we lay together on the plinth, but when I tried to open my eyes, I was dizzy and closed them quickly, focusing on breathing into my belly to still the imbalance.

'I sense the Great Mother reassuring me all is well, although I do not understand what happened between us,' I whispered.

He sat up, putting a hand on my chest as I lay there. 'Stay down for a while, my love.'

PART II

CHAPTER 9

I woke in his arms to the crackle of a campfire on the grotto beach and the smell of bread ready for our breakfast, another day of honeymoon bliss ahead. After the grandeur of the wedding and feasting, the eyes of the entire city constantly on us, it had been a relief to depart for the grotto.

From where my head rested on Adam's shoulder, I gazed beyond our open-sided tent to see a mighty ibex buck halfway up the near vertical grotto wall. The creature looked right at me, the base of each of his monumental curved horns nearly as thick as my thigh. He turned to ascend in a series of impossible leaps, then looked down at me once more from the top. His magnificence coursed through my blood, and I nuzzled Adam's neck in appreciation of his own masculine spirit.

Reaching down, I fondled his shaft, warm and soft in my palm for a few moments before I relished its swelling. Half awake, his lips brushed my cheek in their search for my mouth, and effortlessly we joined, our lovemaking like languorous swells in the sea, the surface glossy with light and the depths rolling endlessly.

After, ravenous, we wandered naked from our tangle of sheepskins and blankets, perfumed with our lovemaking and patchouli oil, to the grotto beach. We sat on the waiting cushions as Tadez served us steaming barley bread with honey and dates, and yoghurt courtesy of Lala and Dodo, the grotto's resident goats.

At the ground level camped 50 guardians, ready to ensure our safety in this new era of threat. I'd instructed them to stay well back from the cliff edges so we could enjoy our privacy, but I didn't mind Tadez and his beloved Udul-Kalama nearby. The grotto caretaker was as calm and soft-footed as his wolf, Teba.

With each couple so in love, the four of us carried the same sparkle of life-force and sensual celebration. Adam and I smiled when we heard the cries and moans of the two men coming from the cave in the cliffs surrounding our campsite where Udul-Kalama had made his home.

Adam and I had spent the previous day in an altered state of sensual pleasure, revelling in having nothing to do other than enjoy one another. We'd made love passionately before breakfast and refreshed our bodies in the cold grotto pool, swimming to the far side of the dome where the underground waterfall, framed by masses of maidenhair ferns, splattered from a rocky cleft. We'd let the water gush onto our heads, and when Adam felt my shivers, we had returned to the beach to lie in the sun.

When my cold-stiffened nipples had softened, Adam had begun to lick them, heeding my request to be careful as they were already so sensitised from our days of passion. So replete was I with our endless lovemaking, it was a joy to relax without fiery urgency. Gradually, the sun climbed higher in the sky and pleasantly burnished our skin, and Adam continued at my bosom, my head tipped back such that I put our temple cats, who excelled in sensual relaxation, to shame. In time, the sensations seeped into my heart, and out beyond my physical body, and my ecstatic trance grew deeper and wider, my explosion beginning with a slow rumble and rolling lazily out through my belly and heart into the sky and Earth.

After lunching on barbecued squab, one of the variety of birds the grotto attracted, we swam again then lazed in our tent, this time Adam's hands exploring my every part as we gazed into one another's eyes, or while our lips locked for long stretches, or my nose buried in the smokey richness of his underarms as if the perfume were the finest on all Inanna's Earth.

The only irritations in this paradise were when one of Adam's favoured guardians, Balih, came down the steep slope at some point each day to report on any signs of rebel threat and the army's status. Adam always took leave of me immediately to speak in hushed voices with Balih, and when he came back to me, the soft swell of love in his eyes had hardened a little. But he would not indulge my petulance, sweeping me in his arms to run into the cold waters and make me squeal with happy dread, or burying his face between my legs or at my breast to distract me with his skills, and I quickly forgave his transgressions.

Every morning and evening at milking time, Udul-Kalama called 'Lahlaah' and 'Dohdooh' in long melodic tones that echoed around the cliffs, and we enjoyed this simple rhythm to the day. On hearing the call, Adam and I paused to listen for the rustling of bushes and crackling of twigs as the goats pranced from their grazing spots to offer their milk, sweeter than any I'd tasted before. Once, we spied on Udul-Kalama teaching Tadez how to massage out the goats' milk, and we enjoyed their flirtatious hilarity when Udul-Kalama offered his shaft to Tadez to practice his milking skills. This was a side of Tadez I had never seen. With my heart kneaded wide open with love and the joy of life, I was touched by Tadez's happiness and struck by the realisation that men also shared in the aspect of the Great Mother that enjoyed bawdy humour. I decided to allow Tadez to spend more time at the grotto.

On our fourth night, Tadez served us a delicious meal of roasted mallard duck, brought down by Udul-Kalama that day with his slingshot. The flesh was rubbed with sumac and salt, served with lentils stewed with leeks and raisins. After dinner, Adam and I lounged by the fire and sipped blue lotus-infused wine, not strong enough to cause us to vision but enough to heighten our senses with euphoria and flourish our already insatiable desire for one another. The evening was tranquil, the moon nearly quarter-sized and the stars brilliant in the clear sky. Laying back together, I pointed out some constellations to him.

'Which constellation were you born under?' I asked, apologetic that I had never considered this.

'I don't know. Nobody remembers when a boy is born.'

My heart sank a little at this truth. A girl's birth astrology was studied to guide which of the 100 topics of the Mes she might focus on to best flourish her gifts and higher purpose, but a boy's fate was chosen based on what the city wanted from him. I took Adam's hand tenderly to acknowledge the unfairness and he squeezed my own to show he held no sulk.

'Look, there is my own birth constellation, Ophiuchus, the Sky Snake Goddess.' I gestured to a patch of sky, trying to point out the shape of a woman holding a long snake.

'Is that why you love Yasmin?' He chuckled.

'Yes, she is my own Sky Snake. She is powerful and beautiful, bringing the wisdom of the Heavens down to the Earth.' I trawled my fingertips across his chest.

'You describe yourself, Lotus of Lilith,' he murmured. His eyes were bright with a love that moved me so profoundly, I felt I must express it somehow. I offered him my truth, whispering, 'I will love this way only once, and you are the one.'

'I would go to the depths of the underworld and back to truly know your love,' he whispered, tears shining in his eyes. We held a long gaze filled with knowings that went far beyond my mind's comprehension, yet I understood them as surely as I did not. A fathomless sense of both heartache and love spun passionately, tenderly, through my being as my own eyes teared.

'Let me give you something,' I said huskily, sitting and repositioning myself on my belly, my face in front of his spread thighs. We priestesses joked about taking a man's shaft in one's mouth, putting cucumbers and carrots to use in our merriment, and we knew the men who lay with other men did this, but it was considered undesirable for an incarnation of Inanna—any woman but none more so than I—to practice. But I loved and desired Adam so utterly that my mouth filled with juice at the notion of knowing him this way, and I wanted to witness the ecstasy I would surely yield in him.

He gazed at me with wonder, and I kept his eyes as I kissed his figs and stroked his flanks, skilled in the art of building and holding sexual energy as I was, allowing him to experience how the wait made the prize all the sweeter. My delight increased as I watched his shaft shed a tear of anticipation, and the tip of my tongue dabbed it. I marvelled that the fluid tasted and felt as slippery as a woman's nectar. Instinctively, my right hand swept up his belly and I lay my palm over his heart as my mouth took in the hotness of his tip, and I felt his whole body levitate upwards, his head resting back in a gasp of sublime bliss.

Swooning with the urge to devour his shaft, I savoured the feel and taste of him, occasionally pulling my head away to rejoice in the spectacle of his body, to see his face with his mouth open in surrendered ecstasy, the still black void of the sky extending behind him and holding us in infinite peace. I could feel his figs rising and knew his explosion was imminent. I sat up and pushed my palms on his hips, crawling to slide over his thigh before positioning myself above him.

'Wait,' his voice was choked with desire. 'Lie beside me.'

We moved into position, and he slipped inside me, and so passionately did I wish him to penetrate my core, to be one with me, I allowed him to roll on top. He strained to hold back his release, but I wanted to offer myself entirely to him. I whispered in his ear, 'Beloved, give me your essence,' which sent him into a frenzy as his eyes entered me as deeply as his shaft. I felt again as if he wielded a wand of light that pierced my soul. My throat opened in a silken cry, joined by his own, and I felt my womb eagerly draw in his liquid.

'Why did you receive my milk?' he asked after we rested. 'Priestesses never allow a man to do so.'

'Because I love you so much I wanted to welcome your nourishment. I want to know and receive every part of you.'

'Do you think the Great Mother will soon bless you with a child?' he asked, his face glowing red in the firelight.

My heart shadowed. It pained me to lie to him again and again about the physical process of making a baby. I yearned to tell him the truth but the oaths of secrecy I'd taken ran deep in my bones. It saddened me I could never experience pure intimacy with him while lying, but I could not betray the secret that sought to protect my society from an unthinkable future.

'Perhaps.' It was all I could say, and I sought to distract him with my kisses.

I was woken by the sound of rocks tumbling down the cliff. Perhaps it was Lala and Dodo, but their sure-footedness was unlikely to cause such a scuffle. Sitting up, I peered out and saw something red move on the steepest part of the cliff, the fastest route down. I rolled my eyes. It was Balih, intruding as the sun was still rising to make some fuss to impress Adam, who remained asleep beside me.

When Balih saw me watching him as I lay with my arms behind my head, I sensed his dread at having to speak to me.

'High Priestess, please forgive my intrusion so early in the morning,' he fumbled as he stood by the edge of the tent, unsure of whether to look me in the eye or at his feet. His eyes darted between both options and I remained silent. Let him flounder.

'High Priestess, I am sorry but I must speak to Adam. There is alarming news about the heretics,' he said.

'You report to me, man. I am the ruler of this land and all decisions pertaining to it are mine.'

'I'm sorry, of course,' he said, his tone conciliatory.

Adam stirred beside me and sat up, tense. 'What is it, Balih?' he asked.

'A runner from Uruk informed us now. In the early hours, a travelling merchant reported the presence of a heretic camp north east of Uruk. He guesses there are two hundred men, accompanied by women and children, perhaps three hundred people altogether. The men were sparring and sharpening what looked like fighting weapons, possibly bronze. We think they're planning to attack Uruk.' Balih spilled all this out in a panic.

Adam was already on his feet, rummaging for his kilt, which he'd had no need of since we'd arrived.

'We must go back to Uruk immediately. How soon can you be ready?' Adam reached to help me stand.

My chest thumped with anxiety even as anger bulged in my throat at the way Adam presumed to tell me what to do, and that this damned situation ruined my honeymoon. I snapped at Balih, 'Get away from my tent, man.'

Both men went outside to talk on the beach.

'Tadez,' I called in irritation, beckoning him over from where he tended to the fire. 'A rebel attack on Uruk may be imminent. Go up the slope and fetch the other servants. I'm sorry, but you must bid Udul-Kalama farewell.'

Adam came back to tie on his walking sandals, brow furrowed in worry. 'I need to see that camp as soon as possible. We need details on how many men there are and what weapons they have.'

'I will send a runner ahead to organise a council meeting to decide our strategy,' I said.

'Can you ensure Sabium is there?' he said over his shoulder as he walked away towards Balih without giving me a chance to answer.

My core was quivering with an energy I didn't know or welcome. I calmed myself—*Only two hundred men, and our own army is one thousand strong.*

As I put on my sandals, Adam returned to stand before me. 'I need to move swiftly. I'm going ahead. You can follow with most of the guardians to ensure your safety.' He was distracted, his voice panting with aliveness. He kissed me but his lips were empty, and I pushed him away. How could he run so hot and cold with me, the notion of anything to do with the military immediately taking his priority?

'Go. I'll see you at the council meeting,' I said stiffly, his coldness infectious. 'Ensure you take time to visit the barber beforehand.' I looked pointedly at the stubble I had allowed him to accrue over our honeymoon, the dark patch strange in contrast to his shaved head, where regrowth had not yet become so visible.

I looked up as he ascended the slope, the sky in the distance filled with thick cloud. He turned to wave at me briefly before he disappeared.

CHAPTER 10

'What on Inanna's green Earth are they doing?' hissed Gemekala as I led the priestesses down the temple steps towards the green dome of the council chambers.

'News travels fast. They've heard about the heretic camp,' I muttered, keeping my expression serene and my lips barely moving, blocking the penetrating gazes of the men below me. The entire army shuffled in a sea of agitated movement on the plaza, wearing their protective leatherware and daggers at their hips.

Sweat ran down my back beneath my official blue mantle. I'd had time to bathe and prepare for council after the long walk back to the city early that morning, but still my body had not cooled.

The men fell back to open a pathway, stilling as we passed. Since the first day of training, they'd changed. They were more confident, at ease with their weapons and identity as an army. Without directly looking at them, I sensed their muscles were bigger. Their eyes burned into me with a different emanation to any I'd felt before. They were ready to fight for their city and temple, and so for me...so why did my skin crawl? I tried not to inhale the odour of their sweat, amplified by the humidity in the midday air, an effect of the grey clouds lingering on the horizon.

The council chamber was clanging with combative voices when Urnina swung open the double doors, the fraught atmosphere offering no reprieve from the plaza. It looked like every one of Uruk's matrons and guardians was there to view proceedings. I stood inside the main entrance and radiated my presence until they quieted, and they all stood to receive us.

The advisers and matrons filled the benches running the room's round perimeter, leaving no choice but for the guardians to sit on the floor. The men pulled in their brown hairy legs as the priestesses stepped past to reach their reserved area on the front bench.

It was a shock to see Sabium at the council table. He wore a copper collar studded with blue stones, sodalite I guessed, the kind of adornment a man simply did not wear, and I didn't know where he had sourced such a thing. Probably one of Semiramis' old pieces he'd found in what used to be her apartments. I'd given permission for him to move there until a new councillor of copper was appointed, and there was no appropriate contender. For now, Sabium was leading the district, and residing in some of the most privileged accommodations in Uruk.

My eyes turned to Adam. He had asked if temple resources could be used to dress him better once we were married, and I'd agreed, but still it was strange to see a man so well presented. He had groomed himself, his body lightly oiled, the gold wedding cuffs I'd given him on his wrists and wearing a smart leather kilt with a copper-studded belt. But his face still carried a shadow of stubble.

He was the only person in the room still standing, with no space for him at the council table. He looked pointedly at me—as my husband and military leader, he did not want to be put on the floor. I gestured at councillors Dudu and Benni to make a space for him, and they tucked their chins in at having a second man at the table. Adam frowned as he sat on the stool Tadez brought to him, obviously annoyed I hadn't invited him to sit by my side. His hostility disappointed me after the intimacy we'd shared on our honeymoon. Was it not enough he had a seat at the table?

'The stench in the plaza, and this room!' said Amarazen to Zamug, glaring at the guardians. The dome structure of the council chamber carried the councillor's words easily throughout the space, and I was sure she was deliberately making her displeasure generally known. 'Since these men have been fighting, they've become more malodourous than ever.'

'Yes, and eating meat every day is making them even more fetid,' replied Zamug.

'See they aren't clean-shaven? Apparently they don't have time to groom because of army training.'

'If you don't mind, councillors?' I said to them, my eyes cold but my voice deceptively calm. Zamug did not have her baby with her today and

I worried for his welfare. I would inquire into it later but for now, I took a fortifying breath and prepared myself for the meeting.

'Greetings, councillors,' I said, nodding to the group. 'The unusual circumstances we now face require us to have additional people at our table. We have my husband, Adam, joining us in his capacity as a leader of our army. And an infill to advise on the affairs of the copper district, Adviser Sabium.' Even among women, he was the shortest seated figure.

I looked around the table. 'A travelling merchant came to us this morning to report a sizeable heretic camp near Uruk, and it looks like there could be an attack planned on us sooner rather than later—' I began.

'Excuse me, High Priestess,' interrupted Sabium, raising a hand with his palm towards me, as if to block my words. My blood ran cold. He was bolder in his subversiveness than usual. 'If I may note, it was actually late last night the merchant knocked on my door...' He paused, ensuring we registered he had personally received the warning.

'Do not speak without permission, especially of petty details,' I snapped, weary of his attempts to undermine me. 'You are only here because Semiramis was dismissed for her incompetence. Show yourself worthy of your *temporary* place.'

He looked down, his jaw twitching in rage. 'I'm sorry, High Priestess.'

'With the urgent situation,' I continued, 'I have called this meeting to decide our strategy for protecting Uruk.'

Mutterings began and I raised my hand to command silence. 'Our options are to attack the camp with our fledgling army, or gather more information before we make any decisions. Does anyone wish to state their view?'

The table was silent. I waited, the tension growing as nobody dared to give an opinion.

'High Priestess, if I may?' said Adam eventually, standing, and when his eyes met mine, they were full of the one-pointedness he always had when talking of army plans. It felt like he didn't see me.

'Sit, then you may speak,' I said, my command causing his throat to bob with irritation. He took his seat.

'I wish to offer myself to spy on the camp to assess their numbers and weaponry, to help you decide our next move,' he said, his voice resonant with a sense of his growing authority. 'I can approach the camp before dawn to find out what I can then hide nearby to watch their daily activities.'

Olgana made a grunting sound from where she sat on the bench, her chin dimpling in distaste at a man proposing strategy. Adam ignored her and pressed on.

'Before this meeting, I met with the merchant who saw the camp, after I was pulled away from my honeymoon with the High Priestess...' He paused to affirm his esteemed status, although he did not look at me. '... and he told me there are rocky outcrops around the camp that offer a place to hide. It will be a matter of time before someone comes to void his bowel or such and I will take a prisoner to interrogate.'

'High Priestess, may I speak?' Olgana burst out. I looked at her with a frown and she took this as my consent, continuing. 'Those men could be planning to attack us tomorrow for all we know. I propose we gather the matrons, with support from the army, and make a surprise attack before dawn tomorrow.'

'Excuse me, Matron,' Sabium used courteous words but his eyes spoke his hatred of Olgana. 'Our army is barely trained, nor properly armed, and the same can be said of the matrons. We need more time or you send us to our slaughter.'

Olgana pulled her shoulders back in an effort to look more impressive, causing her bosom to lift higher. 'We must act now to kill those heretics in their beds!' she spat, eyes bulging with vitriol.

Exasperated, I glared from her to Sabium. This meeting would not be thrown around by the squabbles of these subordinates.

'Sabium and Olgana—and Adam,' I added, since he was also being lippy, and treating me with a frosty distance. 'You will all be silent unless asked for your opinions.' My right foot tapped three times as I anchored my stand on the matter. A few vindictive mutterings of support for my order sounded from around the table and benches.

Olgana looked at the floor and Sabium squinted repeatedly in frustration. Adam's face remained impassive, attempting to disassociate himself from the situation, but I knew he was angry that I'd put him in his place alongside them.

'Councillors, your opinions?' I asked, giving them barely a few moments to speak before I continued, ready to bring this meeting to my desired outcome. 'Very well, I will give you mine. Sending our ill-equipped army to fight an enemy we know little about is unwise. The estimate of two hundred men in this camp is only that, a guess by an uneducated man. I will question him further after this meeting but we can't expect much reliable intelligence. We need better information before making any decisions about going into battle, so I endorse the spying mission with the taking of a prisoner for interrogation.'

Adam's energy rose in glee as he registered my support for his preferred plan, but the room remained silent.

I continued. 'Adam and Balih can go late tonight and be back in a couple of days. Do we agree the plan?'

The councillors voiced their agreement, except Zamug and Amarazen, who looked unconvinced. Their bruised egos were not inconsequential factors and I preferred to have at least their token cooperation, but my decision was what mattered and under my pointed gaze, they nodded. They did not want to displease me and face the same fate as Semiramis.

Adam gave me a small smile for my support of his spying agenda. It left me cold.

I sat taller when I heard the thud of heavy sandals approaching. Adam—he had decreed on our honeymoon he would no longer use the servants' entrance now we were married. When he'd said it I'd smiled, malleable with love, but now it felt more like an encroachment.

'What do the stars tell you?' he asked when he found me in my garden. In front of me was a stone astrolabe disc inscribed with a map of the Heavens, with units of angle measures on the rim.

I sensed his prickling mood. It was understandable since he was heading out on a dangerous mission before this night was out. I was also worried, loathe to imagine he may be captured or even killed.

'Jupiter and Venus are in beneficial aspect to the moon, boding well for you tomorrow, thank the Great Mother,' I said, touching the smooth stone of the alabaster bench to invite him to sit, although I was annoyed with his behaviour in the council meeting and that he had come to me so late in the evening. 'But in the longer range, the stars show trouble. The planet of challenge and loss, Saturn, is not well placed, and the planet of fight and aggression, Mars, will soon conflict with it. We are in for a struggle over the next number of moons.'

I did not tell him Saturn was now returning to the same place it had held in the skies when Sabium and I were born. Known as one's Saturn return, it marked a difficult and long rite of passage into hard-earned wisdom. I suspected Adam was of a similar age so would also soon be subject to his Saturn return.

'Then I will make the most of the beneficial rays to find out more about our enemy and take a useful prisoner,' he said, sitting beside me.

I was silent. Until he explained why he was so late, I had no desire to speak with him further.

'I've been seeing to the final preparations for the mission and settling into my new apartments,' he said finally to explain his tardiness, as usual showing unusually good mind reading skill for a man. I had agreed on our honeymoon that Adam could take what used to be Matron Shagshag's apartments in the copper district as soon as we returned to Uruk. With Sabium living in what were previously Semiramis' apartments on the grand western edge of the plaza, it made sense to also let Adam also move to more sumptuous accommodations. It was fitting now he was the husband of the High Priestess.

He continued. 'Did you question the merchant about the heretic camp?'

'It was a waste of time,' I said, thinking of the bumbling man who stuttered in my presence and revealed nothing new. 'Are you ready to leave on your mission?

'I am. After I leave you tonight, Balih and I will walk out to arrive at the camp before first light.'

I waited, knowing he had something more to say.

'Why did you silence me at the council meeting like I'm just another of your inferiors?' he said, the muscles at the front of his neck twitching.

I rolled my eyes at his huffiness. 'I don't know what you're talking about. I agreed your plan could go ahead. You should be thanking me, not berating me.'

Expecting no answer, I reached over to stroke Yasmin's head, which peeked out prettily from the blue lotus pond, the blooms closed into buds for the night. She looked at me with eyes becoming an opaque blue, giving her enhanced sight to the otherworlds. This change occurred before she began her annual shedding of skin, after which she would be rebirthed with eyes blacker and deeper than ever before.

'Must the snake observe our conversation?' said Adam.

'Do not speak of her in that tone,' I said, keeping my head turned from him and continuing to pet Yasmin, though my belly sank deeper in disappointment at the distance between us. 'Would you like Tadez to bring you some washing water?' I found the scent of his stale sweat unattractive.

He took my shoulders and turned me to face him, the sudden move causing Yasmin to dip back into the watery depths, and kissed me aggressively, tongue probing my mouth.

Despite his blundering approach, my loins lit to receive him, but I couldn't allow it. His roughness wasn't born of passion—there was a disconcerting quality to it. I shoved him away.

'Perhaps I won't return alive from my mission, so best you lay with your husband now,' he said, pulling me closer again and crushing his mouth to mine. I allowed the kiss this time, afraid he may be right. I wanted to know his love, as sweet as it was on our honeymoon, here in this same place where we had first lain together. Had that really only been a couple of moon turns prior?

He pushed me back on the bench, unfastening his kilt and letting it drop to the ground, burying his sharp stubbly face into my neck in biting kisses. He gave me no time to catch up, groping at me like the crazed males who had to be banded for their munted approach to the sacred sexual arts.

'Slow down,' I said, pushing his shoulders back. 'What is this?'

'If I'm to be captured tomorrow risking my life for your city, tonight let me have you as I wish. I want to be on top.' He spoke gruffly, returning my push until I lay beneath him. He pushed his swollen shaft between my legs, opened by his knees. It had to be his nerves about the spying mission and the tension so palpable in the city making him act like this. I surrendered a little, letting my legs open, and he pushed into me quickly. As he began to pump on top of me, the feeling was one of invasion, and my girdle of fire shuddered in recoil.

'Off me now, man,' I snarled, shoving him back. 'How dare you touch me with such disrespect.' My eyes flared in outrage as a hollow sickness invaded my heart.

'Disrespect?' he panted. 'Your hypocrisy knows no bounds. The way you treated me at council!' He got to his knees, his shaft jutting in an aggressive point up his belly as I struggled to sit and adjust my shawls.

'I have given you the greatest esteem ever accorded to a man,' I snapped, his shaft wilting before my glare. 'I have broken with tradition on so many levels to treat you more like my equal, risking my reputation and the displeasure of my people, of the Great Mother herself!'

'Men are not only equal to women but in many ways, superior,' he spat. 'Women are fools when it comes to battle—look at the matrons—and war is the way of the future.'

I stood to face him, shock reeling through my heart. This, the same day we returned from our blissful honeymoon? Was the man I'd seen in that paradise his true nature, or was he this heartless aggressor, this...heretic?

I shook my head in disbelief. 'What is this, Adam? Why do you turn against me so suddenly?' I felt as if a rock had been hurled at my chest.

'Me turn against you? You have been against me right from the start, as you are against every man simply for being who he is. You women should drop to your knees to thank us for going to fight for you in your Great Mother's name while you sit around priding yourselves on your fertility.'

'You walk a dangerous line! You are jealous because you cannot create new life but you are proud of your ability to destroy it through fighting.'

He stepped closer to speak in my face. 'You say only women create new life and men have no use, but I don't believe you. I think men have a far greater role than you give us credit for.'

'You are speaking shepherds' foolery, and you know what comes of that.' My voice was a low growl and I injected it with threat, but the words felt empty.

'You cannot trick me. It is obvious men's milk creates babies, and Sabium agrees.'

A small sound rushed out of my mouth at the stab I felt in my heart. After I'd told Adam how profoundly Sabium hurt me, he had spoken against me with him. I allowed my anger to rise and swamp my hurt in its fire before I spat a reply. 'So you and Sabium conspire behind my back?'

'You can be outraged all you like, but Sabium is the only other man brave enough to raise this topic.' His voice was far too loud. 'Would you try to dictate whom I can and can't talk to now?'

'Sabium hates me! He seeks to turn you against me.' I was slipping in my control of this situation, as if there was an energy spiral of increasing sway pulling me down. In an effort to take back my power, with a blast of will I surged out the mesmerism as a cobra flares its hood.

'Answer me this,' he said, as unphased by my expanded energy field as Sabium always was. 'If men are unnecessary in creating a child, why do the women who do not lay with men so rarely birth babies?'

'The sacred love between two women will not be questioned by you! Such women generate enormous power to serve creation, on vaster scales than just creating a baby.' This was at least partly true.

'Lies! Why do priestesses almost never allow men to emit inside them, and only have one or two children each?'

'You know why. We have important work to do at the calling of the Great Mother, and She will not have us constantly with child or suckling a brood.'

'And what of Menna's three sons? They are replicas of Demsar. It is clear his milk has created them. Explain that.'

'Menna has willed her body to create them in his image, you fool. Everybody knows that.'

I held his stare but as he continued to search my eyes feverishly, I felt stripped of the ability to deceive him.

'The men of Sumer have long quaked in the face of the temple's tyranny, but I will not,' he said. 'I know the truth. It is felt in my core.' He held his arm out to show me the stippled flesh that made his hairs stand out. 'See, my skin crawls with it. Men's milk creates babies and women's bodies are tools that carry them.'

I gulped, struggling with the dryness of my mouth.

'Do you deny it?' he demanded.

My throat ached with the desire to speak truth. The lies were becoming more dangerous. He was taking the situation to the extreme in claiming men create children and women were merely the carriers. It would not do to swing from one extreme to another, each demeaning the sanctity of the other's purpose in creation. Surely men and women could honour one another's roles? Yet I could not discuss any of this with him.

'You are wrong, and you and Sabium wade in dangerous waters with your sacrilegious statements. If you incite these ideas among the men of

Uruk, you will have their deaths on your hands when the matrons put you all to the waters.'

He gave a spurt of bitter laughter. 'That's all over. You need men to protect you because this threat is growing faster and harder than any number of matrons can control.'

'You have crossed the line. Instead of thanking me for all I've done for you, you speak the unthinkable!' A sickening and foreign feeling gnawed in my gut.

He snorted angrily. 'Wish me well, for before sunrise, I risk my life to protect you and this city. Instead of your lies, I suggest you pay me the respect I deserve.'

A ragged gash opened deep in my heart as I listened to him leave, my throat thickening until I couldn't hold back my tears. The force of sorrow sucked the energy from me and I sank onto my bench, my shoulders crumpled. I had changed the traditions of the society I ruled to please him, accepted him completely into my being, and just the day before had trusted him with all I was. Was our love untrue?

In the far distance, somewhere far into the desert, I saw a flash of lightning, but no thunderous voice accompanied it.

CHAPTER 11

The aroma of the herb gardens wafted in the overcast morning heat as I spotted Gemekala. She stood stock-still, her braid reaching down her bare back, holding a tightly drawn bow aimed at a wild boar rooting in a row of plants. She'd mentioned she was waiting to take down this bold creature that had been tearing up the temple's herb beds, outsmarting the novices who'd tried to stop him.

Gemekala's powerful arm released the arrow and an instant later, the boar's thick grizzled shoulder was pierced, his squeal breaking the serenity. The arrow must have gone on to puncture his lung, as he stumbled only a short time before keeling over, screeching in pained outrage. She walked towards him briskly, drawing another arrow from the quiver at her hip and, at closer range, shot his heart to finish the struggle.

'He can't be blamed for scoffing your fine fennel, Gem,' I called weakly as I approached.

She turned to greet me with a grin. 'This rude boy has been scoffing more than my fennel—see what he's done to the lemon balm.' She pointed to one of the rows of medicinal herbs she managed meticulously. 'He'll be a tasty one, that's for certain.'

I gave a half-hearted laugh and she peered at my face, asking, 'Is everything well?'

'No, I fear it is not,' I said, my voice wavering.

Gemekala waved over two novices who had been watching at a safe distance then gestured for them to remove the boar's body. All novices spent time here on rotation to study herb cultivation under her exacting eye, and they moved swiftly to follow her order.

She took my arm and we walked between a row of calendula and thyme to move out of hearing range of the novices as they dragged the boar away. Gemekala waited for me to speak.

'Adam tried to push his way on top of me last night.'

Sucking in her breath, she stopped in her tracks. 'That is an unthinkable offence!' She shook her head in disbelief. 'He must be put to the viper pit. That man is lucky he's away from the city or I would throw him in right now.'

I swallowed to clear the thickness in my throat, but it barely budged, and my eyes filled.

'He was so cold, Gem. He confronted me about a man's role in creating babies, such that it would put the most outspoken shepherd to shame. He's suddenly turned on me, since the moment we ended our honeymoon. We seemed to be so in love...now I'm doubting our love is true.' My jaw quivered with emotion.

'Oh Lilu,' she muttered sympathetically. I knew she considered my doubts valid, and my spirits dropped even further.

'And yes, I know he should be executed. But even if I could bring myself to put him to the pit, he would put up a mighty fight, and I...I think his guardians might back him.' A tremor was beginning in my belly at what I may have unleashed.

'The matrons would prevail if that happened,' she said, but we looked at each other doubtfully. The matrons would not be able to stop so many men if they fought back. She lowered her voice. 'I can take care of him more discreetly. You know I have a nice patch of hemlock growing.'

She eyed me to gauge my response, and I felt my mouth gape at the ghastly idea. Hemlock was useful for lung and breathing problems, if used with precision, and only Gemekala was trusted to prescribe it safely. A touch too much was dangerous and a generous dose was deadly. She continued eagerly, 'We could trick him into taking some during the night, with none of his cronies around, and say he fell down the temple steps. We can do it the night he gets back.'

She was pacing along quickly in her angry excitement and I was forced to keep pace by our linked arms.

'I won't do that, not unless I have no choice,' I said. 'You forget—I love this man. And he is crucial to directing our army. Surely it's the stress making him act so badly, made worse with Sabium smearing me.' I desperately hoped I was right.

'He's rotten and I always knew it.' She was terse. 'We have to manage this before it gets more out of hand. You've given him too much leniency and he is taking advantage. Trying to force himself on the High Priestess!'

Her voice grew louder with every word. Our linked arms felt awkward, but we both hesitated to release the grip for fear of confirming the friction between us. Although we often debated with rigour, we had rarely in our entire lives ever raised our voices to each other.

'What can I do? I know it is disgraceful, but right now, we need him,' I said in anguish.

'Then if he doesn't show a drastic improvement soon, you must commit to strictly subduing him.'

I sighed, thinking a few moments. 'Very well. As soon as we defeat this camp, I will reconsider the situation. If Adam isn't showing himself to be a respectful husband, I will banish him from the city, and if he refuses...I will quietly get rid of him.' I shuddered as I spoke the words.

'Good. We can look for a woman who has what it takes to lead the army.'

I nodded. 'Yes, perhaps Matron Delondra, if Doshina would let us have her. She seems honest and strong.'

'A good idea. We certainly don't want Olgana at the helm. She has not the wit.'

'I will discuss it with Doshina, but I don't want any such changes until we have defeated that camp.'

'Is there not something more you can do this day?' Her voice was now thin with the anxiety that lay beneath her fury.

'Not much,' I said. 'Except cut the army's meat rations. Their emanations are more aggressive than I've ever felt in men, and the meat is making them more foul.'

Releasing my arm, Gemekala stopped by a bed of senna and bent to pinch off some dry yellow petals. She spoke with her face towards her pruning, forcing casualness into her tone. 'Lilu, is it true Adam moved into Matron Shagshag's apartments in the copper district last night? Right after you let Sabium move into Semiramis' apartments?'

'It's true.' My heart constricted again and I sighed heavily, cringing at my decision. 'Adam asked me on our honeymoon and I wanted to give him what he wanted. What was I thinking? And now I realise he and Sabium have been speaking of the shepherds' foolery...they're criticising me and the temple rule.'

A feeling I was unfamiliar with was thickening my gut, as if my body was recoiling to hide. Those two men were making a fool of me, taking the allowances I granted and turning against me. This was...*shame*. A blast of anger ran through me that they treated me this way.

'If you won't have them killed, at least put them back in the communal house under the eyes of the district matrons,' spat Gemekala in a rush of rage, slinging her thick braid over a shoulder so it hit her back with a thud.

I let her bluster, knowing I would not do such a thing to my brother and my husband. If I'd actioned my promise to Sabium to improve conditions in the district houses, it might have been an option, but with the heretic attack and the building of an army, my priorities had shifted.

'I dread to say it out loud, but...I suspect Adam shares the heretic's drive for rejecting our rule,' I said. 'It's as if he has no fear of repercussions, knowing I can't bring myself to punish him. He says he's going to defeat them, but I now fear he wants to dominate our city as much as they do. And the way he treated me last night...he tried to dominate me.'

Gemekala now fiddled pointlessly with the downy leaves of a sage plant, her silence telling me she agreed.

'I'm praying we will crush the heretics soon and the tension with Adam will dissipate,' I continued, hoping for her support, but I floundered as I said it. When it came to Adam, I didn't know if I was sensing true insight, or if I was deluded. My mind started swimming as I doubted myself, and I breathed into my lower belly to steady my thoughts. *Great Mother Inanna, give me clarity.*

Gemekala still did not speak.

'Am I naïve in thinking I could create a more harmonious future where men could stand beside us?' I asked. I heard the tremor of vulnerability in my voice and braced to hear her honest response.

She stood and brushed down her skirt, looking at me frankly. 'You have my support—forever. But those two men are getting the upper hand with you, and that means the army is too. You have the responsibility to manage this situation to protect the city and the temple. To protect *us*.' She breathed out with an angry gust. 'I know we're in times unlike any other and that may call for some change, but an equal footing with men is not possible. You have gone too far in giving Adam so many privileges.'

My throat dried as my eyes filled with wetness. 'I fear I have let things move too quickly. I felt so strongly this was right.'

'Men aren't equal!' she said, impassioned. 'If left uncontrolled, their aggressive natures will soon arise. We need to be tougher, not give them more rights.'

I felt my energy drop lower. This time, it was because I was betraying myself and what I had experienced as truth in my visions in the high temple. I pulled on my strength to trust my knowings, although nobody else did.

'I told you, I have seen it in my visioning and I stand by that,' I said firmly. 'The dance of the red and blue flames and the deeper meaning of the masculine and feminine together. I *know* they are equals. It may be hard to see but that's because we haven't given men a chance to show their greatness.'

'The feminine sits at the Heavens and men are from and of the Earth,' replied Gemekala. 'How can they be our equals?'

'Men could be just as impressive as women. Like an apple and an orange are equal, but different.' I was short with her, unwilling to be challenged further.

'I cannot agree.'

We kept walking in silence along the herb beds, and gradually I sensed her soften in compassion for me and the difficult choices I faced. She met my eyes with wry humour, and I knew her peace offering was coming. 'An orange is superior to an apple. It is more fragrant, sweeter, intricate, stronger. As is a woman.'

I snorted, but let her take my arm again, relieved to have her by my side, even if we disagreed. I could always trust her, but she could not share my truth. There was no point brooding any further on this issue. I must make societal changes slowly and carefully to allow women time to adjust to such radical ideas.

A small movement caught my eye among the reeds between the gardens and the river, and I spotted a hare edging towards a leafy row of the sacred green guide plant.

'Give me that,' I said under my breath, reaching for Gemekala's bow, and we shared a mirthless grin, pleased to reminisce on hunting together in our youth. 'It's roast boar and hare for lunch.'

The cedar grove was cool, its minty aroma soothing the back of my throat as I pressed my cheek to one of the trees. Aea dashed past my field of vision, Humusi following moments later, each holding a bow and fumbling to nock an arrow as they shouted about imaginary prey.

'Be careful, girls!' Gemekala and I called in unison, and we chuckled. The day after our tense exchange at the herb gardens, it was a relief to have restored our bond.

All our lives, we'd loved visiting the temple's cedar groves on Uruk's southern outskirts, the air filled with a mysterious vibrancy and the ground carpeted in flowers. In this place, my mind's eye naturally opened, showing me the dazzling array of life all around in the trees, flowers, soil, the sense of water coursing beneath the ground, and the little creatures of light sparking to and fro like lightning. It took my mind off Adam and his spying mission. He and Balih had been gone two nights and should return today, if things had gone well.

For now, we were choosing trees for building scaffolding at the mines, as I had promised Sabium. We'd already directed the felling of several trees a few days prior, hauled out to the mines. Now we searched for the final trees that felt right for the role.

Keeping my cheek against the cedar and inhaling the sweet woody perfume, I placed my palms on her trunk and closed my eyes. Life-force pulsated through my being. The hectic thoughts and worries swirling in my mind and churning through my solar plexus were replaced with a sense of calm.

'Aea,' I called, waving her over. 'Come and feel this tree. She's a good one to practice your connection.' Aea bounded over, dropping her bow and quiver to the ground to stand beside me in a shaft of sunlight bursting through the canopy. 'Remember, use your mind's eye and heart to connect with the tree's spirit. Once you feel the connection, ask her if she is willing to give herself.'

Aea put her grubby hands on the trunk beside my own and we closed our eyes and breathed into our hearts, then down into our lower bellies. When I felt the full flow of the tree's spirit run through me, I asked, *Are you willing to give yourself for scaffolding to protect the boys?* I was flooded with the tree's response, one of pure love in her agreement to serve in this way. As I communed with the tree, the sense of the mine boys throbbed as a heaviness in my heart. I felt as if Aea was one and the same as every boy who crawled around in those holes to meet my city's voracious needs for new copper jewellery and art, and now, weaponry to kill men who refused to be subdued any longer. Culpability flooded me and I allowed the full experience of it to wrench at my soul. I felt the tree's essence unite with my anguish and transform it into compassion, bringing tears of gratitude to my eyes.

'Mammi,' whispered Aea, and I opened one eye to see her face glowing with light, eyes tightly shut in concentration. 'This tree is so kind. She says we should take her to help the boys and it won't hurt her when she's cut.' She paused. 'But do we have to chop her up?'

'My darling Aea, death is not separate from life, remember. This is in many of the Mes teachings,' I murmured tenderly. 'It's when we look at death with a small perspective that it seems so final. This tree gives of herself knowing her spirit will continue in different forms, her wisdom eternally growing. What's important is we don't take her life carelessly and that we nurture new life.'

Aea began to cry and flung her arms around the trunk. I allowed myself to join her, grieving for the tree, for Adam, for Sabium, the mine boys, and the conflict between men and women that caused all this suffering. When we calmed, I called to Gemekala and Humusi, who had communed with a tree at the other side of the grove. 'Over here. This is our third tree.'

Only the drowsy hum of insects sounded as the four of us held hands around the chosen tree, closing our eyes and sending gratitude into the living being. Long moments later, musical birdsong rang out joyously through the grove as if to complete our ceremony and we met one another's gazes with peaceful smiles. On a whim born of my appreciation, I held my hair up and stooped, asking Aea to unclasp my necklace with its green malachite gems.

'Give this to the tree as our offering to her and the grove,' I said, lifting her high so she could reach a branch and hang the necklace there. I heard her murmur to the tree as if it was her best friend, and she kissed the bark.

With some regret, I turned towards the councillor of building, Amarazen, where she waited at the outskirts of the grove, six of her men ready with stone axes. As I approached, I pointed out the three trees we'd selected, telling her to have the men bury the necklace beside the last tree's stump after they felled her. I kept my back to the group of guardians hovering behind us, charged by Adam with bolstering my security while he was on his spying mission. They annoyed me, posturing with their weapons as if they were my saviours. Olgana and her matron cohort stood a good distance from the men, eyeing them with palpable disdain.

A familiar voice yelled my name and I looked around to see Urnina trotting through the trees, her halo of sandy hair more expansive than ever in the humidity. She called excitedly, 'Adam and Balih are approaching the city, and they have a prisoner with them. Come quickly!'

My heart leapt and I turned back to the imposing woman beside me.

'Councillor Amarezen,' I said urgently. 'Ensure two of your best construction advisers go to the mines on the next transport mission, as well as your woodworkers. They are to stay there until the scaffolding is complete.'

'Yes, High Priestess. The convoy leaves in a few days.'

I nodded and turned to Gemekala and Urnina and the two girls. 'Let's go.'

The violent thumping of the stone axes rang through me painfully as we hastened back to the city.

After sending Aea and Humusi back to the temple, we strode briskly through the plaza towards Olgana's chamber, where I expected Adam and the prisoner would be waiting.

'We needn't have hurried,' said Gemekala, nodding towards the other side of the plaza. I squinted, miffed to see Adam and Balih approaching with a child between them. The child barely reached the top of their shoulders, slowing their progress, and my chest fluttered in irritation.

As they grew closer, I saw it was a young woman wearing a knee-length tunic that covered her bosom, making it hard to distinguish her as an adult. It was not a garment a sophisticated Uruk woman would wear—the Great Mother would be insulted by hiding the female form in such dowdy attire. As I stared at her, my skin prickled and a flash of energy jolted through me. There was a powerful recognition rushing through my blood.

Who is she?

My chin lifted as they approached, each group of three facing the other without words. Adam beheld me coolly and waited for me to initiate a greeting.

'You are safe, Adam, thank the Great Mother. How did you fare?' My words were appropriate to speak to my husband on his return from a dangerous mission, but were stilted to my ears.

'My wife and High Priestess,' he said formally. 'It was a success. I have a better idea of their numbers and laid eyes on the weapons they have. I was not able to take a man, but this woman is from the camp and knows their ways, and she speaks our tongue.' He looked at her with a strange familiarity. 'We can extract all the information we need from her without difficulty. She's already told me she's one of a hundred or so women who live with this group of heretics.' Perhaps he was cool with me because we were in front of the prisoner? But I feared he was still angry about our argument several nights ago.

'Look at me, woman,' I said, bringing my gaze upon her. 'Tell me your name and where you're from.'

She lifted her head a little, showing eyes of an indeterminate pale colour and a docile face, comely in an unremarkable way. Her hair was the colour of light honey, neatly arranged despite the long walk through the desert. Had she taken time to groom herself despite the stress of being a prisoner?

'I am Eve, from the north.' Her words were a little stilted.

'Do you subscribe to the view touted by your tribe that the Great Mother is not the true ruler?' I asked her.

She looked up at Adam, unsure. 'I do not know,' she said eventually. The woman was clearly stupid, without her own opinion. I supposed she was terrified, but still, surely she could speak to another woman with more confidence than this?

'She seems to have little to say,' I said, glancing at Urnina, rolling my eyes a little. 'Adam, bring her inside. Balih, you are dismissed for today.'

The priestesses and I led Adam and Eve into the chamber, where Olgana and several other matrons waited. Their mouths dropped open when they saw the small woman.

'High Priestess, where is the prisoner?' said Olgana, scowling darkly as she looked from Adam to Eve. 'Has this man failed in his mission?'

'This is the best prisoner Adam could get,' I said. My mouth dried as, from the corner of my eye, I saw the rodding bed was prepared, the bright blue rods set out beside it.

Adam left Eve's side to stand in front of the table, blocking her view.

I frowned at him. 'Adam, why do you hide the rods from the prisoner?'

Eve kept her head down as he answered. 'I told her if she cooperated, we would treat her well.'

'She has not yet cooperated.' I turned to her. 'Eve, you must confirm whether or not you subscribe to the ideas the heretics hold,' I said, becoming more agitated by the decision I had to make—could I order the rodding of a woman? 'You must agree or disagree.'

Surely she couldn't agree? Yet how had those heretics come to rise unless the women they lived with were weak and stupid, allowing such despicable behaviour among their menfolk?

'I know what I've been told—that the true divine creator is male,' said Eve.

I snorted. Her stupidity knew no bounds. Olgana leered hatefully at her and picked up rod number one, letting her fingers caress it. For someone under threat of being rodded, Eve did not seem particularly frightened. Did she not realise the purpose of the rods? Her lack of fear confirmed she was simple, or at best naïve, and my jaw clamped together in resolution. I could not inflict such treatment on a woman, especially a childlike one.

'What can you tell us about the men you live with? Do they share their plans with you?' I asked, hoping she would reveal useful information without me having to change my mind about the rods.

'They do not share their plans with me, but I lay in the bed of one of the leading men so I hear what they say,' she said.

'Raise your eyes, Eve. Why do you downcast yourself so? Are you happy to let that man pleasure your lap?' I was perplexed.

She looked up at me through her eyelashes. 'I must do my duty in allowing the man at my lap.'

My mouth twisted in contempt. 'You have a lot to learn, and can be grateful you have come to Uruk. Now, tell me what these fiends are planning?' I probed her with my mind's eye, finding her energy soft and pliant. What a strange and irritating creature.

'They will attack this city on the next full moon. They will target your great tree where they know the priestesses—that is you?—will be celebrating the full moon. They will kill the strong women who look after you.' She looked at Olgana and the other matrons.

A buzzing in my head started, so loud it was hard to think straight.

'How many men are in the camp?' I asked.

'We have two hundred men who fight,' she said, and I turned to share a quick glance of relief with the priestesses standing behind me. They looked as baffled as I about this bizarre woman.

Eve continued. 'But our leader says there are two thousand more coming from the north for the attack, due to meet over the hills past this city just before the full moon.'

My breath stopped and an awful stillness came over the room. The greatest number our own army could reach, based on our population, was two thousand, but we'd so far only started training one thousand men. We had less than one month. My knees felt like buckling, but I kept a composed demeanour as I pulled Adam aside.

'Surely she lies about the heretics numbering two thousand? She appears guileless, but she may be a skilled manipulator,' I whispered in his ear, then stood back to address him with more volume. 'Find Eve a suitable room where she will be comfortable, and tonight you will brief me fully on your mission.'

I turned to Olgana, her tongue tip sliding back and forth across her top lip. 'The rods are not needed. Assign a matron to guard Eve in her room and report to me if you have any concerns—any whatsoever.'

Adam touched Eve's arm, as thin and insubstantial as a reed, to guide her to a chair. 'Come, Eve, rest a moment. Your legs are tired after the long journey.'

My neck bristled.

The dark clouds that had hung in the distance since the honeymoon created a rich orange sunset. I beheld the dramatic vista as I sat on my terrace bench, yet again waiting for Adam. The spectre of war was becoming more real before me, and with the number of heretics Eve had reported, we could be at real risk of defeat. It was unthinkable.

When I heard Adam arrive, my jaw tightened as my heart ached. I could already sense his emanations towards me were cold.

'Greetings,' he said as he strode over to stand before my lotus pond. He did not open his arms to me and I did not go to him. I did not feel he would necessarily receive me if I offered my embrace. His face showed the dark shadow of stubble, longer than I'd ever seen it.

'Why do you come before me unshaven and unglossed?' I asked coolly.

'I have more important things to do than make my face smooth.'

I decided to ignore his disobedience of shaving protocols for now. 'Well, tell me, why did escorting Eve to a room take all afternoon?'

'She told me more about the heretics' weapons and the way they train for battle. I've learned something more of their strategies, and heard about their leader, a charismatic man who leads with clarity.'

'Who is this leader, where is he from?'

'His background is unknown by Eve, but she said he is handsome.'

I snorted. 'And that such men do not bring pleasure to her lap. So where is she now? Is she locked up?'

'Sabium and I agreed to house her in his old room in the copper district.' He looked at me blankly.

My heart dropped further in what I supposed was jealousy. Adam fraternising with Sabium was hard enough, but now they were joining forces to accommodate this woman with such personable hospitality?

'What happened to your plan of taking a prisoner?' I demanded. 'Instead, we have a new Uruk citizen, one you've settled comfortably adjacent to your own new apartments. What an *intimate* arrangement.' I ached behind my frosty glare.

'She is not a prisoner, but willingly stays with us, so I have relieved the matron charged with watching her,' he said with surly confidence. 'We've rescued her from the heretics and she's helping us all she can.'

'That is not your decision to make,' I said sternly. 'Perhaps she lies.' Noticing how his shoulders sloped differently, fraught with strain, I rose to place my hand on his arm. 'Adam, I don't want to argue. Let us embrace.' I opened my arms to him and he looked at me appraisingly.

'Not now. Since you doubt me and the information I bring you from Eve, in service to you, I do not feel so inclined.'

'You seem so taken by a boneless piece of fluff!' I snapped, stung by his rejection. 'So easily you believe her because she obeys you, answering your questions. Perhaps she's manipulating you.'

'I don't think she lies, but she does value what I have to say. It's little wonder I enjoy talking to her without the incessant challenges you throw before me, questioning my every move.'

I turned away, hiding the angry wetness in my eyes. *At any time, husband, feel free to embrace me.*

'Listen to me,' he said. 'If Uruk is to survive, you need to respect my decisions and recommendations when it comes to the army. Why did you cut the men's meat rations? If they risk their lives fighting to protect your city, at least give them the food they need to be strong.'

He had redirected the conversation to banal details about the army, ignoring my insecurity about Eve. Even as my heart ached at his neglect, I knew I mustn't show more vulnerability, instead readying my voice to calmly address his statement, 'The men are still getting more meat than they used to. Right now, our food supplies are good, but the spring rains have not come. We can't assume food will be bountiful this year.'

'This is exactly the kind of treatment that makes men rebel! We need good food as much as women.'

'Women are the creators of new life and bleed as part of that,' I shot back. 'We require meat, but there is no real need in men.'

He scoffed. 'There is real need now your life depends upon us. And another issue you need to address—we need more men for the army. You should allow more refugees into Uruk. Instead of working our own men at twice the rate, I want five hundred more refugees. What use is there in taking in all those refugee women if we are attacked by swarms of heretics? If you don't take those men in, they are likely to join the rebellion—'

'Silence! How dare you tell me what to do!' I spun around to blaze my eyes at him.

He drew a breath to calm himself, and the next time he spoke his tone was mollifying. 'Lilith, please, let me help you defeat this threat. You said yourself a new era is here.'

He reached out to hold my arm, a conciliatory gesture that made me pause. The path before me was tempting—if I pacified him, he would be loving with me once more and the city would be better protected. But it would also mean the erosion of my power. Every concession I made to him, he tried to claw more. It was a pattern that had played out since the day we met, where he'd give me his love while I supported him and turn it off as fast if I displeased him. He was manipulating me.

'My love, come to my arms,' he said, reaching to embrace me.

I shook off his touch, glaring. 'Get off me. Why would I want you after you brought me no pleasure last time?' My voice cracked in hurt and anger.

He exhaled sharply. 'Now my wife refuses me at her lap? It's a good thing you stooped to give me lap rights in marriage so I may be satisfied elsewhere.' My mind's eye flashed a vision of Eve, though why he would desire that meek woman I did not know. She could never meet him at the gates of Heaven.

'If there's any woman who wants the bleakness I found between your thighs last time, she's welcome to it,' I said.

We glared at each other.

'I'm sorry,' he said finally. 'I'm driven to speak out of turn. This stress is making me tense.' His gaze lifted to meet mine but I sensed something disingenuous. It felt as though the walls of a trap were closing around me. I needed time to think.

I nodded—it was best I kept him on side. Removing him from power would likely cause the guardians and the army they led to become mutinous, and then how would our city fare under attack? Or worse, would my own men join the rebellion? I swallowed my pride. The safety of Uruk had to take priority over my power struggles with Adam. For now.

'Leave me alone now,' I said quietly.

As he stomped away, I stared at the darkening horizon with fierce focus to hold my sobs until I was alone.

CHAPTER 12

'I'm sorry, High Priestess, could you repeat that please?' asked one of the novices, several others nodding in support of the request. None of us were concentrating—in 21 days the full moon would rise and the heretics were supposedly due to attack.

Preparing the army was turning Uruk upside down. Even with the two hundred refugees I'd taken on to help with daily chores, our labour resources were stretched to the limit with the sudden doubling of our army. Some women had resorted to picking figs and cutting lettuces for themselves.

The army was the priority, but to encourage temple life to go on as usual, I'd gathered the novices on this sultry morning to continue Mes lessons on their terrace.

'I will show you again,' I said to the novice, recognising her as one of the women I'd lain with on the full moon night I'd first met Adam. I knelt and held her ankles to display the technique used to draw a type of fever out of the body, applied in combination with the incantation I recited.

In touching her skin, memories of that night filled my mind. Meeting Adam had been a turning point in my life. A strange sensation washed over me and I looked up to see he now stood at the vestibule. My heart panged at the sight of him, handsome and distant, and I yearned in anguish to unite with him. Knowing it was futile, I turned back to my novices. It was only when the lesson was complete that I called him over by raising my eyebrows, slightly surprised he had waited so long.

I had not seen him for several days, not since our argument on my garden terrace, sensing it best to avoid him until the full moon came and went in the prayer we would prevail against the heretics. If things did not improve between us, he would have to go, as I'd discussed with Gemekala. I hoped there was no need for such action, but I was growing less optimistic. I would no longer be manipulated. Heaviness and a sense of despair clawed at me and I gathered myself to stay focused on what must be done in the best interests of the city.

The novices watched as we greeted one another reservedly, and I led him behind a thick bank of bird of paradise flowers to talk in more privacy. It was still too quiet, the flow in the nearby pond a trickle now the men were too busy with the army to fill the reservoir that fed our temple waterways.

'Where have you been the last few days?' I asked quietly.

'Busy with the army, of course.'

'What have you been doing?'

'A great deal, since we are doubling our fledgling army in such a short time.'

'I've been visiting the relevant districts to oversee army preparations too, but I've not once seen you,' I said, suspecting he was also avoiding me. I heard from Lahamu, who had gone to the leatherworks district to visit her son, that she'd seen Adam and Eve discussing the design of protective garments. Apparently Eve was explaining what she knew of the rebels' kit, and Adam had immediately instructed enhancements to Uruk's own designs based on the advice.

He shrugged, refusing to respond.

'Why do you come to me now?' I asked.

'I want our army to practice a full-scale battle at the new moon, and I seek your permission,' he announced, no hint of request in his tone.

With two thousand heretics due to attack us, I didn't have the luxury of calling him up on his tetchy attitude. We held each other's gaze for a long moment, the silence broken by the fluttering of two white doves landing beside us on the mud brick floor.

'What would that involve?' I said.

'While you and all the city women take your red moon retreat, my guardians and I will run an extensive training exercise. We will take the army, all two thousand men, to the north of Uruk and split them into two groups. They can storm one another where we believe the heretics will approach. Practicing in the dark of the new moon will help them fight better when the moon is full.'

Rehearsing violence on Uruk's doorstep was a shocking concept, but there was no denying we were preparing for war. 'I see. And who will do the essential works in Uruk?'

'Perhaps the city women can fetch their own water and do a few chores.'

'The women will be bleeding! We must ensure there are enough men here to attend them.'

'Very well, they can keep their key servants to bring them honey cakes and beer.' He maintained a blank expression but I recognised his scorn.

'And what of the safety of the women in the city? And we priestesses, who hold our red moon retreat at Huluppu?'

'You shouldn't have to make any changes to your new moon rituals. I will double the scouts from now and through the new moon to check for any suspicious activity within range of Uruk. For your added security, all the matrons should camp around Huluppu.'

I was silent.

'Well? Do I have your permission?' he asked. 'This could make all the difference when our army engages in real battle.'

I still hoped he would step towards me and seek reconnection, but he did not. I held his gaze, probing him to understand more of what he felt. I detected nothing.

'Very well.'

Under cover of night, I approached the entry to the copper district. My chest thumped with fear at what I would find when I arrived at Eve's room. I had already decided—if Adam lay in her bed, or I found her in his apartments, I would enact the plan to be rid of him. I would find a way to manage the army without his leadership. Yes, I had given him lap rights, but never imagined him using them with such a woman, an ex-prisoner who all but supported the heretic agenda, and looked up at him with fawning eyes. My naïve decision to give him lap rights, alongside my hypocrisy in refusing him use of them, sickened me now.

From the shadows of the communal house's vestibule, I peered into the common dining room. A group of matrons sat around a table at the far side of the room, each with a long straw drooping from a beer jug. Several empty jugs lay on their sides on the table and floor.

One of the matrons yelled at a serving man to bring more beer, and as he leaned in to place the jug on the table, she shoved her hand up his kilt. The seven other women hooted as the man flinched and tried to back away. The matron stood, and with one hand still gripping his figs, slapped him hard, the sound snapping across the room. She shoved him and as he fell to the floor, his legs opened to show his recoiled appendage.

'How dare you disrespect me with your limp teat,' the matron spat. 'When I offer you my attentions you should be grateful, but you wave that silly thing around. You will make it up to me with your tongue. What do you say, man?'

'I am sorry, Matron Ninbanda.' His words were weak.

She sat back on her chair and pulled up her leather skirt, long thighs spread and her gates barely visible among the mass of hair. Folding her arms under her bosom, she leaned back and nodded downwards. 'You'd better hope you make me forget your insult or I'll twist your ears so far, they snap.'

The other matrons snorted with laughter and settled back to watch as the man shuffled forward on his knees to see to his task. She took hold of his ears and twisted them so he yelped into her folds and, judging by his muffled cries, she was either relieving or increasing the twist in alignment with his performance. Another matron, her appetite whetted by the scene, stood to leer at the group of serving men stacking plates at the back of the room.

'Get on your knees and crawl over here now, one for each of us,' she yelled, hoarse after the night's carousing. The women hoisted up their skirts in preparation, one of them grabbing the first man who approached on his knees. She slurped from her beer straw as she ground his face into her crotch with one hand and grasped a half-eaten piece of bread in the other.

Revolted, I crept around the dim perimeter of the room, staying close to the walls in an effort to evade the matrons' attentions. I had no desire for anyone except Eve to know I was here, so acting on my wrath at witnessing such abuse must wait. I took the same path the teenager had taken me on just a couple of moon turns prior, taking a lamp from a wall to guide me past the sleeping men, then the boys and babies in the next room, until I made it out into the fresh air. I moved swiftly towards the garden courtyard until I stood before the room that had once housed my brother and now belonged to Eve, casting a glance at the double doors with ibex horn handles, where Adam now resided.

Straining to detect any sound from beyond the door over my own heaving breath, I paused. Nothing. Without knocking, I opened the door with a shove, and relief swept through me as I saw Eve was there alone in the dimness.

'Do I disturb you?' I asked coldly, watching as she scrambled to sit on the sleeping pallet, drawing the blanket up to cover her nude body, her hair tumbled. She reached for the shift sitting in a heap on the floor beside her and quickly put it on, galling me with this bizarre act of dressing in my presence. Why on Earth would she cover her body?

With an immature urge to intimidate her, I held the lamp below my chin to give my face a daunting glow.

'Is everything well?' she asked in guileless tones.

'Tell me more of who you are and where you come from.' My tone demanded her immediate compliance, for I had no patience for coy games.

She stared at me as she reached to tidy her hair, assessing the situation.

'Very well,' she said, and I sensed she would speak truth. 'I was born in a small settlement in the north of Mesopotamia. A sickness came upon our people when I was a young girl and my mother was among many who died. A passing group of itinerant men took pity on me and took me with them.'

'Those men were heretics.'

'Yes. They choose to wear beards and defy protocols. Some of them were originally from Uruk or had dealings here trading gems, and they taught me your language.'

'You're saying this group of heretics has existed for many years? And other groups like it?'

'Yes.'

The simplicity of her affirmation and what it meant for my society scared me. 'What of the other women in such groups?' I said as if unconcerned. 'Are they held captive?'

'We women agree men deserve a fairer place in our world. We see their value and so obey their will. The daughters born among us grow to see men very differently to you.'

'Do you find this acceptable?' I was truly baffled. 'You could have run away. A woman would find welcome in any settlement.'

Her eyes showed compassion, as if I were the one who were simple. 'I had no desire to live differently. It is not in my blood to stand above men.'

I stared at her in disbelief. The visions in the Weird Sphere had never shown that women might be complicit in the tyranny of men.

She continued. 'In truth, men want only the chance to create, to choose their own destiny, to pursue their own purpose. It is fair that they do so. They have been pushed down long enough.'

A vision of the cowering man on his knees before Matron Ninbanda brought a quake through my spine.

'I accept men should be treated fairly and not subject to abuse,' I said. 'But that women should obey them? Never.'

'What do you call fair? Women have had their turn forcing men to their knees, so now...' She let her sentence dwindle, as if in consideration of how finishing it may aggravate me.

Part of me wanted to rant at her, to strike her docile cheek and make her see sense, but I could not. There was more to her than I'd assumed, and even if she was abnormal in her willingness to submit to men, she spoke her truth, some of it even aligned with my own. I could not condemn her for that.

'We each have our own destiny, High Priestess, and I respect yours. But my life has taken me on the path of helping men rise.' Her voice was gentle.

I shook my head slowly. Even while I felt some personal respect for the position she took, she was deviant in touting the ideas of the heretics. She had to go.

Without further comment, I turned to leave, frustration rising as I considered how I could evict her in an ethical manner. Perhaps I could have her taken to Ur and ask High Priestess Dagartum to keep her under control.

I felt overwhelmed by the challenges coming at me from every direction, including from this pest of a woman, Eve. My breath began to rise in angry puffs as I rushed through the district house, all too cognisant of the abuse that went on under my rule.

The night was now deep and nobody saw me enter the plaza. I broke into a run, allowing my pent-up frustration some release, and came to a stop outside Olgana's door.

I thumped my fists on the wood. 'Olgana! Get up!'

Scuffings and scrapings sounded as she roused herself and opened the door.

'What's happened, High Priestess?' She moved in anxious jerks, eyes darting about the plaza as if checking if we were under attack.

I had no time for her fears. 'Go to the copper district now and banish Matron Ninbanda. She must leave the city before sunrise and never return.'

Olgana's bottom lip dropped open as she stared blankly at me.

'That district is foul,' I said. 'Perhaps it is from the infection of Semiramis' cruelty, or are all of the district houses as grim? I will get rid of every matron who unjustly harms men and neglects children. As head matron, you will ensure no more abuse takes place and if you fail, you will be ejected just as quickly.'

She managed to scowl and cower at the same time.

'Go now,' I spat. Ferociousness seared through my eyes into hers, and I cared nothing for how she flinched.

Queasiness nagged my gut as I stomped away. What kind of ruler was I to intimidate Olgana or Eve, or anyone else? In no way did my wretched expressions of dominance help address the vast issues my people faced, and no longer did they comfort me with a false sense of control. A major societal transformation was demanded, and I would have to call on my greatest strength if I were to bring it.

CHAPTER 13

That night, a dream haunted me. Two boys, dirty, yet radiant with light. One of them stepped forth, his eyes burning with golden fire that reached deep into my soul.

'We are you,' he said, expansive peace filling us.

But a darkness began to seep into our joy, and their faces crumpled in terror as they covered their heads with skinny arms against the earth falling upon them. We were united in despair, and I woke filled with it, lying still until the dimmest light permeated my chamber.

I knew I would join the convoy leaving for the copper mines today, a three-day walk east of Uruk. All these years in rule and I had never contemplated going before, unwilling to confront what I was ultimately responsible for.

Pulling on my shawls and lacing my walking sandals, I went to the chamber next down from my corner suite.

'Gem,' I whispered, touching her shoulder until her eyes opened a little. 'The transport convoy leaves today for the mines, and I feel called to join them. I'm leaving you as my proxy.'

She sat up, and I hastened to finish my words. 'Keep my departure quiet. Tell the priestesses and Adam I'm going to see how the scaffolding is progressing and to check on copper production. You'll look after Aea? I'll be back in seven days, at the new moon.' We'd still have half a month before the expected attack.

Before she could do any more than nod, I was gone, in no mood for questions. If the other priestesses and Adam found out my plan, they'd fuss over details and security fears, although the transport convoy travelling regularly to and from the mines had never reported any suspicious activity.

As the golden glow of the sun emerged above the horizon, Tadez and three sturdy servants followed me down the temple steps and across the plaza. A strong desire to invite Menna filled my being, and I stopped at her apartments and stood beside her bed. When she sensed my presence and woke, I whispered an invitation to join my journey and she immediately accepted. She had never been to the mines either.

I waited as she wrapped orange travelling shawls about her waist and shoulders, Demsar sitting up to watch her. When Menna went to rouse her attendant, Baba, I met Demsar's blue eyes. Star, laying at the foot of their bed, issued a melodic chirrup and a sense of gentleness filled the room. Messages passed silently between Demsar and I, but I did not know what it all meant, only that this trip was crucially important. I felt a restless urge to arrive at the mines and experience what I must. Without forethought, I stepped towards him and squeezed his hand in affection.

Outside Menna's double doors, she and Demsar stood in a long embrace. Her small stature fit perfectly into his manly frame, and they kissed and spoke quiet words. The soft fullness of love filled the air and I looked away, their moment too intimate to watch. Never had I seen a man so loved. A pain seared my heart as I registered that what I shared with Adam did not carry these qualities, and never had.

Demsar watched us from their door, Menna turning to wave to him several times as we set out to join the rest of the convoy.

With our servants and attendants surrounding us, Menna walked beside me along the path etched into the rocky ground. The two advisers from the building district and the woodworkers trailed behind us, then the 12 men of the transport convoy, each driving a white ox, pulling sleds and hauling the tree trunks. On our second day, the immense Zagros Mountain range came into view as we trudged through a broad brown valley. This was the furthest I had ever travelled east of Uruk. Late on the third day, one of the transport men called out that the mines were ahead. Squinting, I surveyed the foothills bathed in shades of deep brown and orange, and made out a series of holes and ledges on the face of an early slope.

'Come, Menna,' I said, increasing my stride and causing the servant walking beside me to break into a trot to keep the shrivelled palm frond parasol above my head. I waved him away—the sun was low, although the air was still hot enough to keep the waistband of my skirt soaked in sweat.

A rocky overhang at the base of the slope became visible, with a group of perhaps 30 matrons lounging beneath it, beer jars dotted around them, empty jars lying on their sides, and cooking fires smouldering. Low trees surrounded the clearing, with a dozen mud huts interspersed between them. I surveyed the slope above the clearing for evidence of the miners, seeing only a dozen very young boys standing across the rockface, along with a few goats chewing thickets of pale green brush.

When the matrons noticed there were women walking ahead of the usual transport convoy, one of them stood, adjusting her skirt and the leather sash across her chest as she looked at us. Her lanky frame began moving towards us, calling over her shoulder to the rest of the matrons. As she grew closer, my hackles prickled at her coarse energy field, cruelty emanating like a stink.

'I am Hyene, head matron of the great mines serving Uruk,' she called, sounding put out by our presence. She bowed her head slightly as she took in the dusty forms of Menna, me and the two advisers, all in travelling shawls. She didn't know who I was—I doubted she'd ever set foot in Uruk and thus had never laid eyes on me, especially not out of my regalia. The mine matrons were a breed of their own, with a reputation more loathsome than the city matrons, and I had no cause to encourage them to come to Uruk.

I straightened my back wearily to deal with another woman I sensed understood only domination and manipulation.

'I am High Priestess of Uruk's Temple of Inanna,' I said coldly, looking at Hyene and ignoring the other matrons now standing behind her in an odorous clump.

Hyene was tall but not so much as I. Her gangly posture shifted into a more diminutive pose to make herself smaller, her shoulders and chin dropping a little. 'Welcome, High Priestess.'

'This is the retired High Priestess Menna,' I said. 'We're here to assess the conditions of the mines and the boys, and my advisers and workers will build scaffolding. Have you prepared the first load of wood?'

She shrunk a little more and I knew she had not.

'High Priestesses and advisers,' she said, her muddy eyes gazing up from her lowered head in a way she must have thought humble. 'As yet we're still planning how to best cut the wood. We were just now talking about it.'

'You've had seven days since the load arrived with clear instructions to prepare it,' I said, holding her gaze. 'Are you incapable of managing such a task without endless discussion?'

'I'm sorry, High Priestess. We've been so busy extracting more copper to meet Uruk's increased needs.' Her tone was offended.

'You will work through the night to have the wood ready to begin work tomorrow morning.'

Her eyes bulged with a rage she must keep repressed, and she nodded.

I turned to look at the two advisers Amarazen had nominated to design the scaffolding, apparently Uruk's best building minds. They stood stiffly, their faces twisted in disdain for the matrons gathered before us. It was easy to read the advisers' minds—they were sour they'd been removed from Uruk and forced to work with these coarse women for the benefit of dehumanised little boys, building common scaffolding. It was an insult to their experience, normally applied to designing elegant buildings with articulated buttresses and clever recesses.

I gestured at them as I spoke to Hyene. 'Advisers Ludo and Sapurtum and our woodworkers will stay here to ensure the scaffolding is up within one turn of the moon, and you and your matrons are at their disposal. This is a temple priority.'

'Yes, High Priestess. However, some of the mine tunnels are too small for an adult to enter so the task is difficult...' The matron's voice trailed off under my glare. I had no patience to make pretences of diplomacy for this matron and her cronies, nor the haughty advisers. Squirming urgency twisted in my gut, a drive to push forward.

'You are unable to do as ordered?' I demanded.

'No, no, of course we will do as you say,' Hyene blustered. 'We've been tasked with extracting more copper to meet new targets set by Councillor Semiramis. Apparently it's to produce weapons because there's some kind of threat from men.' She scowled in disbelief at such a notion. 'Last month, we had one of the district advisers here—that man!—telling us we had to increase quantities even though he hindered our efforts in doing so.'

She didn't seem to realise she spoke of my brother and continued complaining. 'He didn't want the boys working extra time, so I don't see how Councillor Semiramis can expect us to deliver if her own adviser thwarts us. But fear not, High Priestess, for the new mine we're now digging is showing plenty of the Great Mother's coppery veins running through it.'

She gestured towards the base of the rockface at the outskirts of the mine settlement, looking pleased to deliver what she felt was good news.

'If the mines collapse and kill the boys, how can we progress at all?' I said abruptly. 'Speak no more of Semiramis. I've removed her from the council for her improper conduct and got rid of her head matron.' I eyed Hyene to ensure she felt my threat—she would experience a similar fate if she did not please me. 'And do not speak of my visit to that adviser when he comes again. It could impact my investigations into how things are run in the copper district.'

I wanted to hide my visit from Sabium, as if I didn't want him to know I'd seen where he had laboured as a child. A wave of guilty nausea ran through my belly as I turned from the matron, putting a hand above my eyes to shield the tip of the sinking sun as I looked up at the rocky façade. A number of young boys stood on narrow ledges beside the holes as the dull thudding of hammers funnelled out through the wormlike holes.

'Where are the other boys?' I asked. 'I see only some young ones.'

'The miners start to come out from about now,' Hyene said. 'The young ones are waiting to collect the lamps and ready them for tomorrow.'

Movement caught my eye and I saw a boy crawling out of a hole not far above where we stood, his skin so white it shone from beneath the dirt covering him. Squinting at the shock of the soft sunset light, he untied ropes from his ankles to which a reed basket was attached, filled with copper ore. How such a small boy could drag so much rock was beyond me. More bedraggled boys emerged, wearing filthy loin cloths and strips of linen wrapped thickly around their knees and hands, and tool belts holding flint picks and wooden hammers. Beside me, Menna's aura quavered at the deplorable sight, and I sensed her distress as she thought of her own three sons being in such a position. We watched the boys drag their bounty towards a ledge, where a few matrons inspected the baskets. Most boys were permitted to tip their basket's contents into a pile of greenish rock, but I noticed a matron berating one of them and gesturing him to join a small group standing to the side.

'What's happening with those boys?' My hand dropped to my heart so my knuckles could rub my aching breastbone. Some of the boys were crying as blood trickled down their legs from cuts on their knees.

'Those boys have not filled their baskets to the standard required. But don't worry, they'll all go back in and work until they do their job. You'll get the copper you need for your weapons.'

How many times had Sabium been in such a situation, or left sick or injured as these heartless women neglected and overworked him? Bile rose in my throat.

'No. Tell those matrons the boys will not be working any longer tonight.' I glared steadily at her. Sourly, she waved at one of her matrons to deliver the message.

'We're tired after our journey,' Menna said, stepping forward. She placed her diminutive hand on my forearm, and I realised my knuckles were still grinding at my heart. 'Come, High Priestess, shall we rest? Then we can sit with the boys for dinner. Matron Hyene, where and what do the lads eat?'

Hyene pointed to a dusty expanse further along the ravine. 'That's their sleeping and eating area—downwind from us,' she said with a snort of contempt. 'They eat bread and goats' cheese, and they can help themselves to dates and nuts from the trees.'

I looked around. The date palms were picked bare, and the young almonds and pistachios were sparse due to the drought. At any rate, they would not be ready for eating until late summer.

'The trees are not providing, so what are they eating beyond bread and cheese? What about meat? And vegetables and other fruits?' I demanded, eyeing the scrawny forms of the boys climbing down the rockface.

'Oh, not a lot.' The matron waved dismissively. 'It's best they stay lean to move through the mines. But we are excellent huntresses and often bring down desert gazelles, and we give the boys the scraps. Tonight, we have two to roast, a most fortunate provision of the Great Mother on this day we have the honour of hosting you.'

'Tonight, the matrons will eat bread and cheese and the boys will eat the meat. Our attendants and servants will direct the meal.' I stared her down hard to check for any sign of impudence.

'Of course,' she choked.

A group of boys gathering at the base of the slope looked at us from behind mops of hair as they removed their tool belts and threw their knee and hand padding onto a filthy pile.

'Matron,' I said, and beckoned her close. 'Do not tell the boys who I am. I want them to be comfortable in our presence. Tell them we're visiting from Uruk to make the mines safer, and will join them for dinner. Now, where is best for us to make camp?'

Hyene made a loud show of telling a group of matrons to move out of a mud hut for the duration of our stay. I eyed the huts with distaste, imagining the crude and stuffy spaces.

'Hurry!' Hyene yelled at her women. 'Can't you see our guests are tired?' Her tone dripped with theatrics as she looked sideways at me. I shared a smirk with Tadez.

'I prefer to stay in that cave,' I said, pointing to a rocky overhang to the north of the matron's area, a good distance away. I turned to Menna with raised eyebrows and she nodded. 'High Priestess Menna will join me. Advisers Sapartum and Ludo will take the hut.'

As soon as Menna and I washed and dressed in fresh skirts and shawls, I sent Tadez and Baba to oversee preparations for the boys' dinner. Menna and I rested outside the open-sided cave as the other servants swept and arranged our bedding, and readied fires to burn through the night to warm us and keep animals away.

When the smell of roasting meat drew us for dinner, we kept our expressions aloof as we passed the matrons' dining area, from where a group of women sourly bid us a good evening. Next, we passed a brewery, provisions store and bakery set up under another rocky overhang. Menna and I exchanged a smile at the many cats sitting on rocky perches to enjoy the early evening, paying us no attention. Their bodies were thicker-set and their faces flatter and rounder than our elegant temple cats, though I supposed they could rat just as well.

As we approached the two hundred or so boys seated on the dusty ground, they did not look up. I wasn't sure if it was their lack of self-worth preventing them gazing upon us, or that they couldn't spare the energy. If I hadn't known how Sabium had once been a vibrant child, perhaps I would have thought as most women did—that these boys were simple, animalistic even, and not aware of their poor living conditions, or at least not developed enough to be bothered by them.

'Boys!' Tadez cried cheerfully, standing beside the makeshift kitchen, a series of woven reed mats upon which meat and bread were piled, with two large cooking fires a short distance back staffed by surly matrons. 'I will make a deal with you all. Tell me your name and your favourite animal and I will serve you meat. Come forward.'

The boys remained still, silence hanging in the air. Their faces looked almost featureless in the dimming light. They looked ghastly.

'Come, boys!' called Tadez. Behind the friendliness in his voice, I heard the crack of emotion. It seemed they could not believe what was happening. Still the boys did not move, so Tadez stepped forward to take one gently by the hand to lead him to the food. With ongoing encouragement, more boys stood to form a line, holding their rough wooden plates shyly, and Tadez said a kind word to each as he served them.

Tears blurred my vision as I watched some of the boys taste the meat, tentatively at first, before they wolfed it down gaping throats. The more reluctant boys now joined the queue. A new aliveness rose in the crowd as the boys ate, many of them lifting their gazes to look around, and the sound of light chatter emerged.

A servant brought plates of meat to Menna and me, and we sat on the pebbly ground among the boys. The smell rising from the filthy boys and their sweaty loincloths was disgraceful, but hardly their fault.

I put a piece of meat into my mouth. It was unsalted and not to my usual palate, but in my hunger, so mild compared to that of the boys, I ate gratefully. Probably the boys were never given salt, beyond what was in cheese, and I made a mental note to have additional supplies brought out with the next convoy.

'What is your name?' I turned to one of the boys next to me. The child's head did not rise. His stick-like limbs and narrow shoulders suggested he had lived no more than nine springs, but perhaps he was older. I knew how life in the mines stunted growth. He muttered something, and I did not push him.

I turned to another boy, who was looking up at me shyly, one skinny arm wrapped around his plate and holding it tightly to his bare chest, as if afraid he could lose it. I smiled and asked for his name.

'Bazi.' His eyes were too big for his skinny face, swamped by matted hair. 'This is my brother, Eluti.' Bazi nodded to the smaller boy beside him.

'How did you two come to be at the mines?' I asked, keeping my tone light despite the lump in my throat.

'Our mother couldn't look after us because she was busy, and the city needed us to help here. We also have a big brother who hauls bitumen and tends the smelting furnaces.' His lack of bitterness caused my eyes to burn. He didn't have the sense of worth to be saddened or angry at these fates.

The boys cleaned their plates, and looked as if they could eat the meal ten times over.

'What do you get to eat each day?' I asked Eluti.

'A piece of bread at breakfast, and another with some goats cheese before bed,' he said, looking without self-consciousness into my eyes.

'And whenever the important man comes from Uruk, he brings sacks of dates and nuts,' said Eluti. 'He worked in the holes once himself and now he's got a big job in the city. He says one day, we can all leave the mines so we mustn't give up hope. He says the mines are going to be made stronger and we'll be safe.'

'Adviser Sabium?' I asked, my throat catching. The boys nodded.

I looked away, breathing into my belly to control the emotion rising like an ocean tide within me. Menna was examining Bazi's hands, with their broken nails, cuts and many callouses. He explained proudly that he doesn't suffer from blisters now because his hands had become so tough.

'Do you ever have the chance to play a game, or swim in the river?' I turned back to Eluti with a bright smile.

'We've been to the river a few times to wash but not for a long time. I heard the water doesn't gush over the rocks now because of the drought. Have you ever seen water rushing over rocks? It's pretty.' He was more chatty now.

I swallowed hard, blinking, as I pretended to contemplate his question.

'I have, Eluti, and you're right—it's very pretty.'

Bazi wrapped his arms around his chest and shivered in the rapidly cooling air, and I placed my hand on his bony back in hopes of bringing him some comfort, his snarled hair unpleasant to touch.

A hush came over the crowd and I looked up to see Hyene striding towards us with a rangy gait, towering above the seated boys. She plonked down in front of me, almost crushing Eluti, who scrambled out of the way.

'I hope your meal is suitable?' she asked. All the boys had shrunk in her presence, and my jaw tensed in anger.

I ignored her question. 'Tomorrow, the boys will take the day off to go to the river to wash and play. Tadez and Baba will oversee them, with my other servants.' Her mouth dropped open in dismay at my words. I continued, 'Ensure your matrons bake double the usual bread supply ready for the morning—the ones who won't be cutting the wood through tonight, that is. While the boys have some time off, you can show us the mines, and Advisers Sapartum and Ludo—' I looked around, unsurprised to register they weren't dining with the group, '—can start designing the scaffolding.'

Bazi and Eluti peered at Hyene to see her reaction.

'But copper production will fall behind!' she spluttered. 'The boys are already lazy and failing to meet targets...but yes, yes, as you wish.' She wilted under my glare.

'We will see you in the morning. Good night.' I dismissed her, and as she stood and stomped away, I offered a small grin to the two wide-eyed boys.

Later, I lay on my sleeping pallet, and although my body was exhausted, I was enlivened with desire to help the boys. Thoughts on how I could improve conditions ran through my mind. If we must mine, we could do it with the sophistication we applied to agriculture or building.

'Are you awake?' I whispered to Menna.

'How can I sleep? Treating little children like this...'

The magnitude of our guilt hung between us. I drew a shaky breath, and forced myself to speak the dreadful truth. 'I can't believe I have ignored what goes on under my rule.'

'As did I,' said Menna, her dark head shaking slowly in regret.

'The time was not yet ripe in your reign—but now the time has come. I must bring about great change, not token measures. And not only to moderate the dark future towards one of greater balance...but because it is right. There is no choice now.'

Menna's voice was reverential. 'It's true, circumstances now drive you hard. Still, it takes great will to make changes in a society so deeply ingrained in keeping men and women separate.'

Knowing flashed through me; how the agony of my rift with Sabium taught me men and women must not be separated by dogma nor life conditions; how Adam had shaken my foundations and forced me to look at what I stood for, beyond the grandeur and creed of my station.

Gratitude swelled in my chest. 'Without my love for Sabium and Adam and all they've made me see, I wouldn't find the will.' My voice caught with emotion. 'They are the divine guidance I've long prayed for to help me create a better future. It's only now, right before the prophecy activates with a heretic war, that I realise it.'

'It's not too late. You have heard and seen the guidance of the Great Mother.'

Hope rose within me. 'I'm so glad you're beside me. My priestesses don't truly support me, not yet anyway. I need your help.'

She reached her small hand to touch my cheek, her tenderness filling my being.

'Tomorrow, we'll learn more about the conditions here, and head back to Uruk the next day to order major changes,' I said excitedly.

I thought of Bazi and Eluti, their light still within them, and wanted nothing more than to ensure they never lost it.

The mine opening stood taller than me and wide enough to open my arms at full stretch.

'As is usual, the boys have filled the oil lamps so our way will be well-lit,' said Hyene, waving a long arm towards the lamps dotting the walls of the tunnel as far as we could see.

Sapartum and Ludo shifted nervously, holding their measuring reeds and soft clay tablets, ready to inscribe dimensions.

My eye was caught by movement further down the slope, and I saw the familiar faces of two little boys poking over the top of the narrow ledge we stood on.

'Bazi! Eluti!' I beckoned them forward then turned to Hyene to hiss, 'I hope you did not keep these boys back because they were talking to Menna and me.'

Hyene's eyes widened in a display of innocence as the boys scrambled up the slope, eyeing her warily.

'Fear not, boys, this matron won't give you any trouble,' I said. 'Why aren't you at the river?'

'We were worried you might leave before we saw you again,' said Bazi, meeting my gaze without hesitation.

'The boys will come on the tour to tell us how this mine compares to the others,' I said to Hyene as she scowled at the brothers. She would not present the situation honestly to us, but they would. 'Come, boys, we're glad of your company, but after the tour you should go and have fun at the river. We won't be leaving until tomorrow.'

We walked into the well-lit tunnel, with its neatly swept ground, and after a hundred feet or so we passed a table holding a water jug and loaf of bread. I raised my eyebrows at Bazi and he shook his head, as if his mind's eye read my question on whether this was a normal provision. I looked fondly at him, imagining him and Eluti well-groomed and wearing fresh kilts. They were smart boys and would scrub up well, capable of standing as bright and rosy as Aea, if given the chance.

The mine narrowed as we proceeded, but still allowed me to walk mostly without stooping. Eventually, the space opened into a larger chamber.

'See the green veins?' said Hyene, pointing to one of the walls. 'This is still one of our most productive mines. As well as plenty of copper ore, it produces the finest malachite for your eyeshadows and jewellery.'

I nodded, running my hands over the lumpy rocky walls and sensing the security of the rock. It felt stable.

'As you can see, the mines are secure and at low risk of collapse,' said Hyene, hovering over my shoulder. 'And with the scaffolding, they will be even safer.'

'This is by far your largest mine and it seems stable, but what of all the others?' I said.

'Oh, they may be small but they are generally stable,' she said evasively, turning to project her voice away from Bazi and Eluti in a futile effort. The chamber easily echoed every word, and the boys' miffed expressions showed she lied.

As Hyene talked with Sapartum and Ludo, who were measuring the height of the ceiling at different points, I stood by Menna and the boys.

'Show us another mine,' I said to the boys. 'You've been working on the new mine low on the slope, haven't you? Take us there.'

The four of us began to exit the mine, with Hyene and the advisers left with no choice but to follow us.

'So you think this one is safe?' I asked Hyene once our cohort had picked our way down the steep slope and stood before the hole. My chest constricted with dread as I looked at the opening, as high as my bosom and not a lot wider than my shoulders, the gravelly floor quickly disappearing into a black abyss. I looked up the rockface at the other mine holes riddling the slope. All those tunnels would surely make this lower level mine particularly unstable.

'It's safe, but still, I don't think it's a good idea for you to enter. It would be uncomfortable and far too grubby for a woman of your elegance.' She attempted to smile sweetly. Sapartum and Ludo shuffled from side to side, eyeing the dark hole with abhorrence and standing as far from Bazi and Eluti as they could.

Menna and I shared a look, and I knew we felt the same—we had to enter. It was my duty to experience the conditions the boys were working in. I owed it to Sabium and all the boys for whom I was ultimately responsible.

'We're going in. Advisers, it's too tight for us all at once, so Menna and I will go in with the boys, and you'll go in to take your measurements once we come out.' I ignored Hyene, unwilling to have her with us.

Standing before the hole, I gathered my will to enter.

'Are you ready?' Bazi asked, looking from me to Menna. 'Your backs will ache in the tunnel, but in the chamber, you might be able to stand. It's easier to crouch if you don't carry a lamp but I'll have one. Follow my light, and don't be scared.'

'You need to bend down low because you're so tall,' Eluti said to me encouragingly.

Exchanging a fortifying glance with Menna, we watched the two boys disappear into the hole. Menna went next, her small frame bending over to fit in. Pushing away my apprehension, I took a few breaths before stooping low to fit my far taller frame in the hole. I made my way forward on a slight incline for the first stone's throw, in almost total darkness, following the whisper of shuffling feet ahead. The tunnel grew smaller, and with my head crouched low, I could not see Menna, nor hear her over my own panting. The tunnel turned downhill abruptly, causing additional discomfort at the bend as I stooped lower, turning my shoulders to the side to squeeze through. My heart lurched as I was pulled to a sudden stop, my skirt catching on a jagged rock, and I couldn't fit my hands behind me to release the hold. It was pitch black. Forcing myself to breathe more slowly, I tried to quell a rising panic.

'Lilith!' Menna called back to me, her echoed voice filled with anxiety.

I firmly instructed myself, *Be calm*. My fear was disproportionate to the situation, but still trembles rumbled through me and clouded my head with a roar, making me think I was swamped in my own dread. Then gravel spattered on my head, puffing dirt into my open mouth, and the walls of the tight tunnel shuddered against me as a roaring sound sent shockwaves through my body.

Utter terror consumed me. Cracking and thudding shook the tunnel as rocks crashed into each other, falling to the ground, then a thump reverberated through my head, stunning me into nothingness.

A hacking sound brought me back to the horrifying moment—my own coughing.

More dust and dirt entered my lungs with each inhale, causing me to choke and cough uncontrollably. The structural strength of the bend I was stuck in had saved me from being battered by the rocks that had thudded to the ground. Horror spread like thick black pus throughout my being as I realised the direness of the situation.

I calmed my coughing with a rush of will. The rumbling and cracking of falling rocks had stopped with only the sound of pebbly debris raining down now. Ripping and tearing at my skirt to free myself, I held a piece of the fabric over my mouth and nose.

'Menna!' I rasped loudly, not daring to yell for fear it would further destabilise the mine. I tried again, louder. 'Menna! Bazi! Eluti!'

The reply was another smattering of dirt on my face. Holding my hands in front of me in the lightless space, I reached down to feel the stones that had fallen on the ground, some as large as my head. A small relief emerged as I recognised—for as far ahead as I could reach, there was a small space I could crawl through. I would not think further ahead or behind me than that.

Getting to my knees as best I could, I part crawled, part writhed like a snake, wriggling and twisting as rocks cut my skin. Pain would be a luxury I could experience later—its presence would be the mark of my survival. At some points, the walls were so close they were like a second skin, such that little air could come past my feet towards my face. *Focus.* I could only go forward, and with each small section I passed, I was filled with the miracle that another space large enough for me to crawl through was ahead. *Great Mother, stay with me.*

I had no idea how far I had travelled, hoping the larger chamber would open before me and I'd find Menna and the boys. I didn't dare to think about how I might drag them out if they were injured.

Fear pushed me on, and the common sense that panicking would do me no good. I recalled my initiation in the sepulchre, entombed for three days in an almost airless space. In there, I had to apply all my training to master fear, of the close airless confinement and the doom of being lost in hell if I fell into fear. I had made it through my initiation, and I pulled upon the knowing of my own strength to continue.

I heard a muffled cry, stopping my movement for a moment to listen carefully. Again I heard it—Menna's voice.

'Menna!' I called, the echo telling me there was space ahead of me. I doubled my efforts, my bare breasts dragging painfully across the stones beneath me. I wasn't sure if the dirt hitting my face and head were kicked up by my scrabbling hands or coming from the upper tunnel wall.

I sensed the space around me increase as I emerged into the mine chamber, disoriented as my hands reached around and made contact with rocks and dirt.

'Stop,' said Menna with a weak cough. 'Not stable.'

I could barely hear her. 'Where are you? Are you injured?' I spoke at what I hoped was a normal volume, impossible to tell in the black space that gave no contrast to measure anything against.

I tried to quiet my panting breath, my heart banging as loud as a deerskin drum. The gritty feel and musty taste of dirt filled my mouth.

'The boys...' Her voice was close.

I reached out blindly as I edged forward, touching rocks, dirt, knocking my head on a jutting sharpness that brought fresh warm liquid down the side of my face. I must slow my frantic movements and focus if I was to be of help. I let my senses rise as I ran my hands lightly over the rocks, sniffing at the dank black air, trusting I would be drawn to her and the boys. I felt a patch of skin as my fingers reached into a gap. A child's limp foot. Tears ran from my gritty eyes, uselessly open.

'Bazi? Eluti? Make a noise if you can hear me.' I tried to sound as comforting as I could, as if I were making normal chatter. In the total silence that followed, I felt wetness running down my cheeks, my tears and blood.

'Menna, I think they're dead.'

She made a low moan, and my throat convulsed in a sob. Desperately, I began feeling around again, lifting some smaller rocks, afraid I would cause a further cave-in if I pulled at the wrong one.

'Bazi! Eluti!' I cried, pushing my fingers into the spaces between rocks. I sensed there was no life. 'Menna...where are you?' The blackness pressed upon me as a weight so heavy, I could scarcely pull a breath out of it. She did not speak.

'Help!' I cried. A wave of panic engulfed me and I turned to scream back towards the way I thought I'd come. Maybe a rescue team was on its way to us. 'Help us!' More dirt fell in my eyes, still wide open with terror.

'Leave me.' Her voice was a weak rasp. 'Tell Demsar I love him forever. My sons.'

I continued to crawl forward, gasping as I found her shoulder. My hands ran over her chest and neck, up and down her arms, over her head, feeling for injury. There was no wetness, no open flesh. Maybe she wasn't badly injured.

'Lilith...' she murmured.

With deep dread, I let my hand move down her torso. A sickening wave rolled through me as I felt the flatness of her crushed belly, how it tapered abruptly downwards, and I coursed with horror as my fingers made contact with the huge slab of rock on top her. From the waist down, she was near flattened.

Resting my head beside her shoulder, I groaned from the depths of my core. 'Oh no, oh no.'

'The Mother calls.' Her voice dwindled. I held in my sobs and tenderly touched her hand, the bones as delicate as a quail's. This hand had given me endless strength and affection through my life.

She was breathy, speaking in less than a whisper. 'What I let happen to all the boys...now here I die.'

My tears ran onto her face as I gently kissed her cheek.

'No, don't give up.' I felt for a grip beneath the huge rock lying across her middle, feeling with despair how it extended to her thighs. I could never lift it, and her body was ruined beneath it. I gave a mangled sob, feeling as if two claws tore my ribcage apart and ripped at my heart.

'Menna.' My utterance was ravaged, helpless.

She sighed, and I waited for her to gather the monumental effort required to speak. 'You always knew the truth...of equality.' She paused, gasping for breath.

I wept, stifling my coughing, kissing her in a mess of salty tears and blood. The depth of my grief could never be satisfied, but for now, I let my body wrack in sobs at the imminent loss of Menna and the death of the dear little boys, so like Sabium had once been, unspoiled by the conflict among men and women, as we grew and were told and believed that one was more or less than the other.

'I love you forever,' she whispered.

Stilling, I held her limp hand to my cheek. The darkness changed and greater love swelled in the space within and around me, lifting the density of fear and grief into the peace of the Great Mother's womb of creation. Menna was expanding out from her body, and I calmed myself to be present with her. It was quiet a while, with a faint scent of roses suddenly on the thin air. I thought she was gone, but again she spoke, miraculously stronger.

'Men and women...are not just equal...' She paused to pant a little, as if in ecstasy. 'We are one.'

Great swathes of light ran through my being in an epiphany fantastic in its obviousness. The red and blue flames were not only equal partners— they were one inseparable being, able to differentiate so they could create with their contrast. *We are one.*

'Thank you, thank you,' I whispered with passion, my cheek slippery against her palm.

'We will live again to see all unified...some day,' she murmured, her voice enraptured in the loving blackness we were now held within. 'Oh, the flames...beautiful...'

'Tell me what you see, Menna.'

'Perfection.'

In the silence that followed, I knew it as pure truth. Her spirit ran out of her palm and through my cheek, into my being, fortifying me to emerge from this underworld and return to Uruk to do what I must—make a better future where men and women could stand united.

CHAPTER 14

As Tadez helped me ascend the temple steps late on the afternoon of the new moon, dusty and exhausted, gloomy rain clouds covered the sun and gave the appearance that darkness had already settled.

Aea and Fancy ran down the steps to meet me halfway, and I smiled a little as I pressed my trembling legs onwards, each step painfully cracking the split skin on my knees. Tears flowed freely down my face as I bent to receive Aea into my arms, Fancy's pointed muzzle nudging moistly at my cheek.

'Mammi, what's happened? You're all cut!' Aea's forehead pushed down in worry as she beheld my wretched form.

From the first tier of the ziggurat, Gemekala and Urnina waved and craned their necks to watch us coming towards them. Sobbing and smiling, I soon fell into their embrace, Aea with us. The women rubbed my arms and back and kissed my grimy cheeks, still streaming with tears as my grief erupted anew in the relief of being back in the bosom of the temple.

Placing her hands on my shoulders, Gemekala looked at me in angst. 'What happened?'

'Sisters,' I said, my lower lip trembling. 'Aea, come here, my darling.'

I bent to lift Aea onto my hip, holding her close to cushion the shock of my next words. 'Menna is gone. We were in the mines and there was a collapse. She is dead.'

Aea pulled her head back to frown at me, confused, and moments later tears spilled from her eyes.

'What!' Gemekala gasped.

'I cannot believe it! I'm so sorry,' said Urnina, eyes flooded with compassion as she grasped my hand.

'Whatever were you doing in a mine?' sobbed Gemekala.

Urnina took my forearm and rubbed it tenderly. 'You're covered in cuts! Oh, your poor knees, and that gash on your head.'

By the time I had managed to escape from the partially collapsed tunnel, my body was severely cut and bruised. I'd crawled and writhed my way to the earlier parts of the tunnel, where the two advisers frantically cleared rocks. On my exit, my first words were to order the immediate closure of all the mines and the banishment of Hyene. I appointed one of the woodworker men I'd sensed was kind to see that the boys were taken care of until I decided how to progress. We could recycle the abundance of copper in Uruk—masses of jewellery, art, pots and plates, wall reliefs—for weaponry if required.

'Come,' said Gemekala. 'Tadez will have ordered your bath, then we must dress your wounds.'

While several boys prepared my bath, I sat at the far end of my garden terrace with Aea on my lap, the two priestesses either side, and Fancy licking my dusty feet with great gentleness. I crumpled into heaving sobs, my companions shuddering in grief around me.

When I calmed myself, I told them the story briefly, revealing my epiphany and plans to banish the false barriers that lay between men and women. My chest and throat constricted in despair as I forced myself to express the truths I knew Gemekala and Urnina could not yet embrace.

'I know you are right, even if I can't see it fully myself,' said Gemekala in earnest tones.

'I don't think I'm strong enough to do this,' I quavered, my voice vulnerable as a young child's. 'I must go forth alone to foster unity among the masses and the task is too great. They will think me mad.'

Gemekala's dark eyes implored me. 'Even if I can't give you the support Menna could, I will help you.'

'We stand with you, Lilith!' wept Urnina. 'You are strong enough.'

Aea climbed off my lap to face me, and I crumpled forward with my hands to my breast in despair.

My words were barely comprehensible amid my sobs. 'As Menna left her body, I promised I would create a fair future where we all stand united.' I took frenzied breaths in an effort to speak. 'I promised it from my deepest core but...I don't think I can do it.'

Aea stood silently with her hands limp at her sides, her honesty as pure as a white dove as she awaited my lifted gaze.

'But Mammi,' she said with quiet strength, reaching beneath her shawl to draw out the black obsidian arrowhead, hung on a reed string about her neck. She must have taken it to give her strength while I was away. 'You taught me that an arrow cannot change its course. You already released your arrow when you made the promise, so I know you will do it.'

I pulled her into my arms, my being expanding with love.

'It's true, Lilu,' said Gemekala with devotion. 'The arrow flies far before it hits its target, and you have set its path.'

The four of us now sat in silence, peace entering our hearts as we were held in the bosom of Menna's love and the truth of these raw moments.

'The sun has started to set,' said Gemekala eventually. 'We must help you prepare, then we go straight to Huluppu. The other priestesses will be waiting to begin the new moon retreat, and you need the tree's comfort more than ever.'

'No, first I must tell Demsar about Menna.' My heart sank at the thought.

'For now, you must focus on yourself,' said Gemekala, her gentle yet firm tone the same one she used with birthing mothers. 'Besides, he's out with the rest of the men on their army exercise, remember?'

The sun had set when we left the temple for our new moon retreat at Huluppu, the red sky darkly spectacular as the dying light shone behind heavy clouds. I'd gathered the other priestesses and their children to announce the death of Menna, and many of them keened their grief as we walked to the tree.

Instead of the usual throngs of city women waiting to call blessings upon our promenade, only the matrons stood at the bottom of the temple steps, carrying their provisions for their three nights camping as our guards.

'It's quiet, isn't it?' I asked Aea, seeing how she looked tearfully at the empty plaza. 'But that's just because the sun has set, so the city women have already started their red moon retreat,' I explained. 'And most of the men are out on their fighting exercise.'

It was a moody and solemn atmosphere. Some city women and children stood in their doorways, barely discernible in the dimness, but few blessings were called and no songs were sung. They watched us in worried confusion, wondering why we were so maudlin. Some of them stared at me, trying to understand the cuts and bruises visible on my exposed skin, although I'd covered the worst of them with shawls. The city was already tense, frightened by the prospect of the expected attack, and I knew the women could tell something further was amiss, their sensitivity more attuned than ever as they began their monthly bleed.

When we reached the tree, I lifted Aea into my arms to press her head into the crook of my neck, whispering, 'I'll see you tomorrow.'

She was quiet, her moist hands clasped firmly about my neck.

'Ask Tadez for warm milk with honey tonight, hmm?' I said. 'And ask for one of Gem's herbal pouches, the one that helps you sleep. Tadez will be back at the temple soon to look after you.'

She reluctantly allowed me to put her down and I reached to straighten my obsidian arrowhead amulet she still wore. I watched her and Fancy begin walking back to the ziggurat with the other temple daughters.

With rain threatening, the servants had hung a huge tarpaulin made of greased goatskins over Huluppu's greatest bows. Blankets were set out with plenty of cushions, and piles of fresh barley grass sprinkled with cypress oil lay in the nooks and crannies of the root system, ready to receive our blood. It would be mulched and spread over the crops of Uruk to help ensure ongoing bounty.

Low fires burned around the inside of the tree boughs, and the campfires of the matrons made a second ring around us, their own new moon retreat disrupted by the need to guard us. I curled up in front of Huluppu's gateway and sipped the lygos tea Tadez brought in to help bring on our flow. The servants distributed bowls of barley and lamb broth and as we let it nourish our bodies, we were mostly silent, lost in our feelings and thoughts about Menna. More silent tears flowed down my face for Bazi and Eluti, as if they represented the innocent purity of all souls, regardless of what body they wore. Their loss heightened the despicable injustice of my society and strengthened my resolve to change it.

As the evening deepened, Sabit stood to place her finger between her legs. With her first blood, she painted a downward pointing triangle on her lower belly. Dipping again into her gates, she marked the slit of a crescent moon inside the triangle. Now and then, as the evening deepened, another priestess stood to paint this symbol of reverence to the moon to mark the commencement of her flow. Although I should not be surprised my blood did not come, every time I checked between my legs, my chest lurched with the realisation—I carried a child.

My feelings were mixed. I felt excitement and hope for better times at the idea of a baby I'd made with Adam, but also feared I'd made a mistake. I didn't feel like speaking of my pregnancy yet, although there was no way I could hide my dry thighs from these women. When every one of them had stood to paint the triangle and crescent moon except me and Beihani, who was of an age that she bled no more, still they waited for me to speak of it.

The occasional silhouette of a matron moving about was visible outside Huluppu's boughs, or the dark orange glow on one of their faces as they sat by a fire. Anxiety churned in my gut about the heretics' plans to attack us here at the full moon. How would the matrons fare in real battle? They had never been involved in any fighting. A sinister chill shuddered through my core, and a horrific vision threatened to rise. I blocked it wilfully. We could not let such an outcome unfold.

Despite our heavy moods, Lahamu and Sabit encouraged us to sing our best-loved new moon songs, and Urnina told one of our favourite stories, applying her usual dramatisations to amuse us. The rituals were of some comfort in their familiarity, but there were no soft chuckles and happy whispers that usually punctuated the performances.

I rested as Gemekala applied more healing lotions and poultices to my wounds and Urnina took a cedar comb to work through my knotted hair. Lahamu lay next to us, belly pressed to the earth between two rambling roots, her eyes closed in repose. Anunit and Sabit snuggled in each other's arms. Nisaba sat cross-legged in meditation, her face serene. Beihani massaged fragrant oil into Tiamat's shoulders. Ku-Aya lay on her back, gazing beyond the boughs to the thick bank of clouds that had lingered for weeks, finally moving overhead.

Will this storm ever break?

When the night grew late, hot stones wrapped in blankets were distributed for our comfort, although the evening was humid. We drifted into the quiet depths of the Great Mother's void, facilitated by the new moon, embraced in the fecund tang of creative blood. We used this time to rest, to meditate, to quietly contemplate the nature of life and receive messages and visions while the veil between the physical and energetic realms was so thin.

As most of the others slept and our lamps were extinguished, Gemekala laid beside me and embraced me in the fullness of her love. My eyes pooled anew with tears and she stroked my forehead until I grew sleepy. I drifted between the worlds in the altered state so easy to access in the bosom of Huluppu and among the priestesses in their blood flow, the new life within me also serving to connect me strongly to the otherworlds.

A swelling of peace and love came up softly within me, and the whitish golden light I'd experienced on the morning of my wedding arose within my heart and mind's eye to speak to me without words.

You have realised the feminine can never be less than the masculine, and vice versa, because they are one. Now understand that in the great cycles of evolution, the halves appear to separate as one rises above the other, before they eventually reunite. The purpose of this contrast is to flourish creativity, for nothing new is created in stagnancy and sameness.

You are a harbinger of the still-distant era of unity. In this lifetime, you pass the baton from the era of the feminine on top to that of the masculine on top.

Hold to the perfection.

The message disconcerted my mind. I embraced oneness and that men must now take a stronger role, but I would do it without one being on top of the other. The overbearing feminine rule I knew all too well showed me the suffering of such a path. I wanted to set a different foundation— one based on equality and respect—for the new era where men would take their rightful place in society. The beautiful golden-white energy held me in love and acceptance through the night, and by the time Gemekala stirred beside me in the early morning, I felt peaceful, ready to manage the intensified challenges I knew were coming in the fairest way I could.

The servants came in to pour us hot cinnamon tea and set out our breakfast of figs with honey and pistachios, sheep's yoghurt, and a fresh batch of crescent moon-shaped cakes drenched in honey. When the humid day grew hotter, the servants took the bloodied barley grass ready to bless our crops, and fresh grass was laid.

We entered the warm river shallows so the moon blood could bless the river with fertility and channel it downstream into our irrigation systems. The river was running very low, but at least rain looked imminent. Lolling around, we all laughed a little as we watched the familiar romp of otters tumbling on the bank upriver. I swear the little animals knowingly cheered us. With the mood lighter, I decided it was time to speak of my revelations.

'I must share something of great importance with you,' I said to my priestesses as I lay on my side in the ankle-deep water, head propped on my hand. 'It is an epiphany Menna shared just before she died, one that stirred the depths of my soul.'

They were silent a while, a mystical peace filling the air and heightening the sounds of frogs croaking and birds singing. The sun suddenly burst through a small gap in the clouds.

I spoke softly, unconcerned as to whether they believed me. 'As her spirit began leaving her body, she told me the masculine and the feminine are not only equal, but in higher truth are one unified energy, no matter how we believe ourselves one or the other depending on our body.'

I exchanged a long look with Gemekala as she lay on the sandy beach at the water's edge, her eyes full of wisdom, the sharpness gone in this moment.

'I do not yet understand it,' she said. The other priestesses looked at me with eyes of innocence, and I sensed they felt as Gemekala did.

'This truth is not ripe to be widely understood,' I reassured them. 'Its full realisation is of a far distant era, but my path requires me to know it now. My entire life has prepared me for it, and Menna's death, and the little boys that died by her side, allowed me to receive it. My message to you is that men are destined to take a greater place in our world. If we manage that with fairness, we need not have a mass rebellion on our hands. I used to believe fate couldn't be changed, but as oracles, we know visions show only the most likely future if we continue on the path we're on. We can shape a more positive future and that starts with honesty and fairness.'

The priestesses stared at me silently, sensing the profundity of the moment.

'To that end,' I continued, 'I have already closed the mines until we find ways to manage them without the labour of little boys.'

Most of them nodded, able to accept this decision. Now I needed to state my intention to make far more shocking changes.

'Sisters, you know I carry the child I've made from Adam's milk. I want him to know he is part of its creation. I have decided to tell him the truth of procreation, then share it with all.'

As expected, this shocked them out of the peaceful moment.

Doshina's sharp exhale brought our attention to her. 'Lilith, your wisdom is deep but the world is not ready for it. Our men will be furious if they hear the truth of procreation now—they could turn on us! Look how they hate the matrons.' Doshina's lithe arm waved as she spoke to punctuate her words. She was extra sensitive to this issue in her passionate love of Delondra.

Lahamu spoke next. 'Treating men better is all very well, but they are not remotely ready to understand the complexities of creation.'

I paused, reminding myself to be patient with their limited understanding. I rested my gaze on Urnina as she sat in the shallows, swishing a red tendril of blood in the water. She drew in a breath to speak, then paused, dreading to speak against me.

'Tell me, Urnina,' I said.

'Change is inevitable, but telling men the truth in the midst of this rebel uproar feels out of control. Can it wait?' Her face was pained.

'The truth must be revealed now. Men must be embraced as our equals, and we must even accept they will rise to some degree,' I said, my clarity complete.

'But the feminine sits above the masculine. How can they rise?' said Ku-Aya, her face wrought with confusion. 'The Great Mother sits at the top and all creation is born from Her. Even babies begin as female. The feminine comes first.'

'I ask you to trust my knowing,' I said. 'Think of it this way—the top half of an apple is not superior to the bottom half. You could turn the apple over so the other half is on top, and it matters not. Either half could be on the top or bottom and remain of equal value.'

Ku-Aya stared at me in bafflement, and I sighed deeply. There could be no forcing the natural rhythms of truth.

I looked around at them. 'Sisters, the cyclic nature of life goes far beyond the 13 monthly moons of one year and the shifting of the seasons. Perhaps the men are sensing the changing of a giant cycle and are rightfully asking to be treated better, as the first step towards realising we are unified in some far-off era. If we reveal the truth of procreation and start teaching them the Mes, their anger may subside and we can progress with peace.' I felt good about this.

'We are the creators of life,' said Ku-Aya fiercely. 'Men's small role in activating a pregnancy is nothing for them to feel proud of. Next thing we know, they'll be insisting on taking ownership of the babies we create, and even of our bodies. We've all seen it in the Weird Sphere. See how my hackles rise at this notion!' She thrust out her arm to show us the prickled flesh. 'It is a mistake to tell them anything.'

'Men's role is essential to creation, and the sphere has shown us only the worst potential of the path we're on if we do not make changes,' I said. 'For now, I ask you to simply consider what I have shared.'

After lunch, we took a lump of fine red clay from under moist linen cloths, and through the afternoon, each woman created a pot. Once painted and glazed, these red moon pieces were given to the populace, who dearly valued them for storing beer. The pots brought the Great Mother's blessings from her heavenly home and anchored them in the clay of the Earth.

As I handled my clay, smoothing the successive layers of coils into a thin wall before tapering it into a neck, I contemplated leading such great change. I thought of Adam and the baby we had created, a joy rising that our child would be the first born under the shared truth of procreation, therein birthing a new and more just society. Allowing my consciousness to expand, I sought to connect with the babe's soul in celebration, but it was still deep in the bosom of the otherworldly realms, unable to communicate with me.

In the late afternoon, we put our pots aside and took another foray into the river. When we dried off on the sandy bank under Huluppu's great limbs, Aea and the other young temple daughters visited with sliced blood oranges. As ever, the girls were proud to be among bleeding women and we thanked them excessively in indulgence of their awe.

'Mammi, where is your blood?' said Aea, perplexed as she studied my thighs. 'You must be using it to grow a baby. Is there a sister for me?'

I embraced her. 'Yes, indeed you will have a sister, or maybe a brother. Are you excited?' A beaming smile lit her face, and she called out the news to Humusi. Their childish joy cheered me and I let them stay longer than they should.

'A baby girl is just what we need,' said Tiamat, a small smile on her face, perhaps the first since she lost Anba.

'Yes, a baby girl,' said Gemekala, smiling tenderly. 'But if it is a boy, I will love him just the same.'

Gemekala's eyes teared, and I felt her opening to the concept of accepting men in a spirit of love and trust. Hope burned brighter within me that my priestesses could come to share the vision for unity.

As the priestesses chattered about the baby, my spark of happiness grew and I felt a mother's hunger to hold her babe at the breast. Of course, Adam would be angry for a while when I told him the truth, but I was certain he would soon come to be as delighted as we all were. Menna would have been so joyous I'd decided this path.

After her initial excitement, Aea was quiet.

'What is it, my precious white bird?' I asked, stroking her hair.

'I can't believe I will never see Menna again. I feel empty. And the streets are empty too. It feels like something is wrong.' Her voice was tiny. Fancy sat by my side with her ears lifted and head cocked, looking at Aea in rapt concern.

I also felt the eeriness of the empty city, palpable even from our removed place at the tree. There was a silence, a gaping absence, heightened by the damp and heavy air that left the tree's boughs hanging limply. A shudder ran down my back and I drew Aea into a tight embrace.

'All is well, my love. The men will be back tomorrow and they will be stronger than ever.' My words felt hollow, so instead of trying to comfort her, I said, 'I love you forever.'

I held her tightly to me. She looked up at me with her clear grey-green eyes full of intelligence and purity.

'I love you, Mammi. And I want the world to be fair too, so we're all kind to each other. I'm glad you are going to make things right.' The ever-present tear in my heart opened wider, the space filled by a swoon of love for my daughter.

'Look!' I cried, staring in delight at a butterfly hovering about our heads. 'I've never seen a purely orange butterfly before.' Peace filled the air as we watched the creature for a few moments, and Menna's love swelled around us. My throat thickened again with emotion and I prepared my throat to speak calmly so as not to overwhelm Aea.

'Come, rest in my arms tonight. The other girls must go back to the temple now, but you can stay this time, since you're upset about Menna.

But you need to go back before sunrise.' No one would challenge me for flouting the rules of the red moon retreat in these circumstances.

She smiled with relief and nestled deeper in my embrace, and I placed a hand over her brow to shield her mind's eye from the wisps of fear lingering in the air. Fancy slept along the line of Aea's back, and in between the dog and me, she was peaceful.

Under the black sky, with no moonlight and thick clouds snuffing out the stars, I lay awake and wrestled with the fear wanting its way with me. I was woken before dawn by a screech owl's trill, knowing it was the bird that had visited me several times since I'd met Adam. The owl perched on a bough in front of me, and her eyes glowed yellow in the darkness as she stared at me, unblinking.

A sharp crack of thunder sounded. Long moments later, a flash of brilliant light filled every space. Aea stirred and I whispered she should return to the temple before the storm broke. I watched her silhouetted form leave through the hanging branches, an intensified awareness filling the air and the aura of every black leaf throbbing with life-force. A sinister weirdness filled me, but I pushed it away. Dangerous times were ahead and I needed sleep to build my strength.

CHAPTER 15

Something was wrong.

Without moving my body, I opened my eyes, seeking information, recognising that the priestesses still lay around me, sleeping.

It was dim under the tree in the early morning, little light coming through the laden sky, and I strained to look further. A sludge of fear ran through me.

Through the foliage, a group of men stood stock-still in a wide circle around the sleeping matrons.

Aea. Had she gone before they arrived? Great Mother be with us now.

I stood up, their eyes immediately focusing on me with the force of a gust of wind.

Adam, where are you?

The air was cool on my bare body as I took a few steps forward, beyond the edge of the tarpaulin's cover. Black terror flooded me as the realisation dawned—blood, everywhere. I focused on the lump that was Olgana, a gaping red slit at her throat, head tipped backwards, eyes open and surprised. Around the perimeter of Huluppu, the matrons were all dead, their throats cut.

My flesh began to crawl as if an army of ants marched upon me as I registered—the men wore red headcloths. Adam's guardians were traitors.

'Sisters,' I said quietly to the priestesses, dread thickening my voice so it sounded like a stranger's. One by one, the women slowly got to their feet and came to stand behind me. In complete stillness, the 13 of us stood naked and staring through the leaves at the men holding bloodied daggers who were just as frozen, as if each group feared the next action as much as the other.

I took another step forward, expanding my aura.

'What have you done?' I said uselessly, looking around at them.

They stared at me in silence. Finally, some of the men stepped aside, and Sabium walked towards me.

How could I not have realised? He stopped at the border of Huluppu's boughs, as if an invisible field of energy prevented his admittance.

'Lilith,' he said, a lifetime of bitterness distilled into this utterance.

We stared unblinking at one another, a vastness that felt strangely peaceful holding me, or perhaps simply my denial this was happening. I heard the rapid breathing of some of the priestesses, feeling their shock and fear pulsing through the air.

'From the moment you brought me back from the mines I've awaited your downfall,' he said. 'It's...perfection.'

My skin raked in a tingle of recognition. *Perfection*. My mind was confused, scrambling to understand my sentience at his words.

'You take pleasure in this,' I said, more saddened at that moment than afraid. But then—*Aea*. The thought flashed through me like a bolt of lightning. I cannot die now, I must protect her, Humusi, the temple women and children. My city. The entire land. The future.

'Adam will destroy you,' I spat. 'However you've orchestrated this attack, you will not get away with it.'

He laughed, choking a little on the phlegm in his throat, and turned to look at the guardians as they parted to open a pathway. The dawning was natural to me, somehow, as Adam stepped forward.

'Adam.' I stood tall and unmoving as he came to a stop at Sabium's side.

'Lilith.'

'Where is the army?'

'My army is busy at military practice. When they return later today, I will expose the lies that have kept men degraded for aeons and they will follow my new rule gratefully.'

'So you are one of the heretics you denounce,' I said, keeping my face blank even as confusion engulfed me.

'I am.'

A powerful sense of fatedness ran through my veins.

'You manipulated me to let you build an army against them, and you are one.' It was sinking in like the weight of ten thousand stones.

Adam's mouth turned up in a grim grin. 'Not only am I one of the heretics...' he said, moving towards me in a few slow steps. 'I *am* the heretics.'

My stomach dropped deep inside me, deeper than any feeling could go.

He snorted. 'There was never any threat. I made it all up to build my army, ready to turn it against you. The rebellion is *me*, with a few friends from the north and desert wilds, and my devoted guardians. Especially my top collaborator.' He nodded at Sabium, addressing him. 'I would never have been able to do this without you.'

My belly flipped over. I made myself bigger again, shielding my priestesses as best I could.

Now Adam was standing inside the perimeter marked by the tree's branches, getting closer. He continued. 'You were so focused on your own superiority, it was easy to fool you. It made forming an army easy, and that was the best way to resuscitate the flame of purpose within the men. See how they livened in the army and how they love me?'

I closed my eyes, opening them when I began losing my balance.

'And now my army will help me take down Inanna's rule across Mesopotamia, then all the lands beyond. I will release men from the chains you have kept them in for so long. From this day on, we will obliterate the Great Mother, and where we cannot erase her, we will relegate her to the realms of obscurity.'

A high-pitched drone sounded beside me and I turned to see Doshina, the strange noise coming from her mouth. She stared at one of the many bodies on the ground. Delondra.

Doshina dashed past me and dropped to her knees beside her beloved's body, a ravaged cry coming from deep in her throat.

'You treacherous fiend!' she shrieked at Adam, her face white as milk. 'May the Great Mother damn your soul!'

She stood suddenly and flew towards Adam, Delondra's dagger in her hand. The nearest guardian caught her arm well before she reached her target and, in my horror, all movement slowed to an unstoppable crawl, filling an eternity as his dagger entered her gut and moved from one side to the other. My mouth gaped as the priestesses screamed behind me, watching as Doshina's delicate body lurched back, her eyes round with disbelief. She looked at her belly, and turned to stagger towards Delondra's body and collapse upon it. The killer held his dagger high in a macabre gesture, dripping more blood down his stained arm.

'What have you done?' I looked at Adam, my voice aghast to my own ears. 'You cannot do this.'

'You no longer rule.'

'No! No, no...' I erupted a low wail, my eyes stuck on the heaped forms of Delondra and Doshina, and the puddle of blood in which they lay.

'Ah, but yes, Lilith,' said Semiramis, stepping forward from among the guardians and eyeing me triumphantly. 'Yes, yes, yes!'

I felt my forehead twist in confusion at the sight of her, the red birthmark on her cheek fairly pulsating in bitter joy. Shagshag, the matron banished after Anba's murder, appeared at Semiramis' side, her lips stretched in the semblance of a grin.

'So now you have also had your title stripped,' Semiramis crowed at me. 'Our mighty High Priestess no more. But I hope you can be happy for me. I will have a position of great power in the new order, ruling beside these men.'

Adam and Sabium exchanged a glance and I knew Semiramis would never see such a day. They had used her to bring them to this point, and would quickly rid themselves of her. She faced as great a threat as me, and my heart almost tugged for her idiocy.

'And Priestess Tiamat,' Semiramis said, focusing her stare behind me. 'Your squealing pig Anba begged for you the night we killed him, the fool. He was so deluded in the grip of your thighs that he wanted to betray the rebellion.'

Semiramis was coming closer to the tree's edge, peering through the boughs at us. In an effort to distract attention from Tiamat, I took another step forward. 'I always hated you, Semiramis.'

She continued to glare at Tiamat. 'Shagshag and the two other guardians had to kill him, and that matron who tried to get a message to you. It all worked out very nicely, an opportunity for us—' Semiramis waved to take in Adam and Sabium '—to inflame your fear by saying those guardians ran away to join the heretics. I do believe we've now welcomed them back to be part of today's events.'

Tiamat's energy was raging behind me, and I willed her to calm.

'Your wretched souls will meet Anba and me in the next life, and for every life after, and we will torment you in all ways,' Tiamat spat, looking from Semiramis to Shagshag with bitter hatred. My mind's eye pitched a message to her. *Be silent!*

'What of the man put to the snake pit?' I spoke to Adam, floundering for something to say to take the focus from Tiamat even as my legs shook beneath me. 'Those men that attacked us were your heathen friends from the north, hired to convince me a rebellion was rising...now I see why the prisoner screamed such hatred at you. It wasn't in the deal you made with him, was it, that you would capture him and allow him to be tortured and killed? Do your guardians know how you betray your own men?'

'That man was desert scum and no loss to the world. You would not have believed there was a threat without the dramatics of his sacrifice,' said Adam. 'He was one life in exchange for the cause.'

His guardians muttered agreement.

'Your every breath is a lie,' I spluttered. What a fool I was.

'You call me a liar? You lied to my face over and over about procreation. I gave you the chance to tell me.' His voice rose. 'I have known the truth since I was a boy and overheard my mother laughing about it with her priestesses. They scorned men as you do.'

'I was planning to tell you. I decided yesterday.'

'Hah! That is convenient.'

'I am with child. I do not bleed now.' I looked at my legs and his eyes followed mine. 'I chose to receive your milk to create our baby, and I was going to tell you the next time I saw you. And I have,' I added with a tiny snort.

'It's too late. Men create babies. Today, a new word is born from my lips—man is the creator of life and the word for him is "Father".'

Nausea roiled my gut at seeing him act out the prophecy with exactitude. 'Adam, stop. I was coming to tell you I carry our child, that you are the—' I paused, trying to remember the word he'd proclaimed '—father. That you created the child in partnership with me.'

'Eve carries my child also, and will give me many more at my decree,' he sneered.

'But we have been blessed by the Great Mother, She—'

'Silence, woman!' he thundered. 'The *real* divine force is the Great Father and I am His messenger. In my visions, He's proclaimed women should only lay with one man and bear his children alone. No man wants women who open their thighs to anyone. No one wants you or your Great Mother anymore.'

As Sabium and the other men jerked their heads and cawed support, the deeper realisation of this complicated plot sank in. How could the Great Mother have let me be so blind to this conspiracy? I thought She was guiding me to a better future. Instead, I was foolishly paving the way to allow this betrayal.

'We are the ones with knowledge of the Mes,' I said, frantically thinking of how I could find a way to calm him. 'Without our knowledge, how can Uruk continue as the world's best city? We can teach you.'

I had no intention of doing so, but sought to gain time. I had to find Aea.

He ignored my offer, stopping to look us all up and down. 'Look at you women, worshipping your blood as though it is sacred. You celebrate the blood that shows you have denied a man his child.'

'Does Eve agree her womb is your property?' I asked archly. 'Is her blood unwelcome as an insult to your greatness?' My eye was drawn to the diminutive figure standing in the background. So small was the space she took up, I just noticed her now.

'Eve accepts her place under the Great Father.'

'Eve,' I called. 'What do you say for yourself? Or do you have nothing to say? Does this man speak for you?' She remained silent, as I knew she would. I snorted.

For the first time, I took the chance to turn around, meeting the horrified gaze of Gemekala. Her eyes were blacker than ever against the ghastly white of her face. Blood trickled down her legs, delicate and pure in contrast to the horror outside the ring of Huluppu's embrace. I turned back. *Keep talking.*

'How long have you been planning this?' I looked from Adam to Sabium, preferring to understand the logistics of this betrayal than to focus on the men standing with their knives drawn.

'You forget, woman, we no longer answer to you,' said Sabium, but he continued speaking anyway, desperate as ever for recognition. 'Adam is the brother I never had. Since we met many months ago, we've shared our passion for justice. I helped him take over Uruk through your weakness. I taught him how to use his mind's eye so he could block your mind invasions and receive visions from the Great Father. Adam is the chosen one now, and you bow to us.' His upper lip twitched.

'No one will bow to *you.*'

'Perhaps not, but Adam and Eve will attract the adoration of the people. You will soon be forgotten.'

'Oh Sabium, wake up!' I cried desperately. 'Don't you see? Adam has targeted you, manipulated you to help him do this. Everything he does is calculated. He is not your friend!'

He pursed his lips as he glared at me, narrowed eyes absent of his soul.

Giving up on him, I turned to Adam.

'What do you want? If you wish to slaughter me, proceed, for my body is but one form of my soul. You think I wither because you say so?' I paused as I focused my will for my next statement, upon which so much hung. 'But I trust you will look after Aea, or do you stoop so far as murdering children?' I took a risk challenging him on this. I had to trust the affection he had shown her was genuine.

The dark sky suddenly dimmed several shades.

'I saw your daughter upriver,' said Sabium, voice breathy with excitement. 'She was calling for you. Didn't you hear?'

My blood stopped in my veins.

He walked towards me, holding out something in his hand. 'I have a gift for you, sister. It's something I know you'll value.'

My gaze dropped to the piece of folded linen on his open palm, and I shook my head. A spasm of panic racked me.

'Very well,' he said, whipping the linen in the air so the dark hair it wrapped fell to the ground. 'I suppose a few bits of hair is a poor keepsake for someone's lost childhood.'

A thousand fists choked my solar plexus. My legs began to take me towards the river, feeling as insubstantial as air, and Sabium stepped aside to let me pass. He wanted me to look for her.

'Let her go,' said Sabium to Adam, a quaver in his voice. 'She will not go far.'

I began to run. Eyes down. I didn't want to see the river flowing past in slow motion. Denial begged me in a violent thudding through my ears—I would not believe this was happening. I blinked hard as I ran, smacking my palm to my mind's eye, desperate to discover this was merely a vision, a nightmare I would wake from. I stopped and stared ahead blankly. Fancy was there, on the riverbank, but I refused to focus on the shape at the edge of the water line, the registering of it opening a new vortex of horror within me. I smelled clay on my fingers, my hands over my mouth.

My mind wrestled to enact my trained responses to intense stress and pain. I must disassociate myself and enter a hovering awareness from where I could take control.

I couldn't.

The darkness was pulling at me relentlessly, far bigger than I could make myself. My energetic hands clawed at the edge of the lightless hole, its suction fighting to take me. A new thought came, pushing me into movement. *I can resurrect her. I can take her to the high temple and use every incantation and spiritual tool we have. The Great Mother will not allow her to die.* With this hope, I found the strength to look where she lay on her back, feet in the river's flow, the remaining strands of long dark hair plastered across her white face, the arrowhead amulet still on its string around her neck.

Fancy's eyes lifted to meet mine as she rested her chin on Aea's heart. I found the will to make my legs bend and, in a jerk, I dropped to my knees. A gasping sound came from my mouth, *Oh, oh, oh.*

My hands rubbed over her bruised arms where Sabium had held her under the water. I pulled her into my arms and moaned.

My arms had no strength. I sobbed with the overwhelming effort it was to pick her up, her slippery skin hard to grip, her body denser without the light of her spirit inhabiting it. Staggering, I carried her along the riverbank, mindless of anything but my grief.

Birds broke into a warble that cut through the thick air as I approached the tree, their daily song carrying on without care for the ghastliness before them. Ahead, my priestesses stood on the outside of Huluppu's perimeter, gripping one another in anguish. I counted them. Nine. It took me a few moments to register Tiamat and Anunit were missing. And, of course, Doshina.

Dumbly, I watched as Adam's men dragged the last of the matrons' bodies into the tree's canopy, adding them to the growing pile of dead women lying among the trampled and broken pieces of our pottery.

My eyes drew to Semiramis, watching the scene smugly from the edge of the tree, covered in blood. I knew it was Tiamat's. Anunit must lay among the other shapes beneath the tree, along with Doshina.

Adam held a blazing torch. He looked at me, my arms drooping with exhaustion so Aea's body hung low in front of my hips. His eyes burned with grim resolve as he walked closer to the tree and held the torch to one of Huluppu's branches. The tree's size made him look pathetic, his flame bringing no response from the tree. Eventually, a patch of leaves started to smoke, black and copious, but nothing burst into flames.

Eve stood beside Sabium and Semiramis, the guardians behind them, watching for the tree to become ablaze. Huluppu would not. I was the first to laugh, a mix between a screech and a wail, and soon the priestesses joined me from where they stood, all of us spurting mirthless cackling as the men took more torches to the tree.

'Bring more torches! Smear the trunk with bitumen! And take those women back to the temple!' Adam shouted in a rage, ugliness ravaging his face.

His men surrounded the priestesses and led them away. They did not resist.

No longer laughing, as though my throat closed over, I turned and walked away. But I had no destination, and realising the futility of my efforts, I collapsed to my knees and lay Aea on the riverbank. I could not raise any sound. Fancy pressed herself to my side and whimpered, softly at first, then louder, coaxing an odd noise from my own stiffened throat until I bent to rub my forehead to and fro over Aea's heart, eventually sounding an ululation worthy of my agony. In exquisite sympathy Fancy broke into an anguished howl, lifting my expression of grief into the vast terrain it belonged.

Someone was tapping my shoulder. With effort, I opened my eyes to see Balih hovering over me.

'High Pries...stand up. Please.' I closed my eyes again, resting my cheek on the sand, feeling it cup my cheek, my nose pressed into Aea's arm. 'I'm taking you back to the temple.' He pulled my arm, trying to make me stand, and I held tighter to Aea.

He tried again. 'You must come with me now, or I will have to use force. Please, stand. I will carry, uh...your daughter.'

'You will not!' I shrieked, causing him to cower.

Then I thought of the temple women and children, my city. I began to get to my feet. Lifting Aea made me stumble and Balih caught me. I let him steady me a moment, then began walking towards the concourse,

Fancy at my side. Balih strode to walk in front of me, turning anxiously and reaching out his arms several times to indicate he would carry Aea. I stared straight ahead as my shaking legs took me onwards, my numb arms clasping my daughter against my breast. I would not look back towards Huluppu, needing all my focus to continue forward.

Deafening thunder cracked and lightning flashed almost simultaneously, and fat drops of rain began to smash on my head and run down my naked back. Women and children stood silently at their doors along the concourse watching us pass, mouths agape in horrified confusion. Rising wind shuddered the fronds of the date palms, a wet rustling noise louder than my own panting breath. Several times, I stumbled and my knees buckled beneath me, and I had to let Balih haul me up. I would not let him touch Aea.

At the base of the temple steps, I looked up with my eyes squinted against the pelting rain. How could I make it up those steps with Aea? I took one step at a time, shuddering through my every muscle and bone, considering surrendering to the pull to fall backward. My gaze drew up through the fuzzed greyness to see a figure running down the steps towards me.

Tadez.

'You can't touch her,' Balih said as Tadez pushed past him to embrace me.

'Aea...' I rasped over the noisy splats of rain, meeting Tadez's appalled stare. 'Sabium drowned her.'

'Oh, my lady. Oh no.' Tadez clasped my arm and laid one hand on Aea's back, his face aghast. 'Great Mother, no.'

'Where are the priestesses? Have you seen Humusi? Nanni?' I choked my words, rain running into my mouth.

'I saw the priestesses brought in by the guardians. I did not understand...' Tadez paused, his mouth moving silently in horror. 'He...Adam shouted at me to stay away. I haven't seen Humusi or the other children. Oh my lady, there is a great betrayal afoot.' He stepped from one foot to the other in his anguish. 'Please, let me carry Aea.'

Dumbly, I let him take her heavy form.

'My lady, put your hand through my elbow and I will help you on the steps.' Tadez's eyes implored my cooperation, and I took his arm. We finally reached the vestibule, Balih hovering around us uncertainly.

'You must go to your priestesses now,' Tadez said, waiting until I met his eye, and through my shock I realised he was trying to tell me something. 'I will see you soon,' he added pointedly.

Clasping Aea to his chest, Tadez turned to Fancy, her cream ears plastered flat to her head in the rain, and yelled in a shrill voice, 'Go! Go now!'

The dog cowered, her whimper throwing salt water on my heart's pain, and she cocked her head and looked at me in hurt confusion. 'Go!' This time Tadez's voice boomed, and Fancy's tall chest drooped as she turned and descended the steps. He sought to save her from having her throat slit if she entered the ziggurat, but perhaps she would prefer that than be turned away like this. I had no strength to influence her fate now.

'This way,' said Balih, taking hold of my arm. I flicked it off, but followed him through the vestibule and onto my garden terrace.

Sabium stood alone in the shelter of my verandah, looking out through the grey haze to the city. Black smoke rose from Huluppu, the pouring rain ensuring it was impossible to burn her, for now at least.

'Ah, Lilith,' he said, absurd in his red headcloth, a red kilt around his scrawny hips, watery streaks of women's blood on his feet and legs. 'Do you like our new set-up?'

Clanging came from my chambers as the guardians ransacked them, pieces of my jewellery and cosmetic pots hurtling out into broken piles. The potent sweetness of my perfume lingered in the air, rising from broken flasks.

Tombaya honked wildly, his head dipped in aggression as he darted about on my terrace, turning to swish his long tail feathers one way then another before charging at the nearest guardian.

'You're insane,' I said, turning to stare at Sabium. 'You killed my daughter, part of your own flesh and blood. '

'I could kill her a hundred times over and you would still not know the pain I experienced when I was cast out, nor what you inflict on the boys in the mines and district hovels. She was a spoiled brat, as haughty as you, thinking she would be the next woman to rule the world.'

I walked towards him and sensed his recoil, though he tried to hold his body proud. His hand clenched at the dagger at his waist, and I relished that he feared me.

Standing close to him, I looked down into the drab pallor of his face and hissed, 'There is nothing left of you. How could you lose yourself so completely?'

He gulped. Razing hatred swelled in me, easing the pain.

'My own brother, the one I loved the most. Why couldn't you forgive what happened?' I spat, penetrating him with my eyes. 'But there is no point speaking to you.'

His eyeballs quivered.

'You are not so strong now you stand alone before me.' I shoved his left shoulder with all the force my drained arm could gather, and he tumbled backwards onto the ground. 'You have fallen into darkness. Rot there.'

Scoffing in disgust, I turned away, my eyes falling upon the shining surface of the looking pond beside him. The water showed a horrifying image—a demoness, blood running from her twisted mouth, eyes empty of all but evil as she stared into my own, her malevolent power pulsating in waves through my system. I lurched in shock. *I am not that.*

'Who is it you see?' Sabium asked, as if he knew the darkness I beheld.

I walked past him to the place calling me—the high temple.

Standing between the marble lionesses guarding the high temple's open doors, I let my eyes adjust to the dimness.

Scattered and trampled on the floor were the black obsidian eggs and crystal wands, visioning diadems, other crystals and temple paraphernalia rifled from the storage chests, and I knew—Adam sought the Weird Sphere. It would not be long before he tore the place apart and found it. How would that vessel of knowledge be misused in the hands of men? Priestesses had always claimed men were incapable of accessing the sphere's secrets, but both Sabium and Adam showed some ability with their minds' eyes. Perhaps they could use the sphere for their ill purposes.

Movement drew my eye to the plinth. Adam heaved up and down on top of Eve, kilt bunched up around his waist, his back glistening with the rain that splattered through the star-shaped incision above him. I gaped at this sacrilege, my mind's eye bulging open to show a blur of Adam's red energy swamping the blueness around Eve beneath him. Eve, lying on her back on my white dove feather mantle, made small, breathy sounds as his body landed on hers. My gut roiled and, clasping my belly, I doubled over and threw up, the bitterest, blackest of biles rising in me and imprinting its taste in my mouth.

Adam turned with glazed eyes to note my presence, continuing to pump on top of Eve for a few moments before he let out a grunt and collapsed. He kissed her cheek and murmured something in her ear, casually getting up and adjusting his kilt. She climbed off the plinth, pulling her shift quickly over her body, her shoulders caved in with an effort to shield her breasts and belly from my eyes. A flicker of disdain ran across her face as she squeezed her legs together, then she resumed an inoffensive expression.

'Where is the sphere that shows the weird future?' He demanded of me, an echo carrying his voice in a ghostly wave around the temple.

I looked at him blankly.

'You know I will find it,' he said, cocky. 'But for now, I must address the army. They will be back from the desert and I must tell them the truth.' Eve came to stand behind him. Now it was plain to see they had been together since before I met him. Had he been visiting her tribe of heretics, conspiring with them and Eve for some time? Then the realisation swept through me—the same group of itinerant men had raised them both. Adam and Eve had known each other since childhood.

I spoke to Eve. 'Why do you eat of this foul fruit?'

'It is my fate to be his wife.' Her tone was patient, gentle.

Standing naked and shivering before them, water dripping down my body, I stared at her in disbelief. Where was her dignity, her independence?

'You've lost yourself, woman,' I spat.

'Eve,' said Adam, keeping his sights on me. 'Go down to the public terrace and wait for me there.' She left quickly.

The moment stretched between us, and I wondered if he would try to kill me now. But instead, I saw his eyes mist.

'Lilith...' His voice cracked. 'If you'd let me rule this could have been different. Though of course, you never would.' He looked at me, witnessing the expression on my face that I knew must reflect my tortured heart. 'I did love you, in many moments, but it could never be.'

'If you loved me in any moment, you could never do this,' I said in a strangled sob.

His eyes threatened to spill over, a look of agonised love. 'I had to forsake the love I had for you for the higher good. Helping men rise is of far more importance than any feelings I have for you.'

'I understand you want equality, and I was bringing it forth. I planned to tell you the truth and give you a place beside me, and credit you as an equal in the creation of our child.'

'It's too late,' said Adam. 'You would never have let me rise. It's not in your nature the way it is in Eve's.'

'I don't know why you want a weak woman who can't meet you eye to eye. I offered you a place at my side.'

'Eve is not weak. She's tender. She's soft. She hears what I say and responds. She respects my strength and the guidance I offer.'

'You will never know passion with her.'

'The passion you and I knew was true, but the price is too high. I want a woman who will yield, one I do not have to fight at every turn.'

My head shook slowly. 'You will never be satisfied. You'll always want me.'

'That may be so, but what I want more now is a woman who will let me rise.'

The agony in his eyes was at odds with his compulsion to be with a woman who would lie beneath him. I recalled the message I received from the golden white light the previous day—I am to pass the baton from the era of the feminine on top to the masculine taking his turn. *So be it.*

The knowing in our shared gaze extended far beyond our human characters, and my pain melted away for a fleeting moment. Then the bulls' horns blasted across the city, and he squeezed his eyes shut hard until the sound died. When he looked at me again, the hardness had returned to his stare.

'It's time to address the people,' he said, turning and walking out, and I heard him say to his men lingering outside the temple entrance, 'Bring her down.'

Two guardians took me by the arms and pulled me down several flights of steps and out to the public terrace, the entire population watching from below and sounding a collective gasp as they recognised me. The rain had stopped, the wind stilled and the sky was close and dark. At the end of the concourse, Huluppu continued to send out plumes of black smoke that came to hang low and acrid over the city, but still she would not burn.

With a short burst of relief, I saw the priestesses standing along the side of the terrace, each with her arms pinned behind her back by a guardian. Gemekala watched me as I was brought to stand beside her, her face haggard with horror. In dismay, I saw the priestesses wore brownish, coarse shifts, similar in style to that Eve wore but of inferior fabric. Fresh redness dribbled down their calves to the ground and I took small comfort their blood refused to stop flowing no matter what betrayal these men wrought. My arms were yanked behind my back tightly.

From the other side of the terrace, Sabium and several other guardians sneered at me, staring openly at my breasts and downward pointing triangle, and a strange feeling arose in me such as I'd never felt before. It made me want to turn away from them or put on my priestess shawls, but I shook the feeling off and expanded my aura with what strength I could muster.

Adam walked out of the vestibule, staring straight ahead at the crowd below. He stopped at the front of the terrace, and Eve came to stand behind him, her face down and hands folded demurely in front of her.

'Men of Uruk.' Adam heralded the packed plaza. There was silence. 'All men, step forward and take your place at the front.' He waved them forward. In one of his hands, he clasped a staff of red cedar wood, topped with a fat red jasper stone resembling the end of a man's shaft. He wore a red leather kilt studded in gold and the gold cuffs I'd given him at his wrists.

The crowd murmured in confusion as the message was passed from person to person back through the plaza.

'Men of Uruk, I command you, step to the front. Women, go to the back. Now!' He yelled the order, and among the crowd, the red-clothed heads of some of his guardians could be seen pushing and pulling people to bring the men forward. Despite some shouting from the women, the crowd shifted in compliance.

'Today is a turning point in civilisation as I reveal what has been hidden from you,' he called. 'The temples of Inanna across all lands have been feeding you lies to hold onto the power and riches you should all fairly share, and none so badly as Uruk's own temple.'

Despite the thousands of people in front of us, there was silence across the city. Lightning lit the plaza in a blinding flash, and Adam turned to look at me as the subsequent roll of thunder shook the world, the vibration shuddering through me as I saw he had painted the red upward pointing triangle on his brow.

The people remained silent, baffled by the men being brought to the front and perplexed as to why Adam was addressing them while their High Priestess and her priestesses stood behind him.

'The feminine is not the creator of life—men are!' he boomed. 'The very bones of women are made by men!'

The muttering of thousands of men began, loudest at the front half of the plaza where the army now clumped. The howls of outrage from the women at the back seemed further away than mere distance dictated.

Encouraged, he continued with more gusto, 'A woman's womb is an empty hole, useless without a man's power as wielded with his staff. And her blood is not magical—it is sacrilege. Every month it flows, it bears witness to her disrespect for a man's creative power.'

The city's men talked more loudly, the voices becoming urgent as they conferred on these staggering claims.

He continued. 'Men, you will be anointed with the red triangle this day, heralding the new rule of the Great Father, the true heavenly power.'

One man cheered loudly from the plaza below, setting off a smattering of cheers nearby.

'Betrayers!' shouted another man, echoed by several more. Soon, fists were flying as the division between those who supported Adam and those who objected erupted in violence. The red headcloths of several guardians pushed through the crowd to quieten the row, forcing my loyal men to their knees and holding knives to their throats. Anguished sounds came from my throat, or those of the priestesses beside me, for it was unclear to me in the dreadful chaos. The baying of men, perhaps confused about what to do, was punctuated by the distant yells of the women.

Adam raised his arms again to command silence and boomed with greater fervour. 'Some men are so accustomed to being controlled by women they may find it hard to accept today's sudden revelations, but they will soon wake up. All men breathe freely as of today! I have removed the evil matrons who dealt the hand of feminine abuse. No longer will you be threatened at the purifying pool, nor forced to satiate their laps. Nor will you be ordered around by the council!'

I looked around, already knowing I wouldn't find Semiramis. By now her body would be lying among those piled under the Huluppu tree, perhaps with the other councillors too.

More men cheered, encouraging others, and soon many of the men of Uruk yelled victoriously. Gemekala managed to press her arm against mine, our hands still held behind our backs, and as I turned and met her eyes, I saw the sorrow beneath her outraged horror. We knew these moments birthed a long era of suffering, for us and all womankind.

Adam raised his spread arms to receive the growing adulation, holding the staff high, yelling, 'You will see the councillors of Uruk no more, nor heed their absurd protocols. This day, you throw away your blades and primping oils, and embrace the hair on your face and head as does the mighty lion!'

The men cawed louder at their unexpected freedom and leap in status, their triumph heightened by another flash of light then a vicious crack of thunder that seemed to come from a new force in the sky.

'Women, heed me!' Adam roared, beckoning Eve to his side and holding up her hand as if she were a prize. 'Eve is the woman you will model yourselves on. She is my real wife, promised to only me under the rule of the true divinity, our Great Father. She submits to me and gives her body only to me. She will teach you the sacred way, and we will give you mercy as you adjust, for the Great Father is compassionate about your foolishness.'

He turned to look at me and I shivered, my nipples stiffening anew as water dripped from my hair down my body. Adam eyed them, his mouth twitching.

'Give Lilith the tunic,' said Adam to Eve, nodding his head towards the shapeless shifts the other priestesses wore. He leered at my body, a swirl of lust and repulsion.

'I will not wear it,' I said, standing as tall as I could with my arms painfully twisted behind my back.

A guardian put a tunic in Eve's hands, but she made no move to give it to me. Her head dropped further as she held the garment with a limp grip. She lacked the appearance of defiance, yet she did not obey him.

'Bring her here,' Adam spat at the guardian who held me, and I was yanked to stand before him.

'See how she flaunts her body?' he yelled to the crowd, gesturing at me. 'For far too long, women have used their wiles to overawe men, but no more. From this day, good women will cover their form, and we will choose when we view it.'

He grasped my shoulder and pushed me to my knees, my chin shuddering with helpless rage. I looked up to see the black smoke of Huluppu's protest, her refusal to be destroyed. The murmuring of thousands of people buzzed in my ears, and looking out at the sea of shocked faces, I resolved myself. I must speak against this outrage.

'People of Uruk!' I shouted, pulling on the depths of power I knew were mine. 'I am your High Priestess, hear me now! I offer men equality! I promise you great change as I already decided before this traitor revealed himself—'

Adam struck my cheek, flinging my head to the side with the force, and I was dragged back to the priestesses with a guardian's hand over my mouth, my eyes wide as I met the appalled stares of the priestesses.

'We no longer listen to her!' yelled Adam. 'Hear this! From this day, the truth is lived by all—the masculine rules the Heavens and the feminine belongs on the Earth.'

The crowd was swelling in its outcries for Adam's proclamations, both calls of support and wails of outrage.

'The thirteenth star sign, Ophiuchus, is struck from the zodiac,' he yelled. 'All the temple's symbols of despotism will be destroyed, for the good of all. Bring the staff to me.'

A guardian placed my ebony staff in Adam's hands. He raised it high to show the people before smashing it against the edge of the terrace, the sickening crack of the wood reverberating in my bones as the copper serpent that had twined around it and the carved pine cone atop it broke away and clanged down the ziggurat's front wall.

'This is the new staff of life,' Adam cried, holding the red cedar rod high to the cheering of the men in the crowd and the guardians. 'This is the symbol of a just and Great Father, who honours rationality to see what's true, not the nonsense women claim comes from their feelings.' He flicked his hand at me dismissively.

He looked at Sabium. 'Now, bring me the serpent.'

A new low of dread pumped through my blood as Sabium came forward, holding a wriggling sack. Adam reached in and pulled Yasmin out, holding her head high as her length twisted and writhed in panic. He squeezed her throat, his fingers just meeting. With incredulous horror, I watched as her jaw opened with the force of his grip, her tongue waving.

'No!' I screamed, my feet scrambling on the slippery mud bricks beneath them, my strength unsteadying my captor's feet, but I was no match for him.

A clicking noise came from Yasmin's gaping mouth, her bones breaking, jaw dislocating. Her eyes bulged until they popped out grotesquely on their stalks. Sobbing, my legs crumpled beneath me, the man at my back holding me up with pinching grips on my arms.

There was cheering from some men and a faint wailing from the women, weakened in the dreadful display taking place before me.

Adam held Yasmin's broken form up for viewing and bellowed, 'The snake no longer resides in the skies, but on the ground, along with the women she represents.' He flung her body off the terrace to the plaza below.

'Now hear me!' he cried. 'Uruk has the first and best army on the Great Father's Earth, men of courage and strength.'

He paused, raising his arms again to encourage the self-congratulatory cheering of the men.

'We have two thousand trained men, ready to restore order and truth to the land of the two rivers and beyond. There are no so-called heretics but us! We are the heroes of the new age and we will take what is ours!'

A burst of colour took my eye to Huluppu, where orange flames appeared in patches. For every moment I felt the pinnacle of destruction was upon me, another rose. The betrayal knew no bounds, no bounds.

Back on our terrace, the priestesses and I stood along the balustrade, Adam, Eve and Sabium facing us, the guardians behind them.

'Women, are you willing to teach us the Mes?' asked Adam. 'If so, you may live in the communal copper district house under the guard of my men, so long as you do not speak of the Great Mother or her ways again. If not, you and your daughters die this day.'

He strode back and forth in front of us.

'Lilith,' he said, stopping in front of me. 'What is your choice?'

'I am beholden unto no man.' I met his eye, my clarity complete.

Lahamu spoke next. 'I would rather die, and my daughter too.'

Sabium sighed theatrically, stepping closer to Adam and looking up at him. 'I fear these stubborn women will cause more trouble than they're worth. Remember, I know something of the Mes, and will teach you all I can,' he said eagerly.

Urnina leaned forward from the line of women, her anguished stare bringing my focus upon her. *I must look after the children*, I heard her silent cry. I nodded imperceptibly and she stepped forward.

'I will help teach the Mes, so long as all the temple children are kept with me,' said Urnina, her words hoarse and stilted. She turned to embrace me, whispering in my ear, 'I love you forever.'

Adam pulled her from my arms and pushed her into place behind Sabium, then turned to look expectantly at the other priestesses. A long moment passed.

Ku-Aya took a step towards Sabium, tilting her head in an effort to be charming. 'If my daughter and I are cared for, I will be your wife, as Eve is Adam's. I will teach you more of the Mes, and no longer follow the hem of Lilith's shawls.' She tried to look meek.

Sabium looked her up and down and, after a pause, lifted his chin in joyless acceptance. When Ku-Aya took her position behind him, gazing downwards, I felt sorry for her, for we had seen the same prophesied future. She knew as well as I that many women would have to give themselves away in this manner to protect themselves and their children, and she had begun that path already, presumably finding that preferable to a long, slow subjugation.

Gemekala and I shared a look, exchanging an ocean of grief. She stepped forward to address him. 'Sabium. I am also happy to serve under you as a herbalist and adept in the sexual arts.' My mouth gaped to see her walk towards him with undulating hips, her aura shrunk and shoulders stooped as she used the reverse of the mesmerism to make herself seem small enough to be with a man of his stature.

'I will try you out,' he spluttered in an attempt at bravado, but I heard the fluster in his voice. He clearly had little experience with women from the way he gawked clumsily at her, shuffling from one foot to the other. Unlike Ku-Aya, I knew Gemekala could never be serious about her offer, and I dreaded what she would do as she tipped her face low into his neck as if to whisper in his ear. Suddenly, she wrenched his dagger from his belt.

'No!' I screamed at her, but it was too late. She jabbed the dagger in a lightning-fast movement to navigate between his ribs, finding an entry point and plunging it into his heart. A dreadful squeal emerged from his lips, his face animated with shock. Instinctively, I wailed at seeing my twin collapse, despite what he had done, my pain compounded by Gemekala's foolish belief that this act would somehow benefit us.

A guardian stepped forward to grab the base of Gemekala's long braid in his fist. In one swift movement, he yanked her neck back and slid his knife across her throat. Her eyes rolled to meet mine with a gleam, a victorious gurgle erupting from her mouth as she stumbled a few steps towards me and fell to the ground.

A noise, high-pitched and awful, rose in my ears, and I realised it came from my throat. I dropped to my knees beside Gemekala, her throat open like a wide mouth spitting throbs of blood. I took her still pristine hand and clasped it to my breast. My head flung from side to side in disbelief, looking at Sabium on his back, squinting at me in agony, then to Gemekala, her eyes drooping as her life-force left her. Within me, vast anguish and futility wrestled with the love I had for them both, no matter what they did. I felt Gemekala's spirit around me, breaking my heart wide open and gusting her light through it, lifting me.

Hold onto yourself, she whispered through my being.

Dully aware of Urnina's screams as she leaned over Gemekala's body, I looked up to see Lahamu step onto the bench and atop the balustrade, removing her tunic in one swift movement. She turned to look at me and the priestesses with wild defiance, spread her arms wide and leapt from the great height, bellowing a triumphant cry. I looked around in spinning confusion from one scene of horror to another, meeting Sabium's eyes one last time. A moment of pure intimacy passed between us as I saw the remaining life go out of him.

I was unable to take any more. I desired to finish this life, to join my lost ones in the otherworlds. I locked my gaze on the man who had slit Gemekala's throat, the knife held at his side, barely bloodied from the swiftness of its contact with her flesh. I stood, my calves warm with blood, and tried to take a step towards him. My slimy feet would not move. When I opened my mouth to scream at him, to invite his blade to my throat, I could make no sound. *You must carry on.* Was it Gemekala or Menna I heard?

'She will not yield,' said Adam, his voice flat as he looked at me. 'We will need to make a show of her death. The city needs to see her reign is finished, and what happens to women who will not submit.'

Eve's hand touched Adam's forearm as her face tipped up to him, her voice quiet but every word crisp to my ears. 'My husband, Uruk wants to see more of you, not her.'

I met Eve's eyes and bile rose as I heard how her words placated him while still she tried to orchestrate what she wanted. She sought to gain me reprieve, if only temporary, from the deathblow of the new male order. For all her weakness, Eve was not cruel, and I sensed she wanted mercy for me.

Adam frowned, pondering my fate as if he owned it, then waved his hand. 'She does not deserve the attention of the city any more this day. She cannot escape.'

As my gaze penetrated his eyes, there was something more. I saw his true essence, a flash of it as I had seen in our deepest intimacies and in his recent moments of sanity in the high temple. A glimpsing, within, of Adam and I embracing in another time and place, bathed in light.

A lull came upon the moment, as if a blanket of stillness fell over us, and instinctively I backed away a few steps. When I turned and walked out through the servants' entrance, nobody spoke a word or raised a hand to stop me, as if an unknown force allowed my departure.

Inside the door, Tadez stood in the shadows where he'd been watching everything. Tears slid down his cheeks as he threw a shawl around my shuddering shoulders. He bent to lift Aea's body from where she lay beside him, and I took her from him and hugged her tight. I followed him mindlessly down the stairs, heedless of the cries of my trembling arms and legs and refusing his offers to carry her. He took a torch from a wall to guide us through the lesser used passageways and we went deeper into the ziggurat's belly.

'Lady, listen.' He stopped and turned to me. 'Adam let you walk off the terrace, as if a divine grace was brought upon the moment, but he will soon look for you. I once heard you say there's a tunnel down here somewhere, leading to the herb garden. How do we access it? I've sent a boy with a convoy sled and an ox to await us.'

Wordlessly, I led the way down more stairs and passed through gloomy passages, beyond the bakeries and brewery, past the storerooms and coffers, finally stopping in front of a blank wall that hid the secret entrance to the initiation chamber. I passed Aea to him and found the lever that allowed a block of stone to swing back, so well designed that my weakened arms succeeded in pushing it open. We entered the large chamber holding the initiation sepulchre, dimly visible in the light of the torch Tadez carried, and swung the block closed behind us.

Soon after I was initiated, Menna told me of the secret tunnel, dug as an emergency exit by our temple foremothers. It had always struck me as strange, since they faced no threats. On a whim, Gemekala and I came down here once to crawl through the tunnel to the herb gardens. The journey had been long, dark and frightening, and we had never wanted to repeat it.

I opened the lid of a wooden chest and threw out its contents, tossing linen cloths and a black cowhide at Tadez's feet to wrap Aea's body. Shoving the chest to the side, I uncovered the loose bricks covering the tunnel's opening. Tearing strips from the linen, I wrapped them around my knees and hands, my cuts and grazes still fresh from the copper mines, gesturing at Tadez to do the same. He insisted on dragging Aea, and I helped tie the linen cloths to the cowhide and then to his ankles. Tadez entered the tunnel first, and I watched the black bundle holding Aea's body move in jerks until it disappeared.

Then I too crawled into the dark.

CHAPTER 16

As the sun lowered against the clearing sky, we prepared to bury Aea's linen-shrouded body near the grotto's beach, next to an ancient cedar tree surrounded by pale pink primulas. She still wore the obsidian arrowhead about her neck and I reached to lay my hand upon its form. Silently, in honour of my love for Aea, I gathered all my will to pledge to her, 'I will hold to our vision of a fair world, and love you through the ages until the arrow hits its mark.'

Waves of energy ran through me at the enormity of what lay ahead, of how the soul of my darling daughter, the souls of all my loved ones, of all humanity, would suffer through aeons until we might find unity. My stunned heart wavered, threatening to unleash something that might annihilate me when it broke. I kept it down, managing to sound a final whisper to my daughter. 'Goodbye, my precious white bird.'

Tadez and Udul-Kalama covered her with soil, both sobbing raggedly. I lay on top of the grave, and the men put rugs on me and lit a fire nearby, leaving me alone at my whispered request.

Late in the sleepless night, I heard Teba whining, and someone coming down the slope, followed by low voices. Shortly after, the cold wetness of Fancy's nose touched my cheek, and a familiar woody scent filled my senses as strong arms embraced me. Demsar. He cradled my head to his chest, and although I'd never been in such intimate contact with him, I let him hold me. Menna's spirit ran through him, and I felt her in his heart's silent wails.

Eventually, sound came from my throat, and Demsar and I joined in wild waves of crying, the dog pressing close in concern and licking my tears.

Later, Demsar stood to put more wood on the fire then returned to sit beside me, his hand on my back as terrorising visions pinged through me. I buried my face in Fancy's soft fur in an effort to dull the scenes, but smelling the geranium scent dabbed there by Aea tore at me beyond measure.

Knowing I could not sleep nor speak, Demsar pulled me to a sitting position, giving me sips of water and pushing tiny pieces of barley bread into my mouth.

'I brought you the Weird Sphere,' he said finally in a rasping voice, the sound strange after our speechless communion. 'Menna told me where it was hidden as you left for the mines, telling me to bring it to you if something happened. I couldn't shake my foreboding, and all through the army exercise I felt something terrible stirring. I rushed home as soon as I could but she wasn't there, and I hoped it was simply that you had not yet returned. Then the city was in chaos and I saw you on the terrace, pushed to your knees by Adam. I still didn't know where Menna was, just that I had to enact her request.' He paused, and a sob erupted from deep in his throat.

I stared dumbly at him.

'Late last night, I got past the two drunken men guarding the high temple where the priestesses are being held,' he continued in a voice shaking with grief. 'Priestess Urnina helped me find the sphere, and said she sensed I would find you here. Then she told me…about Menna.'

After squeezing his eyes shut a few moments as he gathered strength, he went on to tell me how he'd then taken Menna's bow and quiver, travelling shawls and other supplies for me, and slipped out of the city. Fancy had appeared at his heels as he'd navigated the backstreets. He told me he must leave the grotto before sunrise to arrive back in the city before anyone dangerous noticed his absence. It would be easy as most the city's men would be snoring well into the morning following their celebration of the coup, for which Adam had opened the ziggurat breweries.

He took a linen bundle from the sack beside him, unwrapping it to reveal the Weird Sphere. When he placed it in my limp hands, the roundness as cold and smooth as ever, immediately its power throbbed through my palms and into my being. A tiny relief arose that it was not in the hands of Adam, although, what harm could he wreak with it now? The fate promised in the Weird Sphere had begun unfolding already at his hands, my hopes for a more balanced future ruined.

My hands spanning the sphere, I closed my eyes and let it amplify my connection to the otherworlds. Silently I called, *Help me. Why has this happened?* Instantly, love enveloped me, the familiar golden white energy rising to soothe the deep tremble in my core. I lifted higher and higher until I popped past all turbulence and into pure peace.

Without words, the golden white light communicated with me.

Beyond what you see now, your great soul sees the perfection.

You are part of turning the cosmic seasons towards all people living in unity, but much is asked of you. Before the unity can arise, six thousand years shall pass when the masculine takes his turn on top.

As the separating and reuniting of the feminine and masculine occurs, the universe writhes in ecstatic creation. This feels an insufferably long time to a human perspective, but is a blink in the cycles of creation.

The souls of Sabium and Adam agreed to take on many dark veils to do what they must to help shift this cycle. Born from love, they bear the agony it takes to enact the so-called betrayal upon you. This plan requires great sacrifice from each of you, the purpose to agitate you to remember what you have forgotten or not yet realised about your true unified nature, in service of all humanity. The risk is you play the game so deeply, you forget the truth of who you are, causing you to become lost for many lifetimes, making the experience far denser than it need be.

The seed of your destiny is to help bring unity to humanity, but that seed must lie underground, unseen and denied before it sprouts. Although the world will forget your greatness for a long time, you need not. You felt the truth that the feminine and masculine are one. This realisation was offered in compassion to help you hold onto higher truth through your difficult journey.

Lilith, you are more than your mind could possibly recognise.

When I opened my eyes in the pre-dawn dimness, I was thoughtless for a few moments, feeling the peace of truth. But slowly, like a seeping stain, a density spread from one sense to another, quickening as I remembered my reality. The pain conjured in its path opened ever-new ripples of horror, and the connection with the golden white light faded to wisps.

'Did you find guidance?' Demsar sat among the flowers in the grey light.

'Yes. I am helping turn a great cycle to a time when men put women beneath them.' My voice broke.

'In their hearts, men will yearn for you to stand by their sides. They will miss you so in their deepest soul, as you have missed we men.' His eyes held mine, pouring strength into me. We sat in silence for a while, then Demsar gathered his things. Sunrise was approaching.

Tadez and Udul-Kalama came to sit with me, one on either side.

'High Priestess,' said Tadez. 'Adam will look for you. We can all hide in the caves when they come, Udul-Kalama knows his way around. There are escape routes that take us a little back from the grotto at ground level. They will never find us.'

'No. I must warn High Priestess Daggartum in Ur. All the other temples across the lands, they must be warned. We can gather forces and fight back.' My words were weak with futility.

'You can't travel to any of the cities or bigger settlements,' said Demsar. 'I heard Adam is asking the refugees you turned away to look for you, and they are spreading across the land of the two rivers. He's promised them if you're caught, he will reward them and welcome them into Uruk. They will soon come here looking for you. You must hide.'

'I will not hide. Nor will I endanger Tadez and Udul-Kalama by staying. Yes, Adam will expect me to be here,' I said, thinking aloud. 'Or he'll think I've gone north along the river or south to Ur. So I must go the other way. I'm going west, to the Red Sea.'

Tadez's face streamed with tears. 'But lady... that's more than a full moon's turn across the desert, perhaps two, and that's if you can cross the Euphrates first. I will take you and help find a place you can settle.'

'I'm going alone. That's how it must be.' The finality in my voice frightened me. 'You and Udul-Kalama will stay safe until you can escape and start a new life together.' Love for Tadez swelled my raw heart. I could not endure the thought of never seeing him again, but I must go forward alone. That I carried a child hovered in my awareness but I pushed it away, unable to think of it now.

Demsar came to kneel before me, the three men in a triangular formation around me.

'My place is in Uruk,' Demsar said, taking my hands in his. 'I will look out for the priestesses and novices as best I can, and the children. I will ask Priestess Urnina what they need and find a way to get it to them. She's already asked me to help Dax, and I will find a way to take him from the temple to live with Star and me.'

I dipped my head in gratitude. 'Tell them I love them. That I'm sorry.'

He held my hands more firmly. 'Go to the Red Sea and find a village where you can keep the truth of the Great Mother alive. Many others will do the same, if only in secret.'

'It seems in this new era, the Great Mother will be pushed aside,' I said in a quaver.

'I will not give up who I am and what I know, even if I must pretend it to protect Menna's sons.' His tone was bold but I heard the naivety.

'If you pretend to be less than you are, eventually you may become convinced it is true,' I said with all the passion I could muster. 'And know they are your sons also.'

Reaching into his kilt pocket, he drew out a small pouch. 'Take this with you. It's some of the sacred green guide, grown by Menna in our courtyard. She prayed over it every day. It might help when you most need guidance.'

I enclosed his outstretched hand for a long moment, a connection filled with Menna's essence flowing between us.

When he reached the top of the grotto cliff, he turned to me, the beginnings of sunrise behind him. His lower lip trembled as he tried to smile, his hands lifting to form the downward pointing triangle over his heart to honour me, and I returned the gesture.

As he turned and disappeared, the ibex buck I'd seen on my honeymoon stepped into view at the top of the cliff, his two massive horns curving up against the brightening sky. Reverently, the great beast dipped his head to me, then backed away, until he too was gone.

As the sun climbed higher in the sky, all trace of storm clouds gone, Tadez and Fancy escorted me to the grotto's clifftop to bid me farewell.

'Thank you for all you are,' I whispered, embracing Tadez tightly.

He pulled back to hold my shoulders, his eyes swimming with tenderness. 'I love you forever, High Priestess Lilith, and I will see you again, in this life or another.'

My heart found another depth to crack to as we embraced a final time.

I knelt to farewell Fancy, her gaze transmitting purest love, and I pressed my brow to hers as my hands cupped her feathery ears. Then I stood, slapped the ox's flank, and walked away without looking back, my soul shrivelling with every step taking me from them.

I walked west, wearing Menna's orange shawls, her bow slung over my shoulder, the ox pulling the utilitarian sled tightly packed with supplies. Once I crossed the Euphrates, my survival would rely on crossing the path of the wadis used by Uruk runners or merchants on missions to Egypt, and I prayed they would still carry water.

On my first night, I drew a big eight-pointed star of Venus on the ground and rested within it, clutching my nocked bow. Hyenas screeched and chuckled in the distance but none came near. The deep shuddering in my core would not abate, nor let me sleep beyond fitful grabs.

The next morning, I reached the Euphrates. I drove the ox upriver until the sun hit the mid-sky, waiting for the banks to widen as Udul-Kalama told me they would. Gradually, the river broadened and looked shallow enough to attempt a crossing.

Accustomed to passing through the Tigris River on her way to the copper mines, the ox strode into the water without pause, and I quickly pulled off my shawls to follow her. The sled began to float as she progressed, and I steadied it from behind, grateful for Tadez's meticulous securing of the supplies.

Wading in the waist-height waters and wrestling with the sled was a tremendous effort. I prayed we would not be swept away. At the quarter point of the crossing, the water was already at my chin, the ox's white head tipped up as she swam, emitting sharp bursts of air with the effort.

I fought to keep the sled steady, kicking my legs or scrambling to touch my toes to the bottom in hopes the waters were shallowing. When the riverbed was untouchable, I kicked with all my strength, angling my body to push the sled upriver against the pull of the current. Relief seeped through my trembling muscles as the depth receded. When I collapsed on the far bank, the ox turned to look at me patiently.

I lay panting for some time, the baby magnifying my fatigue. How could I continue to grow a child on my wretched journey through the desert? If I managed to hold the pregnancy and find people to take me in, I prayed Aea's soul would be part of the baby, giving me enough to love that I could forget Adam's part. It gave me something to hope for.

Drinking my fill and topping up my water bags, the ox and I set off as the afternoon deepened. We headed into the desert, continuing through days and nights, leaving the fertile land close to the river further behind us with each step as the dryness took all signs of green life away.

Sometimes I tried to rest on the sled, awkwardly perched on top of the supplies, although I felt for the ox, who pulled the weight along in jerky movements, her once glossy black nose now dry and matte. I sensed she did not lament the thirst and hunger, continuing forward with epic strength and endurance. Sometimes she stopped and insisted on being given precious water, or dipped her head looking for grass that did not grow on the dusty desert plains, and I would offer some of the dwindling supplies.

On the cold, wind-stirred desert nights, I lay beside her and rested a hand on her flank, taking comfort from her solid warmth and dusty scent. Sleep did not come to me, my senses too ragged. Visions of Aea in her joy morphed into her dead body lying on the ground. Scenes of blood and women's bodies ran across my mind's eye, or the black bitter smoke of Huluppu, or Adam on top of Eve in the high temple.

Using the stars, I steered the ox south west, towards the Red Sea.

We walked endlessly on the burning sand, following the rise and fall of the desert floor, the water rations more dire with each passing day. My blood moved sluggishly through my veins, thickened by thirst. If we didn't find water soon, death would be a few days away. Thirst was a powerful foe, torturing with its desperate need, but it served as a salvation, taking my mind from worse torments.

Sometimes, I felt I hovered above myself, strangely carefree and beyond thirst. I laughed with Aea, who was right there with me. Or with Gemekala, when she replayed her death gurgle and laughed at how she enjoys dramatic life departures. Doshina and Delondra showed me flashes of their next lifetime, and how Doshina will be a burly male warrior and Delondra a delicate serving girl. Tiamat said Anba is her true love and they agreed to this lifetime as their contribution to the turning of the ages.

Adam. I had no thoughts for him yet, preferring thirst.

Sabium. The notion of him hinted at an explosive pocket of grief I keep quashed. It was not a sharp pain, but far worse, the feeling so vastly empty, I'd take it as a pinpoint any day to know what I was dealing with.

I held as best I could to Menna's dying words, and the message the golden white light gave me. But with every day, my hold grew weaker.

The ox was to thank for bringing us to water. She insisted on heading towards some gently sloping hills that took us off our trajectory. She jerked her head to the left and showed me the whites of her eyes as she rolled them in that direction, snorting heavily. The ground became rockier and the ox's hooves clinked and clacked as the sled shuddered over the bumps. Eventually, we neared the base of the hills.

A sea of dazzling yellow emerged, revealing itself as a mass of sunflowers, thrilling to my senses after the endless vistas of sand and rock. And this time, when I saw shimmering light, it was not one of the mirages that had tormented me, but a wadi meandering between the flowers at the base of the hills.

The ox and I drank in a frenzy, my fears and pains gone in the blissful moments of wetness on my throat. I stripped off my sweat-crusted linens and rolled in the ankle-deep water. I splashed the ox and rubbed my hands over her, a small rightness rising in my heart when her nose was black and shiny again. She ate green grass while I caught locusts as Udul-Kalama had instructed me, roasting them by the small fire I lit with a flint. I cried as I ate them, their deliciousness somehow tragic.

We lay in the shade of shrubs, and I kissed the ox's forehead, telling her, *We might stay here a while.* My tears flowed once more now I had water to drink, and endlessly they fell as untold pain pulsed through me with my heart's every beat. Days passed, my time spent picking sunflower seeds and catching prey, laying fast-burning fires with the scant fuel I could find, and scouring my sleeping area for scorpions, crushing them viciously.

The full moon came and faded back into the sliver of a new moon. I sat still for long periods, surveying the area for creatures to shoot with my bow. During the month I stayed at the wadi, I took several desert hares, barely cooking them in my haste to devour the meat. My pregnancy continued, and I did not know if I welcomed the tiny spark of life.

One evening, I stared at the stars, despair pulling me down in a heavy spiral, sucking and clawing me in. *I know who I am*, I repeated, a feeble proclamation as fear and doubt swamped me. I was not so sure who I was, removed from my glory as ruler of the world's greatest city, stripped of my loved ones, wearing rags and eating insects.

I found the pouch of the sacred green guide, burning several buds in a bowl with my shawl over my head to inhale its smoke through my mouth. I let the mellowing effects stroke my ravaged energy and help me escape the pulsing of my mind. Taking the Weird Sphere from one of my sacks, I began invoking the 13 secret names of the Great Mother, used only in the most powerful and secret of all invocations. I swayed in a comforting rock for timeless moments, repeating the names over and over, calling for guidance.

Light splayed me open to the endless black sky so peace could pierce my every sense, and the golden white light rose within me. She spoke.

Birth requires intense disruption, and a new era for humanity is being born. Can you allow the illusion of separation as the masculine has his time on top, while holding to your true self? Will you dance with creation in this way?

Even in my expanded state, I could not agree. *I am not that.* I knew to the core of my soul that I could not support the illusion of men being above women. I felt Her complete acceptance of my choice.

Very well, beloved Lilith. But know your destiny was chosen by you. You agreed to step aside to allow the masculine to rise, no matter how your human self cannot believe it. Your commitment to equality is what was needed to disrupt the cyclic energy and allow the new era its foothold. You have played your role perfectly. Let me show you the big picture.

Instinctively, my eyes opened and in the scarce light of the fire burning beside me, I stared into the Weird Sphere, falling into its glossy depths. The deeper I fell, the further my awareness streamed outwards, until I was filled with simultaneous awareness of all life.

I felt the cycles of evolution turning as the stars and planets rotated their way around the centre of the galaxy in perfectly timed exactitude, moving Earth from times of light as we aligned with the galaxy's heart, then plunging us into darkness as we turned away.

Through impressions and flashes, I saw a beautiful civilisation that existed thousands of springs ago, during an era when the Earth was aligned with the galactic heart. The elegant people were united and peaceful yet they were inexperienced, never having gained the wisdom that comes of living through adversity. They were technologically advanced, far more so than the people of Uruk, and used the immense power of the Earth's crystalline structure to run their civilisation. When the planets and stars inevitably turned from the light, that civilisation fell into greed and ignorance. Its great cities sank under massive seas caused by their foolery with the Earth's gravitational field. They were trying to shift planetary movements to avoid the future they saw coming—a fall into separation, and the vast pain that would cause them and future generations for many thousands of years. I knew I was part of that foolish attempt to change the galactic cycle, and that those most important to me in my current life were somehow involved too.

Following the demise of that ancient civilisation, the inevitable era of separation began with the rise of feminine energy. I saw how the dense consciousness caused women to repress men, to diminish their masculine energy by depriving them of purpose and the ability to take focused action, to dismiss them as simple, without creative ability, wisdom or universal connection. This era I now completed. The level of imbalance was of the same magnitude as that which would occur in the forthcoming era of masculine emphasis, as the energy must swing equally both ways. My naïve hope that I could have forged a more balanced future would never have come to pass.

I saw that within the feminine was the masculine and vice versa, no matter the era, and the effects went far beyond the relationship between men and women. When we believed ourselves separate, greed and fear held great sway, though always our eternal light was present, even if just a dim spark within the cruellest or most fearful of people. The shadow in women expressed masculine energies of violence and control, and the shadow in men expressed feminine energies of manipulation, secrecy and neglect. And in their best expressions, women were strong and focused directors, and men were sensitive and nurturing. I saw we are each in all of it.

In the coming six thousand years from now, a blink in the ongoing cycles of evolution, the masculine would sit higher than the feminine. I saw the best expressions, where a woman held to her essence within the limits of the masculine-dominated era, but that relatively few would experience this. Intuitive feminine wisdom, creativity and sensitivity would be dismissed, causing a shrivelling of the pineal eye. This contempt would be expressed in myriad blatant and insidious ways through language, laws, education and culture which would seem to advantage the masculine, but it would suffer as much as the feminine.

In the worst expressions, I saw men, or masculine-ruled structures, controlling anyone or thing that could be overpowered. The Earth would be seen as feminine and Heaven as masculine, and disrespect to the feminine would be expressed in how men sought to tame the planet into never-ending productivity, whipping people and the land mercilessly to produce without rest, opening great gashes in the Earth and pocketing the profits as if it all belonged to them, feeding off each other in fear of lack. The most domineering peoples would increasingly seek to control others, so those who did not look like them, carry their skin colour or follow their beliefs would be segregated, subjugated and persecuted.

As I visioned, I was held by an immense hand from which all seemed lighthearted. Like a cell dividing into two whole parts then dividing again, creation continually blossomed through the interplay of the two forces.

I knew that after the era of masculine domination was complete, starting six thousand years from my life as Lilith, the red and blue flames within each willing soul would reunite as the Earth faced the light of the galactic heart once more. Many souls of that era would be wisened in their unity, having gone to the depths of the underworld to know themselves in every facet, and peace would reign on Earth. Those unripe to enter the unified era would continue on another cycle of separation, for there were cycles within cycles, and each soul was graced to take its own journey without judgement, just as no one condemns a babe for not walking before time.

This great cycle was like a gigantic out-breath and in-breath, flourishing creation. I knew as humanity evolved, it would not invoke such extremes and the accompanying suffering.

But my truth remained—I could not pretend to be less than the masculine.

The golden white light spoke again. *So be it. Remember what you have seen, and most of all, remember who you are in your greatness. It is possible for you to experience the illusion of separation without losing yourself within it. Your challenges push you to the edge of your endurance. But if you fall, you will rise again, stronger than before.*

I assured Her, *I will not lose myself.*

The next morning I got to my feet, faith buoyed. How could I have outrun the weird future? The masculine was to have his turn on top, and my quest for equality was ahead of its time. I had misunderstood my role in the great cycles of change, thinking I would remain at the centre with the ability, even the responsibility, to change the fated path.

The truth was that Adam and Sabium had taken that central role, and I was relegated. I must accept fate and take comfort that there was nothing I could have done to change its course.

There was less and less to eat, and the wadi would soon dry up. We must keep moving. The Red Sea was calling me on with the hope I could find a settlement along the coast and birth my baby. I discussed it with the sweet ox, and her liquid eyes urged me to keep going after one more night of rest.

We headed out at sunrise and soon the searing sun burned my lungs with each breath and roasted my skin. I resented each trickle of sweat that ran down my face, my back, willing my body to stop wasting water.

In early pregnancy, my body was doubly ravaged by the desert. Dread flashed through me. *How can I love this baby?* What if this child was nothing but a cruel reminder of Adam's betrayal? My thoughts tormented me. *I know who I am,* I repeated to myself, keeping my mind on the visions the golden white light had shown me.

Days later, our water was almost gone. Dying of thirst now seemed worse than any fate. Two days later, still we walked, no water or food, no sign of the sea.

The ox stopped. She looked at me, and dropped to her knees. I shook our remaining dribbles of water into her dish, but she refused it. She made a grunt, the best her dry throat could conjure. She was saying goodbye, unable to endure any more.

Go on, she said, and moved her once powerful neck back to offer her throat to me. Her chest rose and fell with her rasped breaths, nostrils flaring limply. My cracked lips could not pucker to kiss her, but I put them to her head with a tenderness unfound within me until that moment. When I took out my knife and looked questioningly into her eyes, I fell into them. I sensed she could see higher truth perfectly, and I wished I could see what she did, for her gaze showed pure love. Like the Akitu bull, I knew she also felt sorrowful for me, without condescension, as if she knew that accepting the veils that fell over a person's eyes when entering the earthly realms entailed great sacrifice, keeping us from seeing the truth she was incapable of doubting.

When I sliced her throat and drank her thick blood, she gave me her life-force with the grace of a mother's breast. With this strength, I sobbed tearlessly a while, then the flies and smell of her sun-baking body pushed me to walk onwards. Leaving the sled beside her, I carried a sack with the Weird Sphere, my spare shawls, a knife, flint, a cup and bowl, two empty water bags and the bow and quiver.

As the sun intensified, a new feeling started to pull me apart. When my ox lived, she could see me, interact with me. With her, I existed, with a sense of who I was in contrast with another being. A massive terror swamped me. My ox was gone, everyone and everything was gone and I was alone, as if I'd vanished into the swirling emptiness, the end of the world and far beyond in magnitude.

But worse, I could not escape through death. My predicament was direr, with my inescapable awareness for what was to come far beyond this lifetime. The guidance I'd received, once offering me hope, now confirmed a sentence of suffering for aeons, for me and all people.

Or was I mad? I didn't know which was worse—to be madly confused about reality, or that the vicious turning of the cycles was real, and I had helped bring it about at the urging of the Great Mother. If that was true, She was surely a cruel force masquerading as love. Fear froze me. I clawed for something to hold onto. What is it I know to say, to pray for?

I thought of Sabium, of the way he had lost himself to his pain and bitterness, how the light had extinguished in his eyes. How he had let his pain destroy him to the extent he could kill a little girl, part of his own flesh and blood, with his bare hands. Was I imagining it? I heard Sabium's voice in my mind now. *Lilith, I showed you what happened when I lost myself to anger and pain... Do not lose yourself now.*

I seized at this message, calling to my brother for help, but I could not reconnect with him. I began a silent chant—*I know who I am, I know who I am.* All day, I repeated it in line with my plodding steps.

That night was wholly sleepless. I watched the stars spin, occasionally feeling expansive peace, but when I grabbed at it greedily, I was plunged back into my deplorable reality. Confusion made my mind swim—was this happening during my initiation in the sepulchre? Was this an initiation test I could pass, would I realise it was not real? The mastery of fear I thought I had achieved in the sepulchre was unreachable now, my losses too great and my body and mind too weak to rise above the inescapable horror. *I know who I am, I know who I am.*

I was desperate to sleep and never wake, to escape my hell, but I could not. Instead, nightmarish states tormented me with many scenarios, all of them putting me in different times and bodies, this time without the hand of the Great Mother to hold me. I was on my own. I was a baby girl, shivering wildly then feebly on the ground, watched through a window by my distraught mother and merciless father who hoped I'd be dead by morning and there'd be one less worthless mouth to feed.

I saw nuances on the theme of me as a woman, festering in shame and rage as men scowled or leered at me, called me a whore, a witch, crazy, or charmed me with scraps of love and then used me. Baby after baby came from my wretched womb, and I knew the pain of losing them, of wanting them when they wouldn't come, of not loving them when they did, of loving them so much my heart split, of dying in agony trying to birth them. In some far future lifetime, men in white garments tried to force me to give birth supine, and I screamed with all labour's power, 'I won't fucking lie on my back!'

In another vision, I swept a dark hallway, a man trampling dirt on it again each time I finished, and I justified my enslavement to the part of me that watched, 'It's just something he likes to do.' Then I picked up my broom to begin again.

You ask me to see the perfection?

CHAPTER 17

It was a relief to hate Adam.

Rage enlivened me to push one foot in front of the other, burning sand streaming into my disintegrating sandals, tied with linen strips to my feet. Each time I crested a hill, my hope was swallowed by the vastness of the terrain, another sea of dust and scrub shimmering in waves of heat. Relentlessly, I continued to apply my training in ignoring physical torment, using it to keep going despite my miserable future prospects.

I came upon a small pool in a shallow valley, just in time to survive. It was the remnant of a wadi that no longer flowed, as spring deepened into summer. A number of days passed, with me drinking the warm, stagnant water and eating whatever I could find—dates fallen to the ground, frogs and crickets I barely cooked on scanty fires.

I still refused to connect with the baby spawned by the bitter milk of Adam. He was as responsible as Sabium for Aea's murder. It felt disloyal to Aea to nurture the life so connected to the destruction of her own. I did not expect this baby to live, yet I felt it flutter when I drank, clinging to life greedily. I refused to offer any response.

Futility pumped through my veins as I contemplated continuing on to find the sea. For what? My hopes of finding nomads or a settlement of fishing folk that might take me in withered. If I ever found such a group, why would they look past my starved body and the rags on my back to see my worth? In their fear of me taking something from them, they'd turn a dismissive or contemptuous eye to my temporary need for help, as I had done to the male refugees who came to me. I had failed in my responsibility to care for the people of my lands when I was in the position to do so. Now I must accept that I would face the same harshness.

Imprisoned by the impossibility of my situation, still I felt a small pull to continue. Again, I saw visions of Aea performing in the play at the grotto, leaping up from the ground with her smile, having been reborn after the merciless descent to the underworld. I tried to remember the divine guidance I'd received without feeling angry doubt. Perhaps there was some meaning to this wretchedness.

Under the weight of my filled water bag and the Weird Sphere in my sack, I staggered away from the puny wadi pool. Through the coming days, the rockier terrain harangued my battered feet with a new bruising pain. A burning wind blew every day, swirling up sand that scoured my legs and arms.

Was I walking in circles? Cloud cover the previous night confused me on which direction was west. In desperate exhaustion, I dropped to the stony ground, gazing at the beginnings of a deep rose sunset. A flock of ibis flew above me, the vertex of their 'V' formation lining up with the middle of a pair of hills in the distance. I had to trust passing through that valley would take me to the sea and nearby drinking water. Through the night, I walked under a shrinking quarter moon, refusing to doubt my knowing.

At dawn, the smell of salty sea air lifted my heart. A colony of white gulls with black heads and white rings around their eyes squawked happily above me, flying in a haphazard formation as if celebrating my arrival at the coast.

When I crested a peak and laid eyes on the sea, there were great blotches of water as red and thick as blood floating among the blue. Since childhood, I'd heard stories about this strange red growth that occasionally stained the Red Sea. I'd never imagined it would be so extensive.

Three date palms stood on the endless brown row of squat cliffs lining the coast, offering a glimmer of hope that I could find fresh water. In a flush of gratitude to the ibises for guiding me here, I gathered my strength to climb down to the shoreline to look back up at the low-slung cliffs.

The dark mouth of a cave gaped below the palms, where I might find access to the water that moistened the earth, and my chest thumped with desperate faith. In the open-sided cave, relief made me dizzy when I found a place where fresh water bubbled up from a spring, and although the cracks in my lips meant I could barely open my mouth to slurp, each drop was an explosion of sweet bliss. Inside me, the baby quickened with renewed life. That this child still lived was unbelievable.

The front of the cave was far enough above the high tide watermark to stay dry. I swept the sand on the floor into one area to sleep on. I could stay here a while, build strength. I could not think beyond that.

Sensing food, I pulverised one of the knobbly discs attached to the rocks visible at low tide, and slurped the cloudy, salty flesh. Soon, I learned to prise open the black lips with more precision. When I found the first sphere of milky radiance, I realised they were oysters. As the days passed, I gathered a growing pile of pearls to keep in my cave, touching their glow to my brittle lips. Sometimes I stuffed a large pearl in each ear to drown out the nightly moans of the wind and the relentless slaps of the sea against the rocks at high tide, or held a handful to my shattered heart as I cried.

I looked down at my hands, the bones protruding. My wild-knotted hair hung about me, some stuck in the dried tears of the wounds and insect bites covering my burned skin. I barely recognised myself. I wondered what my face looked like, but could not imagine. *Who am I?*

In my fear of annihilation, I grabbed at rage. *Adam.* My hate surged at him, and I felt a strengthened sense of myself. I let it build. *Vile betrayer, murderer. You want endless Eves to worship your boneless shaft, as though it is the creator of life, and say women's bodies are storerooms to be stuffed with your progeny. For thousands of years, the zealotry you birthed may rule, but there'll come a time when you realise you're half a being, and by then, I'll have found a way to make myself whole without you. Who will want you when even the Eves of the world have been forced by your neglect to become whole unto themselves? When even they reject the scraps you toss? I offered you a place at my side, and you spat upon it. The rotten future is on your hands, demon man.*

Bitterness rose higher, threatening to submerge me. Part of me boomed, *I know who I am*, struggling to keep me from drowning in the spiral of grief and rage to which Sabium had succumbed. But a bigger part didn't care.

I scowled at the Great Mother and blasted her with all my will as I surrendered to the darkness, *Who I am is what you've made me, in your game of so-called perfection!*

I took the Weird Sphere from my cave and, in an eruption of rage, hurled it with all my strength into the red viscous layer swamping the blue waters in front of me. Its impact made a sickening plop, sending red water splashing high, then it was gone. My rage seethed to be satisfied, to find a target on which to blame the loss of the Weird Sphere, the loss of everything, everything. My vitriol at the little life inside me increased.

Why would I harbour this baby after Adam's betrayal? It sucked me dry, uncaring of my needs, putting its existence above mine. It could never replace Aea, dead because I let Adam manipulate me. A woman gives life through her body as a sacred offering, and I had no will to offer life to this child, the symbol of the desecration of my world.

What woman could thrive in Adam's new world, where men denounce her moon blood and treat her and her babies as property? A baby born from this disparagement will surely feel the taint, and go on to birth more generations that continue the curse.

Through the day, I fumed. At high tide I sat above the water, looking down at the swell of my belly above my starved legs. I closed my eyes. For the first time, I let my mind's eye probe my belly.

There was a delicate thumping, like layered drumbeats. Two tiny heartbeats. A sob rose from my core and erupted from my mouth, becoming a long wail of anguish. Twins. I knew immediately they were male and female.

The curse Sabium and I carried must not be repeated. I could not bring them into this life where men and women hated and disrespected each other, where their own mother was cursed with the downfall of the feminine and their father the one that caused it.

'You call this my grand destiny?' I yelled into the sky, at the Great Mother. 'You take all from me and make me responsible for the downfall of women! You used me and my brother to turn your awful cycle. I'm not going to give you these children too.' My chest heaved, blood dribbling down my chin from my lips, split anew from the force of my twisting mouth. 'Like you, I am both creator and destroyer of life, and I reject this curse. I will not carry on my line in a world that peddles the vile untruth of men's superiority!'

Raggedly, I sobbed for my innocent babies, contaminated by the curse they carried. I stared at the patch of red below me, edging over a new area of blue water, and my bloodied lips pressed together firmly. The sea confirmed the appalling truth—men had taken over and the prophesied future was here in full. I hadn't been able to change it—rather, my choices had accelerated this ugly new order into being.

Dragging my flint stone over the top of the sturdy stick, I sharpened it to a point. I put my finger pad on the point and pressed lightly, wobbling it around, not hard enough to pierce the skin, but the tiniest change in pressure would do so.

Standing, I opened my legs, carefully guiding the stick inside me. The gulls appeared suddenly above me, swooping and squawking, their white bellies flashing as air gusted from their wings to touch my face. A single white feather drifted in front of my eyes, as if suspended in the air before me, and I screamed at the birds to be gone. I was unwilling to be swayed from my choice, despite the bile that swelled in me like an ocean of seething dread. I drew on my hate and breathed power into it.

A groan rose from my throat as my body trembled and the point touched the throat of my womb. I waited, swaying a little as I shut my heart and closed my mind, and with a sickening grunt, I plunged the stick inside me and made three quick jerks, the agony rising with each puncture. Collapsing to the rocky ground, gasping, I squinted at the light pink water gushing out of me.

My babies. I'm sorry.

By sunset, the cramps felt like labour pains and warm blood was pouring from me, clots falling in heavy splashes. I sat for a while with my legs open, watching the blood and liver-like tissue join the rising red water. The sea was indifferent as to whether I offered the blood of life or death, each inseparable from the other to these waters.

It was so easy for the Great Mother to be indifferent, but what of a person?

In darkness, I crawled into my cave and lay on my side, clutching my belly, my wails echoing around the space and drowning the screaming wind. I bled all night, wincing and convulsing, my legs slippery with blood as I writhed. Before sunrise, I felt the urge to bear down, and I birthed the twins with an agonised scream. In the light of the new day, I examined the bloody mess, and saw the tiny bodies.

I promise I will make your life hell, Adam and Eve, and that of all your progeny.

I sneered at the Great Mother, who made grand triumphant stories out of the shit of life.

A heat began to rise in my body, dancing with shivering cold, and I knew I had womb fever. Another day and night passed, and the shivering fits struck with increasing violence. Every muscle in my body trembled and my teeth chattered and clacked, my heart raced uncontrollably, my swollen belly agonised. Life and death struggled over me.

A shard of rage broke through my fevered anguish and I grasped it. I spat at those dead babies. *Hah! You want my life in return for yours, children of Adam?*

Deliriously, I drifted in and out of consciousness. The torment knew no end.

Hurry up and die, I told myself.

When a calm took over and the shivering stopped, I faintly recalled a woman I had watched die from this fever. She told me she was better, with no more pain in her distended belly, but it was because her womb was dead and she soon followed, eased with the mercy of poppy tincture. I now underwent the merciless destruction of my womb, the symbol of my glory as a revered creative power, now turned against me.

The stench in my cave was hell, the drone of flies deafening even as the sun slid down and light drained from the sky. I dragged myself to the edge of the rocks, the water gently lapping in a rhythmic pulse below me, the blue and red sea offering me its bosom and strong arms. I wanted no part of it. Turning my eyes away, I felt the wind whistle through me to loosen my spirit from my wrecked body. With my last strength, I looked up at the barest slit of a shrinking crescent moon surrounded by infinite points of light, and felt the golden white light calling me to the Heavens.

I rejected it, and my body died.

PART III

CHAPTER 18

Without the confines of my body, I liked to visit Uruk.

Adam and Eve had moved into my chambers since he'd made himself ruler of my city. When I monitored the swelling of Eve's pregnant belly, she felt me as I entered their space and her pleasant face whitened with fear. She shook Adam awake to tell him my spirit was present, and I knew he was scared, though he said she was an irrational woman for imagining ghosts.

It was harder to get to him in his waking hours because he didn't have a woman's sensitivity to the other realms. But it was easy to enter his dreams and make them nightmares. I came to him in the form I chose—sometimes beautiful, nude, offering red distended nipples to his lips through my strands of long silky hair. I showed him the poison pooling at the top of my thighs that lured him in as surely as a man dying of thirst gasps at water, and he couldn't help but spill his precious seed as I sated him with it.

Other times, I appeared with blood running down my thighs, clutching the bodies of our babies, my hair a mass of writhing red clay snakes to remind him of his origins—the red clay, as his name defined him. *Remember? You may say the feminine Heaven is now of the Earth and that you and your god sit above Her, but I know who you are, red dirt man.*

Sometimes, I flung the slime of my cunt on him and slid it up and down his shaft as I tugged on the beard he was so proud of, and he was powerless in the force of his desire. He would wake excited and revolted by the depth of his fear and longing.

Eve. I reminded her, *It's not your baby is it? It's his, and so are you.* She'd agreed her babies belonged to him, as her body did, and she would never share herself with another man. She was doomed to be bored by his rutting whenever he wanted her beneath him.

She was terrified of me, but with a ghoulish fascination. She tried to deny I existed, but she couldn't because I was part of her, buried within her every sense. She'd made her choice to submit to him, to remain endlessly smiling, sacrificing her desires, keeping her hair neat. *Why, woman?* I would not make it easy. She wouldn't drag me down with her to suffocate under a man.

She complained more about me to Adam and to pacify her, he said he'd have an amulet made against me. I sniggered in their ears, *You think that will make me go away? You drive me deeper into your bones when you deny me.*

As my body rotted at the edge of the Red Sea, my spirit watched as Eve began her labour. In wordless whispers, I said I'd take the baby and then what worth would she offer her husband? But she had the baby—I couldn't stop her. It was a boy.

Bored of her predictability, I moved on to others in Uruk. My power extended further than I'd assumed, and I could visit all the women at once and taunt those who gave themselves up as the property of men. Almost all of them let me harass them as they quaked in fear, ignorant of their power to turn me away. Increasingly, they used amulets given to them by men to repel me, but the only reason they worked was the strength of each woman's intent, nothing to do with the chip of carved stone they were so ready to assign their power to.

Now my old body was a shrivelled, blackened scrap, covered in persistent crabs picking at my bones. Viewing it, I saw a fishing village lay a day's walk south of my cave. Alternative futures tried to flash through my awareness—me setting off down the coast in hopes of finding people, being welcomed when I came upon the village, birthing my babies with the assistance of their women, befriending a man who looked at me with tenderness. I could have lived a quiet life there, slowly coming to accept the fated new era while holding to my essence. But it mattered not. My choice was what it was, and my anger fuelled my spirit onward.

I turned my attentions across the entire world, continuing my reign of terror as the turning of the earthly seasons flicked over and over. Adam's creed spread; priests took over from priestesses, gods from goddesses, men claimed the Mes as their own creation, controlled and diminished women as much as my society had men.

With disdain, I watched Adam's lifetimes flounder. When incarnated in a male's body, he enjoyed the booming surety of his own greatness, ignoring the sorrow he suffered for polarising women as mothers or whores. When born into a female's body, he experienced the gradual loss of the worth each child is born with simply because of the sex his soul wore. Those lifetimes diminished his confidence so that in the next as a man, the insecurity would see him even more tyrannical about keeping his place on top. Back and forth his lives went, spinning nowhere on the wheel of karma. My spirit was always there to amplify his loneliness, bringing him dreams of helpless imprisonment and sorrow that would make him all the more vicious about claiming power when he woke.

As the men of the world slept, I visited them and teased out their precious seed. They quietly agonised that their desire for a passionate union with a woman was ever out of reach. I sucked out their rotten life-force and spat the venom of my hatred to fill the void. They didn't want to resist me. They woke with wet loin cloths and their wives exclaimed in horror that Lilith the demoness had visited their bed. The men lamented their lost seed that could have been used to make more brats, so precious to their god.

Sometimes, I implored women to remember their lap rights by filling their dreams with eroticisms, and indeed they would mourn the loss of their sexual truth, waking with a gaping emptiness and dissatisfaction they were forbidden to lament. They'd started to believe men's lies that it was sinful to revel in their sexuality, and that their only respectable function was to breed men's progeny. Their fertility and lusciousness withered more. Pride in their wombs' abilities to bleed and grow new life dropped into shame, and their misaligned girdles of fire screamed offence with excruciating labour pains and red moon cramps and torments. The flame burning in their bellies dimmed so no longer were their words as powerful, their intentions as potent, their clarity as focused, their sexual bliss so easily swelled.

My legend was impressive. The cunt-fearing masses reviled me, although secretly they wanted me—man and woman alike—as much as they dreaded me. They condemned my existence and commanded my exile, blamed me when babies couldn't be made, or when they died. They cursed me for the pain and suffering of women in childbed. They called me a whore, a seductress of men and awakener of sexual desire, as if that was evil. They named me a succubus, a vampire and denounced me for almost everything their new god deemed wicked, and I took pleasure in provoking them more, sucking their lifeforce and that of their babies to burgeon my power.

The more they feared and rejected me, the more I controlled them. They could pray all they liked to their god, but he couldn't stop me, because there was no god, nor goddess, there was just each of us, and we could do whatever the hell we liked.

This went on a long time, my rage wreaking havoc, my power beyond my imagining as I expanded my mastery of the powerful tool of fear to control people and feed upon them. Gradually, though, I lost interest in their reactions, the curses and hatred they flung at me, the way they acted out their anxieties and repeated vile patterns. There was nothing more for me to do.

Lilith.

It was loud, but it wasn't a voice. It was mine and yet not. I faintly recognised a light energy, but fineness had been so long removed from me that I barely registered it. It persisted, and I felt drawn in. This was the golden white energy that used to come to me an eternity ago, when I was High Priestess of the greatest city in the world.

You're worse than I ever was. A familiar voice spoke.

Sabium? I asked. *Adam?*

There was a kind laugh, deep and resonant. *In a way. Have you had enough of this game? Are you ready to come back to yourself?*

I told Sabium or Adam, whoever it was, for they felt one and the same, *You betrayed me.*

Stillness followed, then understanding flooded my being—I'd done the same to them. To myself.

A deeply buried sob rose from the depths of my being in a release that shook the world. The golden white light swirled, erupting in bursts of rainbow colours as it embraced me in pure love. A knowing washed through me—I was not what I had been doing, what I had been feeling.

The light continued. *I come to you because you are tiring of your experience of who you are not, and until now, you would not have paid me any heed.*

Who are you? I asked it.

We are one and the same.

I asked, *Why have I been singled out to take the fall of the feminine on my shoulders?*

Together, the golden white light and I rose higher as the reply came in a swell of sweet tenderness. *Beloved Lilith, did you not ask to serve this way?*

A memory began to emerge from my depths. My soul's wish to serve was two-fold; to plunge into darkness to flourish new creation and turn the wheel of evolution and, as I awoke to the truth of unity, to pave the way for others to follow. My soul was one of many with the same purpose, for it is easy to get lost in the darkness, with so many souls forgetting themselves, cycle after cycle, stuck in endless suffering. When almost all forgot the oneness of the red and blue flames through these long and turmoiled aeons, I wanted to assist humanity to evolve without unnecessary stagnation.

I realised that when Menna died, she had embraced the blue and red flames and her soul ascended in unity, assisting the masculine to rise, as was his due. When I died, I had rejected the blue and red sea, assisting the sinking of the feminine and affirming separation. I chose to lead this fall, requiring me to take on density that blinded me to the truth of unity. I knew now I could have carried out this mission without losing myself completely. In my life as Lilith, support was always there to help me walk the knife-edge of holding to myself through even the most harrowing stages. But in that cycle, I could not find the wherewithal to do so, and bitterness and rage had taken me to a path of evil. For a while.

Self-compassion rushed through my being for the sacrifices I had made. Now, I had made it to the bottom of the bottom.

Yes, Lilith, it is time for you to come back to the light, from where you will begin your new incarnations on the journey to know who you are in all your magnificence, such that you will be awed beyond measure. In doing so, you forge a path to assist all, for we are one and the same.

I had a long way to go on the second half of my mission, and I'd known enough devilry.

Melding with the light, I expanded out of the dark realm I had been in. Looking back on it, the darkness was tiny, tinier, infinitesimally tiny, nothing.

CHAPTER 19

It is time for my soul to resume incarnations on Earth. Having fallen to the bottom of the underworld of my soul, I begin the return to wholeness. From the vastness of my soul's essence, in the space between lives, excitement and wonder fill me as doorways open to reveal visions of the lifetimes ahead.

I am a woman wearing rags, she's a slave with blank eyes, thinking only of miserable survival.

A thread of energy pulls me from that scene to another.

I'm a woman lying in a bed with a man on top, fucking me as I stare blankly ahead.

A woman is strung up and raped by six men, one of whom finally lets her body drop dead to the ground. I am that man.

The scenes flash faster, a woman sobbing, 'I'll be good, I'll be good', her eyes crumpled in shame.

A boy biting his cheek until blood fills his mouth as he struggles not to cry.

A priest hiding his stiffening shaft as he curses a woman as the devil's whore, his face twisted with hate to cover his yearning for what he believes he must condemn.

A woman so lost to herself she cannot find or trust her instinctive knowing, heeding shortsighted opinions on how she and her young should be treated with harmful medicines, ready to hand over her power and comply.

I am all of them, my denied and unforgiven darknesses enacted and received over and over. In the soul's realm where there is no time, I have yet to embark on these lifetimes and I have completed them already.

Gradually, two steps forward and three steps back, I see how the veils of separation are slowly removed. I revive the many aspects of myself festering in the buried chambers of my heart, my gut, my closed mind's eye, my doused girdle of fire.

I recognise my beloved soul companions who appear in each lifetime, helping me awaken through a variety of themes and situations. Slowly, slowly, I begin to make peace with the souls of those who most challenge me, in whichever characters they play—parents, spouses, siblings, offspring, friends, enemies, authorities. Each player shows me a place I've lost myself so I can reclaim it.

For many, many lifetimes I cannot open my heart in love, playing out the same themes as I stubbornly hold to a resentment or fear. It is difficult for my energy to accept another into my being, while the Eves of the world are all too ready to dissolve themselves for another. Both of us are equally challenged in relationship—Eve types without boundaries, me with too many. I know we are two sides of a feminine collective soul. Eve represents the more feminine side and in shadow, her gentleness makes her a doormat. I represent the side of femininity that is more masculine and in shadow, my force makes me a bitch.

On cosmic schedule, as the Earth starts to align with the galactic heart once more and the age of unity returns, my wholeness blooms.

I embrace my soft and yielding parts, the parts Eve represents, and balance them with my fiery force. Eve and I make peace with each other, no longer accepting the rules that said a woman must only be one of us or the other. We're finished being pegged as a mother or a whore. *We won't take any crap, but we're pretty nice about it*, we laugh. *We are the whole woman*, we tell Adam and Sabium lovingly, and they embrace us as such, Adam's masculine aspect of the whole man at one with Sabium's feminine.

That soul—the unity of Adam and Sabium—is my eternal beloved. Through many lifetimes, we play out the depth of separation in every nuance only to realise there is none. It is a sacrifice necessary to create a deeper experience of unity, a love beyond anything we could have reckoned. It is our gift to the One.

If this were Eve's story—or that of Adam, Sabium, or any other soul—it'd be the same, for we all live this path in our own way. We are one, yet with individualised purposes and perceptions so that we may create ever-new. All are expressions of the red and blue flames, each carrying the two flames within them, on and on into infinity, and we play out creation with and within them.

The masculine and feminine, once seeming so opposed, begin to merge within me. Their ins and outs grow closer until finally they merge in my heart to form the Heaven and Earth star, made up of the blue downward pointing triangle of the feminine and the red upward pointing triangle of the masculine. They can never be separated, though I lived the experience of believing they could. They are creation itself.

In the eternal moment, with the lens drawn out far enough, the game is easy to see. The penetration of otherness—of what appeared to be separate—brought me to experience who I am. Otherness allows creation, alive and moving, and in its coarse expressions, it moves in and out with harsh thrusts. Awakened, it allows for the exquisite lovemaking that is the higher truth of creation.

I didn't want to be only unchanging light forever, but to hone and define myself for the joy of knowing who I am, and I did just that. I continue to expand in ever higher and more beautiful spirals of creation, for that is my purpose.

I am whitish gold light, pure love and intelligence. I am one and the same as my veiled aspects of self in all my incarnations, ever-present with loving guidance, always dwelling within no matter how far parts of me fell. Sometimes my essence reduced to a mere spark, ever ready to revivify at my will. As the creator and the one perceiving the creation, I explored every facet of human consciousness in its highs and lows.

And when I look down upon my cosmic garb, I adore every stain, every tear, every wrinkle. For if I had not known what it is to be who I am not, then I could never come to know who I am, so deeply that I can never waver again.

It's been one hell of a ride, but from up here, seeing the scope of my earthly lives, it's easy to see the beautiful truth of who I am.

And who is that?

I go by the name of Lilith, and billions of others, but I am much more. I am Her, one with Him.

I am You.

AFTERWORD

I used to be deeply enraged and saddened by the way the feminine has been treated by the masculine. This was not only about females, but also how feminine qualities—like nature, feeling and sensitivity, and the cycles of life including ageing and death—were pushed into submission, feared and depleted of some of their mystery and worth.

Through investigating this over the years, in 2017 an epiphany emerged about the interplay between the masculine and feminine that left me flabbergasted—I realised that the feminine was just as overbearing and disrespectful to the masculine.

I'd read in a variety of sources there was an era of feminine rule in our far distant past, which I resonated with, and it was presented as a time of peace and goodwill to all...until the masculine era came along and ruined it.

But by drawing the lens out, I saw a larger story which made sense, as in the laws of energy the pendulum swings equally both ways. Suddenly, the playing ground between masculine and feminine became more equal to my eyes, even though one or the other seemed to dominate at different points in the game.

As an astrologer, I'm fascinated by an ever-evolving 22,000 to 26,000 year astronomical cycle (average of ~24,000 years), in which the Earth's spin axis in space appears to trace a circle. This is not only an astrological cycle but also an astronomical one, recognised by scientific bodies such as NASA. It's called the Precession of the Equinoxes. The cycle is made up of ages representing the 12 zodiac signs, for example, the age of Aquarius, which we are now entering. In astrological understanding, the energies of each sign set the gist for what is experienced on Earth.

In the work of astronomer and astrologer, Nick Anthony Fiorenza, further meaning can be applied to this cycle. Fiorenza's model shows a separation then reunification of the feminine and masculine energies. Kind of like a macro 'she said, he said' before we reunite, with the purpose of evolving consciousness.

Fiorenza's model is called the Grand Precessional Cross, which becomes exact when the Earth's vernal point is perpendicular to the galactic equatorial node. You can learn about the astronomical and astrological details at his site, lunarplanner.com/HolyCross.html.

In the Grand Precessional Cross, we're now at the stage in the cycle when masculine and feminine energies can most easily reunite in our earthly experience after about 12,000 years of appearing to be separate, with feminine then masculine energies taking a turn on top.

This unification can be expressed within the self or with a partner, and from there, with the way we relate to all life. One's sex organs and sexual expressions are unimportant. This shift towards unity may be associated with the shift in consciousness birthed in 2012 as most famously predicted by ancient Mayan astronomers and astrologers. The more years that pass since then, the less tolerance there is between the finer energies of unity and the denseness of separation. It is now that we must choose which path we are on, as the galactic cycle continues regardless.

Why must we appear to be separate in the first place? The game of evolution we've played involves us falling from paradise—Heaven—and returning to it after our heroic journeys, wisened and expanded by what we learned in exploring duality.

To play, we believe in opposites. We think the two sides of any opposite are separate things, though they are not. There is no precise point of separation, but a relative contrast between the two. When does black become white, or sad become happy? Heaven, hell? Or masculine energy become feminine? Each pair operates in one circle of relativity—cold gets cool, then warmer, then hot, then cooler, and so it goes around in one unified energy. In playing with the concept of opposites, we open a massive new range of creative choice. To create, we need contrast and as we evolve, we become better at it. We can create without suffering.

The journey of separating then reuniting is a common theme in many creative expressions, such as movies—a peaceful society or character that has never known real contrast experiences some kind of shadow force and through the struggles, they find the greatness of who they are. Just think of Simba in *The Lion King*. Without challenge, we would not know the joy of experiencing our greatness.

The story of Adam and Eve kicked off the masculine-dominated era we're now ending

As a lover of Lilith, I wanted to write a novel with her at the centre of the story.

The ~24,000 year Grand Precessional Cross is split into four segments, each of about 6,000 years. I initially chose to set this novel 6,000 years ago from our current day because it aligns with the point in the Grand Precessional Cross that marks the change from feminine to masculine energy domination, suiting the themes I wanted to explore through the eyes of Lilith.

Incredibly, I went on to discover this point in time is also when Adam and Eve are believed to have existed. Based on chronological and genealogical biblical history, a number of experts estimate the beginning of humankind as referred to in the bible with the lives of Adam and Eve began about 6,000 years ago. These esteemed scholars include the discoverer of calculus and the laws of motion Sir Isaac Newton and Polish mathematician and astronomer Johannes Kepler.

Also of relevance is that 6,000 years ago is where the line is drawn between pre-history and history, probably because of the Adam and Eve story. Further, the Hebrew calendar begins just under 6,000 years ago.

This novel tells a story of the turning point from a time of the feminine being on top to the era of masculine superiority, while holding the context of evolved unity as the cycle's purpose.

Who is Lilith in mythology?

According to Jewish mythology, Lilith was Adam's first wife, before Eve. Lilith left Adam after he insisted she submit to him, including demanding she lay beneath him during sex.

Some bibles state the first woman and Adam were made from the same soil or red clay, but that woman is not named as Eve. It was 100 or more years after, based on biblical chronology, that Eve was said to be made from Adam's rib. Lilith is not named in any bible as the first woman... perhaps her name was removed in this context. She is referred to as a wilderness demoness in Isaiah 34:14. This is her only mention in the bible, but her legend continued to grow in ancient Judaism.

Lilith is first mentioned in ancient Babylonian texts as a class of winged female demons that attacks pregnant women and infants.

What does Lilith symbolise?

Lilith would not submit to Adam, and paid the price during the forthcoming aeons of patriarchal rule, when she became the scapegoat for fear of feminine power, sexuality and fertility in a number of regions and cultures.

She paid dearly for her refusal to fit into the narrow model of the all-sacrificing wife and mother that the patriarchal era prescribed, and was called a demonic child killer, evil seductress, a wicked serpent and the first vampire. Her inspired sexuality saw her called a whore. She was associated with abortions, miscarriage, fertility problems and the deaths of babies and children, and known as a predator of pregnant and birthing women. Through thousands of years, countless people had amulets and used magical inscriptions to ward off Lilith's evil.

After a long era of being rejected and demonised, it's time for Lilith's voice to come out from the shadows. She's taking her place as an archetype of the empowered, sexual and passionate feminine within every person, and especially women. She is ready to stand beside Eve in harmony and balance as the whole woman.

The illusional era of masculine or feminine being on top or made of this womb or that penis is over. They can never be separated. The true nature of the masculine is to cherish the feminine and her boundaryless dynamic creative nature. And her true nature is to adore his structure, his focus, and how he forms the banks that shape her wild river. They are creation itself and exist within every form, every creation, every moment.

Why wouldn't Lilith go under Adam, but Eve would?

These are my theories, which use archetypes we're calling Lilith, Eve, Sabium and Adam, to demonstrate how the unified feminine and masculine plays out a game of being separate.

Eve's role in the story was to let the masculine be on top, because it was his turn and the cycle called for it. Lilith's energy could not submit, because she carries the yang or masculine aspect of the feminine collective soul, which will not bow. She was exiled through the patriarchal era, unheard and rejected in her fullness. In many ways, Lilith took the rap for the fated—which in ancient language is known as 'weird'—fall of the feminine. It is time to clear her name.

The feminine or yin side of the feminine collective soul, represented by Eve, also made great sacrifices to turn the wheel of evolution, but this part of the collective feminine was more welcomed and suffered less in being submissive through the patriarchal era, her yin nature allowing this more easily. For Lilith, it was pure hell, but a necessary evil required by the creative cycle through that stage of human evolution, when we hadn't yet learned to create without suffering.

If we were to use Adam and Sabium as similar representations for the masculine collective, we could say Adam's yang half took the lead in the last 6,000 years up to now, while Sabium's yin half was pushed down as feminine qualities in men were rejected. In this era, both Sabium and Lilith have been denied.

All four archetypes are present within all people, in shadow and light expressions. Our relationship with each of them, and the level to which we've faced and integrated their shadow and light, reflects our balance and wholeness as a person.

In our current day, the part of the game that saw Lilith and Sabium exiled, and Adam and Eve elevated in a sense, is complete. This coincides with the point in the Grand Precessional Cross, where masculine and feminine can begin to reunite and re-enter the Garden of Eden as wisened grown-ups. The evolved masculine integrates Sabium's sensitivity with Adam's active assertion. The evolved feminine integrates Lilith's active passion with Eve's gentle receptivity.

At this point in the cycle, the poles of feminine and masculine expressions can more easily merge in the Heaven and Earth star, made of the feminine blue downward pointing triangle and the masculine red upward pointing triangle. I say 'can', because it is a window of opportunity—like a launch window—that can now be accessed most easily, but to do so, we must have a strong willingness to do the self-development required to master ourselves. The more people that do so, the greater the helpful drag pulls others forward, as does the front of a peloton.

There are many paths to soul realisation. The path I take and recommend is through the teachings and methods offered by the Melaney Ryan Institute of Applied Consciousness (Mahat Meditation and Integrated Therapeutic Alignment energy medicine), which provide the keys to aligning human consciousness so it can enter the realms of unity at this crucial time.

Those people not ripe to move into unity at this time will continue on the wheel of karma, and it will seem we are living in entirely different dimensions even while sharing the planet.

The hope is that many millions of humans will take the leap when the launch window is open and the fling into the unified realms can more easily be made. If enough of us do so, we can better care for the Earth and continue to live here.

Exactly how long this launch window is open is not known, but my sense is that it is starting to close. The time is here to realise we stand side by side in unity, and the groundswell we're now seeing in equality and liberated self-expression, regardless of gender and biology, will continue to deepen.

Was Eve made from Adam's rib... or his penis bone?

I was fascinated to learn that Adam's rib may have been mistranslated—it may have been his penis bone. Modern biblical scholar Professor Ziony Zevit proposes that Eve was created from Adam's penis bone, also known as a *baculum*, as explained in his Yale University Press article[1].

The concept that Eve may have been made from Adam's penis bone is surely metaphoric, yet isn't it funny humans don't have one? Of the primates, apparently only humans and spider monkeys are missing such bones.

It makes sense that Eve was made from the yang symbol of Adam to symbolise the era of the masculine on top. For me, a rib never made sense.

The Heaven on Earth star

This symbol is used in different religions, often with different colours, and is strongly connected with Judaism. It is also used in Hinduism. Wherever it is used, it holds the same essential meaning around uniting Heaven and Earth, and the feminine and masculine polarities of oneness.

I look at the star through the eyes of my spiritual beliefs and an understanding of the Grand Precessional Cross. I see the downward pointing blue triangle is the feminine energy reaching down from the Heavens, and the red upward triangle is the masculine energy of the Earth. Now is the time for the reuniting of the blue and red triangles, in accordance with astronomical cycles which are like a game board of creation.

Should we use Ophiuchus as a star sign?

Ophiuchus (*oh-few-kuss*), meaning 'Serpent bearer' in Greek, is a constellation of stars situated behind the sun from November 29 to December 18.

It may have first been acknowledged under another name in Babylon, or prior in the days of Sumer, or perhaps even further back. It has not been widely used in astrology for thousands of years, and I am not alone in suspecting its alchemising qualities saw it removed as we entered a structured masculine-dominated era. Its qualities as a sign are currently not well defined, with little consensus as to its element (fire, water, earth, air), modality (cardinal, fixed or mutable), ruling planet, or even whether it's masculine or feminine, although most consider it feminine.

Ophiuchus is actually more than one constellation, as it is considered together with the Serpens constellation. Serpens is made up of two disconnected parts of a snake (Serpens Caput, representing the serpent's head, and Serpens Cauda, the serpent's tail), with the serpent bearer or charmer in the middle. The snake halves represent duality—poison and cure, life and death, feminine and masculine, or any other expression of opposites. The serpent bearer has the ability to unify these dualities. Unifying the serpent signifies the awakening of our intrinsic healing and spiritual power that lies within our sacred sexual energy, which is creativity expressed through separating then re-unifying the poles of creation. It isn't necessarily about physical sex—it is about creation. The imagery for Ophiuchus shows a man holding a serpent, but perhaps it was originally a woman. When you consider the higher meaning, the gender doesn't matter.

At present, Ophiuchus in rarely used in astrology, with little software available to calculate charts using a 13 sign system. Whether or not Ophiuchus can be used as a zodiac sign depends on which of the two main astrological approaches you use—tropical or sidereal. Because of the way Western or tropical astrology is set up, it cannot include Ophiuchus as a sign, but Eastern or sidereal astrology can incorporate it.

Western astrology does not account for the Precession of the Equinoxes, which shows the change in the position of constellations due to astrophysical parameters that vary over time. Rather, Western astrology is based on the seasons we experience on Earth and uses 12 zodiacal signs (named after the constellations), divided evenly into 30 degrees each on the ecliptic belt. It cannot accommodate a 13th sign, so if you're basing your star sign on Western astrology, it remains the same, regardless of the existence of the constellation of Ophiuchus.

Having trained as a Western astrologer, I find the tropical 12 zodiac sign system works accurately to analyse the energies of a person, place or event. Undoubtedly, the sidereal approach, whether or not it uses a 13 sign system, works every bit as well.

More than one approach can be applied to understanding something. An object seen from its side is as true to itself as when seen from above, but each gives a different perspective—the intent to see and understand something is of the greater importance. We are the ones who assign intent and meaning and the power of that goes beyond what our left brain can compute. *We* create meaning.

Swiss psychiatrist and psychoanalyst Carl Jung saw the human collective unconscious as shared structures of the unconscious mind populated by instincts and archetypes, encompassing the soul of humanity at large. This is key in how we understand life, ourselves and create meaning as a race. The archetypes of the 12 well known astrological signs have long been part of the collective unconscious, so we all connect to them at some level, even those who do not believe in or know about them. If you consciously resonate with your Western star sign, it can feel disconcerting to consider you may be another sign, which may be the case if you apply an astrology system incorporating Ophiuchus.

If Ophiuchus was removed from astrological systems a long time ago, its archetypal power will have diminished in the collective unconscious, making it feel mysterious and more difficult to grasp as a zodiac sign. I suspect that from now on, as many people enter a new era of unified consciousness with balanced feminine and masculine energy, Ophiuchus will become more accepted and active in the conscious and unconscious collective.

Taking the window of opportunity for unity

The ~24,000 year Grand Precessional Cross cycle gives a broad explanation for the journey of evolution, but within it, each soul plays at their own game according to their will.

So what happens next? As the Grand Precessional Cross cycles continue to occur on a colossal timeframe, I believe we will keep spiralling higher, into finer expressions of the feminine and masculine, whether or not it continues to take place on Earth. We are creators in the process of creating, and we can do it without suffering.

The time is truly now to take strides to exit the wheel of karma and enter a new era of unity, and all those with the will can do so. Every person that reads this book is well on the way, because if you got this far, then we are truly on the same page! May we stride forward in unity, no matter the details of how we choose to see or action it. We are One.

Footnote 1 – *What Really Happened in the Garden of Eden?* By Zevit, Ziony. Pp. xxvii, 368, New Haven/London, Yale University Press, 2013

ACKNOWLEDGMENTS

Thank you to my beloved husband, Wayne, the most important person in my life—your devotion, love of life, wisdom and creativity are vast. Every day you are by my side seeing my best, always asking, listening and encouraging, and your ideas are intuitive and lusciously creative. This book is a realisation of the unity between us that has taken the unconditional love, compassion, perseverance and sacrifice of a scale only you could offer, my holy Ferdinand the bull.

To our adored sons—Luc, 'light', you are a soul of great depth, intelligence and presence, who awakened the light in me and set me on my destined path. I see you. Remy, you are of the heart of the heart, the embodiment of wise joy and creative expression, and you lift this world beyond measure. I know who you are.

Profound thanks to my spiritual mentor and friend, Melaney Ryan of the Melaney Ryan Institute of Applied Consciousness, without whom this book would not have made it into form—thank you for seeing me and offering me what I needed to achieve my destiny, and showing me an example of an enlightened woman. I'm delighted and humbled to work beside you to help restore unity in our world, in this lifetime and beyond.

Deep gratitude to the other great souls who continue to bring tremendous light to my life—Grand Master Choa Kok Sui (2007); Lama Geshe Lodoe Gyatso (2011); and Padmasambhava, the enlightened being who lived in 8th century Tibet and is part of the spiritual lineage of my greatest teachers including Melaney Ryan. My sincere gratitude to astronomer and astrologer Nick Anthony Fiorenza (2020), whose incredible work greatly inspires me.

My soul sister of many lifetimes, Jenna Lambert-Porter—on a daily and cosmic basis, you have been part of this creation, brainstorming ideas and spiritual mysteries until we ripped in sacred goosebumps or hysterical laughter, encouraging the sex scenes, offering clarity, wise advice and loyalty, and always getting it. You are a complex and adorable muse for Gemekala. This book soars on the wings of your faith, and would not be what it is without you. Thank you.

Many have helped as beta readers and supporters. Thank you to each and every one—your help will always be appreciated. An extra call out to early readers Janina Norton, Marie Hoy and Anita Bennetts for your depth of response.

I greatly appreciate the global Mahat Meditation community—this collective fuels me and in many ways is the foundation upon which I stand. *We are one. We are unified. We stand in pure love.* Thank you Melissa Crier for your belief in me and for being a wonderful muse for Urnina. Christine Lomangino (aka Christine America), thank you for your insights into Atlantis. I am grateful for my Mahat Meditation writers' trio—Lee Lenyk, Signe Hovem and myself—as key in the early days when I needed a lot of energy to move the book forward.

Thanks to my developmental editor, Alida Winternheimer, who got this creation humming with outstanding skills and an intuitive knowing of the book's heart. Thank you to my structural and line editor, Libby Turner, who took on the book at a later stage and expertly and sensitively made it so much better. She knew just what to do.

My gratitude to my parents, Colleen and Graham Hubbard, for the gift of life, teaching me so much and letting me expand my wings.

I honour my beloved Siamese-Oriental cats, Star and Adam (Startrill Ek Zeru Dax), who left this world and entered it, respectively, in the week that I began writing this book in 2017. These loving feline spirits knew what they were doing.

Thank you to the many authors who have inspired me over the years towards writing this novel—this includes but is not limited to Elisabeth Haich (*Initiation*), Neale Donald Walsch (*The Little Soul and the Sun*), Rosalind Miles (*Guenevere: Queen of the Summer Country* among others), Naomi Wolf (*Vagina*), and Esther Hicks of Abraham-Hicks.

About the author

Melanie Dufty lives in Perth, Western Australia, with her husband and
their teenage sons. She is an astrologer qualified by the
Federation of Australian Astrologers.
Melanie lived for nine years in London and Sydney, working in corporate
communications for the banking and retail industry bodies, all the while
highly sceptical about the non-material realms. During the homebirth of
her first son, and in the year that followed, she hit the spiritual road.
I Am Lilith is her first book.

Head to melaniedufty.com to sign up for the newsletter and hear more
about the understandings behind this novel.

Made in United States
North Haven, CT
28 December 2023

46726201R00178